A Heart Needs a Second Chance

To: Helen Fanning.
The best and greatest caring
person that I have ever met.
Your son-in-law.
Tom Adornetto

TOM ADORNETTO

First Edition

PAGE PUBLISHING, INC.
New York, NY

First originally published by Page Publishing, Inc. 2019

ISBN 978-1-68456-420-0 (Paperback)
ISBN 978-1-68456-421-7 (Digital)

Printed in the United States of America

Fact and Fictions

This novel is a true story. The names have been changed to avoid any lawsuits for potential slander. Some of the dates and times are slightly altered. Why is it so popular to sing about love? Could it be because love is the most important emotion?

According to the American Bar Association, there are currently over one million lawyers practicing in the United States, which relates to about one for every three hundred people. Women initiate divorce much more than men. Presently, the divorce rate is increasing at an astounding rate, and close to 50 percent of children are growing up in a single-parent environment.

Battering is the single major cause of injury to women, exceeding rapes, muggings, and auto accidents combined. A woman is more likely to be killed by a male partner (or former partner) than any other person. According to the US Census Bureau, fathers make up approximately one in six custodial parents.

In custody situations, more and more courts now favor equal consideration of both mother and father as the custodial parent. This was not always the case in past decades. It was presumed that mothers were the preferable custodial parent as they tended to be the primary caregivers.

The United States lawmakers ignore that unfair custody laws can cause custody disputes that result in one of the high numbers of murder-suicides. Fathers don't abandon their children. They are driven away.

Chapter 1

It was late in the afternoon. Three old acquaintances, Pete, Vinnie, and Bob, were at a cocktail lounge with their new friend, Tom Connelly, a younger man. He had traveled with Bob on Memorial Day from California. The three men dressed in business jackets except for Tom and were reminiscing about "the good, old days."

Peter Devigne said, "Yeah, we did a lot of crazy things when we were young. Gary was crazy. We were around fifteen or sixteen years old. Gary made a spare key of his mother's car. At night, we would take the car and drive around, trying to pick up girls. We drove to the old ice cream place in South Orange. We were talking to a couple of girls in the parking lot. They drove off. One had to be seventeen. We decided to follow. We walk to the spot where we thought we had parked the car. The car was gone. Gary said, 'Oh shit, I must have left the key in the car. My mother is going to kill me.'"

They all laughed.

Pete said, "Wait, it gets better."

Tom said, chuckling, "How!"

Pete added, "We tried hitchhiking. No luck. We had to walk. Gary got yelled at for getting home late. The next morning, Gary's mother could not find her car. She walked up and down the street, looking for her car. She called the police and filed a report. Gary felt like shit. She had to take a taxi to work." Pete was laughing and jerking forward. He enjoyed being the center of attention. "Her car was found five days later."

They all laughed with Pete. He was founder and president of Micro Research, a company involved in the designing, manufacturing, and retail sales of computer parts and accessories.

"Yeah, we couldn't wait to grow up and become adults," said Vinnie. "I have a wife, two children, a house, a dog, and all the responsibilities of bringing home the bacon. We didn't know how good we had it back then—no responsibilities, no stress, no worries, just fun."

"Can you believe it? I'm a father of four," said Bob Dorsete, staring at his drink and gently tapping the table with the glass. "We're nearing forty. Not much to dream about." His glance was sentimental. "Hey, I got one. We were around fourteen years old. Vinnie had his first girlfriend."

Vinnie interrupted. "No, no. Don't go there."

"Okay, I got another," said Bob. "We were around fifteen or sixteen years old. It was me, Vinnie, and Phil. Remember Big Phil?"

Vinnie jumped in, "Yeah, I remember. He had a big mouth."

Bob said, "Yeah! We hitchhiked to South Orange. We sneaked into a private swimming club."

Vinnie added, "We changed, in the woods, into our bathing suits and left our clothes there."

Bob interrupted. "Let me tell the story. We walked in our bathing suits and immediately jumped into the water. Not one minute in the water, a young lifeguard was pointing at us, saying, 'You, out!' Vinnie and I got out, but Phil ignored the guy. The lifeguard jumped in the water and started pushing Phil toward the edge. Phil did not move."

Vinnie said, "It took two of them to get Phil out."

"They told us to leave. Phil insisted that his aunt was a member…Culo…Culograsso. He insisted that they check their membership files and look up Mary Culograsso."

Vinnie, laughing, said, "Yeah, he made up an Italian name, which means fat-ass!"

Bob continued. "I keep whispering to Phil to shut up. The cops showed up and took us to the police station. Phil kept insisting that his aunt was a member. He threatened to sue the club, the cops. At the police station, the cops had us sit on a bench, in our bathing suits, and keep our mouths shut. Phil continued, saying, 'I have rights. You cannot treat me this way. I have the right to call my lawyer. I want to call my lawyer. He will sue you for false arrest.' I finally told the cop that we had sneaked in, and we were sorry. The cop said that they were going to let us get our clothing and drop us off at the city line. *No.* Because of Phil's big mouth, they kept us at the station for two hours and dropped us at the city line, in our bathing suits."

They all busted out laughing. Tom Connelly sat in silence, enjoying the stories.

Pete said, "I'm very optimistic about the West Coast operations. Gary thinks that Tom is a good technician and he'll be a good technical manager. Bob, you have the experience. And, being married to my cousin, I trust you."

"Well, thank you, Pete," said Bob.

Pete asked Tom, "How is Gary treating you? Are you okay with staying at his house?"

"Yeah, everything is cool."

"It was Gary's idea to get to know you." They paused as they glanced at the television screen.

"The news is on," said Pete. "It's getting close to dinner time. I should go home."

"It's rush hour now," said Bob.

Pete chuckled. "You don't have to worry because your wife is three thousand miles away. Okay! One last round," said Pete, as his hand moved to his jacket pocket.

"No, Pete," said Bob, "I'll pay for this round." He reached for his wallet. "Oh shit, I can't find my wallet," he said, with his hands searching every pocket. "I had my wallet out to get a telephone number. I must have left it in the phone booth. Excuse me!" He quickly retraced his footsteps.

Ten minutes later, Bob Dorsete returned and, in discontentment, said, "No luck. It's gone. I had over five hundred in cash. I tried getting in touch with my wife to cancel the credit cards. She's probably out, picking up the boys. I have to go. Need some cash?" asked Pete. He reached into his jacket for his wallet. "I'm sorry about your wallet." He glanced at Vinnie. "Make a cash advancement for Bob tomorrow."

Vinnie had recently joined Micro Research as a controller. He acquired the job through Bob. Vinnie said, "See you tomorrow. I have to go or suffer the consequences."

Bob and Tom had been busy on Tuesday, visiting the warehouse and stores. Today was spent meeting the company executives and discussing business. Bob was staying with his mother (nearing eighty years old). His father had passed away a year ago. It was almost nine o'clock, and he had made many attempts to reach his wife. He wondered why she was not home. *She should be home by now,* he thought. Bob, going over his mind how he was in the phone booth, took his wallet to find Marion's number. He placed his wallet on the tiny ledge to dial the number. He was thinking of the strange way Marion asked if he had called his wife. Becoming apprehensive, he decided to call his next-door neighbor.

"Ray, this is Bob. Bob Dorsete, your next-door neighbor. I'm in New Jersey, and I have been trying to get in touch with Ann. Is there something wrong?"

"I don't know. I haven't seen anything unusual," said Ray.

"I'm a little concerned. Can you please go over and check if she is home or outside?" asked Bob.

"Yeah, I can do that. Give me your number, and I'll call you back."

The waiting was making Bob edgy. After several minutes, the telephone rang, and he quickly picked up the receiver. It was Ray. "No one is home and nothing unusual."

In a polite and disappointed voice, Bob said, "Thank you for your effort." Bob's concern for his family increased, and he worried that something bad had happened. He called Pete Devigne. "Sorry for calling. Ann is not home. I have a strange feeling that something is wrong."

Pete asked, "Is there a friend or neighbor you could contact to check the house?"

"I did. I called my next-door neighbor, and he told me nobody was home."

Pete sensed the concern in Bob's voice. "I'll make some phone calls, and I'll get back to you."

It was nearly 10:00 p.m. Bob was pondering on the past few days, the arguments with his wife, and him not calling for three days. He stayed in the kitchen, sitting on a kitchen chair close to the telephone to not disturb his mother. He sat on a chair and rested his legs on another chair. He dozed off and was awakened by the ring of the telephone. "Bob. It's Pete. Are you awake?"

"Yeah. Just thinking. Must have dozed off."

"I called your local police department." Pete paused. "Bob, you're not gonna believe this. Ann is at a shelter for battered women."

Bob was in disbelief. After a long pause, he asked, "Why? What happened? Where are the boys?"

"The boys are with her. I was told that she's in a safe place and they're all fine."

Bob, unable to grasp the situation, felt a cold sweat slowly invading his tired body. He desperately sought answers. "Why are they in a shelter? What do you mean that they're fine if they're in a shelter?"

"That's the only information they gave me," said Pete. "I'll try to contact Ann. I'll call you back if I get more info."

"I won't be able to sleep tonight, so please call me the moment you find anything."

Pete reassuringly said, "I'll call you the instant I know more."

Bob was concerned and feeling helpless. He needed something to drink. He searched the pantry and found a bottle of rye. He poured himself a tumbler of rye and nervously smoked one cigarette after another. He opened the kitchen window for some fresh air. The cool air felt good. The room was dark, except for the light coming through the window. He nervously ran his fingers through his hair and placed his hands over his face in disbelief. He waited and waited, anxiously, for the telephone to ring. It rang, and he quickly picked it up before it finished ringing.

"I finally got in touch with Ann," said Pete rapidly. "She and the boys are at a shelter because of you."

"Me! What are you saying?"

"Boy, she's pissed! She's angry. She talked about divorce."

Bob was almost in shock. "Over one argument, she talks divorce."

"I asked her to give you a call. She said that she might. If she calls, don't quarrel with her. Listen to what she has to say."

"Thank you, Pete. I'll see you tomorrow."

"Good luck!"

Bob was thinking about what Pete had told him. He hoped that Ann would call. He was too tense to think of sleep. He stayed in the kitchen table, smoking one cigarette after another, waiting and hoping that the phone would ring. He sat quietly in the dark, except for the glowing light of the bright June moon penetrating through the shade of the small kitchen window. He continued to smoke. The room became filled with smoke. His body and mind were tired and numbed, yet he inhaled vigorously. The smoke was becoming thick and taking form. Bob envisioned the silhouette of Ann. His eyes closed, and his head swayed as if severed from his head.

The telephone rang. Bob jumped and quickly picked up the telephone. "Ann! Thank God! Are you okay?"

Ann, in a loud and furious voice, "I don't love you. You hurt me. You hurt the boys."

Bob apologized. "I am so sorry. I love you."

"You don't love me. You don't love the boys. You said it."

Bob replied, "I didn't mean all that stuff. I have been under a lot of pressure. I was angry."

"I don't need you! I'm attractive. I'm intelligent, and I can stand on my own two feet!"

Knowing that she was angry, Bob searched for words to calm her down. Not sure of what to say, he paused to ask, "How are the boys?"

"The boys are fine. Here, talk to Bobby."

Bobby, sobbing, said, "Dad, how come you don't love us anymore?"

There was little that Bob could say to his thirteen-year-old son. "Don't cry. Let me talk to mom." Ann was back on. "Is Tony there?"

"Yes!" said Ann coldly.

"Let me speak to him."

"Dad, how come you want to hurt us?" said Tony sobbing.

Bob, in near shock, had difficulty finding words to say. He paused to think. "Son, how can you think I want to hurt you? Remember the time I spend playing with you?"

Tony replied, "Yeah."

"What have I have done to hurt you?"

Tony made no reply. Ann was back on the phone. "You'll never see the boys again. I told the police that you threatened to kill your boss." She hung up.

Bob was tense and feeling helpless. He called Pete and related to him the conversation that he had with Ann and the boys. Pete was reserved. "What did you do to her?" he asked.

"I told you, when I arrived, that we had an argument. I never put my hands on her. I never put my hands on the kids."

"All right." said Pete, "We'll talk tomorrow."

Bob Dorsete was at the office, but his mind and his heart were not on his work. He wanted desperately to talk to Ann and find out why she took such drastic action. He waited anxiously for Pete to come in. Every half hour, he checked with Pete's secretary. Pete arrived near noon. Bob immediately went to see him. He knocked on the door, slowly entered, and stared at the large man sitting behind the desk. He had long, dark, curly hair, a dark complexion, and a mustache.

"Sorry to bother," said Bob. "Have you heard from Ann?"

"No, I haven't," said Pete coldly. "I have urgent things to do. We'll get together later."

Bob felt the coldness and understood that Pete had a company to run. As he turned to leave, Pete stood up, displaying his big physique, over six feet tall and overweight. In a loud voice, he said, "If you put your freaking hands on my cousin! She's right for what she's doing! If you didn't, I'll help you."

Bob was holding back the tears as his hands were busy twining and twisting. He looked at Pete and said, "I didn't hurt her. I didn't lay a hand on her! You can check with Tom Connelly. He was at the house that night. He saw her that morning as she bid us goodbye."

"Okay, Bob," said Pete. "I'll talk to Tom. I'm not saying that I don't believe you or that I'm taking sides. I'm thinking that you must have done something for her to take such drastic action."

Bob was in an office. He tried to work to take his mind off Ann and the children. He felt very helpless—three thousand miles away, with no idea of his family's whereabouts. Vinnie walked in. They were the same age and height. Vinnie was pudgy, showing the signs of midlife. "I'm your best friend. If there is anything I can do to help, all you have to do is ask."

"Thanks!" Bob acknowledged his words. They had been friends since the age of nine. They always kept in touch and always confided in each other. For the past three years, Bob had been living in California.

Vinnie asked, "Like to go for a drink after work? I want you to know that we have been friends for a long time. You have always been a good friend."

The two embraced. "Sure. I need someone to talk to. I'm trying to make sense of this whole thing," said Bob. "I need to talk to Pete."

Vinnie replied, "I'm trying to make sense of it. I just saw you guys last year. She was happy and proud of you."

"But the last year, I have had problems."

Pete walked in. "Bob, I want to talk to you. My office?"

"Sure, Pete," said Bob. He hoped that Pete had contacted Ann. If anyone could, he was convinced Pete could. Bob turned to Vinnie. "Do you wanna come?" Pete glanced at Bob. "I have no secrets from him and nothing to hide."

The three men entered Pete's office. Pete slowly made his way to his large chair and sat down behind his desk. His desk was a mess, covered with computer journals, unopened mail, and messages. Pete said, "I spoke to Tom. He told me that he was at your house the night before. You all had coffee that night. Afterward, you and Ann excused yourselves to talk over some business matters regarding the restaurant. Tom when to his room and went to sleep immediately. Tom also told me that he heard no arguing or fighting and slept very peacefully. You got up in the morning, and just as you both were on your way out, Ann came down and asked if you wanted breakfast. You told her that you didn't have time. She wished you both a safe trip. You told Ann to take care and to take care of the children, and to make sure to set the alarm in the house every night. Tom thought that it was odd that you didn't hug or kiss her goodbye."

Bob interrupted. "You know that. I told you, when I arrived, that I was kind of pissed off at her and that we had an argument."

"I remember that. Tom also told me that he saw no marks or bruises on her, but he was concerned about the way you left the house."

"Pete, you know that I have been under a lot of stress—my job, the restaurant, and now this business venture! For the past six months, I have been working, morning to night. I only see the boys on weekends. I have been under a lot of stress. I have been critical of Ann for not doing enough to help me. I blamed her for some of my problems." Bob paused. Pete and Vinnie stared in sympathy. Bob continued, "I haven't called her in three days. I screwed up! I made a mistake, but I didn't think that I pushed her over the edge to leave me. I love your cousin more than anything on this earth. I would give my right arm for her."

"I believe you," said Pete.

Bob stood up and paced the floor. "She probably found the money and lost trust in me." Pete glanced at Vinnie. Bob noticed Pete's reaction. "Pete, I trust Vinnie with my life." Pete stared in silence. "I didn't tell her about the money."

Vinnie politely said, "I don't need to know. You don't have to tell me."

"Vinnie! Pete was just trying to help me out since the restaurant was failing. Pete advanced me twenty thousand dollars in cash. It was an incentive to proceed with Micro Research and to close down the restaurant. I didn't tell Ann about the money. I hid the money in the attic of the house, next to her jewelry. I was hoping not to use the money." Bob turned toward Pete. "I have to go back. Tom can stay. I can't wait until Saturday."

"I don't think that's a good idea," said Pete. "The police could be involved. You might be arrested."

"For what?" said Bob in a surprised tone.

"Domestic violence is a serious thing these days. She and the boys are in a shelter. That is serious. The police will not disclose the location. Ann made a serious allegation. You might have restraining orders preventing you from going to the house. Wait a couple of days so that I can get more information and check if there is an arrest warrant for you. At least here, you have friends, and we have the company lawyer available." Bob stared in silence. Pete continued, "You'll be all by yourself if you go back. You just might do something stupid out of frustration. I'll try contacting Ann."

"Why didn't you tell me that you had a way to reach her," said Bob in an annoyed tone.

"I have the hotel number. I have been trying all day to get in touch with her. She has not picked up." They sat in silence as Pete dialed the number. "Room 216, please." Pete placed his hand over the telephone's mouthpiece. "She's at a motel, waiting to be located to a shelter." He paused. "Room 216." Pete, while placing the telephone down and looking straight at Bob, said, "She checked out." Placing his hands over his head, he added, "Last night, you said that you called a neighbor."

"Yes. Ray. He lives next door. Ann is friendly with his wife. She watches Mark a couple of days a week."

"Is he a friend?"

"He is okay. A retired cop."

"But not close?" asked Pete.

"I guess."

Pete, with a reserved look, remarked, "This is weird. A cop?"

"What are you thinking?" asked Bob.

"Cops are tight. And he told you nothing, only that Ann and the boys were not home."

Bob said excitedly, "I have to go back!"

Chapter 2

The five-hour flight to California had been long and painful for Bob Dorsete.

He was uncomfortable throughout the flight, feeling the pain around and inside his head and to the back of his neck. It was not a headache. The pain was inside and outside, rendering him unable to fully concentrate. His body felt numbed and very warm, and the air seemed to lack oxygen. Throughout the entire flight, his thoughts were about his wife and children. He had no idea what he was going to do. He was compelled to return to California as quickly as possible. He had to change airlines to get this flight.

It was dark when Bob drove into the driveway. He carefully made his way to the front door and placed the key in the lock. He slowly opened the door, entered, and stood in the large hall. There were no sounds. No Ann nor boys to greet him home. The house was dark, and he felt an eerie coldness. It was not the usual house that he was accustomed to. He stood still, hoping for the familiar sounds and sights. He thought, *Ann, why are you doing this? Why?*

He went into the kitchen, noticed that the sink was a mess with dishes, glasses, and silverware. He saw the boys' lunch boxes. He opened one of the containers and picked up the thermal bottle. As he tuned the top, out came a strong, foul odor of fermented juice. He opened up the other containers. They, too, had the strong, foul odor.

He returned to the hallway to the table where they kept their bank and checking account books. He opened the drawer, grabbed the checkbook, and noticed that there was a large deposit. It was the end of the month, and Ann typically would make a large deposit to cover the end-of-the-month bills. A check had been written to Will Walsh for two thousand dollars. That was very unusual, thought Bob. He didn't know any Walsh. He grabbed the telephone book, searching the section for attorneys, and found a Will Walsh. Bob wrote down the telephone number, with the thought that he would call tomorrow.

Bob went upstairs into his bedroom closet. He searched through the small metal box where they kept important documents. He examined every folder and noticed that the children's birth certificates were missing. He left, feeling melancholy, and went to their study room. He looked around for anything unusual. He started going through the desk, looking for the folders of letters that he and Ann had written to their friends and relatives. Bob and Ann maintained a journal of events, and on a regular basis, they would send to their friends and relatives back east. The folder was missing. Bob thought that it was strange that Ann would take the letters.

Bob headed for the attic. He had wondered if Ann had found the money. He pulled the door cord, opened the staircase, and peaked into the attic. He reached for the shoebox. Throughout their relationship, Bob had purchased expensive jewelry for Ann—rings, pendants, and earrings of sapphires, rubies, pearls, diamonds, and jade. Ann's favorites were opals. It always pleased her to receive jewelry. He was relieved to see the shoebox. He slowly clutched the box. It felt lighter than usual. He removed the lid and opened the jewelry boxes. They were all empty, and the envelope was missing.

He went into the kitchen, thinking of something to eat. As he searched through the cabinets, his thoughts were of Ann and the children, and he no longer felt hungry. He went into the boys' bedrooms. They were typical boys' rooms with sport trophies and posters of their favorite athletes—shoes and clothing all over the place. He opened the dresser drawers and found that some were empty. He went back to his bedroom closet and found that the suitcases were missing. He thought that they would be gone for a long time.

Disappointed, he returned downstairs, to the kitchen pantry, searching for liquor. He noticed that the pantry shelves were not as full, and he wondered why. They usually kept it full of canned goods and dry goods. For a family of six, the shelves were always stocked. He grabbed the bottle of scotch and a glass from the cabinet. As he set the glass down to pour, he noticed two rings. Ann's wedding band and the one she wore the most, the other with their birth-stones. Tears started to form in his eyes. His eyes became blurry as he poured the liquor. He thought Ann was serious about leaving him. He poured another drink and drank quickly. With each swallow, the pain slightly subsided as he lost coordination.

He walked sluggishly as he made his way up the stairs to his bedroom with the bottle in hand. He placed the bottle on the end table and dropped, face-down, on the bed. He twisted and turned, trying to sleep. His head was pounding, and his throat felt dry. He grabbed the bottle, raised it to his lips, and lifted his head up, and drops of liquids entered his mouth. He was disappointed that it was empty. No use in going downstairs because he was out of liquor and in no condition to drive. He looked at the clock, but the numbers appeared fuzzy. He tried to sleep, but his mind was filled with the events of the past week and was thinking of tomorrow. He hoped that the attorney would be cooperative so that he could get in touch with Ann. His body was tired and in need of sleep, but his mind was active. He needed to find a way to relax his mind. He went down-stairs, grabbed the cassette recorder, and found a tape labeled "Soft Sound." It was a tape of love songs. He returned to his bedroom. He lay in bed as he listened to the music. The songs felt and meant something different now. He felt the pain of love with each song. Even though some of the songs were sad, they comforted him.

He continued to play one song over and over, "A Heart Needs a Second Chance" by Thirty-Eight Special.

> Since you've been gone, I've felt my life slipping away.
>
> I look to the sky, and everything is turning gray.
>
> All I made was one mistake. How much more will I have to pay?

Why can't you think it over? Why can't you forget about the past?
When love makes a sound, babe, my heart needs a second chance.
Don't put me down, babe. Can't you see I love you?
Since you've been gone, I've been in a trance.
This heart needs a second chance.
Don't say it's over. I just can't say goodbye.

The sun, piercing through the lightly drawn blinds, awakened Bob. He looked at the clock, and to his surprise, it was almost 11:00 a.m. He had to get up. He had things to do. He went into the kitchen and drank a large quantity of orange juice and water. His head hurt, yet his thoughts were of Ann and the children. He wanted so much to talk to her. He wondered if Pete was successful in contacting Ann. He searched through the telephone directory's section of community services and found a number for the Women's Transitional Living Center. A woman answered. Bob meekly said, "I'm not sure, but I think my wife and children are in a shelter. I have been out of town. It's important that I know that they are okay. Can you help me?"

The woman asked, "What's her name?"

Bob sensed the annoyance in the woman's voice. "Ann Dorsete and she has four boys with her."

The woman politely said, "If you'll hold on, I'll check."

Within a few minutes, the woman was back. "Yes, we do have an Ann Dorsete at a shelter, and she and the boys are safe."

"Can I please talk to her?"

"I'm sorry, but we don't allow that."

"Where are they?"

"I can't give you that information."

Bob, pleaded, "Can you please get a message to her to call me?"

"I can try."

"Please. I just want to talk to her, please," said Bob, pleading.

Bob decided to call Walsh. He was frightened of what he might hear, so he decided to put it off. Bob hated to deal with the attorneys. Not that they are all bad. He disliked the way they conducted themselves and the exorbitant fees they charge. He sometimes wondered if they work for their clients or for themselves. Win or lose, the attorneys always get paid. In his dealings with attorneys, he found them to be conceited, with an attitude that they are more superior. He thought about all the lawyer jokes and that there must be some truth in them. One came to mind.

Two blind animals bumped into each other, a snake and a rabbit. As they bumped, they both said, "Who are you?"

The snake replied, "I don't know. I'm blind."

"So am I," replied the rabbit. "I have an idea. If you touch me, maybe you can tell me what I am."

The snake said, "That's a good idea." So the snake started touching the rabbit. "You have two long ears that stick up, a furry coat, four short legs, and a fluffy, round tail." The snake excitedly said, "You're a rabbit! Now, tell me what I am?"

The rabbit did the same to the snake. "You have a small head, two large fangs, a long tongue, and a long, slimy body. You're an attorney!"

Bob nervously dialed the telephone with blurry eyes. A man answered, "Will Walsh and Associates, can I help you?"

"Yes, my name is Bob Dorsete. I'm not quite sure, but do you have a client by the name of Ann Dorsete, *D-O-R-S-E-T-E*?"

"Yes. I'm Mr. Walsh. She's my client. I thought that you would be returning Saturday. No matter. I am notifying you that Monday morning, we are filing a petition for divorce."

Bob's heart sank to the floor. "Divorce! What do you mean divorce? She doesn't know what she's doing. Please, sir, let me talk to her."

"Look, buddy," said Walsh in exasperation. "I didn't find her. She found me. On Monday, I am filing a petition for divorce. My advice to you is, get an attorney."

Benignly, Bob said, "I'm sorry for raising my voice. I'm just shocked. Can you get a message to Ann to please call me? I need to talk to her."

"Mr. Dorsete, would you consider going for psychotherapy help?"

"What! What the hell are you talking about?"

"Mrs. Dorsete believes that you need professional help."

"Who the hell are you? Are you a psychologist? You don't even know me. What have I done?"

"I'm only trying to help. You have problems, and you need professional help," the lawyer said, and he abruptly hung up.

Bob was thinking that Walsh had the typical attorney attitude, and he would have to hire an attorney to deal with Walsh.

It was a hot afternoon, and the heat was starting to annoy Bob as he slowly walked into the restaurant. He entered through the back door. "Hey, man, I didn't know that I would see you today," said Skip Rivers, smiling, in a joking voice. "I was all by myself for two days."

Bob, low-key, said, "I want to thank you very much for taking care of business."

Skip Rivers was a tall and slender man in his mid-twenties, with deep frown lines on his forehead and has beetle-brown eyes. At seventeen, Skip quit school and joined the military. He got in trouble after six months of service. He was discharged on a minor offense. Skip's employment record had been unstable. However, Bob took a chance. Bob always believed in second chances. Skip had worked out well. He came to work every day and did a good job. Bob trusted him with the cash and the business decisions. Skip, still smiling, showing his rotten teeth, said, "You look like somebody died."

Bob said, a little embarrassed, "Ann's filing for a divorce. I can't believe it. It's like a bad dream."

Skip was trying to be funny. "Hey, boss, it's not the end of the world. This is California. Everybody gets divorced."

"You don't understand," said Bob seriously. "Divorce didn't exist in our vocabulary. We married forever. We never talked about divorce."

Skip, noticing that Bob was tense, said, "Hey, man, I'm sorry. I was only trying to be funny to cheer you up. Hey, wait here. I got something that's really gonna cheer you up." It was the middle of the afternoon, and the restaurant was empty. Skip returned with a joint and lit it. He puffed on it heavily and held his breath. In a low voice, he said, "Come on, man, you need a hit."

Bob felt uncertain. Perhaps Skip was right. "What did I tell you about smoking grass in the restaurant? I told you that I didn't care if you smoked grass but not here. Now put it out, and open the back door."

With his fingers, he put it out. "Hey, I didn't mean anything by it. I just thought it would cheer you up."

"It's okay. How's business?"

"We're holding our own. I've been taking care of the orders and paying for the deliveries. I've been closing early. I hope you don't mind. I've been putting in long days. Here are the bills."

"How about the cash?"

"Ann took the cash for Tuesday."

"Can you tell me—I mean, you were the last person to see Ann. Can you tell me anything she said to you? What was her mood?"

Skip, with a heartfelt voice, said, "Gee, man, I'm really sorry about you two dudes. I really am. I hated when my parents got divorced, and I hated every man that she has been with. I hope you don't get divorced."

Bob, agreeing, said, "So do I. On Monday, her attorney's filing for a divorce."

Skip murmured, "All week, it was a bummer. Man, she was so down. When we didn't have customers, she just sat at the table, staring outside. I could see that she was sad because she had tears in her eyes. She left early on Wednesday. She called Thursday morning that she would not be in for the rest of the week. She told me that I was in charge and that you would be back on Saturday."

"Anything else?"

"Yeah. Man, she was on the phone quite a bit. Not that I was trying to be nosy. She had a notepad with numbers and was writing things down."

"Have you heard from her?"

"No! I had no way of getting a hold of you. I really needed to get in touch with somebody. Man, I'm really glad to see you."

"Skip, I didn't get a chance to tell you. I have a potential buyer for the restaurant. I have a contract, and I'm just waiting for the property management's approval."

Skip was dejected, thinking that he would be out of a job. "When is this going to happen?"

"I should hear from the landlord any day."

Skip, shaking his head, said, "Man, that's a bummer."

"No, it's not. You're going to be working for us, with the computer company I have been telling you."

"Ann's cousin. *Shit!* What the hell do I know about computers?"

"Don't worry about that. I think you're a hell of a salesperson." Bob said, grinning. "You got charisma."

"What's that?"

"Charm!"

"Yeah, but what're the chances of that deal going through?"

Bob, trying to sound positive and optimistic, said, "That's the reason I went to New Jersey. I wanted to make sure that it was a go."

"Even without Ann? He's her cousin. He might take sides with her and tell you to go to hell. You're not blood."

Bob, with the most confident attitude he could muster, tried to reassure Skip. "He's a businessman. He has to do the prudent thing, and personal matters should not interfere with business. He gave me his word. Come on! Let's get ready for customers."

Later that day, Bob when to the bank and discovered that Ann had cashed in all their CDs and withdrawn all the cash from their savings and checking accounts, leaving only the minimum amounts. Bob cashed the two checks—one from Bennix and one from Micro Research.

Bob was on medical leave of absence from Bennix International, a large manufacturing company. Tom Connelly and Bob Dorsete had met at Bennix. Tom had a stocky build, like a bull and sometimes behaved stubbornly like one. He was muscular and, at times, used brawn instead of brains. He had a strong, bulky face, with curly dark hair and a big mustache covering his square face. Tom and Bob had spent a great deal of time together and had become close friends the past year. Tom had helped Bob with the constructions of the restaurant, building the counters and painting and tiling the floors.

Tom had a genuine liking for Bob. He appreciated that Bob had offered him a job with Micro Research. He was currently working for a small electron company. Tom was concerned how the breakup of Bob's marriage would impact their plans, but he was more concerned for Bob. He was also cognizant that Bob had no real friends in California and was impressed with the friends Bob had back East. He wanted to be the same kind of friend to Bob now and would do whatever Bob asked him to do.

It had been another difficult night for Bob Dorsete. He drank himself to sleep. He was awakened by the light and by the sound of the birds. He looked at the clock. It was past ten, so he decided to get up. He had no motivation to go to his restaurant. Besides, he expected the return of Tom today. He needed the company of a friend, someone to help him sort things out. Bob was lying on the couch, watching television, when the doorbell rang. He opened the door, and the moment he saw Tom, they embraced.

Tom, trying to encourage him, said, "Hang in there. How are you doing?"

Bob asked, "Do you have news from Pete?"

"Pete is still trying to get in touch with Ann."

They talked about the events of the past week. They were interrupted by the sound of the doorbell. Bob got up and opened the door. He stared up at the big figure of a man. Bob was taken by surprise as the man took a step backward. Bob stared at the round, forceful face. Bob said, "Good morning."

Ray Ditler replied, "Good morning! How are things?"

"I don't know. I'm concerned for Ann and the boys."

"Some guys from your company have been trying to get in touch with you."

Bob paused for a moment. He was perplexed, not knowing what to say. "What do they want?"

"I don't know," said Ray with little emotion as he stroked his bent nose, an old football injury. "They said something about wanting to talk to you."

"Well, tell them to give me a call. I'm home."

"Okay," said Ray. "I'll tell them that," and he slowly turned his overstretched stomach and walked away.

An hour or two passed. The doorbell rang. Bob opened the door. "Hey, Bob," said Ray. Bob stared at two strangers dressed in jackets, ties, and sunglasses.

"Hi, Mr. Dorsete," said the black man wearing a nice suit. "My name is Alan Morris, company personnel manager. This is Dave, Bennix security." He was wearing a cheap, undersized jacket.

Bob acknowledged the introduction and said, "Please, come in." He led them to the kitchen and asked, "Would you like some coffee, wine, or anything? Me, I'm drinking wine."

Alan replied, "No, thank you. We have heard that you have had a tough week."

Bob was cautious of the man. *I don't need to have my senses clouded,* he thought. *I need to think clear.* "Would you like some coffee?"

Alan Morris approached Bob and said, "I'd like to talk to you in private."

Bob was curious to know the purpose of their visit. "I have nothing to hide. We can talk here."

Mr. Morris replied, "I think it's better if we talked in private, Mr. Dorsete. Can I call you Bob or Robert?"

"Bob, please."

Mr. Morris said, "Can we step outside?"

"Yes," said Bob as he opened the patio door. He grabbed two folded chairs and opened them. They sat near the edge of the patio, close to the pool. The sun was starting to burn through the June morning mist.

"Bob, we've been trying to get in touch with you," said Alan Morris as he adjusted his dark sunglasses. "We're concerned about your state of mind."

"What do you mean 'my state of mind'? What are you concerned about?"

"Well, you've gone through a tremendous ordeal. The shock of your wife filing for divorce and the allegations of abuse." He paused to remove his glasses. "The fact that she placed herself in a shelter and the problem you had at work with your boss. The company is concerned." Bob was silent, wondering how much Morris knew. He was curious to know how Alan had obtained this information. "We're concerned about your mental and physical well-being… We would like to have you checked out."

"What do you mean 'checked out'? For what?" Asked Bob trying to stay calm. "What have I done?"

"We are just concerned that this is a very difficult time for you, and you need someone to talk to." Bob was only half-listening to what Alan had to say. He was carefully studying this man that he never saw before. Morris was in his mid-thirties. He was articulate, speaking with a certain elegance, and choosing his words carefully. "We've been watching the airport in New Jersey for the past couple of days this week. We hired armed security guards around the clock for your boss. This is costing the company a great deal of money."

Bob replied, "Why all the intense action? Why the security guards? I don't own a gun."

"We were hoping to intercept you in New Jersey. To talk to you. You surprised us when you returned early. Your return flight was scheduled for Saturday." Alan paused to get closer. "You're a street guy from New Jersey. I'm a street guy from Philadelphia. You know people. You can buy anything." Alan paused to select his words. "We need your cooperation. We would like to take you to a place. Think of it as a resort. You'll have some professional people to talk to, to evaluate you, if you need help. It will all be provided for free."

"There's nothing wrong with me. I haven't hurt anyone," said Bob, upset.

"If you get checked out, you'll be able to set the record straight for a lot of people." Bob turned from the man to stare at the pool. He quietly listened, but his mind drifted away. He watched the slight movement of the water as his thoughts were absorbed into the sun's reflection on it. He felt the warm sun against his skin. He heard the sound of the breeze blowing through the trees and the sound of birds. The sun reflecting on the pool appeared so close yet so far, and so were his thoughts.

Alan continued to talk, "I looked through your personnel record. I personally don't believe the allegations made against you. I want to help you. You do this for us, that is, you volunteer to go with us, and I will get involved in your case."

Bob did not answer as he continued to stare at the pool. Morris persisted. "If you are okay, you'll be out in a few hours. The most that you'll be at this place is a day or two. If you get a good report, it can help you with your wife. I promise you that we'll do whatever we can to help you out, financially. How would you like to be relocated back to New Jersey?"

"I'm only concerned about the well-being of my wife and children. I have no idea where they are. But I can imagine, from the brief conversation I had with my children, they're confused and frightened."

"It's costing us a great deal of money keeping tabs on you—security guards around the clock at the facility and around your boss. It's dollars and sense. You understand finance." He paused to hear a reply. "You know, we could fire you right now."

"Why would you think that I want to hurt anybody?" said Bob in a raised tone. "I'm not a violent person. I don't have a gun, nor have I ever applied for a gun permit."

"I believe you. However, you have to look at it from our viewpoint. Allegations have been made that you threatened to kill your boss. We are a large company, and it is our responsibility to protect our employees. It's costing the company a lot of money." Smiling, he added, "This place is like a resort, with a swimming pool, tennis courts, and things to do. You'll have a chance to relax."

They talked for more than thirty minutes. Bob stood up and walked to the edge of the pool. He looked deep into the water as his mind debated. He turned and gazed at the house. How empty it was without his children. How empty it was without Ann. What pushed her to go to a shelter? "Okay, I'll go with you. I have to ask you."

"Sure," said Morris delighted.

"Are you taking me to a mental institution?"

"Oh, no! It's real nice place. You can walk out anytime you want. You understand? You're volunteering. You can walk out anytime. Pack a few things. Can I please use your phone to make the arrangements?"

"Yes. The phone is on the right as you enter. I'll show you."

Bob walked into the house, and Tom stared at him in solitude. "Tom, I want to talk to you," said Bob. "Come upstairs with me. I have to pack."

They were at the top of the staircase, and with a blank look in his face, Tom asked. "What's going on? Where are you going?"

"I can't tell you everything right now. Alan Morris wants me to go to a place to get checked out. Ann has made allegations that I threatened to kill people. They have been watching the airport for my return, and they have security guards around the facility. Morris is putting pressure on me." They enter the bedroom. Bob grabbed his suitcase. It was still packed. He checked the contents. "The thing that bothers me the most, they know more about Ann's actions than I do. Tom, I want you to stay here in the house. If Pete calls—no, better yet, try to get in touch with Pete and tell him where I'm going."

"But, where are you going?"

"I don't know yet. They haven't told me. I'm finished. Let's go down."

"I think that you're making a mistake. They can't threaten you." Bob did not answer. He walked down the stairs, with Tom directly behind him.

Bob approached Alan, "Okay, I'm ready to go. I would like to have a number so that Tom can get in touch with me."

"Sure. No problem," said Alan.

"Better yet," said Tom, "I'll follow you so I know exactly where you're at."

"No need for that," said Alan, distressed. "We'll get in touch with you. He'll be safe. I'll give you a call once he gets checked in."

Tom moved toward Bob, grabbed his arm, and pulled him into the next room. "Bob, I don't like this whole thing. You don't know these people. I have been with you the whole week. You haven't done anything!"

"Thanks for your concern. I gave my word. I'm going to prove them wrong. Please, get in touch with Pete."

"Okay! Good luck! I'll be here if you need me."

They walked outside, with Dave walking close to Bob. Alan Morris made his way to the driver's side. Dave opened the front door for Bob and sat directly behind him. No one spoke. Bob's mind was preoccupied with thoughts about what kind of place he was going to, and why he had agreed to go. Fearing the unknown, he became confused and concerned. He wanted to change his mind. Twenty minutes later, they drove into the driveway of a white, six-story building structure on the left side and four on the right. Alan drove around to the back and parked the car. They walked to the emergency entrance. They walked to the admittance window. All the time, Dave walked close to Bob. A woman sitting behind a glass booth asked, "May I help you?"

"Yes," said Morris, "my friend would like to be admitted."

The receptionist asked, "Does he have medical coverage?"

"Yes." Alan pulled out a medical card and handed it to the woman. Bob stared in disbelief. How is it that this guy is prepared, including medical card? Bob had lost his. Bob was mystified in trying to figure out their involvement.

Alan calmly said, "Why don't you just take a chair over there? I'll take care of everything."

Bob walked toward the chairs and slowly turned toward the door. Dave seized Bob's arm and asked, "Where are you going?"

Bob replied, "I'm going outside for a smoke."

"I'll go with you." They walked outside. Dave offered a cigarette to Bob. They smoked in silence.

Bob broke the silence. "How long have you been working for Bennix?"

"Ah, for some time."

"What office do you work out of?"

"Oh, I work all over."

Bob was trying to be friendly, trying to strike up a conversation in an attempt to get a feel for this man. Why did he have such a hard-cold look? He was tall and thin, over six feet. He never removed his dark sunglasses. Bob was looking at the man's cheap jacket for any bulge of any kind, checking to see if Dave had a gun. Bob heard his name get called and entered the building.

Alan said, "Okay, Bob, you're in. A doctor is going to examine you. I'll be right here with you. But first you have to sign these papers, just hospital procedures. Sign right here." Alan handed Bob a pen. Bob grabbed the pen and tried to read the papers, but his eyes were blurry. "It's okay. I read them."

Bob was in a small room, sitting on a patient's bench as the nurse was taking his temperature and blood pressure, and was drawing his blood. Bob broke down and started to weep. With tears running from his eyes, he called out for Ann. He tried hard to focus, but everything around him became hazy. A small woman, with dark hair, wearing white, entered the room. She asked, "What's the matter with this man?"

Bob said, weeping, "I'm concerned for my wife and children. They're in a shelter, and I don't know where they are. I miss them. I want to see them."

The nurse calmly said, "Just relax. We'll take care of you."

The dark woman turned to Alan and asked, "What's the matter with this man?"

Alan Morris said, "I'm a friend of his." He gently pulled the woman to the edge of the room. Bob watched with unclear vision. Minutes later, Alan approached Bob and said, "I'll be in touch with you. You take care, and thank you for your cooperation."

The small woman approached Bob and said, "Don't worry. We'll take care of you. We're just waiting for someone to escort you to your room." Within minutes, a hospital security guard entered the room. A big young man. Bob was in a trance and never questioned the reason for the security guard. The guard escorted Bob through the hallways, into an elevator. They stopped at a door with a small window with metal mesh around it. The guard rang the bell, and the door opened from the inside. The guard told Bob to go in. Bob walked through the door. He stopped as he heard the key turn behind him.

Bob was approached by a medium-built man with a short, dark beard and glasses. "Hi, my name is Salle." He extended his hand out.

"I'll show you to your room." Bob followed in silence as they entered a simple small room. "Please open up your suitcase. I need to check the contents."

Bob replied with a light laugh. "Why? Are you afraid I might have something to kill myself?"

Salle gazed at him, half-grinning, "It's procedure." As he was going through the suitcase, Bob thought, *This is no country club. It's a fucking hospital. I'm locked up. I'm really stupid to believe that I was going to a country club. That fucking Morris!* "By the way, where are the tennis courts?"

Salle replied, with a half-smile and a little chuckle, "Who told you we have tennis courts?"

"That's what I was told."

"By who?"

"By the people that brought me here. Look," said Bob, now a little frightened, "I don't think I belong here. I want to leave."

"Sorry. Let me explain you your rights," said Salle. "You have been admitted as an involuntary patient, and I'm here to advise you of your rights. The reason you are admitted here is because you are dangerous to yourself and to others. Now you're going to be here for a duration of seventy-two hours. You will be evaluated, and medication will be given to you as necessary. It is possible for you to be released by the end of a seventy-two-hour period. But if the professional staff decides that you need continued treatment, you can be held for a longer period. If you are held longer than seventy-two hours, you have the right to a lawyer, a qualified interpreter, and a hearing before a judge. If you are unable to pay for a lawyer, one will be provided."

Bob, antagonistic, asked, "What the hell are you implying? That I'm crazy?"

Salle handed Bob the leaflet and said, "By law, here is a copy of your admission paper. If you need anything, just ask. Now, let me show you around."

"I'm not crazy," said Bob, annoyed. "I don't belong here."

"Please follow me," said Salle, smiling and thinking to himself, *They all say that.*

Bob was enraged as he was talking to himself to stay calm. *Don't show any anger and cooperate. Stay composed, and don't give them any reason for keeping you longer.*

Salle showed him the dining area, which was also the recreation area. "If you have any questions," he says while pointing to a glass partition, "someone is always there."

"Can I make a phone call?" asked Bob.

Salle pointed to the end of the lounge, "You can make calls and receive calls there!"

"Thank you," said Bob, and he made his way to a chair and sat down, totally oblivious to the people around him. It had been a painful day for him. It was starting to turn dark, and he was feeling a little hungry. Bob walked toward the glass partition. "Salle, can I have something to eat?"

"Sorry, but you missed dinner," replied Salle. In frustration, Bob took out a cigarette. "You can't smoke now. You're not allowed to have cigarettes. You're allowed one cigarette on the hour. However, since you're a new patient, you can smoke now. Please give me your cigarettes," said Salle, extending his hand.

Bob felt dehumanized due to this childlike treatment, deprived of rights and dignity. He handed his cigarettes, his only means of pleasure, to Salle. As he smoked, he looked around in disbelief and thought, *What the fuck did I get myself into? How can I be that stupid? I'd sue that prick. I've got to stay calm. I've got to be careful of what I say. I've got to talk to Pete.*

Bob called Pete several times, but no one picked up, and other times, it was busy.

He finally he got through. "Pete! Thank God I got through to you. I'm in the fucking nuthouse! They locked me up in a mental institution!"

"Bob, how can you be so stupid? An intelligent person like you? I spoke to Tom. He told me. Why did you agree?"

"You're right. But it all made sense at the time. They know everything. They know that Ann will file for a divorce on Monday. They know that Ann is in a shelter. Do you know that the Bennix people were watching the airport in New Jersey? They have security guards around the place I used to work." Bob, becoming more intense and madder, thinking that a smooth-talking guy and his security guy in a cheap jacket made it all so life-threatening. "Pete, he said that Ann is afraid of me. She thinks I want to hurt her. He said that Bennix would help me with the divorce. He convinced me that this would demonstrate to Ann that I'm not dangerous or a threat to her. He convinced me that I had no choice."

Pete said in a strong tone, "I don't give a shit. You don't belong there. Don't you understand what you've gotten yourself into?"

"You are right. Get me the hell out of here."

"I'll see what I can do. What hospital are you in? Give me the phone number there."

"Okay. Thanks Pete. Get me the hell out of here!"

If anybody could help me now, it was Pete, thought Bob. Pete was a smart individual that was good with his mouth. Pete has always been an entrepreneur, confident that someday he would make it rich. So far, on this road to riches, all his previous business ventures had failed, resulting in lawsuits, bad credit, and personal bankruptcies. He survived all of it. It was a long wait for Bob as he sat and stared at the two telephones. An hour had passed until the telephone rang. Bob quickly picked up the handle and said, "Pete!"

"Yeah. Look, I'm not your blood relative. There's very little I can do. I have to get your family involved. Who can I call?"

Bob paused. He found it difficult to respond. "This is very embarrassing. I didn't tell my mother or any member of my family. Let's keep this away from my mother. She's an old woman, and I don't want to upset her."

"Okay. Who do you trust? Who do you think I can talk to?"

"Call my sister, Joanne. She might have a difficult time understanding all of this. Try to keep it very brief."

"Do you want her to call you?"

"Only if she needs to hear from me. I really don't know. I guess so."

"I'll tell her to get in touch with you."

An hour later, the telephone rang. Bob quickly picked it up, hoping that it was for him. It was Joanne. She was weeping, "Pete told us where you are. Why didn't you tell us? Why didn't you tell us you and Ann were having problems? We would have helped. We could have done something for you."

"I didn't know that we had a problem!" Bob said, feeling weak. "I don't know where she and the boys are. Please, I don't want to talk about it now. Right now, I'm in a mental institution. Do whatever Pete tells you to do. I need to get the hell out of here."

"Okay, Bob. If you have that much trust in Pete, we'll trust him. I'll call him."

"Good! Thank you. Please, don't tell mom."

Shortly afterward, Pete called. "Bob, I need some information. Who admitted you? Was the person a psychologist or psychiatrist?"

"I don't know, Pete. I got emotional. The guy from Bennix was doing all the talking. There were two women in nurse's uniform."

"Someone in the hospital had to evaluate you. I have to find out who admitted you. I'll call you back."

"Pete, you promise to call back?"

"Yes. Stay calm. Let me see what I can do."

Bob was sitting in the lounge, anxiously waiting for the clock to reach the hour. He desperately wanted to talk to Pete or to anybody for that matter. The patients were mostly older men. They quietly watched television. Bob was distracted by a woman walking around. She was in her mid-fifties, with hair tied in a bun. She was slender and neatly dressed in a long, brown dress. She was busy wiping the sink, the counters, and the tables. A tall, thin man, wearing baggy pants and glasses, who appeared to be undernourished, approached Bob. "Hi, my name is John Bell."

"Bob Dorsete."

"You look normal. What are you doing here?"

Bob, half-laughing, said, "You're one of the patients and you noticed. What is that woman doing?"

"That's Helen."

Bob, watching the clock, said, "It's time for a cigarette. Excuse me." He walked to the glass partition and asked Salle for his cigarettes. A man in a bathrobe asked Bob for a cigarette. Bob turned to the orderly and asked, "Can I give him one?"

Salle replied, "It's up to you."

Bob sat down to enjoy his cigarette. John Bell said, "Don't give anybody your cigarettes. They don't have cigarettes. If they know you have cigarettes, they'll bother you."

Bob said, "It's something small. As long as I have them, I'll share them."

"Walk with me." As they walked by the tables, a young man said, "Hello!" He was in his late twenties, with a boyish face and a fixed smile. He had light-brown hair and jade eyes.

"Bob, this is Steve," said John.

Bob extended his hand, "Hi, Steve. My name is Bob."

Steve said, "Hello."

John gently pushed Bob to continue walking toward the hallway. "The reason I'm here is because I have a hard time remembering sometimes. A couple of years back, me and my girlfriend were mugged, and I was beaten. I was beaten so badly that sometimes I forget."

"Sorry to hear that," said Bob.

"I'm getting out tonight. Do you want to get out?" Bob did not reply. "We can get out of here. I know the whole layout."

"And where are you gonna go?"

"Oh, I have lots of places."

Bob liked the temptation but not the risk. "I don't think you should. You're here for help?"

"No, I don't belong here."

Bob had noticed that some of the patients were in bed. He asked, "How come these people are in bed so early?"

"It's the medication. They spend most of their time in bed. They're up for one meal a day. Do you want to get out?"

"I think we should stay here."

John, in a low voice, said, "On weekends, they have new people. They don't know the patients and place. I know how we can get out. I have friends waiting outside."

The temptation was in Bob's mind. "You should stay here."

"I don't belong here," said John in an upset tone.

The telephone rang. "I think it's for me." Bob quickly walked toward the phones and grabbed the handle. "Pete, you got good news for me?"

"They're telling me that they can't do anything tonight," Pete said sadly. "I found out that you were admitted by a nurse. A freakin' nurse! A nurse put you in a lockup unit. What did you say to her?"

"I told them that I was concerned about Ann and the boys, and I wanted to see them."

"Well, who the hell told her that you threatened to kill people?"

"That fucking Alan," said Bob, aggravated.

"I threatened them with a lawsuit if they don't get a qualified person to evaluate you. Right now, just stay calm. Don't give them any reasons, and don't take any medication. Just stay calm. Are you listening?"

"Yeah! I hear you. I'm pissed. I need to get the hell out of here. Do you recall the movie *One Flew over the Cuckoo's Nest* with Jack Nicholson? That's where I am. I'm in the cuckoo's nest with a bunch of nuts. Some walk around like zombies. If I don't get out of here, I will go nuts. Pete, get me the fuck out of here!"

"I can't do anything tonight. I'll try first thing in the morning."

"Okay, Pete. Thank you very much."

Bob was beat as he lay on the bed. He stared at the ceiling. He noticed that the room had no door. The bed was flat on the floor. He tried to sleep. No matter how hard he tried, he could not fall asleep. He got up and looked out the window and stared at the lights below, the city of angels. He thought, *It's a big city with a lot of people out there with a lot of problems. It's hard to believe that I am locked up. How could this happen in America?* He looked at the sky and saw only darkness and whispered, *"God, please let her hear these words and what my heart is feeling. Ann, I need you so badly. I need to talk to you. I need to hear your voice. Ann, if I could only reach you to tell you how much I love you."*

Chapter 3

Bob Dorsete was promoted to assistant facility manager and was relocated to California from New Jersey. It was a small facility for a large international company. Since his arrival, he has worked long and productive hours. He found the facility lacking in certain procedures and full utilization of computers. In his first year, he had increased sales by eight percent, and in the second year, by twelve percent. His boss was pleased with the increased sales, however, it reflected poorly on him because Bob attributed the increases to bad contracts that were underpriced and the lack of updated contracts with major customers. His boss felt threatened by Bob and saw Bob as a hotshot.

Two years later, Bob was having a problem with a new female employee. Bob could not understand why she was not able to perform her tasks. He had many meetings with her in an effort to understand and help her. She feared that Bob wanted to dismiss her. She made allegations that he had sexually harassed her. The company had policies regarding sexual-harassment allegations. Bob Dorsete's boss had informed upper management in New Jersey that perhaps the allegations were true. To minimize legal costs and to dismiss the matter, Bob was demoted as the assistant manager. The woman no longer worked for Bob. Bob, who had always been a fighter, filed a complaint within the company. This did not help matters since management was already in support of his boss. Bob feared they were trying to force him to quit or eventually fire him. Because of this fear, he was under a great deal of stress. He became upset about his career and concerned about the finances since he was the sole supporter of his family. Bob had become depressed and unhappy. He desperately wanted to leave Bennix.

California had to be the fast-food capital of the world, thought Bob. There where tons of hamburger, Mexican, and pizza places. Bob had, many times, thought of opening an Italian fast-food restaurant, selling sausage and hotdog sandwiches with vegetables, which were popular back East. The plan was to draw investors and to franchise. He viewed this venture as a way out of Bennix. Ann supported the idea. In early January of 1990, the restaurant was in operation. It had taken Bob six months to find a location, obtain permits, purchase the equipment, and establish suppliers.

They hired two young men. Ann's involvement was to open the restaurant in the morning at 10:00 a.m. and work until 2:00 p.m. After working at Bennix, Bob would go directly to the restaurant to work until closing (9:00 p.m.), clean the place and the equipment. Bob also worked the weekends at the restaurant. The hours were long, and he was becoming exhausted mentally and physically. He was very saddened that he had little time to spend with his children. Their life had changed drastically, and they both were under a great deal of stress. Bob was experiencing anxiety attacks. Bob's doctor had advised that he needed to relieve his stress. He recommended that Bob take a leave of absence from Bennix. After three months, it became obvious to Bob that the restaurant was not going to work out. They were depleting their savings to operate the restaurant. Pete Devigne had visited Bob and Ann. Pete boasted about his company. He had a manufactory facility, a warehouse, and three retail stores. Pete had obtained financial backing, over ten million dollars from an investor located in San Diego. Pete stated that he had plans for a West Coast operation that involved Bob and Ann. But they would have to sell the restaurant. Pete promised that he would try to compensate them for any losses.

Pete Devigne and Ann had grown up together since they were very young. Ann was one year older than Pete. He was the only child. At seventeen, he quit school because he was bored. He purchased an old ice-cream truck, selling soft ice cream. He spent more time repairing the truck and equipment. He was an entrepreneur seeking his own ventures instead of working for someone else. He endeavored in many business ventures. Bob had always praised Pete's go-getter ability. In the mid-eighties, Pete self-taught himself to build, repair, and program computers.

Bob and Pete had had several discussions regarding the West Coast operation. After several weeks, Bob decided to sell the restaurant in an effort to recover some of the cost for the equipment and furniture. Bob decided to follow his doctor's recommendation and take a leave of absences. In addition, Bob filed a harassment suit against Bennix. His boss told the insurance company's investigators that Bob had a restaurant, and his claim was false. It was a means to take time off from Bennix to devote time to his own personal business.

Ann was upset that Bob was drinking and smoking. Bob told her that he needed to deal with the stress. His stomach was in constant knots, and he experienced difficulty in breathing. Sometimes he could not sleep at night but would just lay there, tossing and turning, and he was not eating regularly. He argued with Ann over silly things, which normally did not bother him. Ann was worried about Bob's change in behavior. He seemed to have become short-tempered, with no patience, and unable to cope with simple family situations. She thought that it was just a temporary thing. He was productive. He was busy searching for a location and developing a business plan for the West Coast operation. He had traveled to San Diego twice to meet the investors and some of Pete's managers.

It was Memorial Day weekend. Bob was preparing for his trip to New Jersey to discuss the plans for the West Coast operations, accompanied by Tom Connelly. Bob had estimated the money needed and the cost_for the first three months. He obtained a lease agreement and had three potential employees. He had a potential buyer for the restaurant. The sale was pending the landlord's acceptance of the buyer as a new tenant.

Tom Connelly was in the guest bedroom. Ann and Bob were in their bedroom. Ann warmly and tenderly put her arms around Bob, kissed his cheeks, and whispered in his ear, "Can we make love?"

Bob replied, "I have other things on my mind—the lawsuit, the restaurant, this trip." He gently pushed her away and stared. "I don't have the energy."

Ann put her arms tightly around him and said, "I want to make you happy. You'll be gone for a week. You're going to be gone for over a week, and I want to make love to you."

Embracing her, Bob said, "Okay!"

Ann said, smiling, "Let me get cleaned up and put on something nice."

Bob always enjoyed making love to Ann. She was the only woman he had ever loved. After sixteen years of marriage, he still enjoyed making love to her. He was tired but needed a break from reality and all the problems of life. Bob watched as she dressed. She slowly put on a red garter belt, black stockings, French-cut bikini panties, a transparent, red bra, and a sheer, white dress. While dressing, she peeked a smile to him. Bob was getting excited. She enjoyed turning him on and loved the attention. She was standing by the mirror, brushing her hair. Bob walked toward her. He put his arms around her waist, kissed her neck, and said, "You look beautiful, and I love you very much."

She smiled back and said, "Just give me a moment." Bob's hand moved under her dress, past her thighs, over her stomach, and up to her breasts. He caressed them very gently. He placed his arms around her waist and moved tightly against her. She smiled with approval.

As they lay in bed kissing, Bob stopped touching her. She asked, "Bob, what's the matter?"

"I'm concerned about this trip and all the other problems. I just can't get these thoughts out of my head—the restaurant, Bennix, and this business venture. I don't know if I'm doing the right thing. I've never been in this kind of a mess before. I feel all the weight is on my shoulders."

"Well, while you're in New Jersey, you'll have a chance to see your friends, your mother, and a chance to relax."

Bob was annoyed. "How can I relax? I'm going on business. I have to find out why Pete is delaying things. I'm having second thoughts about this venture with your cousin. I don't know if I'm doing the right thing, quitting my job. Vinnie has been telling me that sales are sluggish, and Pete continues to increase expenditures. I'm giving up my job, which pays for our medical insurance and the rent. How can you think I'm going to New Jersey to relax?"

Ann did not want to upset Bob and meekly said, "I didn't mean anything by it. I just thought that maybe you'd get a chance to see your friends."

"This is more business than social. I also have to see our renters. Vinnie told me that they are not taking care of the property. How can you think I'm going on a vacation?"

"I didn't mean it as a vacation."

Raising his voice, "Then what the hell did you mean by it?"

Ann immediately put her arms around him and said, "Can we just forget about all this stuff for the moment and make love?"

Bob grabbed her by the arms to break her embrace. He stood up and paced the floor. "I'm not in the mood. How can I make love to you when I have too many things on my mind? I have to finish packing." He walked away.

Ann went after him and put her arms around his neck. "Please, Bob, just forget that for a moment. Let me make you feel good. Try to relax." She pulled Bob to the edge of the bed, opened his robe, and started kissing his chest, his waist. He wanted to relax, to make love, but his mind was overwhelmed with anxiety. He felt used and taken for granted. She had no idea what he was going through, and he began to feel angry. He pushed her away. She fell back, hurt and in tears. "Bob, what is the matter? Please, let's make love."

"I can't relax. I'm not in the mood. I have to pack."

"Let me make you feel good. You always enjoy making love."

"I do, but this is not the time. I'm not in the mood!" Bob went to the closet to get his suitcase.

Ann put her arms around him, holding him tightly, and kissed the back of his neck. Bob turned around and gently pushed her away.

She fell against the corner of the door opening and slipped to the floor. "You hurt me!"

Bob angrily replied as he left the room, "Well, I told you to leave me alone! I told you I wasn't in the mood!" Ann chased after him as he went downstairs. He went to the cupboard, grabbed a glass, and grabbed the whiskey from the pantry.

Ann asked, "Bob, do you have to drink so much? Why are you rejecting me?"

"That's the problem with you! You don't understand what I'm going through. You don't understand the pressure I feel. I have the responsibility of bringing home the bacon! I have all this burden on my shoulders."

"That's why I love you," Ann said passionately. "You're very dependable and hardworking. You take on eighty percent of all the responsibilities."

Bob shouted back, "Yeah, eighty percent of all the headaches too! How many times have I asked you to start looking for a job to help me with some of the pressure? How would you like to have all the headaches? That's it. Let good old Bob take care of everything." He paused, looking at a small plant. "Look at this plant. You don't even water the plants. I do." He picked up the small pot and threw it against the wall. Ann became too petrified to say anything. "You see…what happens to plants if you don't water them…they die." He stared at her. "Just stop and think where we would be without my income. We couldn't afford to live here." He turned to walk out then turned around. "Sometimes…sometimes I feel like leaving. I think of divorcing you. Think about that. Then you'll have one hundred percent of the responsibilities and the headaches. Pete is your cousin. Why don't you take this trip? Why don't you go to New Jersey? Why don't you learn about computers?"

"But I don't know anything about business. You're smarter than I am."

Bob, half-laughing, sarcastically said, "Yeah, yeah, that's right! Dump the responsibility on me. That's why I'm the head of the family. Just a figurehead. Everything I do is for this family. What do you do for me? I always have to do what's right for the family. I feel like shit, like I have nothing to live for."

"That's not true! You have me and four boys that love you. You are very special, and I love you."

Bob, walking out, said, "I'm under a lot of pressure, and you're irritating me." He went out of the house with Ann chasing after him.

"Where are you going?"

"I'm going out to the car to get my cigarettes."

He returned inside, turned on the television, and sat on the couch. Ann watched in silence. With a cigarette in one hand and a drink in the other, he said, "Just leave me alone, and get the hell out of my sight."

He had never smoked inside. Ann was as still as a statue. She was frightened and felt as though she were on the edge of a precipice. She had never seen Bob so angry nor heard such violent words from him. She was confused and didn't know what to say or do. Yet she was sure of her love for him and wanted to help. She got in front of him and dropped down to her knees with trembling breath, and, nervously sweating, said, "If you want to hit me, hit me. If it makes you feel better, hit me! Go ahead and hit me!"

Though his mind was filled with rage and anger, he could not. He loved her and wanted to have her but was overwhelmed by the frustration of anger. He reached forward, gently put his hands on her elbows, and, raising her up, said, "Why would I want to hurt you? I just need some time to myself. So please, go to bed and leave me alone."

Ann replied, "How can I go to bed and leave you this way?"

Bob shouted, "Just leave me the hell alone. Get out of here!" Ann, nervous and scared, left. She fell asleep, sobbing. Bob continued to drink and smoke. He fell asleep on the couch.

Memorial Day

It was six in the morning. Ann Dorsete was awakened by the sound of the alarm. She felt around and noticed that Bob was not in bed. She got up to see if he was downstairs, knowing that he was a difficult person to get up in the morning. She found him sleeping on the couch. Gently, she shook him. "Bob, you have to get up. You have a flight to catch."

Bob, still unconscious, said, "It's dark out."

"You have to get up. You have to make your flight."

Bob, rubbing his eyes, asked, "What time is it?"

"Just a little past six. Would you like me to make you breakfast?"

"No, we don't have time. We'll have something at the airport." Bob went upstairs to wake Tom. The two men quickly dressed and were ready to leave.

Ann stood in silence as she stared at Bob. She was still in her nightgown and appeared tired from lack of sleep. She didn't know what to say, hoping that he had slept it off. "Have a safe trip."

Bob, also tired, said, "If the restaurant gets too difficult for you to handle, close it and place a sign, 'Closed for Vacation'. Make sure you set the alarm every night. The most important thing is that you take care of the boys. Goodbye!" He turned to Tom and said, "Let's go."

Once outside, Tom asked, "Why didn't you kiss Ann?"

"It's nothing. We just had a little argument."

Ann was troubled by Bob's threats and could not go back to sleep. The telephone rang, and she wondered who could be calling this early in the morning. "Hi, Ann. It's Pete."

"Hi, Pete. How are you?"

"Okay. I called just to make sure that Bob and Tom left."

"Over an hour ago."

"Good."

"By the way, Bob has some gifts for your children. Make sure you ask for them. You know how forgetful Bob can be sometimes."

"That's very nice of you." He chuckled lightly, thinking that was a strange comment. Bob was not forgetful.

Ann wanted to tell Pete what had happened, but she decided not to air dirty laundry to him. "Bye, Pete."

Ann was in the kitchen, getting breakfast for her four boys. One by one, they walked in. She heard Mark was up. She went upstairs to dress her three-year-old.

She desperately needed to talk to someone. She called Marion Philips, a close friend of Bob. He had been a big brother to Bob. Bob had work at Marion's Arts & Craft store as a teenager. She heard a "hello" on the other the end of the wire. Very meekly sobbing, she said, "Marion? This is Ann."

"Who!"

"Ann Dorsete."

"I can barely understand you. Something's wrong!"

Ann, still sobbing, said, "I'm concerned about Bob. He almost hit me last night. He pushed me hard. He threatened to hurt me. I'm frightened. I don't know what to do."

Marion was astonished. "Ann, just calm down. I can't understand you. Tell me what happened."

"He left for New Jersey," said Ann, still sobbing. "We had a big argument last night. He blames me for all his problems, his job, the restaurant. He threatened to hurt me when he returns."

Marion, again, tried to calm her down. "I've known Bob for a long time. It doesn't sound like him."

She snapped back, "He's changed. You don't know what he's been like. He hits the kids. He threatened to divorce me."

"I'm sure that he doesn't mean it. You both have been under a lot of pressure. I find it very hard to believe that he really would do those things."

She asked, "What am I going to do? I'm afraid of him. I'm afraid he's lost it!"

"Did he beat you?"

"No. Not really," said Ann, a little more in control of her emotions. "He just pushed me."

"Does he beat the children?"

"No. He does hit them. He threatens them when they don't listen or when they fight."

"Well if he's on his way to New Jersey, you're not in danger. He'll get over his anger. You'll see. I know that he loves you and the children, and he wouldn't do anything to hurt you."

Ann was calm. "I'm convinced. He'll get in contact with you. Will you talk to him?"

"Okay! I didn't know he was coming to New Jersey. I haven't spoken to Bob in over a month. I have no way of getting in contact with him."

"I'm sure that he'll call you."

"Don't worry. I'll talk to Bob. You're both just going through a difficult time. You'll be okay?"

"I'll feel better if you talk to him. Don't tell Bob that I called you."

"Okay, I won't tell Bob. You have my word. Bye!"

Ann was feeling the weariness of lack of sleep. She was disappointed and worried that Bob had not called. He always called on every trip to tell her that he had arrived safe and he loved her. She called Bob's mother. Ann told Bob's mother that she had not heard from him and called to make sure that he arrived safely. Mrs. Dorsete told Ann that Bob just left to see Vinnie with his friend. Bob's mother was surprised that he did not call Ann.

Ann tried to go about her daily routine. Ann's thoughts kept drifting to the night before. She needed to talk to someone. She went over to her next-door neighbor, Karen Ditler. Ann nervously rang the bell. She had second thoughts of turning back.

Karen opened the door. "Good morning! Hi, Mark."

Ann said, trying to smile, "Do you have time for company?"

"Sure!" Karen noticed that Ann appeared nervous. "Please, come on in."

Ann followed Karen to the kitchen. "The restaurant has kept me busy," said Ann, shaking. "I hardly get the chance to talk to you. I hope I'm not bothering you."

Karen asked, with a concerned look, "Would you like some coffee?"

"Sure." Ann sat quietly.

Karen said, "Sugar and milk." Karen was dressed in her usual long, loosely fitted dress to conceal her big hips and large legs. She wore her hair in a typical over-processed style, dyed in silver blue, "a young blue bird." She had fleshy, pronounced frown lines on her forehead. She sensed that something was wrong. "I don't know how you two manage a restaurant and four young boys. Ann, what's wrong?"

Ann hesitated at first then answered, "Bob yelled at me. He was terrible." Ann started to sob. "He left without kissing or hugging me. This is the first time that he ever left on a business trip without hugging and kissing me. This is the first time that he left angry." Ann grabbed her tissue to wipe her eyes. "I know that he's been under a lot of pressure. I'm sorry for telling you. I just needed someone to talk to."

"Where is he now?"

"He left for New Jersey. I'm frightened! He threatened to hurt me and the children."

Karen said, in sympathy, "But I thought you were managing everything. I thought that you were happy."

"I think he's having a nervous breakdown." Ann continued to sob. "I have no one here. I am all alone. I'm frightened."

"You should talk to Ray. Do you mind if I call Ray?" asked Karen. "You know he was a police officer, and he has seen a lot of domestic violence. He's outside." Ann was uncertain of what to say. "Talk to Ray. Maybe he can help." Ann was reluctant and embarrassed. The only person whom she had ever confided in was Bob. She and Bob had been very private. "Please talk to Ray." Ann did not reply. Karen opened the back door and called out to Ray.

Ray entered the room. Upon seeing Ray, Ann started to cry. "Bob and I had a terrible fight last night. He threw things at me. He threatened to hurt me!"

Ray, moving closer to Ann, placed his big arm around her. "Where is he now?" It was difficult for Ann to respond. "Karen, get some water." Ray, handing the glass to Ann, asked again, "Where is he? Calm down. Tell me what happened."

Ann said, weeping, "He's in New Jersey."

"When is he coming back?" asked Ray.

"Saturday. I'm afraid that when he returns, he might do something terrible. I'm afraid that when he returns, he's going to hurt me."

"No one is going to hurt you."

"What am I going to do? I have four boys. He's going to leave us."

"He's having a nervous breakdown," interjected Karen.

Ray said, "He needs help. I have seen it many times. Husbands or boyfriends get violent and beat up their wives or girlfriends. You have to leave him until he gets help."

Ann interrupted, "Where will I go?"

"A shelter. You have to take legal action to protect yourself and your boys. You need a lawyer."

"Why a lawyer?"

Ray said, with a slight smile, "You have to get the courts involved."

"But I don't want a divorce! I love Bob."

"He could lose it any time. He could hurt you."

Ann's eyes opened wide. "You don't know him. He always gets his way. You don't know how smart he is. I could lose the boys."

Very sternly, Ray said, "Too many wives don't know what to do or where to go for help. There are groups to help you. It's not like the old days. An attorney can help you get restraining orders and force him to get help. If he loves or cares for his children, he will get help. You will be in a safe, secret place. He won't be able to find you."

Ann, now more in control of her emotions, said, "I don't know if I can do it. We've been together for a long time. I don't know. I have to think about it." With confused thoughts, she asked, "Would you please keep an eye on the house in case he returns early?"

"Sure," said Ray, "I'll do that."

It was evening. Ann lay in bed, weeping and constantly wiping her eyes. She had eaten very little and had not even cooked for the children. She had made them peanut butter and jelly sandwiches for supper. She was tired, confused, and scared. She decided to call Marion. "Hello, Marion. This is Ann. Have you heard from Bob?"

"Ann?" asked Marion.

"Yes, it's me," said Ann.

"It's hard to hear you. I am having a birthday party for a friend."

"Have you heard from Bob?" said Ann in a loud voice. "I thought perhaps that he contacted you."

"No, I have not heard from him. I can't talk right now. I have to take care of my guest. Can I give you a call this time tomorrow?"

"Please do. I'll be waiting for your call." Disappointed, she hung up.

She was unable to rest because her thoughts were on last night. She tried watching television, tried reading. She went to bed but could not find any rest. Twisting, turning, and sobbing, she worried that he meant to leave her.

Memorial Day plus Day 1

Ann woke the children up as part of her daily routine. She helped dress the young ones, fed them, and sent them off to school. Ann was moving slowly as she dressed Mark.

She slowly made her way to Karen's house. She rang the doorbell. Karen, opening the door, greeted her. "Ann, how are you doing?"

"Okay, I guess."

"Have you heard from your husband?"

"No!" she replied, placing Mark down and holding his hand.

"I have some numbers for shelters for battered women."

"I don't know if I want to take drastic actions."

"At least talk to a lawyer as Ray suggested."

"I'll think about it. See you later," replied Ann.

Ann was late getting to the restaurant. They were down to one employee, Skip. Ann greeted Skip the usual way. Ann was despondent. There was not the usual kidding or laughing with Skip. She spent most of the time sitting at a table, wiping her eyes. Bob and Ann had been good to Skip, so he was concerned for her. "Ann, is there anything I can do?"

Ann replied, trying to hold back the tears in her brown eyes. "No. No, thank you." Her eyes became watery.

Skip noticed the tears forming. "I would like to help."

Ann, wiping her eyes, said, "Bob and I had a big argument."

Skip, laughing, said, "Me and my girlfriend fight all the time."

Ann did not laugh. They worked through lunch. Ann was there, but her mind was on other things. She left early, telling Skip she had some errands to run. She had forgotten to make her daily list of inventories.

Ann was home, turning the pages of the telephone book, searching for attorneys. She called several numbers. She called the office of Will Walsh.

"Good afternoon. Will Walsh. Your name, please."

"Ann Dorsete," she nervously replied.

"How may I help you?"

"I think that my husband is having a nervous breakdown. I'm afraid he might hurt me and my children."

"Mrs. Dorsete, this is a serious matter. I need to see you as soon as possible. Can you come to my office this afternoon?"

Ann paused. "I don't think so. My children will be coming home from school soon."

"Tomorrow! I can see you at one."

"I have to think about it."

"Is your husband at home or at work?"

"He is on a business trip in New Jersey."

"I'll schedule you for one tomorrow."

"I have to think about it."

"You decide, but don't wait too long."

Ann anxiously watched the clock, anticipating a call from Marion. It was finally five o'clock. The phone rang. She quickly picked it up. "Marion, I've been waiting for your call."

"Hi, Ann. How are you doing?"

Ann started to weep. "I'm scared. I have been in a trance for the past two days. Have you talked to Bob?"

"No. He hasn't called me."

"I really think he doesn't love me. If he cared, he would have called."

"Maybe he's busy. He is here on business."

"He doesn't have five minutes to call me?" said Ann in a raised tone. "I've been talking to my next-door neighbor, a retired policeman. He's telling me to go to a shelter and hire a lawyer. I've talked to attorneys, and they tell me the same thing."

Marion was dismayed. "Ann, what are you talking about? A lawyer! For a divorce? You've been married for a long time. You've known each other since high school. Don't you think that you should talk to Bob first?"

"I don't know. I'm scared. I have been in contact with shelters for battered women. The attorneys advise me to get a restraining order against Bob. I'm terrified."

"It's not right if he comes home and finds you and the boys missing."

"Perhaps you're right," said Ann, sobbing. "But he's not himself."

"Ann, let me get in touch with him," said Marion, realizing that the situation was bad. "Let me talk to him first. Promise me you won't do anything irrational, and don't do anything until I have spoken to him."

Ann, now composed, said, "Yes, I'll do that. But he hasn't called me."

Marion said in a firm voice, "Call me first before you decide to do any of these crazy things. You promise?"

"Yes," whispered Ann.

Ann prepared for bed. She checked on the boys and kissed them good night. She lay in bed, reading, trying to put the unpleasant thoughts out of her mind. She loved Bob. She thought of the things Ray Ditler and the attorneys had told her. He could be dangerous. She couldn't take a chance. She thought that perhaps if Marion had gotten in touch with Bob, he could be on his way back right now.

She heard the sound of a door. She quickly jumped out of bed and ran to the hallway. She was frightened by the shadow coming up the steps. She gave a gasping sound. The figure's eyes made contact with hers, and it did not say a thing. She slowly walked backward. "Bob, you're home early. Why?" He did not answer. "Bob, are you all right?" He slowly backed her to the bedroom, placed his hands around her neck, and started to close the air from her body. She tried grasping for air. "Bob…stop. Stop! Stop!" She shrieked out for help. She was sitting up in bed, shivering. She felt cold from perspiration. She tried focusing her eyes, realizing it was a dream. She wondered if the children were disturbed by her screams. She listened carefully, and then she pondered if it could become real. She went downstairs to check that the doors were locked and that the alarm was on.

Memorial Day plus Day 2

Worrying about Bob had drastically disturbed Ann's routine of taking care of the boys and the restaurant. She was late in getting the boys off to school. At work, she was withdrawn, making no conversation with Skip. It was a busy day, and her mind was eased a bit. When things were slow, she sat isolated as she had done the previous day, wiping her eyes. She spent the majority of time looking at a notebook and making telephone calls.

Ann said, "Skip, I have to go. Regarding tomorrow, I'll be busy with the boys. I won't be here. I'll leave it up to you if you want to open or not." Skip stared in silence. "If I don't see you tomorrow or Friday, don't worry about me. I'll be okay. I have many things to do."

Skip was uncertain what to say, but he was sure that whatever it was, it was serious. "Anything I can do?"

Ann embraced him. "Thank you, but no. There are things I need to do. I just need time to sort things out. Goodbye and take care. I'm sure that Bob will contact you in a few days."

Ann was in the office of Will Walsh, a white-haired man in his fifties. His face was clean-cut and forceful, with a strong chin and a tiny, firm mouth. Ann said nervously, "I'm afraid of my husband. If he discovers that I left him, he'll burn the house." She began to weep. "I'm afraid that he's having a nervous breakdown. I'm afraid he might hurt me and the children."

"Have you ever called the police?"

"No! What for?"

"Hitting or making threats."

"He never hit me."

"Have you or your children been to a doctor or hospital as a result of your husband?"

"No!"

"Mrs. Dorsete, to protect you, since there are no reported occurrences, we have to take legal action. You have to file for a divorce. You need to prepare a declaration with the courts. You have to make a written certification that you are fearful for your life and your children's. You have to cite events and incidents."

"But I don't want a divorce!"

"Filing for a divorce does not get you divorced. If he hit you once, he'll hit you again."

"But he hasn't hit me. He yells a lot and throws things."

"Mrs. Dorsete, he threatened you. He struck you and the children." In a fatherly manner, he added, "Yes. I know that this is a difficult decision, but you have to think about yourself and your children. We'll try to get help for him."

Ann interrupted, "My next-door neighbor, a retired cop, suggested that I go to a shelter for women."

"Yes, you'll be safe." His eyes, which had a direct, piercing gaze, stared at Ann and detected she was uncertain. "Do you want to live in fear?"

"I'm not sure if I want to file for divorce, but I'm afraid he is losing it."

"Go to a shelter. You'll be safe. You'll have a chance to relax, ease your fears. It will help with your case."

Ann weeping, said, "Bob is not always like this. He has been under a lot of stress—his job, the restaurant, the lawsuit, raising four boys."

"Your husband needs psychological help. When will he be back?"

"He is scheduled to return on Saturday."

"We have to move fast. Find a shelter. I have to prepare motions. Here is a list of things you need to do. Take your valuables and documents and place them in a safe deposit box. Savings! Are they in separate or joint accounts?"

"Joint."

"You're going to need cash. Withdraw the money and establish new accounts in your name. Also, I will need a retainer."

"Why the withdrawals?"

"Once your husband discovers that you filed for a divorce, he will do the same. I need written statements from you by tomorrow. That will give me one day to prepare my motions, and I can file on Monday." He noticed that Ann was uncertain. "Mrs. Dorsete, you are doing the right thing. Don't have any contact with your husband. I'll see you tomorrow."

Karen and Ray helped Ann pack boxes of food. She took the children's birth certificates, her personal notes and letters, and other important documents. As she packed the suitcases, the fear of last night's dream flashed through her mind. She became apprehensive that Bob could walk in any moment and stop her. She hastened to get out of the house as quickly as possible.

The boys entered the house. Ann said, "Take off your backpacks. Go to your room and pack some of your toys. We have to leave."

The older boys sensed that their mother was not herself for the past two days but had no knowledge of the problem between their parents. Bobby asked, "Mom, where are we going?"

Ann gently put her arms around him. "We're taking a trip. I don't have time to explain. I'll tell you in the car." Embracing him tighter, she added, "Somebody wants to hurt us. We have to get away."

Ann nervously followed Ray. She tried to take her mind off her fears and concentrate on her driving. They pulled into the driveway of an old house. The building once had been a residence and was now converted into a shelter for battered women. From the outside, it looked like an ordinary house. There were neither signs nor identification. There was nothing unusual about it except the paved parking lot in the back.

Ann left the children in the car and went inside with Ray. There was an elderly woman with nicely fixed blue-gray hair. Ann introduced herself, "I'm Ann Dorsete. I called yesterday."

The woman, smiling, said, "Oh yes, I'm Allin. Please complete these forms."

Ann felt uneasy. "I'm fearful for my life and my children's."

Allin said, "That's what we're here for. We're here to protect you." She checked the forms. "Please sign here. You have four boys. We need a witness. Will your friend sign?"

"Yes," said Ray.

Ann was shaking nervously as she signed the forms. Allin sorted through the papers. "You agree to stay with us for about forty-five days. I see you have a large family. I am sorry, but we don't have the space tonight. Can you check into a motel?"

Ann nervously said, "A motel not a shelter!"

Ray interrupted, "I can help her."

Allin remarked, "I am sure that we will have a place for you tomorrow. We have several locations. You'll be safe in a motel as long as you don't contact your husband." She paused to hand Ann a handout. "My name and telephone number are inside. Please read and follow our recommendations. They are for your safety. Call me as soon as you check in so that we can contact you. Do you have money for the motel?"

"Yes!"

Ray found a motel just ten minutes from his house. Ann asked, irritated, "Is this place safe? It's ten minutes from home. Why don't I just go home?"

"Ann, you can't go home. Bob could be back anytime. You check in. I'll watch the boys."

Ann murmured, "I hate him for putting me through all this. It's his fault." Ray did not say anything.

Ann and the boys were settled in two rooms. Bobby asked, "Mommy, why are we running away?"

Ann replied, "Daddy is not well, and he needs help."

Tony, crying, asked, "Why does daddy want to hurt us?"

Ann replied, "He is not well. He could do terrible things to us." All the boys, except for the youngest one, were sobbing that they wanted to go home. Ann hugged them and reassuringly said, "We're going home in a day or two. Pretend we are going on a trip."

Bobby asked, “I don’t want to go on a trip. I want to go to school tomorrow.”

“Not tomorrow. Next week. Bobby, remember all the times daddy yells at you. He is not the same daddy. I couldn’t stop him. I don’t want him to hurt you.”

The telephone rang. Ann nervously picked up the handle. “Pete! How the heck did you find me?”

Pete said, chuckling, “It’s a long story. I told the people at the shelter that I was your brother and your mother wanted to talk to you. But you’re in a motel?”

“Yes!”

“With the boys?”

“Yes!”

“Bob is worried! He has been calling the house all day.”

Ann said in a tense voice, “I’m going to divorce him for putting me through all this. It’s his fault.”

“Ann, this is crazy. I just saw you this past March. I have been talking to you almost weekly. You told me that you were happy and about how hard Bob was working.”

Ann in an anxious tone, replied, “He is not the same! He hits the boys. He pushed me. He throws things at me. He threatened to leave me.”

Pete, puzzled, said, “I have known you since we were kids. I have known Bob since I was fifteen years old. Not once did I ever see him abuse you. Ann, he is here in New Jersey. I can keep him here. I will talk to him. Now, please go home.”

“You don’t know. I signed papers. There are rules that I have to follow. I hired an attorney.”

Pete, worried, said, “Ann, are you going to trust strangers or your blood? Please stop all this. I will keep Bob here. You’ll be safe. I have been with Bob for two days. He told me that you had an argument. He feels bad.”

Ann interrupted. “He hasn’t called me for three days. You have no idea how tormented I have been.”

"He has been focused on business. Just today, we were discussing the detailed plans for the West Coast store. He is good. He is okay. He has a lot of things on his mind."

"Don't you dare give him this number."

Pete sensed that she was uneasy and not reachable. "I will not get him the number. But please call him. Just to tell him that you and the boys are okay. He needs to hear from you."

Memorial Day plus Day 3

Ray Ditler been had a police officer in the Los Angeles for over twenty-five years. Now at fifty-five, he retired six months before the Dorsetes moved next door. After his retirement, Ray started a private investigator and security company. He had no need for an office. He worked out of his house. He was in a very competitive field, and business was slow. Ray had no animosity toward Bob. He did have a little jealousy that Bob had a college education, a larger house with a pool, four boys, and an attractive wife. Ann told him that Bob had become violent by throwing things around the house, threatened to hurt her, and threatened to kill his boss. Ray saw himself as a policeman helping a defenseless woman, his neighbor. Ray contacted Bennix, informing them that he feared that Bob Dorsete had a mental breakdown, his wife was in a shelter, and he threatened to kill his boss.

Ann was in the bank, applying for a safe deposit box and creating new accounts. Later, she went to Walsh's office. "This is terrible," said Ann. "I went to the shelter yesterday, and they had no space for me and my children. I had to spend the night at a motel. It was difficult explaining it to the boys."

"The shelter will find you a place, and you'll be safe. Did you make a list of your assets?"

"Yes!" said Ann nervously.

"Written statements and finances?"

"Yes, here." Ann handed several pages of paper.

Walsh looked at the documents. "Good! Do you have a check for me as we agreed?"

"Yes. I can't believe what I found in the attic." She paused, uncertain if she should continue. "I found this next to my jewelry." She handed Walsh an envelope. Opening it, he was surprised to see hundreds of dollar bills.

"There's twenty thousand dollars," said Ann in a surprised tone.

"You found it in the attic? Strange. Did you know about it?" Walsh thought, *It isn't every day you find twenty thousand dollars in your attic.*

"No."

"Where did it come from?"

"I don't know. I have no idea."

"Is your husband involved in drugs?"

"No. Of course not. I don't think so."

"What type of work does your husband do?"

"He manages contracts. He reviews and negotiates contracts and invoices customers."

"Mrs. Dorsete, I think that your husband is involved in something illegal," said Walsh calmly. "Or he wouldn't hide this money and not tell you. It's a good thing that you are in a safe place. When he discovers that you took the money, he could become dangerous." Ann was frightened to hear this. "I'll place this money in my trust account." Walsh paused to review Ann's financial summary.

Residence value	$430,000
New Jersey property	$190,000
Savings and checking	$30,000
Certificates of Deposit	$50,000
Retirement, employee contributions	$34,000

"I see that you are financially sound. Do you have life insurance?"

"Yes. Two for him and one for me."

"Do you know the cash the values?"

"I don't know," Ann melancholically said. "The boys were not happy leaving the house. They talked to their father last night."

"You spoke with your husband?"

"Yes!"

"Did you call him?"

"Yes!"

"Why?"

"My cousin contacted me. He persuaded me to call my husband."

"What did you tell him?"

"I was too angry. I don't remember. I told him I was in a shelter."

Walsh, concerned, said, "Please, you cannot have any contact with him. Your cousin, the computer guy? Don't talk to him."

Ann, frustrated, replied, "My boys are upset that we had to leave the house. I don't know how we can spend weeks in a strange place."

"It's for your protection. I'll contact your husband, the number on your cousin's business card," asked Walsh.

Ann nodded, "Yes."

"I'll tell him that we are filing for a divorce. I'll strongly suggest that he get psychological help. I can suggest places to deal with his anger, to deal with his strong, negative emotions. I want you to call me every day. Here's my card with my home number. Call me anytime."

Ann thanked him and left his office.

Walsh reviewed Ann's written statements and concluded that Ann was an abused woman and that she has causes for going to a shelter. He will need to make stronger statements of abuse and violence in her declaration. Walsh reviewed Ann's finances, and he was content that there were plenty of personal assets for her to begin life as a single mother.

That afternoon, Ann and her children were in a shelter located twenty minutes from her house. Ann had two rooms furnished with a single bed and a bunk bed. Ann was advised that they had set times for meals, responsibility for cleaning their rooms, doing her own laundry, and helping out with other household chores. For the next two days, Ann and the children ate very little. The boys were all apprehensive and uneasy. They want to go home. Ann did her best to assure them that they would go home soon. Ann was in bed, trying to sleep. She couldn't stop thinking. *What choice do I have? Will he hurt us? I can't take the chance. Am I wrong for protecting my children? Is it going to be better? I did everything for him. I loved him. It's his fault. He was wrong. He didn't appreciate me. I can't be holding on to what I'm not sure of. I have to be strong. I can do it on my own. I had one man in my life. I was devoted to him. He disappointed me. Well, it's too late. Things are not the same. We are not the same.*

Chapter 4

Sicily, the largest island in the Mediterranean, known as the gateway to Europe is strategically located two miles from the toe of the Italian boot and not far from the coast of North Africa. Sicily is infamous and best known for the mafia. Some believe that the two-mile opening is the site of Homer's screaming sirens. One must bear in mind the salient fact that Sicily has been occupied by many diverse civilizations. This island bears the scars and ruins of the great armies that have conquered and occupied it—the Greeks in 500 B.C., the Carthaginians, the Romans, the Byzantines, the Normans, the Spaniards and last, the French. All had an influence on this mountainous crossroad of the Mediterranean.

But however magnificent the island is, there are stories of human endeavor. In the fifties, Sicily was a poor, rustic, agricultural society with little interference from the rest of the world. Robert Dorsete was born Roberto in a small, remote town of three thousand people located in the center of Sicily. The "paese" was built into the mountain. The slopes near the town were used for growing grapes and small patches of vegetables. The better flat, fertile land was used for farming, mostly wheat. The town was autonomous and self-sufficient. The mayor and police authorities were one and the same. There was no need for police. The people handled justice in their own way. The most influential men in town were the priests. They were the most educated, most trusted, and closest to God. The people were deeply religious and devoted Catholics.

Very few houses had both electricity and plumbing. The days started from the time the rooster crowed until the time the sun went down. The people worked hard to sustain themselves. The majority of the inhabitants were farmers, farming with the same centuries-old methods of plows drawn by mule or horse. The local laundromat was the nearby stream. The women removed their shoes, tied their dresses, and would enter the stream to wash clothes and then place them on the hot rocks to dry. They were poor in material things but not in culture, family values, and dignity. In the cool Sicilian nights, the men would gather around a fire to drink wine and tell stories of the past. Like their ancestors, they would fight off all those who would try to invade them, even if it took generations. The young boys sat silently as they listened to the history of their forefathers. This was a tradition passed down from father to son. It was part of a boy's initiation into manhood. The women delivered the babies, but the men turned boys into men. At a young age, the children were taught their respective chores around the house and farms. When a boy was able to reach his ear with the opposite hand over his head, he spent the majority of time with his father.

The Dorsete family immigrated to the United States in the late fifties. It was a long and difficult process because of the immigration laws and the Dorsetes' lack of money. Bob was six years old at the time, the youngest of six children—four boys and two girls. The family was separated for almost ten years. Bob's father and his second oldest brother were the first to come to the United States to seek work. After two years, they were able to save enough money and call for the rest of the family. They had to leave the oldest son in Sicily since he was no longer considered a minor.

They settled in Newark, New Jersey, which was the entrance point for immigrants, such as the Irish, Italians, Jewish, and Eastern Europeans. Newark was a melting pot for all types of Europeans and, recently, American blacks. Newark is overshadowed by New York City, hence, New Jersey is referred to as, "the armpit of New York and Philadelphia."

In the late fifties, like most northern cities in the United States, Newark was becoming the home for blacks migrating from the south. The dominant ethnic groups were reflected in the city government and city officials. The South Ward was predominantly Jewish, the West predominantly Irish, and the North and Central dominated by Italians. The Central and East Wards had the largest consideration of Puerto Ricans and blacks.

As more and more blacks migrated into Newark, the whites who could afford it moved out to the nearby suburbs. There was still an influx of Eastern European immigrants into Newark. The large ethnic groups of Italians, Irish, and Jews competed for jobs and struggled for political control of the city. As the City's factories and the equipment aged, companies moved to the suburbs and to other states. The city government was in the hands of greedy individuals. The politicians relied on their ethnic groups for votes. But once in office, they did little for their ethnic group and less for the other citizens. The city started to decline in the sixties and rapidly declined after the sixty-seven riots.

After first arriving to America, the Dorsete family had difficulties adjusting to a new culture, language, and lifestyle. Mr. and Mrs. Dorsete found jobs paying a few pennies above the minimum wage. The older members of the family were also forced to seek jobs. The earnings of every family member were pooled together. Within two years, they purchased their first house. Younger Bob and his older brother of two years were very close. They were teased for the way they dressed, not able to speak English, and their ignorance of the American customs. The boys would tease them, throw rocks at them, and sometimes beat them (some of the boys were American Italians). Bob and his brother always fought back even though they were outnumbered. After the first year, Bob and his brother spoke English fluently, although in the home, they spoke Italian.

There was a neighborhood lot where the boys played baseball. In the summer, the boys would play all day long, one game after another. Bob was rejected because he could not throw, catch, or hit. Nobody wanted him on their team, but every day, Bob would show up at the lot, hoping to play. He did make friends with similar boys like him, who were rejected by the majority of the other boys. But he never gave up. By the time he was eleven, he was a good player and was always chosen as a team captain. He never forgot how it felt to be rejected and made fun of, so he always selected the players no one wanted.

The Dorsetes' neighborhood had the Fourteenth Avenue Hoods. Their base was Jay's, a candy and soda fountain store. The hoods consisted of young white men, mostly Italians. They were the wise guys of the neighborhood. They were also the protectors. They fought off gangs of blacks and Puerto Ricans trying to come into the neighborhood. They made money by hijacking trucks and selling hot goods. There wasn't anything you couldn't buy from the trunk of a car, such as shirts, cigarettes, shoes, and fireworks around July fourth. The hoods sold fireworks to minors, only to be taken by cops a block away.

By the mid-sixties, Newark was predominantly black with pockets of whites in the west, northern, and southern part of the city. The great exodus of white homeowners from Newark to the suburbs was greatly aided by FHA loans. FHA loans made it possible for blacks and Puerto Ricans to purchase a house with a small down payment, regardless of low or bad credit history. The US Federal Housing Administration (FHA) guaranteed private lenders, such as banks and credit unions that issue the loans. If the homeowner fails to pay the lenders, the FHA will pay the lender instead.

Many whites' sellers, who did not want to comply with FHA's requirements for making repairs or lowering the price, had their house burned, known as "Jewish Lightening."

Bob was never taught any prejudices at home. In the streets, he learned to dislike blacks because of their resentment toward whites. The whites, blacks, and Puerto Ricans were competing for jobs and economic advancements, such as the Irish, Italians, Jewish, and Eastern European immigrants had done in the prior years. Thus, it resulted to conscious and unconscious biases among the whites, blacks, and Puerto Ricans.

At the same period, during Bob's seventh and eighth grades, his school's population had risen to fifty students per class. Blacks and Puerto Ricans greatly outnumbered whites. Bob was involved in many fights with black boys. Bob learned that it was more important to fight and get beat up than to run. By the time he was fourteen, Bob was friendly with his black classmates.

Due to the changing population in Newark and the shortage of schools, Bob was bussed to a high school in the west ward of Newark, a predominantly white community. Since he was not from that neighborhood and unknown, he was involved in a lot of fights with white boys. Bob had a reputation for fighting.

From the age of eleven years old, Bob worked as a paperboy, dishwasher, store clerk, and pizza delivery boy. By his senior year in high school, Bob Dorsete had become popular. He was strong, with an athletic build, and participated in school sports. The girls found him attractive. He had a face of a typical Italian with high cheekbones and thick, dark-brown hair. His eyes, eyebrows, nose, and lips were proportion to his face. He had an adult look to his appearance. His high school days were the happiest days of his life. He was popular and had many friends. They always found ways to have fun. But most of all, he enjoyed the company of girls. He was very respectful toward his teachers and authority. That's one thing his father had insisted. Bob had no fear of anyone except for his father. As he matured, he never forgot his birthplace or his roots.

Mario Pellone was a man of medium height, with curly brown hair, and was pudgy around the cheeks, neck, and waistline. He drove a truck for a food distributing company. He was busy in his workshop preparing his camera for his daughter's fifth birthday. Photography was his hobby. He had several cameras, including a darkroom. He spent a great deal of time photographing his daughter, Ann. He had a three-year-old son, and his wife was two months pregnant with their third child. Ann was such a natural for him to photograph. She was so pretty and dainty, and she had a beautiful smile. He wanted to photograph Ann receiving her first tricycle before company arrived. As he left his workshop, he called out, "Ann, are you ready to go outside?"

Rose Pellone responded, "Mario, she'll be out in a few minutes. I'm just finishing her hair."

Mario made his way down the second-floor steps. Once outside, he looked at the sun and set his tripod and camera. It was a beautiful June day. The sun was bright, and it was perfect for photographing outside, he thought. He waited patiently for Ann to come outside.

With a big smile, Ann said, "Daddy, how do I look?" She had her reddish hair in curls. She was dressed in a light lavender dress, white socks, and white shoes.

"You look very pretty. Now turn around," said Mario as he started taking shots. Ann knew exactly what to do. She stood perfectly still, and then she would move, on his instructions. "Hold it." She would hold and smile.

"Daddy, I'm five years old today. Am I a big girl now?"

Mr. Pellone, the proud father he was, with a smile, said, "Yes, you are bigger than yesterday, but you still got a long way to go before you grow up." He put his arms around her, kissed her, and said, "I love you." Ann responded by tightly holding him. "You wait right here. I have a surprise for you." He slowly turned and went into the garage.

Ann, patiently waited, and then she heard sounds of pain. She shouted, "Daddy!" There was no response. Ann shouted again, "Daddy, are you playing hide and seek?" Ann slowly entered the garage. The garage was dark because there were no windows. She could not see over the car. She was afraid of the dark, so she shouted, "Daddy, are you playing?" Ann waited nervously for a reply. She slowly walked toward the back of the garage, calling, "Daddy! Daddy!" She saw Mario on the ground, near the front tire of the car. Ann turned and ran inside the house, shouting, "Mommy! Mommy, Daddy is on the ground…in the garage. He's in the garage."

Rose Pellone, confused by Ann's utterances, turned sharply, made her way through the door, down the steps, and jogged toward the garage. She stopped at the entrance of the garage, calling, "Mario! Mario!"

Ann arrived. "Mommy! Mommy!"

Rose walked past the car and saw Mario on the ground. He was laying on his side, perfectly still. She dropped to her knees and shook him. She quickly left the garage, took Ann's hand, and said, "Let's go inside."

"Mommy, what's wrong with daddy?"

Rose knocked on the first-floor door. "Ann, go upstairs." She knocked again. It was the apartment of her sister, Mary. She glanced to make sure that Ann was out of sight. She rapidly knocked again.

Mary opened the door. "Rose, you're white as a ghost. What's the matter?"

Nervously, Rose said, "Mario is laying in the garage." She paused to breathe. "Please call the ambulance."

By the time the ambulance arrived, the guests for Ann's party were also there. Ann was instructed to stay in the house. She watched from her window and sensed that something was wrong. She thought, if this were a party, how come nobody was happy? How come everybody was quiet and whispering to each other? Her mother told her that her father was sick and that she was going to the hospital with him and her Aunt Mary would be taking care of her. They would have her birthday party later.

Ann did not quite understand what was going on, and she asked her Aunt Mary. "What's the matter with Daddy?"

Mary, sobbing, put her arms around Ann and said, "Your daddy will be okay."

Mario Pellone died in the hospital of a heart attack. Rose had a small, quiet funeral. Her two children were not told, and they did not attend the funeral. Ann asked every day, "When is Daddy coming home?" Mrs. Pellone simply told her that daddy was going to be gone for a while. She finally told Ann that he will never be back and that he was in heaven with God. Ann did not quite understand, but she accepted it. In time, she stopped asking for her father and buried the memories of him deep in her subconscious.

In the months that followed, Rose gave birth to a tiny baby girl. She had difficulty with the pregnancy, and she was not happy. It was not a day for celebration. She was in tears, feeling alone, and thinking, *How am I going to raise three children by myself.* She was concerned about finances. The house was owned by Rose, Mary, and their brother Lou. Lou lived with Mary and her husband, Don. Mary had recently married Don, an older man with adult children, and when employed, he worked as auto mechanic.

Rose missed Mario very much. She was angry at the hospital for not saving him. She was angry with God for taking him. She felt a lot of self-pity for herself and was worried of the responsibility of raising three children without a father.

In the years that followed, Rose Pellone managed. She worked part-time as a seamstress. She received assistance from the state, and her sister and brother helped financially with the house expenses. Rose was consistently busy and had little time to think of men or even Mario. She had taken all his clothing and cameras and stored them in a closet. She kept the room locked at all times.

Rose and her children never discussed Mario. Her children accepted life without a father. Rose had a conviction that the younger children were cheated of time with their father, therefore, she catered to them. She kept a watchful eye on her children and always kept them in the backyard. She would escort them to school and pick them up daily. Occasionally, on Sundays, she would plan day trips. They had to travel by buses since Rose did not drive. Ann hated the long trips because of the time spent waiting for buses.

By the time Ann was twelve, Newark was rapidly changing with the influx of blacks and Puerto Ricans and the exodus of whites into the suburbs. Rose, Mary, and Lou sold their house in Newark and purchased a house in the suburbs.

Mary and Don lived privately on the third floor in two rooms, a bedroom and a living room. They used the first-floor kitchen. The second floor was occupied by Ann's sister and her mother. Her brother had a tiny room that could only fit a bed and a dresser. Ann had her own room. It was the cleanest room in the house, and she was extremely proud of it. Lou had his own bedroom. His room was the worst of all. It was crowded with boxes of clothing, magazines, books, and piles of newspaper. He enjoyed reading. Lou was a bachelor, with no friends, and lived a very thrifty lifestyle. He was the only member of the family to complete high school and worked as a tailor. He had very feminine mannerisms. Occasionally, he would disappear for a day, and no one knew where he had been. He was a very secretive person and kept to himself.

With the passing of time, the house had been ignored and had become dilapidated outside and inside. Some of the neighborhood children called it "the haunted house on the hill," and around Halloween, they would throw toilet paper at the trees. The house was furnished with used and worn-out furniture. It had a strong fragrance of dog and cat food. Downstairs, the hallway, dining and living rooms were cluttered with chairs, couches, lamps and shelves. Ann was genuinely ill-at-ease, inviting friends over.

Lou and Don did not get along. Lou made accusations that the only reason Don married Mary was that he needed a place to live and called him a bum. Don always accused Lou of being lazy. Hence, the two men always irritated each other. Don felt like an outsider, and when he got angry, he would go to the nearest bar. It was a typical Sunday. Everyone was at home. Ann, her brother, and sister were watching TV. Lou was in the same room, reading the newspaper. Don entered the living room and provoked Lou, calling him lazy and a good-for-nothing. It erupted into a verbal confrontation.

Lou left the room. He was in the kitchen, cutting a piece of bread, as Rose walked in, "Lou, don't fight with Don when the children are around."

"Don started it. He walked in, calling me names."

Don walked into the kitchen and said in a loud tone, "Your brother is a lazy son-of-a-bitch. He does nothing around here except for reading and watching TV. He's a bum."

Lou, holding and pointing the knife toward him, snapped back, "You get the hell out of here or I'll—I'll—"

Rose yelled, "Put the knife down!"

Mary walked in and held Don back, "Let's go upstairs."

The two men continued yelling insults. Ann entered, screaming, "I can't stand this! I can't stand this! You're always fighting. You're crazy!" She quickly turned and ran to her room and slammed the door.

Rose said, "You see what you're doing? You frightened my child." She ran after Ann.

Rose knocked on the door. "Ann, please let me in."

Ann shouted, "You're all crazy. You're all a bunch of nuts."

"Ann, please let me in."

Ann unlocked the door, and Rose entered. Ann fell on her bed with her face down, pounding her fist on the bed and weeping. Rose sat at the edge of the bed, and with her hand, she stroked Ann's long hair. Ann said, crying, "I wish I was dead."

Rose tried to turn her over. Ann refused. "Ann, please don't say that. Don't say that."

"But I mean it," said Ann. "I have no friends…and…I live in a crazy house. I'm too embarrassed to invite friends over." She sat up. "Look at this place. Every room is loaded with useless, old, broken-down furniture and junk. The carpet is ripped and smelly. The walls need painting. The kids at school make fun of me, saying that I live in a haunted house. I have to agree with them. From the outside, it does look like a haunted house."

Rose, near weeping, said, "I'm all by myself. I don't have a husband. I tried my best to raise three children. It's not easy."

Ann snapped back, "I didn't ask to be born. I didn't ask to come into this world. I'm not happy. I have no friends, you have no friends, we have no friends. All we have are the aunts and uncles. We never go anyplace."

"But I don't drive."

Ann, weeping, said, "Don't you see we're different? We don't belong in this neighborhood. Everybody makes fun of us. I wish we never moved. I was happy in our old neighborhood. I had friends. The teachers all liked me. We had friends that lived next door to us, across the street from us. Here, I have no friends. The teachers don't like me. I feel like I don't belong."

"What do you want from me?" said a concerned Rose.

"I don't know. I'm just not happy. They're always fighting, always threatening to kill each other. It frightens me."

"They don't mean it. Besides, I'm here."

"But mom, how many times have they chased each other around the house with knives, and you and Aunt Mary were chasing after them?" Ann, with a little more control in her voice, said, "I'm ashamed to bring friends over. The house, it's so terrible-looking."

"You can bring friends over any time."

Ann yelled, "I don't have friends. I'm embarrassed by all of you. You dress in patched-up dresses. You wear old bras with safety pins."

Rose felt hurt. "I have been all by myself, raising three children. You're a pretty girl. You'll make friends."

"How can I? You won't even let me go out on Friday nights. All the kids from school go to the dance. You won't let me go because you say you have no way to pick me up, and it's too late at night."

"Is that it?" said Rose smiling. "Is that what you want?"

"Yes!" Ann replied, pausing. "I want to go out with my friends."

Rose said, trying to please Ann, "If that's what you want, you can go to dances."

Throughout junior high, Ann was a petite girl, an average student with average looks and a pretty smile. Yet a hidden flower, awaiting to bloom. Mrs. Pellone allowed Ann more freedom to stay out late on weekends. Ann made efforts to get involved in school activities. She started going to school dances and made friends. She was invited to birthday parties and sleep-overs. The girls gossiped and talked about boys. They talked about playing games, like spin the bottle and post office and kissing boys. Ann had been invited to the junior prom.

It was a warm Friday October evening in 1968. The Vietnam War had escalated to its highest point. Bob Dorsete had friends whose brothers were currently serving in Vietnam. Bob was a senior in high school, and he was concerned that he would be drafted after completing school. He sat in solitude at a local fast-food restaurant (one of his hangout spots), waiting for friends. Bob's thoughts of Vietnam were strong on his mind as he listened to "Unknown Soldier" by The Doors. It was past 9:00 p.m., and no one has shown up. Little did he know that tonight would be the most important night of his life.

Vinnie Radice and Paul walked in and sat with Bob. They talked about what to do—cruising the strip, seeing a movie, going to the pool hall, or getting some liquor. As they sat there, with no definite plans for the night, an attractive girl walked in. She had long, straight, blonde hair. They watched her carefully as she passed them and continued to walk. They stared in silence, with eyes fixed on her tight blue jeans and the rhythm of her buttocks. They never lost focus as she stood by the counter. She turned around and walked past them with more swaying movement of her behind.

Paul was the first to chase after her, followed by Bob and Vinnie. They saw her entering a car to her waiting friends. Bob shouted, "I've got the blonde." He outran Paul to the driver's side of the car and smiled at the blonde and said, "Hi, my name is Bob." As he smiled, he asked, "Where are you from?"

"Oh, nearby," said the blonde. "I just stopped to buy cigarettes."

Bob asked, "What's your name?"

"My name is Nancy," she replied.

Bob asked, "Where are you going?" He was disappointed that her face was no match for her body. She had a round face, large lips, and distorted teeth. He quickly glanced at the three blank faces of the passengers. He thought that they all appeared to be average-looking except for the little girl behind the blonde. She appeared the most mystified. She had the window up except for a small gap. Bob moved toward the back window and said, "Hi, what's your name?"

The frightened girl replied, "Ann."

Bob thought that she was just a kid, perhaps thirteen or fourteen years old. He turned to Nancy. Paul was now at the door and Vinnie was at the opposite side, talking to the other girls. Their attention was turned to the loud noises of a passing car that quickly stopped in front. They were some of the wise-guys from the neighborhood, the future_mob guys. These guys were always trying to be cool and tough by fighting and drinking. Bob and his friends knew these guys well and did not care for them. It was smarter to avoid confrontation with them because if you fought one, you had to fight all of them. Four guys exited the car, they were talking loud, using foul words. One pointed toward them and slowly swayed toward their direction.

The girls became frightened. Nancy said, "We have to go now."

"Wait!" said Paul. "Do you know where Jan's is, in the Village?"

"Yes."

"Meet us there. We'll make sure that they don't follow us." Nancy nodded her head and immediately took off, burning rubber.

The wise-guys stood still, in surprise and disappointment. One said, "Who the fuck were they?"

Another shouted, "Let's go after them."

"Nah, they're gone," said another.

Paul, Vinnie, and Bob quickly left and turned the corner and headed toward Bob's car. They hurried into the car and looked around for the wise-guys and took off.

Jan's was a typical hangout place for teenagers. They served hamburgers and were best known for their fountain sodas and ice creams. Bob drove into the back parking. They searched for the girls. It was Friday night, and the parking lot was packed with cars and young people walking around and hanging around cars with open doors and loud music. They drove around twice and saw no sight of the girls. By their third drive-through, they saw the girls parked in the street. Bob parked the car behind the girls.

The boys stepped out of the car and walked slowly to the girls. Paul was talking to the blonde, Vinnie was talking to two of the girls. Bob could not decide whom he wanted to talked to. He thought that the young girl was the most intriguing but appeared too young. He decided to talk to her. After a short exchange of words, he asked, "How old are you?"

She replied, "Seventeen."

Bob wanted to be alone with her, so he asked her to take a walk with him. As she stepped out of the car, her long hair bounced and cascaded down her back reaching her buttocks. It was thick, straight, and reddish brown. Her front bangs covered her forehead, almost touching her dark eyelashes. Her eyes were small, her complexion was fair, her nose was petite, and her lips were shapely and wide. She had tight-fitting bell-bottoms and a flower-designed, loose-fitting blouse. She was a bit nervous, thinking that these guys were strangers, and she knew nothing about them. Mixed with concern and interest, she thought Bob was handsome, with his shag haircut, friendly smile, and attractive, brown eyes. He assured her that she would be safe. They walked away from their friends. He asked her where she lived, what school she attended, what they were doing in his neck of the woods. She told him they had just come from a dance, that they didn't particularly like the band, and that they were on their way home. Nancy stopped for cigarettes.

Ann told him that they had been frightened by those loathsome, loudmouth guys. Bob told her about the wise-guys of the neighborhood, the future gangsters of New Jersey. Bob asked if he could take her home. She couldn't answer him right away because she wasn't sure. She didn't know him. However, she was captivated by him. He was polite, gentle, and had a friendly smile. She wanted to be with him, but she didn't think it would be proper since they had just met. She knew nothing about him. Nevertheless, he excited her, and she wanted to be with him. She decided to go with him.

Bob drove for a while. He stopped in an isolated parking lot. As they sat in the car, he kept looking at her. He was bedazzled by her pretty face, especially her smile. His eyes affixed to hers. Slowly, he put his arms around her and embraced her gently. He placed his lips on hers. She embraced him. He delicately opened his mouth and pushed his tongue into hers in search of her tongue. Their tongues met, twined and twisted in uncontrollable excitement. They continued to kiss. He moved his hands from her head to her back and squeezed her securely against his chest. They stopped to breathe. With his hands fixed to the sides of her face, he gazed into her eyes and ran his fingers through her hair and stared for minutes. He put his arms firmly around her, he extended his chest as he pressed his well-developed chest against her breast. With connected lips, their tongues danced once more. They hugged and kissed until they were out of breath.

Bob took her home. As he drove home, he thought of Ann, especially her pretty smile. His body was feeling strange. Something that he had never experienced before. He had dated many other girls. He had experienced sex before, but tonight's feeling was different. His body was tingling, his heart beating with excitement, and his pulse was nonstop. It was a good feeling all around but yet a strange one.

Ann lay in bed, thinking about the boy she met tonight. How kind and tender he was yet assertive. She had never met a boy like Bob, handsome and confident in his actions. She was a little apprehensive that perhaps he was a little bit too forward. Perhaps she shouldn't have kissed him. When she felt his chest against hers, she felt a thrilling sensation that she never felt before. She had never had sex before, so she didn't have any idea what it felt like. She had dated several other boys, and the moment they made sexual advances to touch her, she had rejected them all. One boy was so forceful that he touched her breast, and she had to push him off. But Bob was different. She felt the tingle of her breast through her clothing. She also thought that this feeling was not right. She felt guilty about these sensations. She hoped that Bob would call her. She wanted to see him again.

Ann Pellone was nervously dressing for a date. Her thoughts were of last night. The handsome boy with thick, dark hair, his light-brown eyes, and his friendly smile. She liked him but did not know him. She didn't even know his last name. He appeared a nice boy, and she hoped that he liked her. She had changed several times, trying to find just the right clothing to wear.

Bob Dorsete was proud of his 1960 Thunderbird, painted in a unique bright-blue color. His friends called it, "The Blue Couch." Ann and Bob were at a drive-in movie. They sat in the car, ignoring the movie as they talked, kissed, and embraced. Bob was having a difficult time putting has arms around her because of the steering wheel and high console. He suggested that they go to the back seat so that they could be more comfortable. Ann had been to drive-ins before and knew the purpose of the backseat. She reluctantly told him no. Bob was very persistent. "It's very hard trying to put my arms around you with the high the console and the steering wheel. It's too awkward."

Ann hesitated then answered, "Okay. I normally would not do this. Can I trust you?" She looked into his eyes. "We're not going to do anything but sit close."

"Sure," said Bob. They climbed to the backseat.

Ann asked, "I don't know your last name. What is your last name?"

"Dorsete, D-o-r-s-e-t-e."

"Oh, that's a nice name."

They moved to the backseat and sat closely, embracing and kissing. He noticed that she wore very little makeup and thought she was pretty. He thought of the feelings he had had last night. She also thought of last night, especially the tingling feeling. She welcomed his lips against hers. His kissing electrified her body and sent her head spinning. Their tongues twined, autonomous of their bodies. They squeezed each other tight and kissed for long periods of time. The car windows started to fog up. The illumination from the big screen was like a kaleidoscope, shifting the light inside from bright to dim. They stopped kissing to stare at each other. Bob's eyes, hungry for approval, were fixed on her chest. He gently brushed his hand over her breast and then rested it firmly on it.

Ann quickly grabbed his hand, and in an angry tone, said, "Don't do that."

Bob apologized. "I can't help myself." Placing his hand on her breast, he said, "You're so irresistible."

She again removed his hand, pleading, "Please don't." He stopped and stared at her with passionate eyes. He slowly moved forward to rest his lips on hers. His hands moved all over her body, massaging her back and sneaking ever so close to her buttocks. He pressed hard on her lips causing her head to spin and her body to twitch. He gently removed her blouse from her pants and slipped his hand underneath. His fingers made their way to the hooks of her bra. She unplugged her lips, grabbed his arms, and said, "Please don't." Inhaling heavily, she added, "You have to stop." Without uttering a sound, he gently lay her down on the seat and continued to kiss her all over. He unbuttoned the top button of her blouse exposing the upper part of her breast protruding above her bra. His hands were moving all over her body, lightly brushing over her breast. He slowly positioned his body over her, never breaking his concentration of his lips on hers. He started to nibble on her ear, moving his tongue inside. Ann was excited and started to wheeze, feeling like she never felt before. She was overwhelmed by a tremendous flash of desire. It was new and stunning. He started to press hard against her crotch. She felt the stimulating pleasure between her legs. It felt good. She wanted him to touch her, to do whatever he wanted to. But, she thought it was not right. They just met last night. She didn't know him. She didn't know his intentions. Was sex all he wanted? She had to stop him. Trying to gain control, she said, "Bob, please stop." He did not stop. She pushed him off and sat up. "We have to stop before we go too far."

Bob, in a soft, sensual voice, said, "Please don't fight me. Just let it flow. Just go with your feelings."

Ann said, in a daze, "No, it's not right. I still don't know you. I never did this before. I never let anyone touch me." Fixing her blouse, she said, "I don't know you!"

"I have feelings for you that I never felt for anyone before," said Bob, as his extended muscle in his pants was choking from exhaustion and desiring relief.

Ann was happy to hear this. She put her arms around him. "Give me time. Let's get to know each other."

"Sure," said Bob, disappointed and frustrated.

It had been a warm fall. Most of the trees retained their leaves well into late November. The trees were now bared. The days were becoming shorter, and the nights were colder. Ann and Bob saw a great deal of each other. Bob would always enter the house to pick up Ann. He had negative thoughts of Ann the first time he entered the house. Bob was not pleased to see the dilapidated house, furnished with used and worn-out furniture, the strong fragrance of dog and cat food, and the cluttered junk in the hallway, dining and living rooms.

Ann and Bob socialized with his friends and her friends. They enjoyed going to movies, bowling, ice-skating, and Sunday sightseeing. They often would go to Eagle Park. The park was at a high elevation that the New York City skyline was visible. It was also a place for young adolescents to make-out. They would often walk through the trails, holding hands. Ann, shivering, said, "Bob, it's cold. Let's go back to the car."

"I feel okay," said Bob, looking at her trembling and trying to shrink in her coat. He took a tight hold of her hand, turned, and ran toward the car. He started the engine and turned to Ann. She was still shivering. He put his arms around her and squeezed her tight.

"You're so warm," said Ann, beaming. "How come you're so warm?"

Bob, in a light laugh, said, "It's probably because I'm hot-blooded. You know, I'm Italian."

"You're a wise-guy. A hot, horny, wise-guy," she said, embracing him real tight. "Warm me up. Oh, it feels so good to be with you." Bob moved his hands over her body, touching her breasts, her thighs, and between her legs. She permitted the touching over her clothing. Bob, feeling more confident slid his hand beneath her blouse. He was fumbling with the back of her bra strap. "Please don't. I let you do things that I never did with anyone else."

"We have been going together for almost two months," said Bob, never removing his fingers from her back. "Don't you believe that I care about you? I love you."

"Yes, I think you do, and I love you. But I still have old-fashioned values," said Ann, almost in tears. "I don't want to have sex until I'm married. You promised that we wouldn't go any further."

"I know. But when I'm with you and kiss you, I get so hot and excited. I feel the hardness between my legs." He stared at her with seductive eyes and softly said, "Please…can I see your breasts?"

Ann, with mixed emotions, did not respond. He gently kissed her, and with his fingers, he undid her bra. Ann felt the unharnessing of her protection. He unbuttoned her blouse and slowly opened it. Her bra loosely covered the two mounds of a woman's pride, a man's delight and a young man's ecstasy. With his heart beating ever so fast, he displaced her bra downward, ever so slow. He stared at her young, firm breasts. It was dark, except for the light from the nearby lamp-post. The light was captured by her milky-white chest. Her breasts were not large nor small. They were firm and beautiful, thought Bob. He gently placed his hands over the two mounds and maneuvered his fingers over the nipples. He moved his head over her breasts and kissed them tenderly, with equal time to the left and right breasts. He swallowed her tiny nipples between his lips and delicately bit them as he gently pressed his lips over her breast. He then cupped her breast with his hands, buried has face between them, and slowly moved his lips to the right and the left, kissing them gently. His head spun with excitement. Ann was traumatized, never feeling such phenomenal sensations before. His tongue pressed on her nipple, circling at its base. It grew and became erect. Her entire body swayed in rhythm to his tongue.

Her body was under his control, yet her mind was interrupted by her guilt. She started to sob. Bob continued delighting himself, hoping that she would stop sobbing. She started to shake. He was no longer enjoying himself. He stopped. With his hands on her breasts, he said, "What's the matter?"

"It's not right," said Ann, weeping. "Please stop…Please." She made no effort to stop him. Bob was no longer excited. He did not want to hurt her or force her to do something that she did not want. As hot and excited as he was, he did not want to hurt her, so he stopped.

"Please take me home," said Ann. She fastened her bra and buttoned her blouse.

They were quiet as he drove her home. Her mood was subdued.

He stopped the car in the driveway. "Ann, I'm sorry," said Bob.

"I will never let you do that again. It's not right."

"But I love you. I feel things for you. It's only natural."

"Perhaps for you, but not for me. Do you know how I feel afterward? I feel very guilty. I can't look my mother in the eyes."

"Ann, you're the first person that makes me feel like this. I'm not seeing anyone else, and I'm used to touching girls and doing things."

"Oh. So that's it," said Ann, aggravated. "And if I want to continue seeing you, I have to give in to you?"

Bob said, shaking his head, "No! That's not it. I'm just being honest and open with you. I like you very much."

Ann, getting angry, said, "I'm not ready. I'm not going to have sex with you. If you care that much about me, then you should respect me. If you need your sex," she said, raising her voice, "go out with the whores."

Bob was surprised. "Is that the way you want it?"

"No! But if you have to have it, I'm not going to deprive you." She opened the door and ran to the house.

In the weeks to follow, Bob refrained from touching Ann. He still enjoyed her company, the affection, and kissing. They made an agreement that he could date other girls for the purpose of sex. One night, after such a date, they were together. Ann was bitter and angry. "How was it? Did you get your rocks off? Are you satisfied now?"

Bob was overtaken by her anger. He pulled over to the side and stopped the car. He looked at her and sternly said, "But isn't that what we agreed to?"

"I agreed to it but didn't think that you would do it. I was home last night, crying while you were out fucking! How would you feel if I was out with some else?"

"But I didn't do anything with her."

"I bet," said Ann in a wrath.

"Okay! Okay, if that's the way you feel about it, I'm not going to see anybody else." Ann was relieved to hear this. She became less angry. However, she was still thinking about last night and how jealous she felt that he was out with another girl.

As time passed, their love was in the spring of their lives. Bob took Ann to his senior prom, and they had a happy summer together. Ann started college in September, and Bob had enlisted in the National Guard. Around their first anniversary, Bob was in active duty, stationed in the South. The time that they spent apart was the worst time of their lives. Ann wrote to Bob every other day, and Bob did the same. He hated to be away from her. The training in the military was not difficult, but the time away from her was. Every day, he anxiously waited for her letters. Before he opened them, he would smell the fragrance of her perfume. He was happy to read that she was devoted to him, loved him, and anxiously waited for the day that they would be together again. She closed each letter with kisses and love forever and ever.

Six months later, Bob completed his Army training. He was back home, looking for work, and Ann was attending college. The days she had a light schedule, she would meet Bob at his parents' house. For a few hours, they would have the house to themselves while Bob's parents and siblings were at work. They have not had sex yet. She would undress except for her panties. It was her security to prevent him from penetrating her. She would allow him to get on top of her and press his genitals against her thighs and abdomen. She enjoyed the way her body quivered with excitement as he went up and down, rubbing his genitals between her legs.

As she pulled into the driveway, she saw the next-door neighbor sitting on the front porch. The man stared and watched as she pulled into the driveway. She glanced at the old man, trying not to look. She quickly got out of the car and rushed into the house. Bob and Ann were having wine and talking. Ann said, "I'm a little nervous. The old man was outside again. He watched as I drove into the driveway."

"So what!" said Bob, thinking of her.

"It's just...He makes me feel guilty."

Bob was chuckling. "That's silly."

"I just can't help it."

"I missed you so much. I'm happy to be back with you." He cupped his hands around her face and kissed her.

"Oh, Bob! I missed you so much. If it would have been any longer today, I would have gone crazy. Today, in classes, I had a difficult time concentrating. My thoughts were on the anticipation of being alone with you, holding, and kissing, and you touching and rubbing me. I felt wetness flowing from inside. I just couldn't wait to be with you. Did you miss me?"

Bob squeezed her tight and said, "Yes, I missed you so much. I love you more today than yesterday, more than anything else on earth. Let's get married!"

She was delighted to hear this. "But Bob, we're not ready for marriage. You don't have a job, and I'm only a freshman."

"I know. But if we love each other, we can make it work out."

"I don't want to struggle like Vinnie and Lynn. I want to finish college."

Bob knew that she was right. "It's…it's just that I love you so much. I want to spend the days with you, the nights with you. I…I always want to be with you." They embraced tightly.

They lay on the bed, kissing and snuggling. He started to kiss her all over. Feeling excited, he whispered into her ear, "Take off your clothes."

Ann willingly said, "I'll take everything off except for my panties." He stared at her in silence as she undressed. He watched in excitement, awaiting the unwrapping of a gift. She lay flat on the bed. She smiled and placed her hands to the outer part of her breasts and slowed moved them together cupping her breasts to enlarge them.

Bob felt his pants tighten as his muscle sprang to life. He moved toward her. Caressing her breasts, he kissed her all over. He got on top of her and gently pressed against her crotch. Her entire body was excited, and she responded to his. He started to drive up and down in rhythm. They both started to breathe heavily. He slowly moved her panties downward. They were near her knees. She grabbed his hand. "Bob, please don't."

Reassuringly, he said, "I'm not going to put it in. I just want to touch skin to skin."

"It's too risky. You know how hot we get. We won't be able to help ourselves."

"I'm not going to put it in." She let go of his hand, and he removed her panties. He tenderly and slowly stroked her thighs. He spread her legs and moved his hand to her thick, dark bush of pubic hair. He gently poked his finger into her and felt the secretions of her vagina. He moved down and immersed his face between her thighs and was overwhelmed by the scent. She lay still, twitching slightly and relishing in the sensations.

Bob, gasping for air, said, "You're naked…and…so beautiful. You're so wet. I can't help myself…I'm sorry." He removed his pants. He grappled her hand and placed it on his crotch. She grabbed it and squeezed it tightly. Their eyes were in concert as they stared at each other.

She wanted him inside her. "Yes! Put it in… Please don't hurt me… Don't hurt me." Bob delicately guided his pole to her moist thighs and pushed ever so slow. He continued to push forward, and it felt as no entrance existed. He pushed harder. "It hurts," whispered Ann.

He pulled out and saw the head covered with a light-red film of blood. "Did I hurt you? Do you want me to stop?"

"No! I want it." He tried again, and this time, he penetrated deeper into her womb. It seemed as if her vagina was lined with fingers that just squeezed and grasped his pole and held it tightly. Ann yelled out, feeling the pain and the sensation.

Chapter 5

It was two o'clock, Sunday morning. It was quiet and boring for the two attendants as they watched an uninteresting move. The young, black man looked at his watch and said, "It's two. I'm going down for some coffee. You want something?"

"Si, coffe'," replied the short, stocky woman. The man stood up and headed for the door. His footsteps made a clicking sound that echoed throughout the hall.

A patient jumped out of his bed upon hearing the sound. The tall, thin figure removed his glasses, slowly moved his eye past the doorway frame, and watched the orderly as he placed the key into the lock, opened the door, and walked out.

The thin man listened carefully. He stepped into the hallway, feeling the wall with the palm of his hands. He edged his way toward the door. The man waited for the attendant to return. He stared at the glass opening. He heard the sound of keys. The door slowly opened. As the orderly entered, the man pushed the door hard. The orderly fell back and dropped the tray with coffee. The man attempted to get past the door. The orderly pushed the man back, placed his two hands around the man's chest, and pushed him against the wall. He repetitively pushed the man against the wall. "You think that you're a bad motherfucker?" yelled the orderly as he pushed the man's face against the wall. The man was powerless as he fell to the floor. "Fuck with me!" shouted the orderly as he kicked the man.

Bob Dorsete was awakened by a neatly groomed young man. Bob asked, "What time is it?"

"Seven!" replied the orderly.

"Can I have a cigarette?" asked Bob.

"Not until after breakfast."

"What time is breakfast?"

"Between seven-thirty and eight-thirty."

Bob asked, "Can I shower and shave?"

"Yes!"

He was led to a solid, light-oak door. "You got two minutes to shower and shave. Here." The orderly handed Bob a safety razor. "When you're finished, open the door, and I will hand you the towel. If you ain't out in two minutes, I'm coming in."

It was a small room with a shower head and a small metal plate opposite the shower head. Bob turned on the water and adjusted the hot and cold for the right mix. He turned toward the metal plate to shave. He turned off the water and opened the door. He was handed a towel and started to dry. As he stepped, he asked. "Can I make a phone call?"

"Yeah." They walked toward the lounge and stopped by the telephones. The man pointed to a note. "Them's the rules."

The note read, "No phone calls allowed, in or out, until after breakfast is served." Bob, in disappointment, said nothing.

Shortly after eight, Bob had breakfast and ate everything. *Now for dessert,* he thought. He walked to the glass partition and asked for his cigarettes. The orderly plainly said, "It's a quarter after. Smoking time is over."

"But I was eating," Bob said, annoyed.

"Too bad. Cigarettes are given on the hour. You have to wait until nine."

"Okay," said Bob, trying to stay calm. "It sucks, but I understand. Can you please plug in the phones? I need to make a call."

The orderly replied, "You can't use the phone until everybody finishes eating."

"What's with this horse shit?" Bob said, in an irritated tone. "I couldn't believe it."

"You got a problem?" said the orderly.

"No," said Bob, shaking his head in disbelief. "I understood there are rules that I have to learn." In a civil tone, he asked, "When do you think can I use the phone?"

"I don't know."

"I need to make a call."

The attendant wanted no further discussion but said, "Man, just be cool and wait until they all finish eating."

Bob did not like the confinement, and he didn't like to be treated as a child. He sat quietly, watching the clock and thinking in silence. *Just another few minutes for my first cigarette. Fifteen minutes, just fifteen minutes. When you're waiting for something really bad, the minutes feel like hours. Ah, how good a cigarette would taste. I really need a cigarette. I need to talk to someone. I wonder if Pete is trying to call me. I can't believe this shit. How could I've been so stupid? Okay, I'm here now. The shock is over. I got to deal with the current situation. Shit, the leaflet states that I could be here for seventy-two hours without a hearing. That could be extended to fourteen days. If I'm here that long, I will go crazy. I got to get the fuck out of here. I have things to do. I have to get in touch with Ann. I don't have time to be here. I have to get out of here.*

Bob finally got his cigarette. He looked at the small stick made of paper and tobacco. He rolled it between his fingers, reluctant to light it for fear that it would disappear. He placed the filter end between his fingers and vigorously tapped it on the arm of the chair several times. It was perfect now, he thought. He placed it between his lips to light it but was interrupted by the sound of the telephone. He ran to the phones and placed the handle to his ear. "Is Bob Dorsete there?"

"It's me. Pete, thanks for calling."

"I've been trying to get in touch with you all morning," said Pete Devigne. "The phones kept ringing and ringing, but no one picked up."

"The phones were unplugged until recently."

"Get this. You were admitted by a nurse. I spoke to someone in authority. I told them that unless they had you evaluated by a qualified professional, they would be facing a lawsuit. I was told that they would try to get someone today. But because it's Sunday, it might be difficult to get someone in. They promised me that they would make every effort. If you don't hear from someone by two or three this afternoon, give me a call."

"Did you talk to Ann?" Bob asked.

"No!"

"Okay, Pete, thank you."

"Just stay cool and calm. Don't give them any cause to think you're crazy."

"Thanks. I'll try."

Feeling a bit better, Bob placed the cigarette in his mouth then realized that he had no matches. He remembered that the attendants had taken his matches. He approached one of the attendants sitting in the lounge. "Do you have a match?"

"Hey man, you can't smoke now."

"Why?" Bob asked, surprised.

"It's nine twenty." Extending his hand, he said, "Give me the cigarette."

Bob, infuriated and frustrated, sat quietly with his eyes fixed on the television, feeling self-pity. He was not bothered by the patients walking in front of him. The majority of the patients were dressed in pajamas or robes. Most of the men were unshaved. No one made conversation as they quietly sat watching television or walked around with no place to go. The only woman patient was neatly dressed. She was busy wiping the lounge counter, the sink, and tables.

A young man walked by. He was in his pajamas, covered with a blue bathrobe. He had a tiny smile on his face. He murmured good morning and sat on a chair next to the table. He laughed lightly as he moved a white object over the table. Bob, bored, decided to talk to the young man. He walked over and said, "Hi, my name is Bob."

In a low, choppy voice, the smiling face said, "Hi. You wanna meet my friend?"

"Sure, who's your friend?"

He enthusiastically exposed a white doll-like figure. "This is my friend, Captain America. He is my best friend. He takes care of me."

Bob stared at the two white socks with the tops inverted to create a red-and-blue neckline and two legs. He felt sympathy for the young man and felt luck that he had his sanity. He asked, "Can I see Captain America?"

"Only if you promise to give him back to me."

"I promise."

Slowly and cautiously, the man extended his hands to Bob. As Bob reached for the doll, the man withdrew it and again asked, "Do you promise to give him back?"

"Yes!" Bob examined the doll. "This is very creative. He really looks like a doll. These are your socks!"

The man shook his head. "Oh no. He's Captain America."

"Okay," said Bob. "Can I put Captain America down and talk to you?"

He did not answer immediately, "Okay. Yes, if you will be my friend. You also have to be Captain America's friend."

"Sure," said Bob. "What is your name?"

The man did not answer. His eyes were fixed on the doll. "Give him back to me. Give me Captain America!" The man grabbed the doll. He smiled as he bounced the doll on the table and ignored Bob.

Bob Dorsete tapped on the glass partition. The orderly looked up and slid the glass window open. "What you want?"

"Who's in charge?" asked Bob. The orderly pointed over his shoulder to a desk. A small, thin woman with short, black-grey hair, dressed in a white uniform was busy sorting papers. "Can I please talk to her?" The orderly pointed to the door to his left. The orderly opened the door. Bob entered and walked to the woman. "Excuse me. I would like to talk to you."

The woman was startled. "What are you doing in here?"

The orderly replied, "He is okay. He hasn't caused any problem."

Although yesterday Bob was dizzied and confused and had tearing eyes, he recognized the small, cold face, the small, flat nose, and beanie eyes. Her appearance greatly reflected her personality. He wanted to tell her off, but he decided to be careful with his words. "Do you have news of someone coming in to talk to me to get me out of here?"

In a cold tone, she said, "I no know, what you tak about."

"I was told by my cousin that a doctor would be coming in to evaluate me because I was not examined by a doctor yesterday."

The nurse replied, "Remember why you are here? I tak to you yesterday." Her dull, black eyes gave out a cold stare, and her face showed the wrinkles of her age.

"Yes!" Bob said, bothered. "Do you remember that you spoke to me for a few seconds? You spoke to the black man, who claimed to be my friend, for almost five minutes. I just met that man yesterday. He is a representative of my company, not my friend. He insisted that I check into a hospital for observation. He said that I was going to be in a voluntary unit and that I could walk out anytime I want. I can see clearly that this is a secured area filled with nuts, and I don't mean the ones you eat." The woman never turned to look at Bob. He asked, "What did he tell you?"

"You here, because you need help."

Bob, showing his true emotions, raised his voice. "Are you qualified to lock me in a mental institution? You're only a nurse. You're not a doctor."

"See how angry you get?" said the woman, exposing her gold front tooth. "That's why you here. For help."

"What are your qualifications?" asked Bob as he smiled sarcastically. "You can't even speak English properly."

Feeling harassed, she raised her voice. "I have experience. I nurse for thirty years, here and Philippines."

"Now who's raising whose voice? Who's getting angry?"

"Leave! You go to your room," she snapped as she stared at him with an annoyed face. Bob stood still. Pointing, she shouted, "Go!" He turned and walked out.

Bob was in his room, trying to regain his composure and maintain his sanity. A male orderly walked in. "Hey dude, I got to give your medicine."

"What medicine?" asked Bob in a surprised tone.

"Man, you got the dragon lady all pissed off. She told me to give this medicine."

"What is it?"

"It's a mild tranquilizer."

"Why should I take it?"

"She told me to give you two, but I'm giving you one." Bob didn't answer, so he added, "Look, man, you got one of two choices. You can take it yourself, or I'll force it down." Bob stared in silence. "Hey, I don't know how you got here, but I know you don't belong here. So do yourself a favor. Take it." He waited for Bob to take the pill. "Man are you dumb because I know you're not crazy. If we force you, you'll get a bigger dosage." Bob took the pill and placed it his mouth. "I need to make sure you swallow it. Open your mouth."

Bob was awakened by the sound of metal clatter from the food carts. He wiped the sleep from his eyes. He had very little apatite but ate because of boredom. He was in the lounge, watching television when a Spanish-speaking female orderly, in broken English, asked if he would help her. He nodded his head and followed her to a room. Two elderly people were sitting at the edge of the bed between a young man. The man said, "Can you help us hold my son while we cut his hair?"

"Yes," motioned Bob. He got down on his knees in front of the patient and held his forearms. The father held the patient's face. The woman held the razor. As she touched the patient's head, the patient was annoyed by the noise from the razor's motor and the blade on his scalp. He made angry, growling sounds and sneered at them. "I think that perhaps we should try to relax him," said Bob. He noticed the large ball on the floor. He rolled it to the patient. The man pushed it back. After a short period, the patient ignored the ball.

The mother stroked the patient's face with her hand. "He's okay now."

Bob got down on his knees in front of the patient and held his forearms. The woman tried again. The patient was still for a few seconds, and then he started to move his head. The man attempted to hold the patient's head. Bob firmed his hold. The patient stopped struggling, and Bob loosened his hold. Without warning, he broke loose of one arm and dug his nails into Bob's forearm. Bob felt the pain and let go. The patient's hands were around Bob's neck. Bob placed his hands over the patient's hands trying to break the hold around his neck. The patient had amazing strength as Bob was having difficulty breathing.

The orderly screamed out. A male orderly entered the room. He grabbed the patient, forced him on his back against the bed. The female orderly strapped the patient to the bed. The woman was weeping, and the man stood quietly without showing any expression. Bob was gasping for air.

The head nurse walked in and glanced at Bob. "Why is he here?" She noticed his arm was bleeding.

The female orderly replied, "Man go crazy! We try to cut hair." The nurse pointed to Bob and said, "He does not work here. He's a patient!" The female orderly looked at Bob. "I sorry, mister."

The nurse said, "Come with me." She took Bob to the office. As she cleaned and treated his cut, she murmured, "I have to make report." She looked up at Bob. "Sorry that you got hurt. On weekends, we get new help. You should not get involved. I will talk to the orderly." She finished wrapping Bob's injury.

"It's not her fault. I had no idea that the young man is so imbalanced," said Bob dryly.

Bob was having difficulty passing the time. His thoughts were on his boys, wondering how they were doing or what they were going through, and on his predicament. Bob walked around. He noticed the indentation in the hallway walls. He observed that some of the patients were still in bed. Bob caught a glance of a familiar face laying quietly in bed. He walked to the side of the bed. The thin-faced man opened his eyes to look. He attempted to get up. "Where are my glasses?" Bob grabbed the glasses from the floor and handed them to John Bell. John struggled to place the broken glasses over his bruised eye and cheeks. He fastened one bracket over his ear.

"What happened to you?" asked Bob.

"I tried escaping again." He felt a little pain because the medication was still in effect.

"Again!" Bob said in a surprised tone. "You have been here that long?"

"No! I've never been here before. I have been in other places. I get mad of the way they treat me. I don't want to stay." Bob, uncertain for words, was silent. "I feel tired." Bob left and returned to the lounge.

It was early afternoon when the head nurse approached Bob. She informed him that someone was here to see him. She led Bob through the locked door, past the hallway into another section and to a small room. A man was sitting on one of the two chairs. "Thank you, nurse," the man said.

She turned and left the room. She thought and became concerned that perhaps she made a mistake. He was neatly dressed, well-groomed and civil in his behavior. He helped with the food trays, served the other patients, and assisted the orderlies in cleaning the lounge. Did he belong here?

The man stood up and said, "Hello Mr. Dorsete." He extended his hand. "I am Dr. Bergren, a psychiatrist. I am here to talk to you."

"Thank you for coming," said Bob nervously.

"Please, sit down. It is very unusual that I'm here on a Sunday. I'm here at the request of your family to evaluate you." He paused to adjust his heavy body to the hard seat. He noticed Bob's wrapped arm. He stared into Bob's face. "I'm telling you right now, you are not going to get out of here. You're going to stay here for at least three days." Dr. Charles Bergren was in his late forties. He was dressed in an uncoordinated blazer that did not match his pants. He had short hair with a touch of grey, a thick, full beard, and glasses. He examined the neatly dressed patient and carefully studied his facial expressions. He asked, "What's going on in your life? Tell me how you feel?"

Bob Dorsete openly told him that his wife and children were in a shelter. He stated that he missed them, and he was concerned about them. He was enraged that he was misled and coerced into coming to the hospital. He was annoyed for being here and worried that he was admitted because of the allegations that he was dangerous to himself and others.

Dr. Bergren said, "Perhaps it would be best for you to stay, spend time to relax, and take it easy."

Bob replied, "This place is a nuthouse! I can't talk to these people. They're ill. Their minds are gone. There is a young man tied to the bed and another that plays with his socks."

"I was told that you have been under a lot of pressure. Here you'll have the chance to relax."

"I have a restaurant to run, my wife is filing a divorce, and I need to find a lawyer. I feel stressed and frustrated by just being here," said Bob as he fidgeted on the chair.

"What happened to your arm?"

"I was trying to help the orderly restrain one of the mental patients. His parents were trying to give him a haircut."

"Why did you get involved?"

"I had nothing to do. The orderly asked me."

"Well, that is interesting. Was a report made?"

"Yes, I think so," replied Bob.

Dr. Bergren interviewed Bob for over thirty minutes, "Excuse me for a moment." He stood up. "I need to talk to some people. Please wait here."

"Sure," said Bob.

Waiting for about ten minutes, Dr. Bergren returned and said, "It's obvious that you don't belong here. I will try to get you out of here, but I need your cooperation if you agree to go to the open unit. It's more suitable to your needs. It's a volunteer unit, and you can walk out anytime. The patients function better." He paused, anticipating a reply.

Bob replied, "I need to get out. I have things to do."

Dr. Bergren continued. "You can leave anytime you want, but it won't look good if you do. It's better that you get released." He paused again, staring at Bob's eyes. "Will you give me your word that you will stay until you are released?"

"Okay. You have my word."

"Good. I'll try to do my best to get you out today. I need a couple of signatures, and it being Sunday, it might be difficult. I'm not sure who's on duty."

Bob was happy to hear that something was going his way. He grabbed the doctor's hand, shook it vigorously, and said, "Thank you! Thank you!"

"It'll take me about an hour or two. I'll try my very best."

Bob returned. Waiting anxiously, he sat in the lounge, watching television. He felt delighted that he was getting out. He was uncertain as to what to expect across the hall but believing anything was better than this place. The head nurse approached Bob. Without uttering a sound, she curved her finger toward her for him to follow. She led him to the office. "You going across the hall. I want to say sorry. I thought black man was you friend. He say things and...and you were crying. I try help you."

Bob believed that she was sincere. He extended his hand, touched her arm, and said, "Thank you for getting me the heck out of here."

She gave a tiny smile. "Follow me." She unlocked the door, Bob opened it, and they walked out. She turned to lock the door. They walked across the hall through two open doors and stopped at the counter. She handed a folder to the woman behind the counter and wished Bob good luck and left. Bob turned and stared across the hall as she walked back. He felt the relief. He was there for less than twenty-four hours, but it was the closest he had come to hell.

This unit of the hospital was for patients with negligible metal disorders. The ward consisted of ten rooms, with two beds per room. The women and men were in separate bedrooms. It had two lounges—the eating lounge, with a television and refrigerator, and the recreation room, with telephones and couches. The attendants' area was near the entrance, across from the eating lounge. The patients were able to care for themselves. The usually stay was for two weeks. There were status grades given to the patients. An "A" was achieved if you were a model patient. That entitled the patient freedom to walk outside to the balcony and to the waiting lounge outside the ward. They also ran errands for the staff. The "B" level entitled patients to be group leaders for certain activities. The "C" level was for new patients.

Bob Dorsete felt relaxed and calm as he sat in the lounge, reading the newspaper. He could see the patients' faces as they glanced at him. None stared. They were sitting passively, watching television. A blonde-haired woman approached him and said, "My name is Bonnie. Could I sit here?" Bob looked at the young woman. She was in her mid-twenties, with no makeup, and dressed in loose top and paints. He moved the chair out for her, and she sat down. "What's your name?"

"Bob Dorsete."

"That's a nice name," she said, smiling. "Are you married?"

"Yes," said Bob.

"I thought so. You look like the married type. Do you love her?"

"Yes. I love her very much."

"I wish somebody loved me." Her faced turned sad. "My husband doesn't care about me. I have a baby girl. I haven't seen her for a while. They won't let me see her." She pointed to her head. "I have these pains in my head, and it hurts at times. It's my headaches. They hurt me so much that sometimes I can't do anything."

Bob felt sorry for her as he thought of his children. He was curious, so he asked, "Have you seen a doctor?"

"Oh, yeah. Many doctors. None of them could help me."

They were interrupted by a patient. "Can I sit here?" the woman asked.

"Sure," Bob said, smiling.

"My name is Martha," said the woman. She was in her mid-thirties and ordinary-looking. She had medium-length, dark-brown hair, and a round face with blemishes. She was short and overweight. Martha asked Bob basic background questions then talked about herself. That she had been in places like this many times. She had no place else to go. She had no job, money, nor family. At least here, she had a clean bed and food. Bob expressed sympathy for her. It made her feel good that someone cared. She said, "You're a nice person."

Trying to be polite, Bob said, "Well, thank you."

Bob had dinner with Bonnie and Martha. Martha complained about the food, yet she ate everything, including Bob's dessert. The ladies enjoyed talking to Bob. They liked his gentleman manners and the concern he showed toward them. Talking to them made the time go faster for Bob, and it occupied his mind. Bob excused himself to make a phone call. "Pete, it's Bob." In an enthusiastic tone, he said, "I'm out of the fucking nuthouse, but I'm still in the hospital."

"Why?" Pete asked.

"I had to agree to go into a volunteer unit for a minimum of three days."

Pete felt satisfied for helping Bob and disappointed that he was still in the hospital. "I wouldn't have given them the satisfaction. Walk out right now."

"I gave my word. Besides, I'll be out by Tuesday. I have a pass for tomorrow. The guy in charge said that it's very unusual since I just got here. But it was a legal matter."

"Do you have an attorney in mind?"

"No," said Bob. "I don't know any attorneys in California."

"You have to stop her from filing the petition."

"I'll try my best."

Pete paused. "I want tell you something, but I don't want to upset you."

Bob was inquisitive and asked, "What?"

"You might blow your cool and get pissed off." He laughed. "Then they'll think you're crazy."

"You've got my curiosity. I won't get upset. What is it?"

"Okay. Just don't get excited and don't do anything stupid. I know who's behind all this. You're not going to believe it. It's your next-door neighbor, Ray. I think that's his name."

Bob was stunned. "How do you know? I haven't done anything to him. I've been living next door to him for three years. He has no reason nor cause against me. We're not tight but always friendly. He and his wife have been over my house a couple of times for coffee. But I never broke bread with the man. Ann is friendly with his wife. He's been an okay neighbor."

Pete replied, "Believe me, I am sure that he is behind this whole thing."

"How do you know?"

"I spoke to him early today. I told him I was Ann's blood cousin and I wanted to get in touch with her. He insisted that he had no idea where she was." In a resentful tone, Pete continued, "I told him that I had a suspicion that he knew where she was. The son-of-a-bitch tells me that I can't call the shelters. That is bullshit. Believe me, I know. The shelters are volunteers. They have nothing to with the courts or the police. They allow calls from family members. My cop friend told me."

"I have heard of shelters, but I have no idea how they operate. Pete, thanks for taking all these collect calls. Back to Ray."

"I didn't like the guy's attitude. Who the hell is this asshole telling me not to call to my cousin? Ann is my blood. I've known her my entire life."

Bob found it too unbelievable. He asked, "But why? I never did anything to him. I can't believe it."

"I am convinced. You told me that your friend spoke to Ann. You said that the next-door neighbor suggested that she go to a shelter. So that is one. Two, he had to help. Ann would never do anything on her own. Three, why did your company contact him?"

Bob was confused. "You know, I never gave that a thought. But what's in for him?"

"Didn't you tell me that he was a retired cop and he has some kind of a security or detective business? He has to be making money." Bob, still uncertain, did not answer. "I have an idea, just to make sure. When you get out tomorrow, find a way, very innocently, to stop by his house. Make sure that he sees you, and see how he reacts. Just as important, listen carefully to what he says. If you do it right, you'll know."

Bob felt uncertain. "Okay! I'll do it. I'll give you a call tomorrow night and let you know how I make out in court. Thank you. Thanks for your help."

Pete, a little uncertain, asked, "Bob! Can you handle more bad news?"

"Why not."

"Ann did contact her mother. I spoke to her brother. He said, 'What do you expect. They moved to California. One ends up in the nut house and the other in a shelter.' They are not going to get involved."

Bob, disappointed, said, "I am not surprised. So they know that we are separated. Thanks, Pete."

Bob sat quietly in the recreation room, thinking of Ray Ditler. Why would Ray do this to me? Why would he interfere in my marriage? What kind of person would destroy someone's marriage? Tomorrow, I'll know. He tried to take his mind off Ray by thinking of Ann and the boys. He desperately wanted to be with her and his boys. He felt the pain in his head. The pressure was as if a metal band was tightening around his head. The pain started from the front of his forehead to the back of his head and down his neck. The pain was nothing like a headache or like anything he had ever experienced before.

It was nearly 9:00 p.m. when the announcement was made for medication. All the patients quickly went to the front counter. They eagerly and noisily chattered as they formed a line. They had to be instructed to be quiet. This reminded Bob of the book, *Brave New World* by Huxley, where the workers, the simple-minded people, were kept happy with medication. After all the patients had their medication, Bonnie noticed that Bob was the only one that did not take any. She told him that he was lucky and wished that she did not have to take pills.

Bob enjoyed his newfound freedom. He could smoke anytime, and the dining area was open until twelve. It was well past nine, and all the patients were in bed except for Bob. He was in the lounge, watching television with two of the staff members. He could not sleep. The nights were the worst part of the day. When it was time to relax and go to sleep, his mind would run with thoughts of Ann and the boys. He endeavored several times to write a letter for Ann, hoping that he would see her tomorrow. He was trying to find the words to apologize and to express how much he loved her.

He thought about the patients he met. Most of them appeared normal, and no one went around in pajamas and robes, except for the elderly lady. She moved and walked slowly. The patient, Jim, should be on the other side. He was in his late twenties. The first time Bob entered the dining room area, the man moved his hands forward, up and down. Bob jumped back, stumbled over a chair, and fell on his buttocks. Eleanor, an attractive woman in her early thirties with short, light-brown hair, had a couple of outcries, yelling incoherent to no one. Joe, his roommate, appeared and talked normal.

Joe walked in, looking jittery. The staffer asked, "What's the problem?"

Joe, rubbing his hand over his face, said, "I couldn't sleep."

"Do you want a sleeping pill?"

Joe replied, "Not right now. I'll just watch TV for a while." He slowly walked around, smoking a cigarette.

One staffer stood up. "Break's over for us." The staffers left the room.

Joe sat down next to Bob. He was tall, with a medium build, of mid-forty. He had fine hair and a serious cast to his appearance.

"What are you watching?" asked Joe.

"Some old comedy. I am not paying attention. My mind is elsewhere."

"Like where?"

"Here, there, and everywhere." Bob, thinking of making conversation, said, "Tell me about the patients." Bob was trying to remember their names.

Joe said, "You have to watch out for Jim. He doesn't talk much. I haven't had a conversation with him at all. I don't know anything about him except to watch out for his karate. He's always throwing his hands around." He paused to think. "Annette, she's just old. She doesn't talk to anyone. And Mary, the blonde with glasses, is always sobbing. She's friendly with Eleanor, and when the two get together, they don't want anybody around. I think Eleanor is a lesbian. She hates men. She's always complaining about everything." Joe offered Bob a cigarette. "You look like a clever guy. Can you help me?"

Bob asked, "What's the problem?"

"I need to find my son. The last time I saw him was about six or seven years ago. My wife took him away from me. She ran away."

Bob curiously asked, "Did you hire an investigator?"

"I hired many detectives." He rubbed his face with his hand. "You're Italian. You know people." Bob stared in bewilderment. Joe continued, "You have mob connections."

Bob, a little nettled, replied, "I'm sorry. I don't have that kind of friends. It sounds like you did the best you could." Disappointed, Joe turned toward the television. They sat in silence with individual, wondering thoughts.

Together, Bob Dorsete and Ann Pellone made the transition from teenagers to young adults. Their relationship was one of love, happiness, and dedication for each other. Bob was in his last semester, majoring in business. Ann had graduated the year before and was going for her masters in teaching. Bob financed his education by working full-time as a security guard. Ann financed her education through various scholarships and grants. They had been busy planning their wedding, which was three months away. They were preparing for a large affair with over two hundred people, which included a bridal party of seven couples. Just as Bob was ready to leave the house, his mother called him back for a telephone call. It was Rose Pellone. "Is Ann with you?" asked Rose in a concerned voice.

"No, I was just on my way over to pick her up."

Rose said, "She left this morning. I'm getting a little worried."

"Where did she go?" Bob asked.

"I don't know. She didn't say."

"I'll be right over," said Bob, and he hung up the phone.

It was dark when Bob arrived at the house of Rose Pellone. She was dressed in her usual patched-up clothing and uncombed hair. She was a plain-looking woman but could appear more attractive if she attended to her appearance. She was slim for her age except for a slightly extended waist. This time, she did not express the usual warm greeting. Her face was pale. "Ann is not home yet. I'm very worried. Perhaps she's with your friends."

Bob, also concerned, tried to stay calm and asked, "What happened? Did you and Ann have an argument?"

Rose, in reserve, murmured, "Yes, but I didn't think it was bad enough for her to run away."

Bob headed straight for the telephone and started to make telephone calls. After several calls, he was baffled because no one had seen or heard from Ann. Mrs. Pellone anxiously stood and watched with her eyes focused on Bob.

It had now turned dark.

Their concern now changed into fear as they sat in the kitchen, drinking coffee and making light conversation. They both hoped that Ann would call or be home by now. Bob finally got the nerve to ask, "What did you and Ann argue about?"

"None of my children ever ran away," said Rose Pellone, annoyed. "I don't want my daughter living in your parent's house. I have nothing against your parents."

Bob, feeling a little annoyed, said, "We don't have money. My parents are by themselves, and there is plenty of room."

Rose, displeased, said, "Why not here?" She raised her arms in the air. "You can have Ann's room. What don't you like about us?"

Bob did not answer back. This had been a delicate issue for the past two months, escalating to an antagonistic level, that Bob refused to enter the house for a month. Due to Ann's persistence, he had made a truce with Mrs. Pellone. However, it was difficult to talk to her. She was still the mother. She ran the household, doing all the essential work since Don passed away four years ago. Lou was always too busy reading, and Mary kept to herself. It was getting late, and Bob was irritated by her very presence. He decided to leave.

"I guess I'll go home. Please, if Ann comes in, tell her to give me a call." Mrs. Pellone motioned with her head, and Bob walked out.

Bob spent a disturbing and restless night, worrying about Ann. He felt guilty about the argument they had had last night and thought that perhaps he upset Ann. He was worried and thought the worst. Perhaps she was abducted or possibly hurt. He tried to get those horrible thoughts out of his mind. This was the first real disagreement that they ever had. He tried to understand why she ran away and where she could be. It was early Sunday morning. Bob was disturbed by Mommy Dorsete. "It's her, Rosa."

Bob got up, made his way to the kitchen, and picked up the phone handle. Bob answered, "No, she is not here." This time, she was more receptive. "I'm worried too."

"I've called Ann's cousins. They have not seen nor heard from her. Don't you have any idea where she could be?"

Bob replied, "I called all our friends last night. I just hope that she is okay. I'll give you a call if I find her."

"If you know where she is, please, please tell me."

"I don't know."

Rose was sobbing. "I have to call the police to file a missing person's report."

"Wait. I am going to see some of our friends." Bob had a hunch but did not want to disappoint Rose. "I'll call you in two hours."

Bob had a suspicion. Bob entered the apartment building of Vinnie and Lynn. He and Ann had socialized regularly at their apartment. Vinnie and Lynn were married a year after completing high school. They got married because Lynn was pregnant. The first two years of their marriage was terrible. Vinnie was too immature and irresponsible to support a wife and a newborn child. They went through a rocky relationship and financial problems. Lynn had returned twice to her parents. They survived the early years with the help of their parents. Bob softly knocked on the door. A woman asked, "Who is it?"

"It's me, Bob. Lynn, I'm sorry to bother you this early in the morning, but I need to talk to you."

Lynn Radice, covered in a bathrobe, said, "Bob, I am not dressed."

"Lynn, please. I'll wait here until you get dressed."

The door slowly opened a quarter of the way, and Lynn stood between the opening. Bob noticed her strange behavior. He asked, "Lynn, is Ann here?"

Lynn hesitated for a moment. "No! She's not here."

"You haven't heard from her?"

"No. I haven't."

"Ann has been missing since yesterday. Her mother and I are very concerned. Her mother is going to file a missing person's report. Are you sure?"

"Yes!"

"Is Vinnie home?"

"Yes. He's taking a shower. I'll get him," she said, and she closed the door.

Bob thought, *Ann is here. Why is she lying? Why didn't she invite me in?* In a few minutes, Vinnie opened the door and stepped out into the hallway. Bob, in a very subdued tone, said, "I'm concerned about Ann. We had a fight. Well, not really, a disagreement. I didn't realize that she was that upset." Looking at Vinnie in the eyes, "You're acting strange. Why are we talking in the hallway?"

"The place is a mess. We sleep late on Sundays."

"Please, tell me!"

Vinnie showed no expression at first then a slight smile came over his face. "Bob, she's not here."

Bob, pressing, said, "I can tell by your face that she's here. I just want to know that she's okay. Her mother and I are concerned that she is missing. If she doesn't want to talk to me, it's okay. I just want to make sure that she's all right. Please."

Vinnie smiling, "I'll be right back."

Ann slowly opened the door and stepped outside. She looked like a frightened little girl. Bob slowly put his arms around her, hugged her, and said, "I'm glad you're all right. We were so worried about you. Why did you do this? What's the matter?"

"I'm confused," said Ann in a soft voice. "Between you and my mother, I needed to get away."

"But why? What's the matter?"

"It's this whole situation about where we're going to live. You want me to live with your parents and…and my mother wants me to live in her house."

Bob felt awkward taking in the hallway. He suggested. "Why don't we go someplace where we can talk? Just to talk."

"I don't know. I'm confused. You're both putting pressure on me. I don't know what to do."

Bob said, pleading, "Please, let's just go for a ride and do whatever you want to do. We don't have to talk about it."

Ann wanted to be with Bob, but he was stubborn and too headstrong to change his mind. She thought that perhaps Bob would listen to her and try to understand her feelings. She was also surprised at how smart he was at figuring out where she was and how much he loved and cared for her to do this. After all, she is the girl he loves, and they are going to be husband and wife. She thanked Vinnie and Lynn and said that they were going for a short ride.

It was a cool April morning, with heavy clouds overcast and light winds blowing. As Bob drove, they both sat in silence. Bob moved his free right hand, grabbed Ann's hand, and held it tight. They drove to a park and stopped in an isolated area. They sat in silence for some time until Bob asked, "Are you okay?"

She paused, "Yes, I'm okay… No, I'm not okay. You and my mother are driving me crazy." In a raised voice, she continued, "I don't want to live with your parents, and I don't want to live with my mother."

"I want to do whatever makes you happy," said Bob tenderly. "But we have no money. You have a part-time job. Most of my money goes for school. We have very little savings. Living with my parents won't cost us much. It's just a temporary situation for six months or a year. And besides, it's just my mother and father. I plan to fix the basement. We'll have plenty of privacy."

Ann, sobbing, said, "It's not the same. I won't feel like I'm married if I'm living with your parents. I have nothing against them. I just don't feel that's the way I want to be married. My mother won't—"

Bob interrupted, "I don't want to live at your mother's. Your mother's house is crowded. Your sister still sleeps with your mother. Your brother has that tiny little closet you call a bedroom. The place is a dump. Where are you and I going to live? In your bedroom? How are we going to have any privacy with all those people around?"

Ann said, "You're right. We won't have any privacy. But I don't want to live with your parents either."

"I'm not going to force you to live any place you don't want. The way you feel about living with my parents is the same way I feel about living with your family. I'll feel too uncomfortable."

Ann, sobbing harder, said, "Well, that's why I am confused and needed space." Ann wiped her eyes. "Yesterday, my mother made me an ultimatum. I feel like you two are tugging at me, like I'm being stretched apart. I'm all mixed up. I needed to get away."

"Running away doesn't solve anything," said Bob, feeling bad for causing her such pain. "I'm sorry. I didn't know it was upsetting you so much."

"I told you! I don't want to live with your parents."

"Perhaps you did. Perhaps I wasn't listening. You know I can be stubborn at times. I was thinking of our financial situation. It's just my mother and father. I thought it was the best choice. But I want you to be happy."

Ann stopped sobbing. "Perhaps it is." Crossing her hands, she paused to take a breather, "But I won't be happy."

"Fine," said Bob. "What do you suggest then?" He was looking away from her.

"I don't want to live with your parents, and I don't want to live with my mother." Ann, uncertain, said, "Maybe we should put the wedding off until we can afford an apartment."

"But we waited so long. We've been planning this wedding for a year. I don't want to put it off." He paused to think. "Since you feel that strongly, we'll look for an apartment. It has to be something small and cheap. Will that make you happy?"

"Yes!" She put her arms around him and kissed him. She held him tight. Bob was content to see her happy. But he was concerned about where they were going to live and how they would afford it,

Their wedding day was just as they had planned it. Everything went perfect, and everybody had a good time. They were happy to be married, starting the summer of their life, filled with dreams and hopes they had been discussing for the past five years. It had been a long and exciting day, and they were exhausted. Ann looked forward to their wedding night. She had anticipated this day for a long time.

They had been sexually active. She enjoyed the afternoons at his parents' house, alone.

She was aroused to excitement. The feelings she experienced were so fascinating and satisfying that nothing else mattered. Although she looked forward to the afternoon visits with Bob, afterward, she did not feel good. She felt slight guilt because they were not married. But tonight, it would be different. Tonight, she could have all those feelings without the guilt.

After walking two flights of stairs, Bob reached in his pocket to unlock the door, and Ann was ready to step in. Bob grabbed her arm. "Hold on!" Ann stopped. She was kind of bewildered. Bob gave her a big smile, "Isn't it tradition that I carry you in?" She smiled, feeling special and in love. He picked her up. She put her arms around him, rested her head on his shoulder and kissed his neck. Bob carried her in and said, "Welcome home, Mrs. Dorsete." They embraced in a long, passionate kiss.

They rented a two-room apartment in a two-and-a-half family house. Their apartment consisted of a bedroom and a kitchen. The rent was affordable, and it included utilities. They were in the bedroom, undressing. Bob said, "Boy, I'm tired. It's been a crazy week. I don't think I've slept four hours in the past three days. I can't wait to hit the bed."

Ann, in disappointment, said, "It's our wedding night. Our first night together. Aren't we going to?"

Bob, teasing, said, "What do you mean, aren't we going to?"

Ann smiled, trying to be seductive. "You know what I mean."

"It's past three in the morning. I'm tired," said Bob as he started to undress. Ann was still in her wedding gown. "Why don't we wait until the morning? I need some sleep."

"It's tradition," said Ann sadly. "I'm surprised that you're not interested."

"It's not that I'm not interested. It's just that I'm tired."

"Bob, it's important to me. All those times that we've done it. Afterward, I didn't feel right. I've been waiting a long time for this night. Please!"

As much as he enjoyed making love to her, his body wanted to sleep. He did not want to disappoint her. He forced a smile and said, "Sure!"

Ann smiled. "I'll get cleaned up and put on something sexy." She started to walk out. "Oh, there's wine in the refrigerator. Open it. Light the candles." She bathed, dried, and sprayed perfume lightly under her armpits and private area. She put on the nightgown that her mother gave her. She viewed herself in the mirror. She did not like the way it fit, and it did not make her look sexy. Her breasts disappeared, and it covered her entire body. The straps loosely hung over her small shoulders. She felt a little self-conscious regarding her breasts, thinking they were small. She cupped her breasts and wished that they were half the size of her sister's. All her life, she was teased by her mother and aunt, saying that her younger sister had larger breasts. Bob had always told her that her breasts were just right, and he was more than satisfied.

She entered the dim bedroom. Bob was sitting on the edge of the bed. He handed her a glass of wine and toasted. "To the prettiest bride, Mrs. Dorsete."

Ann sipped the wine and stepped back. Smiling, teasing, and trying to be seductive. "How do I look?"

He raised his glass. "You look beautiful!"

Ann smiled in satisfaction. "The wedding was beautiful," said Ann. "It was everything I ever dreamed of. I think everybody had a great time." Bob too tired to engage in conversation, nodded his head and smiled. Ann placed the glass down and walked around, showing her gown. "My mother bought this for me for our wedding night. It's a little big." She approached the other side of the room by the window. The light from the full July moon penetrated through her long white gown showing the naked silhouette of her body. "Do you like my gown? Do I look sexy?"

Bob did not think so but did not want to hurt her feelings. "You look beautiful in whatever you wear." She approached him. He gently pulled her down to the bed and kissed her. He slipped off the shoulder strap of her nightgown and kissed her breast. He was so exhausted that he felt a headache coming on. He was on top of her, moving his body up and down. His head throbbed with each movement. He tried to continue, but his head was hurting. "I'm very tired. Can we do it in the morning?"

Ann was saddened. She sat up. "It's our wedding night. This is what all the girls look forward to. I can have sex and not feel guilty afterward." She gazed at his fatigued face. "If you really want to wait until morning, it's okay."

He desperately wanted to sleep. He forced a grin, "No, you're too appealing, too beautiful." He grabbed her, gently pulled her toward him and kissed her. He got on top of her, and as they moved in rhythm, his headache was becoming worse. He wanted to stop so badly. He forced himself to perform until he thought that she was satisfied. Ann was disappointed and thought it wasn't nearly the best that she had experienced. She felt no guilt, but she wasn't totally satisfied as a woman.

Chapter 6

Monday

The cool morning wind whisked against Bob Dorsete's unshielded arms. He rubbed his hands across his arms to warm them. He was outside the hospital, anxiously waiting for Tom Connelly. He was tired because he had a restless sleep. It had been a prolonged state of sadness lasting throughut the night. He was awake all morning waiting for the sunlight, for the night to turn to day. He was feeling an unusual blend of uncertainty, the excitement of seeing Ann, and the fear of what the day might bring.

Tom drove into the hospital parking lot. Bob made his way to the car, "Thanks, Tom, for coming."

"It's the least I can do for a friend. It's not bad. The shop is only ten minutes from here."

"I hope that I don't jeopardize your job."

"It's okay with the owner. Business is slow."

Bob was talking very fast. "I have an eight-hour pass. I have to be back before six o'clock. I have to find a lawyer. But first, I have to see Ray."

"He is involved. I am not surprised," said Tom.

"I have to be sure." Tom drove to the front of Bob's house. Bob opened the door and turned to Tom. "Thanks for everything."

Tom replied, "Pick you up at four. Good luck."

Bob rang the doorbell of Ray Dilter. Karen opened the door. Surprised, she quickly closed it. A moment later, Ray opened the door and stepped outside. In a firm tone, "What are you doing here? You are not scheduled to be released until Thursday."

Bob was mad. "How do you know that?"

"Mr. Morris told me."

"Why was Karen white as a ghost, and why did she close the door on me?"

"Because you look drunk. Get out of here!"

"I'm drinking, but I'm not drunk. Why, Ray? What did I do to you?"

"Go home and sleep it off. Get out of here!"

"Where is she? Ray, tell me."

"Get out of here." He approached Bob. "I'll call the cops."

Bob walked backward, turned, and left. And then he turned right. He walked toward his lawn, pretended to stumble. He turned left and turned right.

Ray shouted, "Go inside and sleep it off."

Bob turned with his finger pointing. "I'll get you." Stepping backward, he fell to the ground, shouting, "You know…You know." He got up and entered his house.

It was almost eleven in the morning. Bob was in the lobby of the office of Norman Barber. Bob was having a difficult time completing a questionnaire. He tried to write, but his hand was shaking, and he was too anxious. Two thoughts were going through his brain, attempting to answer the questions and the negative feelings of attorneys. Bob was thinking of all the attorneys that were listed in the Yellow Pages. They were over twenty pages. Probably more than any other profession. He was lucky that this attorney was available, and he is close by. A voice called, "Come in." Bob entered the office. The man across the desk stood up, extended his hand out, and said, "I'm Norman Barber. How can I help you?"

Bob wet his lips and eagerly said, "I'm Bob Dorsete. I called you an hour ago."

"I have an eight-hour pass. I am in a nuthouse. My wife is filing for a divorce. I have to be back before six tonight."

Mr. Barber was confused. "Take your time, one thing at a time. You're in the nuthouse. Where?"

"Long Beach."

"Were you arrested?"

"No! I did a stupid thing. I volunteered." He stopped to collect his thoughts. "My wife is filling for divorce. Are you good? I mean, do you know your shit? Sorry, what I mean—" He was interrupted by the ring of the telephone.

"Excuse me!" said Mr. Barber, and he picked up the receiver.

Bob carefully evaluated the man dressed in casual attire of shorts and flowery shirt. Bob thought that, for a divorce attorney, he appeared too young, about the same age as him. He expected someone in his fifties. He was an attractive man of medium height and build. He had thick, dark hair, and a thin, well-groomed mustache lined his lip.

Mr. Barber hung up the telephone, looked at Bob, and said, "Yes! I know my shit. Please, give me a moment to go through this questionnaire." Bob sat nervously and hoped that he didn't insult the man. Mr. Barber asked, "Do you have money for a retainer?"

"How much are you asking for? How does a retainer work?"

Mr. Barber responded, "Three thousand dollars. A retainer is money that I reserve and I draw my fees and costs from. If anything is left, I return the balance to you."

"I can write a check for two thousand today and give you a thousand next week." Bob said, jabbering, "Something's gone wrong. You have to stop her from filing for a divorce. I want a chance to talk to her. I'll pay you anything. Whatever you want. Just get me a chance to talk to my wife."

Mr. Barber sensed that Bob was nervous. "That's not for us to decide. That's her decision. Do you have the name or phone number of her attorney?" Bob handed him a piece of paper. "I'm not saying that I'm taking your case," said Norman Barber as he dialed the number. "Hello! I would like some information. Do you have a client named Ann Dorsete?" He paused to listen. "I might take this case." Back on the phone, he continued, "Mr. Dorsete said that it is urgent." Mr. Barber listened, and Bob stared in anguish. "Okay, thank you. We'll see you this afternoon."

Mr. Barber placed the phone down, raised his head, and stared at Bob. "Do you have a suit? A dark suit?"

"Yes," said Bob.

"Good, we have very little time. I have to go home and get changed. You get yourself into a suit and meet me on the fourth floor at 1:15 p.m., Department Fifty. You got it?" Bob nodded his head forward. He was more at ease now that he had an attorney. "Here is the address._See you later."

The parking lot of the courthouse was swarming with people crossing streets and vehicles slowly making their way into the parking garage. It was obvious to Bob that it was going to be a challenge to find a parking space. As he made their way to the fourth floor, he anxiously looked around for Ann. He turned his head to the left and right. On the door of one of the courtrooms, a list was posted. He saw "Dorsete vs. Dorsete" scheduled for 1:30 p.m. Bob was turning his head, looking for Mr. Barber,

Bob stared at the men and women in suits with briefcases and the sad faces of mothers with young children. How he hated the word divorce. He thought, *Why did it begin with the letter* d, *like* deceased, deserted, death, departed, disease*? So this is the place where marriages are terminated. You hire a priest to marry and an attorney to dissolve it. How could something so wonderful turn so ugly? Why do we fall in love, get married, have children, and then destroy each other? How is it that two hearts burn with love, and then one day, burn with hate? Life is such a mystery.*

Mr. Barber approached Bob and instructed him. "Once inside, I don't want you to say anything. I'll do all the talking. Just stay calm, and don't say anything. Do you understand?" Bob nodded his head. They sat in the courtroom, waiting for the announcement for "Dorsete vs. Dorsete." Mr. Barber made his way to the bench.

A conservatively dressed older man, taller than Barber, approached. Bob felt sure he was Will Walsh. Bob watched the two attorneys converse with the judge. He could not hear a thing. He sat sadly, with his eyes focused on the judge, with a deep interest of what they were discussing. With butterflies in his stomach, Bob intensely looked for Ann. He was hoping to get a glimpse of her and perhaps a chance to talk to her.

After ten minutes, Mr. Barber approached Bob. Bob excitedly asked, "What's going on? What happened?"

Mr. Barber, in a low voice, said, "We'll talk outside." Once outside the courtroom, he continued. "The judge has accepted her petition for divorce. There are certain conditions that you have to understand."

Bob tried to hold back his tears for fear of the unknown. "What conditions? Where are my children? I want to see my boys."

Mr. Barber grabbed Bob's arm, looked him sternly in the eyes, and with grinding teeth, said, "You better understand! It takes two to marry and one to divorce. Believe it or not, you're getting divorced! Your wife has made some serious allegations."

Bob demanded. "I want to see my children. Where are they? Did you ask for a chance for reconciliation? She doesn't know what she's doing. She is not in her right state of mind. What the hell am I paying you for? You did nothing."

Barber felt the need to control Bob moved to an isolated area. "Get ahold of yourself. She is over twenty-one, and she can file for a divorce. Your children are in a safe place. She made allegations of child abuse. I am not going to sugarcoat it. Child service will investigate. You children are with her in a shelter. She'll be there for forty-five days. Stay calm."

The opposing counselor approached. He had an impressive face, with piercing eyes, gray thick brows, and silver hair. With a pasted smile, he said, "We have a lot of things to discuss. Can I have you card? When can we schedule a meeting?"

Mr. Barber replied, "I just met Mr. Dorsete this morning. I need more time and information from my client. I will call you in a day or two."

"Fair enough. I'll be expecting your call."

Mr. Barber and Bob made their way out of the courthouse, and Mr. Barber handed Bob a copy of Ann's petition. "We have a court date in three weeks," Mr. Barber said. "At that time, we'll make our case to see your children. Also, we have to respond to her petition. I want you to read these documents and write down as much as you can… And I will need more information from you."

Bob dejected, "I have a letter for her. Can you get it to her?"

In a stern disciplinary tone, he said, "Don't you understand? You have restraining orders. You can't go near her. That means no contact with her. The same thing applies to the children. That means no physical contact, no phone calls, and nooo letters.

Mr. Barber paused. In a calmer tone, he said, "You're in the hospital for a three-day evaluation. It could help your case if you get a favorable evaluation. Watch your Ps and Qs."

The hot June sun had heated up the day. The heat annoyed Bob. He felt the perspiration on his neck and back. He sluggishly entered the house. It was dark, empty, and quiet. To Bob, it appeared as if he was in a dark void of a deep cave. His sensitive skin felt the cold air, but his body continue to perspire from the heat of anxiety. He made his way to a chair and sat down. He learned two new words today that he come to use daily; she was the petitioner, and he was the respondent. Bob sat quietly, feeling melancholy. His mind was partially conscious and unconscious. He had a feeling of uneasiness as he debated if he should read the papers. He stared at the papers for some time. Then he read:

> I Ann Dorsete. If called as a witness, I would and could completely testify to the following facts, all of which are known to me to be true to the best of my knowledge.
>
> I am currently residing in a safe place with our four children because I am fearful for our safety and welfare based on the respondent's pattern of unprovoked and unreasonable mental abuse and violence directed toward us.
>
> I am also fearful and frightened of what the respondent might do to us when he becomes aware that I have filed for a course of action with the court. I am particularly concerned about the

> foregone because of the respondent's current state of mind.
>
> I am also fearful that if given the opportunity, the respondent will use his powers of persuasion over me to persuade me to dismiss this action and not to continue to seek the court's help, which I so desperately need for the welfare of myself and our children.

Bob's eyes were filled with water and his vision became foggy. As much as he did not want to read anymore, he continued to read.

> For the past two years and more, particularly for the past several months, the respondent has constantly demonstrated both mental and physical abuse and violence toward me as follows:
>
> 1. Respondent's verbal and mental abuse toward me includes but not necessarily limited to the following: His extreme and unjustifiable verbal outburst of demands and statements of anger. He demands immediate and total domination of my activities, thoughts, and content. He dominates me and acts macho toward me. In the presence of others, he treats me like a possession. He has an explosive temper and is quick to make judgement about my activities and opinions, and he uses sex to demonstrate his control over me.
> 2. Respondent's physical abuse and threats of violence toward me include but are not necessarily limited to the following: He kicks and batters me when he loses his temper. He throws objects around the house. He threatens to kill me if I leave him or dissolve

> our marriage. He demands that I engage in sexual intercourse with him every other day, stating to me, "This is the only thing that I live for and enjoy in my entire life." If I reject his sexual demands, he becomes hostile and belligerent toward me. On a daily and weekly basis, without provocation, the respondent says to me, "You dummy, you idiot. I do everything for this family. If I left you, this family would be a bunch of nobodies."
>
> I declare under penalty of perjury, under the laws of the State of California, that the forgoing is true and correct.

Bob dropped the papers to the floor, sat back, and held back from tearing. He could not control the waterfall cascading from his eyes. He raised his head, searching for help. He cried out "God! what have I done! He reached for the letter he had written for Ann. With foggy and watery eyes, he read:

> I am really sorry for my actions and behavior and for causing you to act as you did. By your actions, you have given me the slap in the face that I needed to knock sense into my head. I miss you and the boys so much and love and need you so badly. Please forgive me. Since the last time I spoke to you, I've had nothing else on my mind but the concern and well-being of you and the boys. Please come home.
>
> I realize that your actions and perceptions were manifested by the false and loud statements I have made. I never meant them. They were only emotional comments of anger. Now I realize that my family is the most important thing to me as well as the physical and mental health of every-

body. Now I realize that verbal comments can hurt like the cut of a knife and take longer to heal.

For all these months, you bottled up your emotions, trying not to add to the stressful situations that I was in. You have been afraid to speak your mind. I have now realized that danger and perceptions that I had manifested in your mind, and the need to change my behavior. Please remember that my behavior was a result of the stressful problems embedded in the complex chain of events that we created and the lack of time to relax.

I have rediscovered the priorities of my life. The good physical and emotional health of the entire family. Marriage is difficult and requires the sincere cooperation of both partners to make it work. Marriage requires tolerance, compromise, sympathy, understanding, romance and kindness; and there should be evidence of this every day.

Our business venture has taken a great deal of time and disrupted our life. Due to the frustrations of the business pressures and the complications we have had, we have spread ourselves too thin, and now we have reached the breaking point.

Because of the personality difference, we have taken different courses of action. We must face the problem and the stress that has occurred in recent months and view them realistically for both short- and long-term effect on the boys and our marriage. We must quickly realize our problems and the difficulties we have gone through and the demand they have caused to us. All of which can be resolved with compromise and love.

> I have never suffered such pain as I have experienced this past week. I have learned to value the ones I love the most—you and the boys. I need to stop to smell the roses, to enjoy the fruits of our labor, and to love and cherish my family.
>
> I fell in love with you for your charm, innocence, beauty, love, and kindness. For your warmth and affection, you are the one who gave me so much to live for. We have been together too long to allow it to end this way. You have fulfilled all my needs, and I didn't show my appreciation. I'm sorry. Please, my love, forgive me and talk to me. I love you very much.
>
> Love,
> Bob

Bob's thoughts were drifting back, reflecting on sixteen years of marriage and the twenty-two years with Ann. The good and happy times together, their dreams and hopes and the birth of his four boys.

Bob Dorsete was back at the hospital. As he walked in, he was greeted by Preston, a hospital counselor. "You missed lunch. However, I did order dinner for you. Oh, we're having a meeting in the dining area in thirty minutes." Preston was a medium-built man with gray hair and a short-trimmed full beard. Preston had given Bob the pass for the day.

With all the confusion, Bob had forgotten to call Skip. He contacted Skip. He was relieved that Skip was still operating the restaurant. He gave Skip the hospital number.

After several attempts, Bob finally got through to Pete. "Where have you been?" Pete said. "I called earlier. Some woman answered the phone. She told me what a nice person you are. She likes you. Then she talked about headaches."

"Yeah, see how lucky I am," sniggered Bob.

Chuckling, Pete said, "All she talked about was her headaches, and if she didn't have them, she could go home." Pete laughed. "You're really with a bunch of nuts."

"I really can't complaint. The food is okay, and I get to keep my cigarettes. The attendants are friendly. I have better conversations with the staff than with the patients. I can't have a constructive conversation with these people. They're like kids. I really feel sorry for them." He told Pete about Martha and more about Bonnie. Pete roared with laughter. "Okay, don't rub it in, and I don't think it's that funny. I can't wait to get out. I have too many things to do."

"Did you see Ann?"

"No! I couldn't stop the petition from being filed," Bob said sadly. "Ann wasn't there. I saw her attorney. This is getting ugly. She made allegations of abuse. You got to talk to Ann."

"She won't return my calls."

"Please keep trying."

"Okay. Did you see your next-door neighbor?"

"Yeah! You were right. He was shocked to see me. He knows that I will be released on Thursday. The asshole knows. But why?"

"The money." Pete noticed that Bob was pissed. "Just hang in there and watch what you said and do. Focus on getting the hell out."

A woman staffer announced, "We're having a meeting in the lounge in five minutes." The group was assembled. "Okay, quiet it down," said Preston. "Before we start, I have your meal tickets here. Please complete them. The meal for the week is posted." He placed the tickets on the table. "Let's get started. We're going to talk about self-esteem. Does anyone know what self-esteem mean?"

Bonnie very proudly stood up and said, "It's when you feel good about yourself."

"Right," said Preston. "What makes you feel good?"

Bonnie said, "When I'm happy."

Preston tried to get participation from the other patients and continued, "Self-esteem is feeling good about yourself. For example, when you do something and people tell you they like it."

Eleanor said, "Like the shirts I did! Everyone liked them." She stood up pointing to her blouse. "I made this design." She had glued sparkles into a colorful flowery pattern. She continued, “I made one for all the counselors. Because they’re nice to us.”

“Very good, Eleanor,” Preston said. “Self-esteem comes from two ways. One from feeling good from accomplishments. Two, by things around us that allow us to do things we like. You can’t do too much about things around you. However, you can do things within yourself to feel good about yourself… Know that you are important. Feel special about yourself, feel confident that you can do it, express yourself in your own way, be proud of your accomplishments. For example, I really like this picture that I painted. Another way to build up your self-esteem is by acting independently. For example, dressing yourself, making your own breakfast. Assume responsibility. Don’t be afraid of something new and don’t give up before you try. Make the effort. If you can’t do it, don’t get mad or frustrated. Try harder. Don’t feel sorry for yourself and don’t say they don’t like me so therefore they didn’t like my painting.” Preston paused to pass out paper and pencils.

“So how can you build up your self-esteem? I would like you to write down how you can build up your self-esteem. Write about things that make you feel good.” He waited a few minutes and called out for volunteers.

Mary said, “Never say that you are too dumb to do something.”

“Good! Joe, how about you?”

Joe covered his face with his hands and moved them to the back of his head and leaned back on his chair with his hands folded behind. “Work toward a goal—something that you can do—and do it.”

“Very good! Someone else? Jim!”

Jim hesitated for a moment. “Never said you’re dumb.”

“That’s good. But someone mentioned that. Think of something else.”

Jim raised his head and stared at the ceiling. “Try to do something to help build your self-esteem.”

“Very good, Jim.”

“Anything else?”

"Don't fe-feel th-that you can't do it," Martha said with a little stutter.

"You all have good ideas." Preston paused then said, "If you don't like yourself, don't expect others to like you. Start by feeling good about yourself. Learn to take pride in those things you can do. Don't be afraid to fail." Preston was interrupted by the sound of the food carts. "Dinner is here. But before we break for dinner, I would like everyone to think about setting a goal for yourself. For the next day, think of something that you can do. Set yourself a realistic goal, and then work toward your goal. Okay, have a nice dinner."

Bob, Bonnie, and Martha sat together during dinner. Martha read a poem she wrote for Bob. Bonnie complained about her headaches and how much she missed her daughter. Martha self-pitied herself that she was all alone, and she cried as she explained her medical problems—leg operation, hysterectomy, and problems with her liver. Bob tried to be gleeful by talking of other things and told them funny stories.

Bob was in the lounge, sitting at the table by himself, smoking. He noticed on the white board activities for tomorrow: "Group therapy, exercise, and arts and craft." A stocky man approached. He had straight, dark hair, a reddish face, and thick glasses. It was Jim. He moved his eyebrows up and down, and in a mysterious low voice, he said, "We can use a man like you."

In a questioning tone, Bob asked, "What do you mean?"

Jim turned his head, looking around, and moved closer to Bob. "I'm a spy for an agency bigger and more secret than the CIA. I can't tell you anymore. I know over twenty different languages." Jim uttered unfamiliar sounds to Bob.

Bob decided to play along and asked, "What language were you speaking?"

Boasting, Jim replied, "In many different languages, I said 'How are you?' I can speak Hungarian, Russian, Polish, Arabic, and many others." He paused and turned his head to look around again. "I've been watching you. You're look strong. How would you like to work with me?"

Bob refrained from laughing. He knew that he had to be careful. He asked, "How long have you been a spy?"

Jim again turned his head. "I'm not patient. It's a disguise." He turned his head. "I'm here looking for somebody."

Their conversation was interrupted by Eleanor. She came in sobbing. She threw a shirt on the floor as she yelled, "If she doesn't like it. I'm not going to give it to her. I don't want her to have it." She stamped her foot and pushed the chairs in a tantrum.

Two attendants came in, and one said, "Eleanor, calm down!"

Eleanor stopped and stood still. The female orderly said, "It's a nice shirt."

"We all like it. It's beautiful."

"Do you really like it?" Eleanor asked in a childish tone.

The female orderly replied, "Yes, it's a very nice shirt. It's one of the best you have made." Eleanor stopped sobbing and picked up the shirt. The orderlies took her gently by the arms and escorted her out of the dining area.

Bob turned to Jim and said, "I have to make a phone call. I'll talk to you later."

"Well, do you want to join us?"

Bob, trying not to laugh, said, "This is very serious stuff. I have to think about it." He got up and walked out.

As he walked out, an orderly called out, "Bob! Dr. Bergren is here to see you." Bob thought that perhaps he was going to be released. He watched as she came around the counter, focusing on the movement of her buttocks covered by her tight white uniform. "Follow me," said May-Gee Kuwahara, smiling. She escorted him to a door. There was a sign on the door that read, "Private." She knocked on the door and opened it slowly. Dr. Bergren was sitting by a small table covered by papers. It was Bob's file. Dr. Bergren stood up, extended his hand and asked. "How are you doing?"

Bob replied, "Fine, thank you." May-Gee left and closed the door behind her.

"Working long hours?"

"My night shift." Dr. Bergren looked down. "I was just reading your file. I'm happy to report that you're doing very well."

"You know that my objective is to get the hell out of here as soon as possible."

"I spoke to Mr. Morris, and he was happy to hear about your progress."

Bob excitedly asked, "Well, thank you! Does that mean I'll be leaving tomorrow?"

Dr. Bergren sat down. "No! You haven't been here long enough. Remember, our agreement was for a minimum of three days."

Bob, in an excited tone, said, "What do you mean three days? I've been here since Saturday."

Calmly, Dr. Bergren said, "Weekends don't count. Today you had a pass. Tomorrow will be your first full day. Perhaps Thursday afternoon if all goes well."

Bob was annoyed. He knew if he got overly excited, they would only keep him here longer. He struggled to get his thoughts and words together. He calmly said, "I need to leave here. I have too many things to do. My restaurant, my new business. I have to try to get in touch with my wife." He paused as he stared at Dr. Bergren. "I'm not going to argue with you. If that's what you believe, fine. But I want you to know. I have personal matters on the outside, and I can't care for them if I am in here."

In a calm tone, Dr. Bergren asked, "Do you have any thoughts of hurting anyone?"

"What do you mean by that?" Bob asked in a surprised tone.

"Do you think an injustice was done to you?"

Bob, getting a little excited, said, "I'm a pissed off for being here. Morris lied to me. And he threatened me to fire me. It was not my idea to get checked out at a hospital. It's all about liability! Look, Doctor, I don't know what's going on, but I know I don't belong here."

Dr. Bergren asked, "Are you thinking of hurting yourself or thinking of suicide?"

"Of course not! Hey, I don't know what Mr. Morris told you, but he's a liar. I don't do drugs, and I just started to drink. I don't know where this whole conversation is leading to."

"You're right. The drug test detected benzodiazepine, a prescription drug, and little alcohol was found. You've gone through a great deal of stress. I'm concerned that you might do something to hurt yourself. I also know that your wife filed for a divorce. I want to prescribe some medication for—"

Bob interrupted, "I don't need that shit. I don't believe in drugs… I don't believe in pills like the little munches here!"

Dr. Bergren paused. He stroked his beard as he stared at Bob. "Okay, I'll make the prescription available in case you change your mind. I think you should take something."

Very benevolently, Bob said, "Thank you."

"If all goes well, you'll be released before the end of the week." Dr. Bergren stood up and extended his hand. "Relax and let us help you."

Bob shook his hand and said, "Thank you for seeing me. But please, get me out of here as soon as possible. I can't relate to these people. They really have problems. Most of them want to be here. I want to get the hell out of here. I've got things to do."

Without showing any expression, Dr. Bergren said, "We'll see. Good night." Dr. Bergren concluded that there was nothing wrong with this man; however, he had to play it safe. Better to be safe than sorry.

Bob was alone in the recreation room until Bonnie walked in and asked, "What are you doing?"

"Thinking," Bob replied reluctantly.

She sat down next to him and, in soft sentiment tone, said, "She's really lucky to have someone like you. You really love her? I wish I had someone to love me." She saw the sadness in his eyes and asked, "What happened between you and you wife?"

"We had an argument. Now she's afraid of me. She made allegations that I threatened to hurt her. I'm here for her, to prove to her that I love her."

Bonnie stared at Bob and said, "You're handsome. I'll lik—" She stopped abruptly. "No, I shouldn't say it."

"Say what."

"I know you don't know me, but if you get divorced, would you consider dating me?"

Flattered by her comments, he politely said, "Well, I'll be your friend. Even if I don't get divorced, we can still be friends."

Bonnie grinned. "I would like that very much." She moved closer to him and placed her arm around him.

He stared at her face and stroked her long downy hair. She was young with a shapely body, attractive eyes, and soft white skin. He thought of Ann and how much he wanted to be with her. He thought of a woman's softness, Bonnie's soft red lips. He moved closer to her. She closed her eyes in anticipation of adoration. He wanted her as badly as any man could want a woman. He needed to clear his mind, to fight off the sexual desire. Bob thought, *This is not right. She has mental problems, and I don't want to add to her problems. I don't need this. I shouldn't encourage her.*

"Can I join you?" interrupted Martha.

Bob said, "Sure," relieved of the sexual flashes. He noticed the annoyed look on Bonnie's face. He wanted Martha there to control his manly instants. "Sit here." He tapped the couch with his hand.

Bob told them jokes and stories of his boys. Martha's eyes became watery. Bob sighed. "What's the matter? Am I making you sad?"

"No, they're happy tears. I'm happy to hear that you have four children and that they love you and you love them. It's a happy story." Martha glanced at him with her childlike and honest eyes, then stared downward. "I think that you are a very nice person and… and you're very lucky."

"Well, thank you," said Bob, smiling. Bob saw the scars on her arms and asked, "What happened to your arms?"

Tears started to form, creating bright crystals over her aquamarine eyes. She said sadly, "I tried to commit suicide several times." She paused to clear her throat. The tears were running harder from her eyes.

He put his arm around her. "You don't have to talk about it if you don't want to."

"No, I don't mind telling you. When I was a young girl, I was sexually assaulted by my stepfather and stepbrother. I ran away when I was fifteen. I met this older guy. We lived together. He made me prostitute for money. Then I had a baby. The baby wasn't his. He left me. I didn't have a job. I didn't have a place to live. I was prostituting to make money. I got arrested. My baby was taken away from me, and that's the first time I tried killing myself. Then they put me in a place like this. When I got out, I couldn't find my baby. I have never seen my daughter. She would about thirteen years old now. I have no idea where she is. I have all kinds of medical problems, my liver, my kidneys." Sobbing hard, she put her arms around Bob. "Sometimes, I don't want to live. I want to die."

Bonnie, feeling that she was not getting Bob's attention, put her hand on Bob's shoulder. "I, too, have a daughter, but I would never try to kill myself. My daughter needs me. My husband needs me. It's just that he's mad at me. And if it wasn't for my headaches, I would be home. Then I wouldn't have to be here, and I could be with my daughter." Bonnie was beaming. "On her first birthday, she told me that she loved me. She is happy that I'm her mommy."

Martha did not care for Bonnie's story. She asked, "Bob, can you hug me again?"

"Sure." He turned, put his arms around her, and gave her a light hug.

"Hug me harder," said Martha. He squeezed her tighter.

Bonnie, feeling nettled, asked, "Can you hug me too?" Bob turned around and hugged her.

As they exchanged hugs, an orderly walked in and stood in silence. Bob immediately said, "We're just being friendly."

Bob was exhausted. It had been a long and disappointing day. He went into his room and lay on the bed with many thoughts in his mind, especial Ann's declaration of abuse. Joe was in bed, twisting, turning, and babbling. Bob was disturbed and could not sleep because of the noises that Joe was making. Bob tried to think of other things, such as movies and songs. But the negative thoughts returned. He switched his thoughts to May-Gee. He thought that she was cute with the long black hair, round face, tiny eyes and lips. She looked like a Hawaiian doll.

Joe sat up and turned his head and looked around. He looked at Bob and threw himself back on the bed. He stretched his arms. "Bob, are you awake? Can we talk?"

"What!" Bob replied.

"Can't sleep…I was thinking of my son."

"I'm thinking too."

"She took him away from me," Joe uttered over and over. "She ran back to her hometown. She changed her name. I found her…"

Bob paid little attention because of own headaches.

Tuesday

As the patients were eating, a woman staffer announced, "After breakfast, we will have group therapy. Everyone must attend." She paused as she looked around at the blank faces. "The meeting will be in the rec room," said the woman as she removed her long curly blond hair from her face to over her ears showing her blue earrings, which enhanced her blue eyes. She appeared to be in her mid-thirties. Her light turquoise dress intensifies her figure. She was tall with long attractive legs. She had an average-looking face but a seductive body raised on high-heel shoes.

The patients were seated around in a circle. At the head of the circle was the blonde woman. Bob was carefully eyeing her long shapely legs and watched as she crossed them from one side to the other. "Good morning, everyone. My name is Ms. Oppenheimer. For those of you who are here for the first time, we start our meeting by everyone introducing yourself." Turning to Bonnie, who was seated to her right, she said, "Bonnie, we'll start with you."

Bonnie had some makeup on and a bow in her hair. Very confident, she said, "My name is Bonnie, and I feel good."

The introductions went around until everyone had spoken. Speaking in a childlike mannerism, Ms. Oppenheimer asked, "Who wants to talk first?"

Bonnie, hoping for attention, said, "I do. I do."

"Okay, Bonnie."

Bonnie stared at Bob Dorsete and in a cheerful tone said, "The reason I feel good is because Bob is here." Her eyes glanced at his. He thought how pretty she looked with makeup and bright-red lipstick. She continued to look straight at Bob and smiled. "I like having Bob here." Bob was delighted and embarrassed as he started to think sexual thoughts.

Ms. Oppenheimer asked, "How are your headaches?"

Bonnie's mood and tone changed drastically. She lowered her eyes. The smile from her face was gone. Pointing to her head, she said, "Yes, I still have my headaches."

"Is the medication helping you?"

"Sometimes…sometimes not. I miss my daughter. She needs me, and my husband hasn't called me. He doesn't love me anymore. He told me he loved me, but I don't think he does. He hasn't come to see me. I asked him to come and bring our daughter, but he hasn't come here yet." Bonnie stopped talking and lowered her head.

"Is there anything else you want to tell us?"

Bonnie, shaking her head, said, "No."

Ms. Oppenheimer asked, "Who wants to be next?"

Martha raised her and said, "I will." Everyone waited for her to speak. Martha did not speak.

Edging, Ms. Oppenheimer asked, "Martha, aren't you going to tell us about how you feel?"

A long pause went by, and Martha said, "Yes, I guess so. I'm happy because I have a friend here." Looking at Bob, she continued, "Bob is a very nice person, and I'm glad that he's here with us. I wrote a poem for him."

"Can I read it?"

Ms. Oppenheimer, "Not now. How are you feeling?"

"I'm not happy because this is my last week here. I have to leave. I like it here."

Ms. Oppenheimer interjected, "Martha, we talked about that last week. There are other places you can go. Don't be worried about leaving." Glancing at the group, she tried not to stare at Bob. How normal he appeared and what a striking influence he had on Martha and Bonnie. "Okay, who's next?" She looked at Bob and said, "Would you like to say something since you're new to the group."

Bob said, "I like to hear some other people." Bob did want to say anything, feeling out of place.

"Joe, tell us how you feel."

Joe, rubbing his hand across his mouth and chin, said, "Oh, okay, I feel okay. I think I'm ready to leave."

Ms. Oppenheimer asked, "Do you think about drinking?"

"Yes, sometimes I think about a cold beer," said Joe as he moved in his chair.

"You know what drinking does to you."

"Yeah, you're right… I'm still thinking about my son."

She interrupted, "Joe, we're not to talk about that."

Joe became more fidgety and a little angry. He turned to Eleanor and said, "I wish she would stop being so pushy and bossy."

Eleanor angrily turned to Joe and said, "If you weren't so damn stupid, I wouldn't have anything to say to you."

Joe stood up. "You bitch! You think that you're so smart."

The therapist interrupted, "Now let's settle down, group. Didn't we talk about this last week, about being nice to each other and getting along?"

Eleanor got up crying and shouted, "He's always calling me names. I hate him!" She left the room howling, "I hate him!"

Staring at Joe, Ms. Oppenheimer said, "This is a repeat of last week. I thought we had an understanding that we would get along."

Mary, half moaning, said, "I came here for peace and quiet. I wish everybody would stop all this fighting and just get along. We would be so much happier here."

Ms. Oppenheimer said, "I agree with Mary. Let's settle down." Everyone was quiet. "Mary, your turn."

Mary, a common-looking woman of fifty, was neatly dressed. In a subdued tone, she said, "I have two children and a husband. I had a high-pressure job, and I was under a lot of pressure. I had no time to relax. I was working, taking care of my children and my husband.

I'm doing much better now, but when I hear the yelling and shout, the name-calling, I get stressed and nervous."

Looking at Joe, Ms. Oppenheimer said, "It's important that we all learn to get along. It's important that we don't addresses each other by bad names. This kind of behavior is abnormal, and that's the reason why some of you are here."

Without warning, Jim moved his hands in karate-chops form. Sitting in his seat, he murmured sounds and continued to move his hands. The patients next to him had to move.

"Jim! Stop that!" shouted Ms. Oppenheimer.

Jim looked down at the floor and then looked up at her. In a slight accent, he said, "Sorry!"

"I've talked to the attendants, and they said you're doing well. You're learning to control your hands and karate kicks around people. You're making a lot of progress, so try to control yourself."

She turned to an elderly man and said, "Cab, tell us how you feel and what's happening with you."

Cab was a thin man of sixty years plus. He had no teeth and a hearing problem. "What?"

Ms. Oppenheimer, looking directly at him, slowly said, "Tell us how you feel."

Cab, slapping his knee, said, "Oh! Oh, I feel fine. I like everybody here. Everybody is really nice. The food is good."

Ms. Oppenheimer asked, "Is there anything you want to tell us?" She tensely moved in her seat, crossing her legs, conscious that Bob was sitting directly opposite from her with eyes fixed on her. Bob tried hard not to stare. It had been over a week since he held Ann. He thought of her soft skin, round buttocks, and delicious breast.

Cab said, "Oh, I like it here."

At that moment, Eleanor returned. Bob was awakened from the trance. Eleanor was poised and quietly as she took her seat. Ms. Oppenheimer turned to Annette, an old thin woman with a sad face. "Annette, we haven't heard anything from you. Can you please say something?" Annette sat still with her head down and her hands folded. She did not answer.

"She won't speak," interjected Eleanor. "She just wants to go home to her grandchildren and son."

Joe broke in, looking at Mrs. Oppenheimer. "You see what I mean about her. See Miss Bossy. She knows everything."

Taking control, Ms. Oppenheimer, "Joe, we're not going to have any more of that. We're not going to repeat what just happened here a few minutes ago. We don't say bad things about people to annoy or to make them angry." The therapist turned to Bob. "How about you, Bob?"

Bob was bored and reluctantly to speak. "What do you want me to say?"

"Tell us about yourself."

"My name is Bob Dorsete. I have a wife and four boys, and I'm here because my wife made allegations that I threatened to hurt her. I was forced into coming here by representatives of my company. They made statements that I was dangerous to myself and others. I have a restaurant, and I'm currently starting a new business venture with computers. My wife has just filed for a divorce, and I want to get out of here as soon as possible because I have responsibilities and to see my children."

Bonnie broke in, "You're a very responsible person. You have a job and a business. You're not like us. Why are you here?"

Ms. Oppenheimer interrupted, "Please continue. Tell us about your problems and how you feel."

"I really don't want to say anymore."

Ms. Oppenheimer was edging, "This is group therapy. It's important that you open up and share your feelings with the group."

"I don't think I should."

"Why not?"

Reluctantly, Bob said, "I don't feel that this group can help me. I don't think this is the type of therapy I need."

Mary was insulted. "Do think that you're better than us?" she asked.

"No," Bob said in a humble tone. "Please don't misunderstand me. I just think I don't belong here for this type of therapy." Bob realized that it would be best if he did not say another word. He turned to Ms. Oppenheimer. "I don't want to say anymore. I apologize if I offended anyone."

Ms. Oppenheimer glanced at the blank faces. "This concludes our session for today. We'll meet again on Thursday."

After lunch, the patients had an hour for rest. Next on the agenda was arts and crafts. The patients crossed the hall to another section of the hospital. They entered a small room with tables and chairs. The light was not bright, and there was only one small window. The instructor's name was Clarence. He unlocked the closets, and the patients were allowed to take anything they wanted. Joe work on an ashtray as he glued tiny little seashells to it. Eleanor, Bonnie, Mary, and Annette were sitting together. Eleanor was trying to get Annette involved in drawing. Mary was doing needlework. Bonnie was gluing different colored plastics into some kind of design. Bob was bored and not interested in the childish projects. He walked around and looked at the anxious faces on the patients. Clarence was busy getting materials out of the closet and helping the patients. The whole thing reminded Bob of his days in grade school. Jim was working with leather. He was making change wallets and boasting that he had already made six of them. Everything that Jim did was at a very fast pace. The old man, Cab, sat alone looking outside.

To keep busy, Bob decided to make the same wallets that Jim was working on. He thought that it would make nice gifts for his boys with their names stenciled on them. Bob had to work with Jim because there was only one stencil set. He watched as Jim gently, with a mantle, stenciled the leather. Before each stencil was stamped, the leather had to be moistened with water.

Bonnie showed Bob her project of tiny color plastics formed into flowers. Martha, very proudly, showed Bob her drawing of a house with a woman, a man, and four children in front. Bob knew that Martha was trying to express her affection for him. In empathy for her, he accepted the drawing and hugged her.

Bob had dinner with Martha and Bonnie. Afterward, they watched TV. At times, they were depressing. Bob struggled to listen to their depressing stories and grumbles. In an attempt to cheer them, Bob told stories from movies that had a happy ending.

Wednesday

The small group walked to the elevator through the lobby and into the cool misty morning air. The sun had not yet broken through the June clouds. The air smelled fresh to Bob, and he thought how good it felt to be out. He looked over the group and saw how happy they appeared. Jim walked quickly as he headed the group. Bob had to walk slowly as he walked with Martha. She complained of the fast pace and that she could not keep up because of her medical problems. Bob felt genuine pity for the woman. He tried being friendly, but there was nothing that he could do for her. He interlocked his arm with hers to ease the strain on her legs. Martha felt good around Bob. She liked his company and attention. Preston had to shout several times for Jim to slow down to wait for the rest of the group.

This was an exercise session, optional. About half the group participated. They walked about ten blocks to a local convenience store. They purchased sweets, snacks, and sodas. Some of the patients were outside, enjoying their treats, waiting for the rest still inside. Preston was busy eyeing to make sure everyone was present. They started their return to the hospital. Bob and Martha were dragging behind. Preston had to stop the group several times to wait for Bob and Martha. Bob informed Preston that Martha had a difficult time walking. He assured Preston that he would stay with Martha. She was breathing heavy, complaining that her legs hurt. Bob stopped at every street crossing, encouraging Martha that she can do it. By the time they arrived to their ward, the group was gathered in the lounge. Preston was conducting a session on self-esteem.

In the afternoon, the patients were in arts and crafts. The females worked in groups and conversed the majority of time. The males worked individually and occasionally conversed. Bob continued working on change wallets for his boys. Bob asked Jim to help him with the stenciling.

After arts, the group was back in the lounge watching TV. May-Gee called Bob. She handed Bob the telephone.

"I spoke to Dr. Bergren," said Alan Morris. "He's very satisfied with your progress and said that you will be released soon. I want to thank you for your cooperation."

In a raised voice, Bob said, "It wasn't right what you did to me. You tricked me. You lied. There's no golf course. How would you like to be locked up with a bunch of nuts? When I get out of here, I'm going to find a lawyer and sue your ass and the company."

Alan Morris, in a calm tone, said, "I can understand why you might be upset, but we had no choice. We had to make sure that you were okay. Look at it this way. You'll get a good report from the hospital. Your wife won't have any reason to fear you. She might calm down, and there is a chance for you and her to get back together."

Bob asked calmly. "What's the involvement of Ray Ditler?"

"Who?"

"My next-door neighbor, Ray. The guy who introduced you to me."

"What do you mean?"

"You know what the hell I mean. What's his involvement?"

"Your wife said that you threaten to kill your boss. We had to get involved. We hired a private investigator. We contacted someone locally. We didn't know he was your next-door neighbor."

Bob said in raise tone, "You're a liar. I am going to sue you." Bob placed the phone down.

Bob glanced at May-Gee and the other attendant. He saw their blank faces and, in a calm voice, said, "As I told you, I was tricked into coming here. They threatened to fire me. He told me I was going to a resort to relax. Once I get out, I'm going to find an attorney and sue them."

Bob was in his room lying on the bed trying to get all the anger out of his mind. He was thinking about Ray, Alan Morris, and more importantly, how his children were doing. He wondered what they were thinking about. Joe walked in and asked, "Can I talk to you?"

"Yeah," said Bob.

"I think you're a smart guy," Joe said in a solemn tone. "I need to find my son."

Bob curiously asked, "What happen?"

"Let me start from the beginning… I was married, and we had a son. When my son was three years old, she ran away with him. She came back after three months. We stayed together for a couple of years, and then she left again. I didn't hear from her for a long time, so I went searching for her. She went back home to Kansas. She changed her name and tried to change my son's name. I found her. I decided to stay, and we got friendly, just talking at first. I spent a lot of time with my son. We had good times. I think that she got jealous. She was telling people that I was calling her bad names and that I threatened to hit her if she wouldn't allow me to take my son back to California.

Her entire family started to harass me and told me to leave. They threaten to kill me. So I left and came back to California. I called almost every day. She would not pick up the telephone. Six months later, she started talking to me. I had conversations with my son. We got friendly. She asked for money. She needed money for a car and clothing. I sent her money. After a year, one day, I called, but the phone was not working. I went back to her hometown, and no one would tell me where she was. She disappeared." Joe breathed a heavy sigh and continued, "That was the last time I ever hear from her and my son. I've been spending all my time and money looking for her. I want to find him. I want to tell him how much I love him and how important he is to me… That's why I need your help!"

Bob didn't know what to say. He wondered how much of the story was true.

Joe said, "Can you help?"

"I'm sorry, I don't know what I can do for you. It sounds like you did the best," Bob suggested. "Hire a private investigator."

"I did, no luck."

"You've got to help me," said Joe. "That's why I drink a lot. I drink because of the pain. I have to find him."

"Sorry!"

Joe stared at Bob. "You're Italian. You got Mafia connections!"

"Yes, I am Italian. No, I don't have Mafia connections."

"You're just saying that because you don't want to help me?"

Bob did not answer. Joe lowered his head, turned, and walked away.

Bob had dinner with Martha and Bonnie. Joe ate dessert with them. Later Bob was in the rec room alone meditating. Bonnie walked in. Within minutes, Martha walked in. Bob could not endure hearing about their depressing lives, especially Martha. To avoid their grumbles, Bob did most of the talking.

Thursday

The patients were in group therapy with Ms. Oppenheimer. There was no new patient, so no introductions were necessary. There was the usual individual talking, weeping by some of the women, outbursts, and cheering. In the afternoon, the patients were in arts and crafts, Clarence had the patients painting with watercolors. Clarence instructed the group to copy his painting. He painted a section at a time. He walked around, inspecting the work and assisted some of the patients. Some of the patients had no interest in painting. Clarence painted a blue sky, a green meadow, and optional to paint people or animals. Bob was called because there was a telephone call for him. Bob entered the lounge; the staffer handed him the telephone.

"Bob, you didn't get me a chance to finish our conversation yesterday," said Alan Morris. Bob did not reply. "We had knowledge of a threat. We had a responsibility. We had to hire a security service. Mr. Ditler said nothing negative about you."

Bob replied, "Do you think that was ethical? You hired my next-door neighbor to spy on me. He tells my wife what to do. He tells her to go to a shelter."

"I don't know anything about that. I don't know his involvement with your wife. We were just concerned about your mental state."

Bob raised his voice. "Well, did I hurt anyone? I will sue your ass."

Alan said in a composed tone, "Do what you think you have to do. I just want you to know that we're satisfied that you're okay, and I want to thank you for your cooperation. We would like to help."

Bob interrupted, "You already have helped. You put me in a lock unit. Your hire my next-door neighbor. Goodbye." He handled the phone to the staffer.

Bob glanced at the attendant. "The reason that I am here is because of my company. They lied to me."

The attendant asked, "You didn't volunteer?"

"No, they threatened to fire me. I am going to sue them."

"I have never heard of that. I don't blame you for being upset."

After supper, Bob lay on his bed. He didn't feel much like socializing. He stretched out as he thought of his wife and their lovemaking. Before the restaurant, they had made love weekly. There wasn't a night that he didn't gently massage, kiss, or touch her. He thought about how much he missed her. His thoughts faded to the knock on the open door. The patients were not allowed to close the doors, and they had to always remain open. "I'm sorry," Bonnie said. "I didn't know you were sleeping."

"I wasn't sleeping," Bob said as he sat up. He examined the young girl. She was dressed in baggy jogging pants and a loosely fitted T-shirt. "I was just relaxing and thinking."

"What were you thinking about?"

"My wife and children," said Bob as he stood up.

With a serious look on her face, Bonnie asked, "You really love her, don't you?"

"Yes," Bob said, nodding.

"Am I your friend?" Bonnie asked as she walked closer.

"Yes, we're friends."

Bonnie asked in a childish manner, "Do you think I'm pretty?"

Bob hesitated as he stared. She had makeup that transformed her girlish face into a seductive woman. "Of course, you are."

She smiled. "If you get divorced, would you consider marrying me?" Bonnie apologized. "I didn't mean that. I meant…be my friend."

Feeling compassion for her, he softly said, "We are friends."

She flushed. "No, not just friends. Real friends." They stood only a couple of feet apart. He knew that it was jeopardous to be alone with her; nevertheless, he welcomed her company. He wanted the softness and the beauty of a woman's body. He stared in silence, uncertain of what to do. Bonnie took his hands and gently placed them over her shirt. She gently pressed them firmly against her breast. She let go of his hands, and he moved them away. She lifted her blouse over her breast. Bob stood back. His eyes were fixed on her breasts. He was surprised that they were larger than they appeared under her clothing. They were perfect, he thought—round, firm, and large. She appeared attractive and innocent with an odd mixture of mature feminine warmth seductiveness and girlish delicacy.

She grabbed his hands and placed them on her bosom. Acting with instincts, Bob gently squeezed her breast and delicately massaged her youthful nipple. He placed his arms around her. He closed his eyes and kissed her lips. Bonnie reacted and kissed him hard as she embraced his body. Her breasts against his chest excited Bob with a bewitching desire. He withdrew and stood back. Baffled, Bonnie asked, "What's the matter?"

"This is not right. I'm married. We're patients in a hospital." He grabbed her blouse and gently lowered it to cover her breast, then he realized that she was not wearing a bra.

Bonnie was saddened by his rejection. "Is it because I'm not pretty?"

"No, it isn't that," Bob said, shaking his head and breathing a sigh of relief. "I really love my wife very much. You're pretty. It's not right…nor the place."

Bonnie sighed. "I know that you're going to get out before me. When you get out, will you call me? Will you come to see me?"

"Yes." He turned and walked out of the room. As he walked out, he thought, if she stayed another moment there is no telling how far I would have gone. I can't get involved with her. She is not well, and I don't need more problems.

Friday

It was nine in the morning, and Bob was ready to leave the hospital. Preston and May-Gee stood in silence. Bob said, "Thank you for your help and your understanding."

Grinning, Preston said, "If you were going to be here any longer, we were going to get you your own private phone."

Bob smiled and asked, "How much longer?"

Preston replied, "Just a few minutes. We're waiting for your paperwork."

"Great!" Bob shook Preston's hand. "Thank you very much." He walked to May-Gee and embraced her.

"Good luck. I hope things work out for you," said May-Gee. "Wait a moment. Some of your friends want to say goodbye to you. They're in the lounge."

"Thank you." Bob walked into the lounge.

Bonnie, with eyes looking downward, said, "You're leaving."

"Yes."

"Are we gonna be friends?" Bonnie asked sadly. "Will you call me?"

"Yes, I have the number."

"Please call... I want to be your friend." She embraced him and kissed his cheek.

Bob walked toward Martha. With tears in her eyes, she said, "You're a very nice person. Your wife is lucky to have you. I hope you get back together."

Bob held her hand and said, "You're very important. You're a very unique person. Don't rely on other people. You have to take care of yourself. I want to see you get better."

Martha sobbed. "I'll try...only 'cause you asked me."

Bob put his arms around her and hugged her gently. "Don't do it for me. Do it for yourself." Bob said goodbye to Joe, Jim, and Eleanor. Bob turned and proceeded to walk out. He stopped to stare at a familiar figure. Joh Bell was walking in.

Bob felt sorry for Bonnie, Martha, and everyone else there, and to some degree, himself. He thought, although I have problems, I had a good life, but these poor people, I feel sorry for them. Do these places really help? Some of these people have been in and out of places like this many times. How can you deal with mental problems? How can anybody get into your head and fix what's wrong?

Tom picked up Bob at the hospital and drove Bob home. Bob drove to his restaurant. As Bob walked into the restaurant, Skip, with a big smile, said, "Hey, boss! Welcome back. Are you going to stick around and help me with lunch?"

Bob, in a half smile, said, "Certainly."

"Good! I could use the help. This morning, I was feeling shitty." Smiling, he placed his hand on Bob's shoulder and said, "I'm glad you're here. I called the hospital a couple of times. Couldn't get ahold of you. So are you crazy?"

"No! Just stressed."

"Man, I didn't know if I was going to make it to work today. I was not feeling good."

Bob happily said, "Thanks for all your help."

"I can't believe you were in a metal hospital." Skip started to laugh. "At first, I thought that you killed someone." He noticed that Bob was not laughing. "Just kidding." Then he added, "Who'd you kill?"

"All right, it's not that funny," Bob said. He turned away. "Let's get to work. Where is all the paperwork?"

"In the paper bag," replied Skip.

Bob emptied the bag. He sorted the bills, counted the cash. "Not much!"

They had taken care of the last customers, and they were alone. "Skip, let's clean up and get out of here early," Bob said. He paused, knowing that he had to tell Skip. "I going to close the restaurant."

"Why?" asked Skip in discontentment.

"Ann will be in the shelter for at least thirty days. She has no desire to work in the restaurant. Why should I? Any day, I'll know if the landlord approves the buyer as a new tenant."

Skip was dismayed to hear this. He had liked working for Bob and Ann and his job. He thought of being out of a job. "Why close it down? I could work by myself… It's no problem."

"Skip, I appreciate that. But I'm not making any money. It costs me more money to keep it open."

Skip was busy cleaning, and Bob was reviewing the bills. "Hey, Skip," called out Bob, "do you have a moment?"

"Sure, boss."

Bob was holding a bill. "This morning, I went to the phone company to get a copy of the current phone bill. I was curious to see the calls Ann made. We've never had a phone bill this high."

Skip defensively said, "Hey, man, I was working long hours, so I made some phone calls."

Bob very sternly said, "I looked at the numbers. You made a lot of long-distance calls. It's over three hundred dollars."

"Hey, man, I was alone," Skip said defensively. "I took care of your business, and you're pissed over some phone bill."

"You bet I am," said Bob sharply. "There is only sixty-four dollars here."

Skip ripped off his apron. "The hell with you." From his pocket, he withdrew a note. "Here are the hours for my pay, and there's your fucking money."

"Just sixty-four dollars for two weeks. You paid yourself handsomely."

"I had to buy some supplies. Here, your keys." He turned and walked out.

Bob was furious as he stared at the money. He shouted, "You owe me for the phone bill." He chased after Skip. Skip was outside, unchaining his bicycle. Bob placed his hand on Skip's shoulder. "You owe me for the phone bill!"

Skip stood up and turned to face Bob. "Hey, man, don't mess with me 'cause I'll kick your ass."

Bob, with an angry look on his face, was not intimidated. "Don't kid yourself. Just 'cause you're bigger than me don't think that I'm frightened. I kicked a lot of guys' asses bigger than you. I'm not afraid of you." Skip stared in silence. "You owe me for the phone bill."

Skip moved closer to Bob. He looked down at Bob and breathing at his face as he stepped on Bob's toes. "The hell with you. You're a goddamn loser and wife beater." He pushed Bob against the wall of the building. Bob's head hit the wall, and he slithered down. On his way down, he grabbed the back of Skip's ankle so forcefully, and quickly Skip fell to his buttocks.

Bob got up, put his hands around Skip's neck, and in an angry rage, said, "I trusted you... You bastard! You probably know where Ann is. She's probably been in contact with you."

Skip grabbed Bob's wrist, trying to remove the hands around his neck. Bob got control of himself, and he let go of Skip's neck. He was looking down at his hands and the spread fingers. Skip was surprised by Bob's strength. He remained motionless. Bob go up and turned. He was by the door of the building. As he opened the door, he was pushed inside by the crushing blow to his back. Skip rode off. Bob struggled to get up. He walked forward a couple of steps and dropped to his knees. He stayed motionless for several minutes. He placed ice on his head. He decided to forget Skip. He didn't want any more problems.

Bob opened the door to let Tom in. Tom walked in, staring at Bob. "What happen?"

"A going-away present from a grateful employee." Bob held the ice pack on his head.

"Skip?"

"Yeah. For two weeks, he worked for himself. We had an argument. I closed the restaurant today."

"Hurt bad," asked Tom.

"No, just swollen." They walked into the kitchen. Tom placed a notebook on the table. "Have a drink. I got mine." Tom grabbed a glass and poured. "I haven't had a drink for a week. Cheers. I'm glad to be out of that fucking place. Thank you for the rides." Bob paused. "Sorry about the chaos I got you in, taking you to New Jersey. Now this."

"I enjoyed the trip until the news about Ann. Gary and Pete paid me for all my expenses, plus a week's salary."

"Good," said Bob as he sorted the mail. Bob was in a subdued mood as he gazed at the mail. The room was mute for a moment.

Tom broke the silence. "How are you handling things?" Bob did not answer. "Tough two weeks." Tom shook his head. "Ann leaving, not seeing your boys, Bennix locking you up, a week in the nut house, getting beat up, and finding that your neighbor is involved. I am surprised that you have not snapped."

"I just might. I am just confused. I have no motivation to do anything. I just keep thinking of Ann. Why?" Bob paused. "What kind of country do we live in when your company puts you away a neighbor fucking in your life?" With a raised voice, Bob said, "Jesus, can I get a break?"

Tom said, "Bob, I got things to tell you. I don't think that Ray liked the idea that I was staying at your house last Saturday. He stopped by. He tried to get information by acting friendly."

"Like what?" asked Bob.

"He asked why I was staying in the house. When did you get in? I was thinking, why is it any of his business? What did you do to him?"

"Nothing!" said Bob, putting his hands up. "I just don't know. I'm pissed at that Alan guy. He called me twice to thank me for cooperating. I'm going to call some attorneys. I think I have a good case for suing them."

Tom replied, "He called me yesterday."

Bob, surprised, asked, "For what reason? What did you tell him? How did he get your number?"

Tom trying not to upset Bob. "I worked for Bennix, remember? Alan said that you were too upset. There was more that he wanted to tell you. He was happy that you cooperated and went to the hospital. He also mentioned about the restraining orders. He told me as a friend that you should beware of that. Alan seemed vague about your next court date. But later on in the conversation, he said the 25th. He mentioned other dates. It was obviously an attempt to see what I knew. He said that the situation with Ann was not irreversible. That's the word he used. He asked if Ann's family was aware and possibly trying to contact her. I told him I did not know her family at all. He asked whether you had ever expressed a desire to return to New Jersey. I told him you never mentioned anything to me." Tom paused. "Let me get my notebook. He insisted that I write it down."

Tom opened his notebook and turned the pages. "He said that you were going to have to listen to Ann. Not to say yes to everything and agree wholeheartedly with everything she says. Alan suggested that you listen to discuss the issues she brings up and understand her viewpoint. This one, I wrote to the tee. *Sympathize with her and adapt accordingly. Show some positive reinforcement for a change instead of constantly criticizing her.* Lastly, he expressed concern about you possibly not being able to return to work. He hoped you would get better and accept what's going on."

"That bastard!" said Bob angrily.

"Oh yeah, he mentioned the lawsuit. He wants to talk about it."

"They know so much about what's been going on. It's obvious they read her declaration... They have been in contact with Ann. Can you believe this? My company and next-door neighbor involved in a divorce? What kind of bullshit is this?"

Tom, in sympathy, replied, "I don't understand the whole thing. There's something weird going on... I don't understand her actions. I thought you two were very happy. You have four great kids. I just don't understand her actions."

Drafting, Bob said, "Ray is getting paid by Bennix. I have to get Bennix out of my life."

Bob Dorsete was going through his mind things to do. He suspected that Ray Ditler was watching him. He kept his car in the garage and entered through the side door. Every time he was outside, he glanced over Ray's yard. No one was outside enjoying the summer's days and nights. Bob thought of Ray's inolvement and decided to approach him sincerely and honestly, man to man. Bob had not done anything to his neighbors.

He rang the Ditlers' doorbell. Karen opened the door slightly and stared in silence. Bob asked, "Can I please speak to Ray?"

"I'll see if he's home," she said coldly. Bob felt the chill as she closed the door.

Within minutes, Ray opened the door. He stepped outside and, in a firm voice, said, "I don't want you coming to my house."

"Can I please speak to you? We can talk in my house."

They were in Bob's kitchen. Bob said, "I know that you know where Ann is. I know that you helped Ann." Ray stared in silence, neither denying nor agreeing. Bob continued, "Please! I just want to talk to her. This whole thing is getting out of hand. I never hurt my children. Did you ever see me hit my children? Did you ever see me hit Ann?"

"I don't know what goes on in your house. All I know is that she wants a divorce." With a lift in his voice, he said, "Besides, it's no big deal. A lot of people get divorced."

Bob snapped back, "You don't understand the kind of relationship we had. The word divorce didn't exist in our vocabulary. We never talked divorce."

"Well, kid, you're getting divorced." He paused to light his cigar. "You need to get help. I have seen a lot of guys crack. You need to be in therapy."

Bob tried not to defend himself, thinking, *I just got out of a hospital.* "Please, tell her I just want to talk to her to tell her how much I love her." He looked into Ray's eyes. "I'm begging you." Ray stared with a blank look. "I know that you're on Bennix's payroll. They retained your services to watch me and provide security guards."

"So they hired me."

Bob tried to stay composed. "Why?" Ray was silent. "I never did anything to harm you."

Ray stood up, overshadowing Bob with his big heavy structure over six feet. "You'll see her in court soon." He turned and walked out. Ray saw it as an opportunity to make some easy money and increase business. He didn't need to follow Bob around. He could watch from his house. This would be good for business to have a prestigious international company on his list of clients. It was easy for Ray to persuade Bennix to extend his contract. Ray informed Bennix that Bob had difficulties accepting the divorce, and he was harboring resentments toward the people involved.

Chapter 7

A battered woman's shelter is a place where a woman and children can get away from abuse; the shelters offer a safe place. The women had one thing in common, bad experience with their lovers. They had been weak, defenseless, and wounded with human emotions. At the shelters, there are people there who will listen and understand what a woman is going through. Counselors to help them sort out their feelings and to decide what to do about their lives. Programs to help the children deal better with battering. Educational workshops and written material to help women understand what has been going on in their lives. Information is available about all other kinds of help in the community, including medical, legal, and social services. The shelters also provide crisis lines for help and support groups. The first shelter for battered women was the Chiswick House. It opened in 1971 in London, England. Today, there are thousands of such shelters throughout the country. These shelters rely on volunteers and money from counties and from nonprofit organizations for their existence.

Each year, millions of women are abused in the United States. Abuse is so common that it causes more injuries to a woman than any other way. More than one million American children are abused or neglected each year. Not so long ago, abused children and women had very few places to turn to for help. Not so long ago, husbands were allowed to hit wives, and adults were allowed to beat children. Today, family violence is a crime. If one family member deliberately hurts another, they can go to jail, or they can be forced get help. It makes no difference whether the injured person is a wife, a husband, a mother, or a child.

Ann was provided with a leaflet: "Domestic Abuse Shelter of the Florida Keys, Information on Domestic Violence."

Domestic violence statistics:

- One out of every three women will be abused at some point in her life.
- Battering is the single major cause of injury to women, exceeding rapes, muggings, and auto accidents combined.
- A woman is more likely to be killed by a male partner (or former partner) than any other person.
- About 4,000 women die each year due to domestic violence.
- Of the total domestic violence homicides, about 75 percent of the victims were killed as they attempted to leave the relationship or after the relationship had ended.
- Seventy-three percent of male abusers were abused as children.
- Thirty percent of Americans say they know a woman who has been physically abused by her husband in the past year.
- Women of all races are equally vulnerable to violence by an intimate partner.
- On average, more than three women are murdered by their husbands or partners in this country every day.
- Intimate partner violence is a crime that largely affects women. In 1999, women accounted for 85 percent of the victims of intimate partner violence.
- On average, a woman will leave an abusive relationship seven times before she leaves for good.

It was Monday morning. Ann Dorsete and her four children made it through the weekend. The boys spent most of the time watching television and playing. The older boys played basketball outside. Ann occupied most of her time catering to her boys to help them feel comfortable and safe. She was instructed not to contact anyone at all. She feared Bob's return and how he would react. She was angry and blamed Bob. She had notified the boys' schools that Bob had restraining orders.

The mothers were feeding their children, and some were getting them ready for school. The agenda for the essential activities for the week was posted. These activities included individual counseling, group sessions, job workshop, apartment search, and recreation.

The shelter was occupied by nine women and twenty-three children. The ladies were assigned chores every day and cooking assignments once a week. Ann found people that were sympathetic toward her and willing to listen to her. It was a comfort to her that people cared about her, and they all had similar experience and fears of their husbands or partners. She made superficial conversations with a few of the ladies. Leaving her home was very difficult, and she found the shelter a bit uncomfortable. Although she missed her house, at least here she was safe, she thought. She had to accept this would be her home for the next thirty days or more. She was troubled about money and the children's schooling, and she was concerned about her entire life. She thought that Bob had snapped and could be dangerous. Her fears confused her. She needed time to be away from him to get her thoughts together.

Ann was told "to accept the help. You really need it. Don't apologize for accepting it, a simple thank-you is enough." Every day there was either counseling or group meetings to verbalize their experiences, their partners, and why they let the abuse go so far. The ladies were educated and informed about abuse and violence and the different types of abuse. They talked about why a woman is battered. The term battered woman is used to describe a woman who has been the target of abusive behavior by a man who is not a stranger to her at all. Abusive behavior takes many forms—physical, emotional, and the cycle of violence. It starts off with people not able to deal with the conflicts and stresses in everyday life. Tension starts to build up, and then battering takes place. He makes some efforts to apologize or make excuses for his behavior, and a woman accepts it. She thinks that things will get better, but they don't.

One lesson dealt with the battering men and what they have in common. The common characteristics are low self-esteem, traditional expectation of sex roles, the male being the domineering sex partner. They are usually jealous and controlling individuals. They come from abusive family backgrounds. They blame others when things go wrong in their lives. They might use alcohol or drugs as an excuse, and they are always denying. They deny their actions and try to make them less significant than they are. They fail to accept the need for change.

In a group session, May Valdez told her story. Her husband stole all the life savings, ran her credit cards to the limit, and left her in heavy debt. She was forced by the court to pay for his debts. After several months of telling her how much he loved her and promised to get help for his drug problem, she took him back. He never sought the help he needed. Instead, he became violent until he finally broke her nose, and that is why she is here today.

Donna's husband at first called her names and said that she was no good. He would insult her or make fun of her. He stopped her from seeing her friends or going out. He would not allow her to work. He controlled the money and always questioned her on her daily activities. He would hit her for no reason. He cut her throat with his hunting knife, and she had to fight for her life. She was cut up so badly underneath her neck that she was in a critical condition for many months. Donna still has the scar of the knife.

Nicole told her story, how her husband was dependable as far as going to work. He would go out three or four times a week, come home drunk, and would force her for sex. If she refused, he would go for days without talking to her and threaten her that if she refused him again he would leave her. He told her that it was her duty as his wife to give him sex whenever he wanted. He was the man of the house and in control. There were times in the middle of the night while she was asleep and tired that he would rape her. He did painful and perverted things to her. It got to the point that she totally disliked having sex.

Debbie was an attractive woman of thirty with fair skin and blond hair. She was intelligent with some formal education. She was creative and charming and had scars of a bad relationship. She said, "I loved Dale when we got married, and I thought he would be the most wonderful husband in the world. He was so handsome and so dependable and good-mannered. He would open doors for me, hold my chair out, and help me into my coat. I thought he was the most dependable person I had ever met. He was also very conscious about his appearance and dressed well. He was thoughtful and concerned about every evening that I did. I thought he really cared about me and all those little things in my life.

"Little did I know that he wanted to control every move I made. Our first year was like a honeymoon for a whole year. Then he started working on my mind. He began to mentally abuse me. He found ways to tell me I was stupid and ugly. No matter how I dressed or what I did and no matter how hard I tried, I couldn't change his opinion of me. He said so many awful things that I finally began to believe them. His abuse became worst. He started to hit me. He would hit me on the stomach. When I was pregnant, he pushed me so hard. I was lucky the baby was not injured. I suffered so much, and I was in so much pain, but I was ashamed to tell someone about it. I had never heard of this happening to anyone, and I was thinking it was me that had done something terrible to deserve such treatment. I thought that it couldn't get any worse, but I was wrong." Tears were appearing from her eyes.

"It got worse as time went on. I never knew when and why he might fly into a rage. He would beat me for every little thing I did wrong and sometimes for no reason at all. He would yell at me when the baby cried. Dale couldn't cope with the baby's crying and blamed me all the time that it was my fault. I became very frightened and afraid that he would turn on the baby and possibly hurt her. Then I kept asking myself why I didn't run away, why I was allowing him to do this to me, why I didn't leave him. The truth is, I was terrified of him. He started to threaten me. Before long, he found a way to threaten me every day. He said he would take the baby away if I ever told anyone or if I tried to leave him. He told me that if I ever left him, he would kill me and the baby. He said there was no place I could run and hide from him. He would get me."

She paused to wipe the tears from her sparkling blue eyes. She continued, "Then he began to sexually abuse me. I can't tell you all the sick and perverted things he coerced me to do. I was always suffering from internal infections. He had a reason for everything, and he said it was because I was getting older and my body was changing. My life was so horrible. I began to wish that I were dead. I even thought about committing suicide. I thought of leaving him and leaving the baby with him, and perhaps he would not come after me. Throughout all those years, I had never once tried to fight back. I was too frightened. He was physically larger than me. He was stronger, and he controlled the money. One night, he was beating me, and I was screaming and hollering. My neighbors must have heard the noise and called the police. When the police arrived, I thanked them for coming. I asked them to help me. I was afraid of Dale. I thought that he might kill me. The police took me to a shelter. Thank God for that 'cause now I found the strength."

This was all new to Ann. She was horrified hearing all these stories. She never had first-hand experience with any abused wives. She thought, *How can men be so cruel and dangerous to those they love?* She held back from relating her story of abuse.

They were told that, in the beginning, it's hard and very difficult to understand everything. But after a while, you will be able to see and feel the injuries done to you, and you might not want ever to see your abuser again. Sometimes during the first or second week, these feelings may change. Your wounds might heal, and you might begin to remember happy times with him. You might want to see him again. The women were instructed to make a most dangerous list. A list of the worst things your partner has ever done to you, including every pain and humiliation. Things that are dangerous to your physical and mental health include the things he said to you afterward, whether cruel or loving. The sheet would help you remember how dangerous he is and how much he hurt you. It will be painful to break up a family, but it could save your life to think about yourself, getting professional help, and the importance for the children.

They were coached to make a list of the good things, the happy times, the hopes and dreams—the things they liked and found very cherishing about their men. Because of Ann's current state of mind, the list was very small. She was told to relive her feelings during the good times and the bad time. Were the good times worth the bad ones?

The women were taught to look at the men who battered them as an alcoholic that needed to help himself. They were told, "Do you have any reason to believe that things will be different in the future? Has he started to make big changes? If he has started to make changes that is good, but for how long? You must see how long that will last. Is it safe to go back to him because he promises something or because he says he has agreed to go to a counselor? If he does go to a counselor, the real test is whether he follows through. And for how many months will he visit the counselor?" They were directed to make a list entitled "Change List." What things would you have to change for you to risk going back? The list should include such things as "Never hit me" and "Never insult me or make fun of me."

They were told that they might find it hard to stay away from their partners and that it would difficult, at first, especial after a long relationship and dependency on a man. They were taught to read the lists anytime they thought of going back to their man. The counselors emphasized to first read the most dangerous list aloud. Relive the abuse again in your mind and always keep the list close to you. Read this list anytime you feel weak. It can stop you from getting in touch with that man. Read the best memory list too. You can look at both the good and the bad. Did the good times make up for the bad times? Those are the things you have to consider for the rest of your life. Then look at your change list. Check the items that he has actually changed and find one item and compare it to what actually happened. Once you make your comparison, that would answer all the questions of doubt you have. They were told that the key was to look out for themselves and the children.

They talked about visitation being the hardest to handle—that is, visitation between the children and their father. They were told not feel guilty or think you are depriving the children of their father. The motto was "One health parent is better than two."

Be careful of visitations. You might be in contact with him. He will know how to play on your feelings of guilt and love. The children may also know how to work on these feelings. He may promise you that he is sorry and wants to change. He will tell you that he needs your help. You have to tell him that he has to change and do it on his own and because he wants to change. And he must change before you'll have nothing to do with him. The best thing to do is not to have anything to do with him. You can avoid seeing him by arranging for the pickups and delivery with a friend, a neighbor, or a relative. Try to avoid seeing him. That is very important, especially after you are separated. After months of separation, you might feel friendlier toward your ex-partner. You might think it is safe to see him now and then. That is the time to go back to your change list and ask yourself why. Make a new list that shows the changes he has made. Maybe he has made some small changes, but you need to wait a while to see if that really means anything. Just remember, you don't have to see him if you don't want to. You don't have to explain to him why. Just tell him that is the way you want it. Look away from him toward a new way, a new beginning for you and your children.

After your separation, your children might not see their father for a while or maybe for a long time. In some ways, the children might blame you or themselves for what is going on. If you get a divorce, it is very typical that some children blame themselves for the parents' breakup. They may even blame themselves for the violence. Build up a communication relationship with your children. Try to get them to talk about it. Listen carefully to the answers and don't ever tell a child that he or she is wrong. Instead, ask questions that help the child think clearly. If you have difficulty with the children, get them to counseling. Make time to have fun with the children and yourself.

The most important thing that was emphasized was not to blame yourself. If you are a battered woman, it is very important for you to realize that you did not make it happen; it is not your fault. You are not responsible for what he did.

As the days passed, Ann felt more comfortable at the shelter. She thought the shelter was a wonderful place, and if she had any problems, they would always help and support her. She felt a bond with the women at the shelter. She was able to relate to the women because of their similar stories. She opened up to tell her own insufferable stories of how Bob mentally and physically abused her.

Ann was an excellent cook and thought that some of the ladies were too basic in the meals they prepared. Ann cooked lasagna and baked pasta with meatballs. They all enjoyed the meals and complimented her on what a great cook she was. More importantly, she was happy to see her children enjoy her cooking. Some of the ladies were very self-conscious about cooking, and they wanted to do a good job and cook something everyone would enjoy. Others were lazy. They would simply open a can of pork and beans, cut up hot dogs, and boil them. Some would just eat cereal all the time. For breakfast, some of the ladies made scrambled eggs and bacon and mixed the eggs with the grease of the bacon. Ann thought how terrible it tasted. The Mexican ladies usually had bean burritos with rice for breakfast. Ann thought that wasn't appealing for breakfast. She did enjoy the egg burritos with the scrambled eggs and melted cheese. She thought that the Mexicans had too much starch in their meals because they ate a great deal of rice and beans. Francis bragged all week long about the delicious pot roast she was going to cook. She boiled it in a pan for half an hour. She mixed whole potatoes and carrots. Most of the ladies thought that it was delicious. Ann thought that it was not cooked enough and the vegetables were too hard.

Ann started to feel good about herself. She was anxious to leave the shelter and return to her big comfortable house and spacious kitchen. Although she felt frightened and concerned about raising four children alone, she decided that she would go through with the divorce. She saw Bob in the courthouse, and she did not fear him now. There were restraining orders on him, and he could not come near her and the children. If perhaps he did change, there might be a possibility of taking him back. She would not worry about that now. She would only concentrate and worry about herself and protect herself and the children.

With each day, Ann became aware of herself and the need to build up her self-esteem. She blamed Bob and believed that he had destroyed her self-esteem. She also started to become angry at herself for allowing herself so many years of unhappiness and her dependence on him and her mother. She felt some resentment toward her mother for being controlling. She left one controlling person for another. This anger gave her the strength she never realized she had. She hated him for what he did, and she wanted him to suffer.

Chapter 8

June 26, 1990

It had been almost three weeks since Ann Dorsete filed a petition for divorce. Bob Dorsete had anxiously waited for this day, hoping that he would see Ann and perhaps the boys. It had been long and painful period without Ann his children. The recent Father's Day was the worst. He stayed home all day, hoping for a telephone call from his children. They did not call nor send a card.

Bob made his way to the fourth floor. He walked through the hallway, looking for the courtroom number. As he made his way down the hallway, it got darker. He spotted Ann sitting on one of the benches. She was dressed in a dull-colored one-piece romper dress. A thin man with sunglasses was sitting close to her. The man sat with his arms crossed and head gawking at Bob. As Bob approached the pair, he stopped to examine the man dressed in a dark undersized cheap jacket and tie. He recognized the man, but uncertain of what to say and do, Bob continued to walk. "Good morning. How are you?" Bob said to Ann.

Ann raised her eyes to glance at Bob and replied in a low voice, "Fine." Her head shook slightly, giving movement to her long lush semi-curly hair hanging over her shoulders.

Bob stuck his hand out and said, "Hi, Dave! Remember me? You took me to the hospital." Apprehensive and cold, Dave shook Bob's hand. Bob turn toward Ann. "How are the boys?"

Ann, uneasy, said, "Fine."

Too nervous to say anything else, Bob slowly turned and walked away in search for his attorney. The hallway was filling with attorneys, clients, and mothers with children. Mr. Barber took hold of Bob's arm. "Good morning," said Mr. Barber. "You feel okay?"

"I got knots in my stomach… I am anxious to my children. It's been over a month."

"Well, let's hope that something could be worked out," said Barber cheerful. "Have you seen Mr. Walsh?"

"I saw my wife at the other side," Bob said, pointing in the direction.

Mr. Barber placed his hand on Bob's shoulder. "Wait here… Don't talk to your wife and stay calm." Mr. Walsh approached them. "Good morning, Mr. Walsh."

"Good morning," said Will Walsh. "Can I have a moment?"

"Sure!" Barber turned to Bob, and pointing to the opposite bench, he said, "Sit there!"

Bob grabbed Barber's arm and anxiously murmured, "The man with the sunglasses works for my company. He's one of the guys that took me to the hospital!"

"Can't talk about that now. You just sit there until I return." The two attorneys walked away together.

Bob sat quietly across from Ann. His eyes periodically would glance across at her, trying to make eye contact. Hers refused. She would turn to whisper to Dave. She appeared nervous as she chewed gum at a rapid pace. Dave was sitting close to Ann, and occasional, he would turn toward Bob. Bob could not see the man's eyes and wondered why he is wearing sunglasses inside the building. Was he trying to disguise himself? What's going on here? How deep is Bennix involved? Why? What did Ann tell them? What did Ray tell them? This whole thing is bizarre.

The two attorneys were standing in an isolated section of the hallway with pens and pads. Will Walsh spoke, "They have expenditures, most important the house mortgages. Your client should pay the two house mortgages." Mr. Barber listened carefully without answering. Walsh continued, "The parties should mutually agree to a family profession for a written family evaluation report, which may be used by either party in this case."

Mr. Barber interrupted, "I don't agree. If you want, you can subject your client to such an evaluation. My client was evaluated in a hospital. Here is the report."

Mr. Walsh examined a letter from Dr. Bergren. Frowning, he said, "Is he in counseling?"

"I'm not sure." Barber, feeling confident, said, "My client wants his children out of the shelter."

"Has social services contacted your client?"

"Not that I am aware."

"The Child Protection Services is investigating my client's claims of child abuse," said Walsh. "Mr. Dorsete needs and should obtain psychotherapy counseling if he wants to see his children." Barber stared at Walsh without saying anything. Walsh continued, "We have to complete the sale of the restaurant. Would you like me to contact the prospective buyer and the landlord regarding the status?"

"You made do so."

Walsh continuing said, "As for child support, can we reach an agreement?"

"No! I believe it to be inappropriate at this time since your client has over sixty or seventy thousand dollars of community cash. My client wants the twenty thousand dollars from the house."

"The twenty thousand found in the attic?"

"Yes."

"It's in my trust account." Walsh threatened, "Your client could be in serious trouble... You know that we can get child support order."

"That's your prerogative."

Wash replied, "If that's your position, I'll file for a continuation and schedule a new date for a hearing."

The attorneys returned to their clients. Walsh handed Ann a copy of Dr. Bergren's letter. Barber, feeling disappointed, approached Bob and said, "You won't be able to see the children yet. It's going to be longer."

Bob interrupted, "Why?"

"Has social services contacted you?"

"No, why?"

"They will."

Bob raised his voice, "Why? I have never hit my kids. What the hell is going on?"

"Calm down," said Barber. "It's because of the allegations of child abuse, social services is involved. There will be an investigation… You won't be able to see the children until they complete the investigation."

Bob, a little calmer, asked, "How long will that be?"

Barber responded, "It's hard to tell. Depends on their workload of cases. It could be a month or three."

Bob, with a slightly raised voice, asked, "Why so long? Why can't I see my children in the meantime? What the hell is going on?"

Barber, feeling hopeless, saw a need to calm his client. "You have to accept what's going on. This is the system. You may not like it and you are not happy with it, but that's the system. It doesn't work at your pace. It works at its own pace."

"We agreed to reschedule a hearing in three weeks. Walsh insists on payment of child and family support and house expenses, and Walsh is handling the close of the sale of the restaurant."

Ann approached them. Holding the letter close to Bob's face, she shouted, "You lied! This letter is a lie. I don't believe this garbage. This is not true. You are a liar and a thief."

"Mrs. Dorsete, please stop," said Walsh as he placed his arm around her shoulders. He escorted her back to the seat as she continued to murmur the same words.

Bergren's letter to Mr. Barber stated:

> In our conversation today (June 13), you asked if I had any indication that Mr. Dorsete would present a danger to his wife or to his children. I have none. He spoke of his family only with concern and tenderness, and particularly a desire to protect his sons from the emotional upsets of being away from home in a shelter.

I have no reason to expect violent impulsive behavior from Mr. Dorsete.

Cordially,
Dr. Bergren, MD

The two attorneys sneaked away several feet from the Dorsetes. Bob sat still staring at Ann, trying to make eye contact. He noticed the tears running from her eyes. She was nervously moving her head in every direction, trying to avoid looking at him. Bob thought how badly he wanted to hold and have her. Bob heard Walsh said, "The guy has psychological problems and needs to be in therapy." Mr. Barber answered with a frown, so Walsh added, "I know his type." Norman Barber turned to walk away. Walsh said, "I'll contact you early next week."

"Yes," responded Mr. Barber. "But don't call until you have a status on the restaurant."

Will Walsh had displayed that he was experienced a strong advocate for Ann. His dislike for Bob Dorsete was obvious. He abhorred men that battered their wives. His own daughter had been abused. His only daughter was married to a man that appeared to all as the perfect husband. Unknown to Will Walsh and his wife, they daughter was consistently battered by her husband. She was six months pregnant when, in an attempt to run away, she fell down the stairs. Shortly thereafter, she experienced cramps, vaginal bleeding, and uterine contractions. Her husband rushed her to the hospital. In an attempted to save the baby, she had a cesarean. She gave birth to a tiny boy who lived for eight days. She was hemorrhaging a great deal that a hysterectomy was necessary. Her husband was charged with assault and received a two-year suspended sentence.

It was days after; Bob Dorsete had no motivation to do anything. He stayed home, feeling depressed, frustrated, and confused. He drank to ease the pain. He drank straight Scotch, rye, or whatever was available. Drinking and smoking eased his pain. He was analyzing his entire predicament, talking to himself in silence. What the hell is going on? Why is she doing this? What the hell can I do? I wish that I can talk to her to try to reason that this whole thing it's insane. The attorneys have taken control of our lives. Why is Bennix involved? Why did Dave pretend that he didn't recognize me? What's happening with the sale of the restaurant? Ah, I miss her and the boys so bad. What are they doing? How are they doing? Are they thinking of me? Do they miss me? What the fuck is my attorney doing for me?

He was disturbed by the ring of the telephone. "Bob, this is Pete."

"Hi, Pete," Bob said in melancholy. "Have you gotten my messages? I've been trying to get in touch with you for days."

"Yeah, I got your messages. Sorry for not getting back to you. It's just that I am so busy. I'm working late every night." Sounding exhausted, he said, "We're a little tight for cash. We're experiencing low sales. I've been busy trying to generate sales. The creditors are constantly calling for payment, and it has been difficult to get material to the stories. I had to fire two store managers."

"I'm sorry to hear that things are burdensome with Micro Research. Sorry for bothering you. But Ann is your cousi—"

Pete interrupted, "What happened at court? Did you see her?"

"Yes, I saw her. I saw the same guy from Bennix security. One of the guys that took me to the hospital. Ann said that was her bodyguard. She wouldn't talk to me." Bob, getting tensed, continued, "The attorneys have taken over the sale of the restaurant and our lives. Ann's attorney appears to be controlling everything." Bob sighed. "She didn't look happy. She was chewing gum vigorously. She kept avoiding eye contact with me, and she had watery eyes."

"Goddamn," Pete said. "If only I could talk to her. I keep calling and leaving messages at the shelter. They keep telling me that they'll give her the messages. It's the shelter people. The freaking feminine Nazism. They don't want her to talk to men. She's listening to the wrong people. She's getting the wrong help."

"Pete, you have your problems, I understand. But I need your help. Here's my situation. My company is involved, security guards at the facility, bodyguard around Ann, putting me in the nuthouse, watching me." Bob paused. "Why are they involved? What the fuck is going on?"

Pete, not sure, said, "I don't know. This is not a just a divorce."

"I'm here all by myself with nothing to do. I'm going crazy. I'm feeling depressed because everything reminds me of Ann and the boys."

Pete hesitated momentarily. "Bob, I can use your help here. Why don't you come back east?"

Bob felt appreciated. "I can't. I have to be in court in three weeks."

Pete asked, "Why do you have to go to court for?"

"For child support, and…and child services is investigating. I'm under a lot of stress. I need to be busy. Tom and I are ready and anxious. I need to keep busy, or I'll go crazy. I need to get Bennix out of my life. Can we go ahead with the west coast venture?"

Pete asked, "Can you go back to work with Bennix?"

"Pete, you are not listening. I can't go back to the facility. Not after this shit. I threatened to sue them. My lawyer doesn't want to get involved." Bob, in affirmative tone, said, "I need to resign from Bennix. I need to get them out of my life."

Pete asked, "How is your financial situation?"

"Well, it is pretty bad. The restaurant deal is still depending. I have house bills I hadn't paid because I had to pay the lawyer."

"Okay, Bob, I understand. I think it'll work. Yes! We'll go ahead with the West Coast operation. I'll get the lease signed. How much money do you need?"

"Based on the financial report that I gave you, about forty thousand for the first three months."

"Okay, I'll try to care of that. We will send you all the fixtures, merchandise, and people to help you get started. Perhaps by the second or third week of July, you can be in operations."

Bob was feeling better. "Thanks, Pete. Thank you very much. Let's keep in touch."

The next day, Bob contacted Alan Morris by telephone. "Mr. Morris, I would like to know, why is Bennix involved in divorce?"

"I don't understand," Alan Morris said in a low, surprised voice.

Bob was in forceful tone. "You know what I mean. Dave! Your security guy. The guy that escorted me to the hospital. Your security guy. He was at the court house as my wife's bodyguard!" Bob shouted. "What do you people want from me?"

Alan, expressing no emotions, said, "I don't know what you are talking about. We are satisfied because you cooperated with us."

Bob was trying to stay calm. "I don't believe you, and I don't trust you. I want you out of my life. I'm resigning."

"Will you send me a letter of resignation?"

"Yes, I will," said Bob and hung up the telephone, shaking his head. "What a lying motherfucker!"

Bob was thinking that perhaps his attorney was weak. He left several messages for his attorney to call back.

"Hi, Mr. Dorsete. Sorry for not getting back sooner. What can I do for you?"

"I called to see if you know what's going on regarding the sale of the restaurant."

"I have not heard from Mr. Walsh."

Bob mockingly said, "He's screwing up. The prospective buyer called me. He's upset that the restaurant is closed and that attorneys are involved. He told me that he received two letters from Walsh—one addressed to him and the other to the landlord. Walsh stated that he will be conducting the sale of the restaurant."

Barber said, "He wanted to handle it, so I let him."

Bob, annoyed, raised his voice, "What the hell is there to conduct? You lawyers conduct shit. You scare people away."

"Mr. Dorsete, just calm down. You are in a divorce. That is what we do. We notify parties."

"I have a contract. This is my restaurant," said Bob in a raised voice. "My business! I negotiated the sale. In my household, I took care of all the business matters. Why are you letting him take control?"

"You're getting divorced. There are two counsels involved. I am trying to save you some money. It doesn't make any difference to me who handles it."

"There is nothing complicated about this deal. We were just waiting for the landlord's approval. I'm an experienced negotiator. The buyer is now stalling. He's trying to take advantage of the situation. I don't blame the guy. It's America, land of opportunity. But I'm hurting for money. I will have to borrow using my credit cards. I can't risk the sale not going through."

Barber replied, "Don't worry, you have a written agreement and his deposit."

"Yeah! And to enforce it, I have to sue him." Bob less excitably said, "I have real concerns. This sale should have been completed two weeks ago. Now, I have to pay an additional month's rent. The guy is looking for a reduction in price." Bob raised his voice. "He's got me by the balls, and he knows it!"

"Don't yell at me. You're getting yourself too worked up."

Bob, a little calmer, said, "I am getting frustrated. Maybe, I shouldn't give a shit like her. She walked out on the business. Maybe I should call the buyer and tell him to put up or shut up."

"You might not like the situation. Your wife filed for a divorce, and she has an attorney. Get ahold of yourself and accept it. If there is nothing else, I have things to do." He hung up the telephone.

Bob slammed his fist on the kitchen table and shouted, "That sons of bitches! Freaking attorneys! They just look for ways to make more money. They want to control your life."

It was midsummer in Southern California. The sun was shining brightly; the birds were active. For the Dorsete family, this was usually the best time of the year with the boys off from school. The boys would be outside playing and jumping in the pool. Bob reflected on the family outings, the fun at amusement parks, and the trips to the desert. It was not the same without them. The house was empty, quiet, and dark; and he felt abandoned. He was living in a timeless zone, a mere existence spent idly watching television and listening to music. He tried to focus on the business. It had been over a week, and he did not hear from Pete. Bob called Pete Devigne. "Hi, Pete, how are you doing?"

"Like shit. I was reluctant to call. I was hoping that things would get better." Pete paused. "I have bad news. We don't have the money right now. We can't support the West Coast operation."

Bob was disappointed. He felt the movement in his stomach and replied, "But it was just a week since I resigned from my Bennix. Now, I don't have any income. The sale of the restaurant is still pending. I need money. I need to work."

"I know, I know," said Pete. "I have my problems. We have money issues. Sales are down, and I have a board meeting in two weeks. My offer is still open if you want to come back east."

Bob replied, "You know it's not practical right now." He dropped the telephone while trying to light a cigarette. He caught the cord between his fingers.

"Bob, are you there?" Pete shouted. "Bob! Are you there?"

Bob placed the telephone to his ear. "Yeah. I just dropped the phone."

"I'm sorry, gotta go. I'll call later you."

"No! Listen!" Pete was not there. A disheartened Bob thought, *If I didn't have bad luck, I wouldn't have any luck at all. Now, what else could go wrong?*

Bob was outside, cutting the grass with his electric lawn mower. A young stranger approached and asked, "Are you Mr. Robert Dorsete?" Bob nodded. The neatly groomed man dressed in a light-blue short-sleeve shirt and tie said, "My name is Edward Muller." He proceeded to hand Bob a business card. "I'm an investigator for the Department of Children Protection Services. I would like to talk to you regarding your children."

The hair on Bob's forearms rose. Bob anticipated and dread this visit. It was like death calling, the coming of the Grim Reaper. He was uncertain of what to say. "Sure, let's go inside." Bob showed Mr. Muller to the kitchen, and they sat down. Bob asked, trying to be polite, "Would you like something to drink?"

"No, thank you." He carefully eyed Bob. "I'm here to investigate the allegations of child abuse. I've spoken to your children and your wife."

"How are they?" Bob asked in a meek voice. "How are my boys doing?"

"They're okay. They are doing fine."

Bob was relieved to hear that. "Thank you for telling me."

"However, they're a little apprehensive."

"That's because of her action," Bob snapped back.

Muller did not reply. He retrieved a notebook from his briefcase. "Your children and wife are afraid of you. They're afraid that you might hurt them. I need to ask you some questions. How do you discipline your children?"

"Many different ways, depending on the circumstances." Bob was getting a little nervous. "It depends on the situation and the moment."

"What do you mean by the moment?"

"If I have the time as for an example if I am working on a project. If we are at a store or at someone's house or if others are around."

"Can you provide some examples?"

"The two older boys sometime have quarrels, and sometimes they get physical. If it is just an argument, I cool them off by telling them to stand facing the wall. After five minutes or a few minutes, the punishment is over." Bob was finish.

The young man stared at Bob. "Please continue, Mr. Dorsete," said Muller.

"If they break house rules or misbehave in school or don't do their homework, we would take away some of their privileges, or they would be grounded from activities."

"Do you hit your children?"

Bob, concerned about the question, asked, "What do you mean? Do I get physical with them? Do I hit them to hurt them?"

"Yes, all of that."

Bob wanted to lie and say that he never hit them. "They are boys, and boys can be tough at times. Sometimes the oldest boy, being thirteen, I have had to smack his face to get his attention. When they were young, we would slap their hand to explain what no means or tap their buttocks. I have never hit them to hurt them."

"Did you put your children in the car trunk?"

Bob paused. He wanted to lie. "That was over a year ago." Muller stared. Bob paused, feeling the need to be defensive and careful in responding. "Wait a minute. It's not as bad as it sounds. Let me explain. Let me tell you what happened. We had just come from the store. I had the two oldest boys. We were in the car, and they were opening the packages of baseball cards we had purchased. The younger one was in the back, and the older one was in the front seat, and they were antagonizing each other. I had told them several times to stop. I threatened that I was going to put them in the car trunk if they did not stop. They continued to push each other. The one in the back cried out in pain. I turned to see. I shouted at them to stop. I turned forward, and a car was coming from my right. I had gotten through a red light and almost caused an accident. My blood pressure went up, and my heart was beating fast. I pulled over, and I told them to get in the trunk. We were only five minutes away from the house. As soon as I pulled into the driveway, I let them out. My youngest boy was laughing, and he said, "Hey, Dad, let's do it again." But my older boy was lamenting. That was over a year ago. It was less than five minutes. All the time they were in the trunk I was talking to them, and they were talking back to me. I knew that they were okay." The man gawked in silence. "What the hell would you do? I almost got in an automobile accident."

In a stern tone, Mr. Muller replied, "I would never have put them in the trunk."

"Let me ask you a question. How many children do you have?"

Very proudly Mr. Muller said, "I have a three-year-old daughter."

Bob thought, *He's a young father with one child, what does he know about rearing four boys?* "I have four boys!" He glanced at the man's blank face. "My wife is a good mother, but she lacks the strength to discipline the boys. She was never forceful. She did not get involved in the disciplining. She would call me at work, complaining about the boys that they would not listen to her. Many times, the moment I walked through the door, she would tell me about the boys quarreling and not listening to her. I was the disciplinarian. I didn't like it, but I did it. The only negative thing I have to say about my wife is that she was not assertive."

"I talked to other witnesses, and they stated that you have struck your children. They saw you slap and kick them."

Bob replied quickly, "Well, that's a goddamn lie. Who are these people?"

Clearing his throat, Mr. Muller said, "I'm sorry, I cannot disclose names. That information is confidential." He placed his hand to his throat. "Can I have a glass of water?" Bob got up and returned and handed him a glass. "Thank you!"

Bob tried to make his case. "We had some creative and constructive ways to discipline. We would talk to them about what they did wrong. We would have discussions about it—the causes and effects of their actions. And then they were instructed to write a letter why their behavior was wrong and the things we discussed. The paper would be graded for good penmanship and correct English." In a half laugh, Bob said, "Of course, the corrections were modified depending on the children's age." Bob paused as he watched the man write. "Wait, I'll show you." He left the room.

Bob returned with a stack of papers. Bob watched as Mr. Muller glanced at the children's report cards, letters from school, letters of achievements, and other certificates of recognition for good performance. It worried Bob that the man made no comment. He felt the need to say something. Mr. Muller raised his head and looked up. Bob calmly said, "Because of all the negative things you heard, you perhaps think I was harsh. I don't think I was. I believe that if you spare the rod, you spoil the child. However, I never caused any physical harm to my children. That is, I never bruised them or break their skin." Bob paused to study the blank, motionless face. He strained as he looked for signs of expressions. Bob stood up and said, "I love my children. I would never hurt them, and I know that I could never hurt them. You will not find any incident of abuse, hospital, or police incident." Bob paused to watch Mr. Muller as he wrote. Believing that he did not convince the man, he said, "Let me show you their rooms."

"No, that is not necessary. I have enough information. I have another appointment."

Bob, pressing, said, "Isn't a picture worth a thousand words? Let me show their rooms and give you a quick tour of the house. I just want two minutes of your time."

"It's not necessary." The man was anxious to leave. "I have other appointments."

"You hold the future of my family. Can you please give me two minutes of your time? Just their bedrooms." The man nodded in agreement. Bob led him up the steps to the boys' bedrooms. Mr. Muller saw posters of athletes, sports trophies, and their closets were loaded with toys. The hallway walls were plastered with family pictures of the boys.

"Would you like to see the family room?"

"No, it's not necessary. Thank you for your time, Mr. Dorsete, but I have to go."

They walked downstairs, and as Bob open the front door, Mr. Muller stopped. "Oh, just one more question," said Muller. "Did you ever hit your wife?"

"No!" Bob responded quickly. "Why would you ask that?"

"I saw the bruise on her leg."

Bob was surprised. "Where was the bruise?"

Mr. Muller pointed to his right thigh and said, "Here, she has a black-and-blue about an inch."

"I don't know where she got that from. I didn't do it. It was probably self-inflicted. I have not seen my wife, except in court last week." Bob was getting emotional. "I mean, I have not seen my wife since Memorial Day. I… I left for New Jersey. She lied to get in the shelter or something like that."

"Thank you and goodbye, Mr. Dorsete, and good luck to you."

"Wait! When will I see my children?"

"It all depends."

"On what? I want to see my children."

"Well, I have to complete my investigation, make a formal report, and submit it to my supervisor."

"And how long will that take?"

"Mr. Dorsete, you have an attorney, discuss it with him. Good day."

July 18, 1990

It was a typical July morning in Southern California, sunny and beautiful. Not for Bob Dorsete. The dark cloud of thoughts hanged over his head. This was his third trip to the building of faith and consequences. The past six weeks had been lonely and empty for him without Ann and his children. His natural instincts dictated that he find his family. Bob was driven by the male instincts of a protector. He searched for his children. He talked to panhandlers in the streets getting leads to shelters. They told him that drug users and prostitutes go to shelters. So, Bob searched places where drug users socialized and places where prostitutes hung out. Some had knowledge of shelter locations. It was suggested that some churches might have shelters nearby. His searches were unsuccessful but it occupied his time.

As he walked toward the entrance, his legs were numbed with each step. He felt the knots in his stomach and_the woozy feeling in his head. His mind elucidated between conscious and unconsciousness as he thought of his wife and boys, wondering if they are coming out of the shelter today. With each encounter, he disliked Will Walsh more and more. The man was always intimidating Bob by telling him that he needed help and implying that he was a thief. Walsh also had control of all of Bob's finances. Bob was trying to be optimistic, hoping that today he might get some kind of visitation schedule with his children. He had a new attorney, Robert Schurer. He released Norman Barber because he felt that he was too weak. This was the most important crisis of his life; he needed a "good" attorney.

The courthouse was crowded as people moved about. The building was filled with men and women dressed in suits carrying briefcases or wheeling hand cards loaded with boxes, mothers with young children, and men and women dressed casually. Bob Dorsete was instructed by Robert Schurer to meet him in the cafeteria. With his eyes, Bob searched for Ann. He purchased a cup a coffee and made his way to the smoking section. Just as he was lighting a cigarette, he spotted Ann. She was alone facing the window. She had a white short-sleeve light blouse, a tan twill shorts, and flat shoes. He wanted to talk to her but felt apprehensive. He decided to go over and talk to her. "Ann, how are you?"

She turned around and, with a sad long face, said, "Fine."

Bob pleadingly said, "Please give me a chance to talk to you. Why are you doing all this?"

Ann responded, "I'm not doing this. This is your doing."

Bob, with a surprised look, pointed to his chest and said, "What do you mean me? You're the one who filed for a divorce."

Ann snapped back, giving him a look to kill. "It's your doing! It's your fault! I'm not going to take responsibility for this."

Bob again pleaded, "Please, stop the divorce proceeding. Let's get counseling. We can be separated in the meantime and see a marriage counselor."

"I don't want to see a marriage counselor," she said firmly and coldly. "You need help. You're sick! That's why I have to do this. You always blame others for all your problems. It's you, Bob. You need help. You're like an alcoholic. You have to recognize that you have a problem."

He did not know what to say. He tried to be careful of his words. He realized that she was cold and fixed. He tried to find the words to melt the ice around the statue of his love. Before he could say anything, she walked away. He called out to her but she kept walking, ignoring his calls.

Feeling the tightening of the band around his head and the pain in his heart, Bob nervously paced the cafeteria as he waited for his attorney. He spotted Robert Schurer as he entered the cafeteria. Bob waved his arm. Mr. Schurer came over smiling. "Come with me. I have to go back to the courtroom. I'm trying to get a hearing."

"What's going on?" Bob asked. "How about our game plan?"

"I don't have time to explain," said Mr. Schurer, smiling through his firm mouth. "I spoke to Mr. Walsh. She wants out of the shelter really bad. She wants to return to the house. That's our bargaining chip." Robert Schurer was a slim medium-built man with fine curly brown hair. He had a dark tan that made him appear too outdoorsy and healthily handsome but not distinctive. He was born and raised in Southern California; he served in the army during the Vietnam conflict and attended law school on the GI Bill; he received many certifies in recognition for his work in the community. He specialized in family law and spent many years as an advocated for fathers' rights.

Mr. Schurer and Bob entered the courtroom; it was not as crowded as it had been earlier. "Find yourself a seat," Schurer said. He walked toward Will Walsh. A hearing was in session.

Bob saw Ann. He walked toward her and asked, "Can I sit here?"

"Yes," said Ann without emotion.

Bob turned to speak to her again. Schurer tapped him on the shoulder and whispered. "Come with me." They walked a few feet away.

"What's the matter?" Bob asked.

"I don't want you talking to her."

"Why!"

In a stern voice, Mr. Schurer said, "Because I'm your legal advisor, and I'm telling you not to talk to her. Do you understand?"

Bob reluctantly nodded. "Yes."

The judge called *Dorsete vs. Dorsete.* Walsh and Schurer approached the bench. The two attorneys had a brief discussion with the judge. The attorneys walked back to respective clients.

"What's going on?" asked Bob impatiently.

"Come on, follow me," said Schurer. "The judge instructed us to work out settlements of the issues."

Bob and Schurer returned to the cafeteria. "Please tell me what's going on." Bob asked.

"They're worried about family support. She's very concerned that you have no job and no income. They said that you quit your job on purpose."

"That's right, I did quit my job. I had to. I couldn't go back to that place. As I explained, I was promised a job by her cousin."

"I know that. However, they're making a big issue about it."

They were approached by Will Walsh and Ann. Will Walsh asked, "Counselor, can we talk in private?" Schurer nodded in agreement. Walsh asked Ann, "Will you be okay?"

Ann signed with her head. She sat opposite of her husband. The moment the attorneys walked away, Bob said, "We need to talk."

"About what?" Ann asked, unconcerned. Bob did not reply as he placed the cigarette between his lips. Ann watched as he nervously lit the cigarette. "Do you have to smoke?"

"Sorry!" Bob exhausted the cigarette. "I was wrong. I made a mistake. I'm sorry. Why don't we talk it over?"

"There is nothing to talk about. I don't want you. I want my divorce. If you get help and if you change, we can get back together."

"That's ridiculous," Bob said in a light chuckle. "Do you know what a divorce is going to do to us? It's going to make us enemies. It's going to make us hate each other. In addition to that, do you know how much it's going to cost?"

Ann snapped back, "I don't care about the money. I want a divorce."

Bob tenderly said, "Please, Ann. Think about what you're doing." He was never one to hide his feelings. "You know that I am a stronger believer that you have to be true to yourself." With tears forming, he said, "I love you more than anything else. I would give my right arm for your love."

She opened her purse and handed him a piece of paper. "Here's a number. If you really love me, you'll get help. You're a violent person. You need help. You get yourself cured, and after a year, if you make progress, I'll remarry you."

Bob paused, not knowing what to say. He had never seen her like this before. He stared and thought how pretty she was with her long hair and soft lips. How desirable she looked. How angry she was. Why was he having a difficult time to reach her? She was not the same person. "How are the boys doing?"

"They're doing fine." She did not want him to know that they were unhappy. "Bobby hit me last week. It's your doing. You taught the boys to be violent."

Bob, with a sarcastic giggle, said, "What do you expect? He's thirteen years old. He's a big boy now. I think that he's angry and confused. You took him away from his home and friends."

"It's your doing! You made them violent," said Ann, piqued.

Bob tried to be calm. "We've both been under a great deal of stress. The restaurant, the business venture with Pete, and my problems with Bennix. It's understandable, but this is not going to help the situation. It's only going to make matters worse. Please think about what you're doing. You are the cause of all your actions. Think before you act."

"I'm not going to take the blame for this. Why did you resign from Bennix?"

"That's because of the allegations you made. You got my company involved. They took me to a mental institution. I could never go back to Bennix. Besides, I needed to concentrate on the business venture with Pete. Your bodyguard, he works for Bennix. He accompanied me to the hospital. I recognized him, though he pretended not to know me."

"He doesn't work for Bennix. He's a friend of Ray."

"He was introduced to me as a Bennix security."

Ann was confused and said, "I never spoke to anyone from Bennix. They contacted me, but I refused to talk to them."

"Did you tell them that I threaten my boss?"

"No, I told Ray that you threaten to hurt me."

"Why?"

"I was scared."

"Did you talk to a guy named Alan Morris from Bennix?"

"Maybe! I don't remember." Ann was confused and annoyed. "I didn't want to talk to them. I didn't tell him anything." Her voice rose, "I don't have to answer you."

"Okay! Calm down."

"Don't tell me what to do. You did say that you wanted to kill your boss."

"Those were thoughts and words of frustration. I never acted. You know that I don't own a gun."

Bob was poised and said, "I resigned from Bennix because they were involved. They hired Ray."

"You didn't have to quit." In a passive tone, Ann said, "I want to return to the house."

"You can. I don't want the boys in a shelter or a hotel. They belong at home. I don't want them in the middle of this mess."

"I want to return to New Jersey. I want to return to my roots to properly raise my children."

"Your children?" said Bob curtly. "How about me? Don't I have a say in this matter. Don't I count for anything?"

"I don't want you around the children." The look on her face changed, becoming less attractive. "I don't want you to see them. You're not a healthy father."

"What do you mean by that?"

Ann certain replied, "You're not healthy. You're sick."

"The children need both parents," replied Bob in a positive voice.

Ann snapped back, "One healthy parent is better than two."

"Who's the healthy parent?" Bob shot back. "How do you qualify as the healthy parent? This whole thing is crazy. You abandoned our business. You took the boys from their home, from their activities and friends. You took them to a shelter with a bunch of degenerates. You took them out of their beautiful home. So who is sick?"

Ann opened her eyes wide and tensed like a wild cat ready to prance on its prey. "You're sick and a thief. Where did you get the money I found in the attic?"

Bob was frustrated. He turned his entire body toward her, placed his hands on the table, and folded them. "From Pete, it was an advancement for the west coast business. That belongs to his company."

"You're a liar," Ann said with a frown and eyes opened wide. "I don't believe you. Why didn't you put it the bank?"

"I was. Once they signed the lease. Talk to Pete if you don't believe me."

"He'll lie. He's taking your side."

Bob, lost for words, paused for a moment. "Ann, where did you find the money?"

"Next to the jewelry box."

"Right! I placed it there the night before my trip to New Jersey in case anything happened to me." Bob paused, hoping to touch her hands. "Please, I don't want a divorce. Give me a second chance. Think about what you're doing."

Ann responded, "I have thought about it. I want my divorce. I'm doing this for the children because you're teaching them to be violent. I don't want them to grow up like you. You've got problems, and you have to help yourself." She was firm, and it showed on her face. She was not going to conceal her feelings. She had no fear of him. She raised her voice and said, "I'm not the same person anymore. The little girl you pushed around. You're not going to get away with the shit you did in the past. I'm not going to let you." Bob thought that this was not the same person he lived with for sixteen years. "For twenty years, I did everything for you, including sex. Whenever you wanted it. I did it because you wanted it. I was available all—"

Bob interrupted, "Except for ten days out of the month and the other times you were too tired because of the boys. And didn't I do things for you? Didn't I provide for you and the boys? What did I do to hurt you? What bad taste did I leave in your mouth?"

"You know what you did. Keeping me down. Calling me names."

"Please, baby," Bob said, trying to cool her bitterness. "I'm hurting. My stomach is in knots and I got this pain in my head. Why are you doing this to me? Why do you want to hurt me?"

"I'm not hurting you. This is all your fault."

"Why don't you give our marriage a chance? Why don't we see a marriage counselor instead of hiring attorneys?"

"It's too late. I asked, but you didn't want to go."

Bob realized that every question and every comment only made her angrier, so he refrained from saying anything further. He sat in silence with his hands folded on the table, staring at her. Finally, he said, "Ann, you hold the fate of six lives… You're in the driver's seat."

She opened a smile on her face, looking right at him, and said, "Yes, I am." She relished this feeling of power and strength. She enjoyed seeing him pleading and begging. After all, she was doing the right thing, she thought. Bob, lost for words, said nothing.

The attorneys returned. Mr. Schurer said, "I think that we're making progress. You have lunch here. I have to go to my office. I'll return in an hour."

Bob was not hungry. He sat in the cafeteria, staring at the people and feeding on tobacco, lighting one cigarette after another. He continually peeked in the direction of Ann and Will Walsh. Her back was toward him. She was just twenty-five feet away from him, but her love was a million light years away. He wanted so badly to put his arms around her, to kiss her sweet lips, to feel her girlish seductive body. Now all he could do was dream.

Mr. Walsh noticed Bob's glances. He approached Bob and said, "Mr. Dorsete, may I have a few words with you?" Bob did not answer. "Are you in therapy?"

"No. Why should I?"

"She cares above you, and we want to help you. The reason you're abusive is because your parents abused you. There is help for people like you."

Feeling harassed, Bob said, "What the hell! You don't know my parents. You don't know anything about them. They were married for over fifty years and always slept in the same bed regardless of any arguments or disagreements. My father was a good person, a hard-working man. So please, don't talk about my parents."

"Calm down. I'm only trying to help." He paused for a moment. "Why did you quit your job? You have four children. Now, you don't have health insurance. You don't have a job to support your children."

"My children," Bob said sarcastically. "My children, then why can't I see them? It's been almost two months. Where are my rights as the father? Why do I have to be here to see my children?"

Ignoring Bob's comments, Walsh said, "They are your children. They are your responsibility." Bob disliked the man. Bob thought, *He is not on my side, and he doesn't answer my questions.* Bob, annoyed, decided not to respond, so in silence, he stared at Will Walsh's face to demonstrate that he was not intimidated.

Will Walsh asked, "Where did the money in the attic come from? Did you steal it from your company?"

"Why the same question about the money?" Bob raised his tone. "I told you many times, it belongs to her cousin. It was an advancement for our new business."

"Don't get vicious."

"I'm not getting vicious. I just don't like what you're leading up to."

In a cheerful voice, Will Walsh said, "Well, it isn't every day that twenty thousand dollars is found in an attic. We do have banks these days. Obviously, you hide the money because you obtained it illegally."

"Why didn't you tell me?" Ann interrupted.

Bob turned toward Ann and said, "Honey, the money was an advancement for us. The restaurant was failing. I was confused. Then I had a buyer for the restaurant." Bob turned toward Walsh. "He contacted you." Bob pointing toward Walsh. "Pete contacted you and asked that it be returned. You told him that if that was his money, to take legal action. The reason Pete hasn't done that is because this is family."

Walsh responded, "It is hard to believe that he would give you that much in cash. You were demoted by Bennix."

Bob turned to Ann. "Ann, speak to Pete. This was a family thing." Bob loudly said, "Talk to Pete."

"What's going on?" interrupted Robert Schurer.

Bob, in an annoyed tone, said, "This guy is making implications that I'm some kind of a crook."

"Counselor, I'm only trying to help Mr. Dorsete," said Will Walsh in his usual polite pleasantries.

"Counselor, this is my client," Schurer said in a firm tone. "If you have anything to say to my client, I would appreciate that you talk to me. You know better." Bob was delighted to hear this, thinking to himself, he liked his new attorney. He put Walsh in his place.

Defensive, Will Walsh said, "I simply told him he has a responsibility to his children." Schurer stared in silence. "Can we sit down to continue our discussion?"

"Yes," said Schurer. He turned to Bob. "Can you please leave us?" Bob decided to get himself a cup of coffee. He walked away. It was past lunchtime, yet the cafeteria was still crowded. The tables were covered with papers, pencils, and calculators. Bob walked around, glancing outside and inside. He kept turning toward Ann. All his thoughts were of her. Every time he gazed toward her, she turned the other direction.

About an hour later, Mr. Schurer approached Bob. Smiling, he said, "It's done! I want you to read this and tell me if you agree." Not having a clear mind, Bob did not want to read the document, but he had to see what he was agreeing to.

1. That all orders of child, family, and spouse support that are payable by respondent to petitioner to be made effective on this date.
2. The family residence located in California is ordered sold. Forthwith, the parties are ordered to list the house with an appropriate licensed real estate.
3. The parties' four minor children shall be evaluated and obtain any and all psychological counseling recommended by an experienced family psychologist as recommended by him.
4. That the respondent is ordered to appear in court on August 22 in Department 50 to show cause why this court shall not order respondent to pay child and spousal support to petitioner.
5. That the court reserves the right to order respondent to pay petitioner's legal and court fees.
6. That the parties and children shall be ordered to attend and be evaluated at the office of Dr. Jule Soble for the purpose of a written family profile, evaluation, and recommendation. The evaluator is requested to submit a written recommendation on or before August 6, regarding custody/visitation schedule pending trial. Until jurisdiction is held, at time of trial, the respondent will be responsible for paying Dr. Soble.
7. The respondent is to vacate the family residence here in California, effective within three days of today's date, and the petitioner and the four minor children will occupy.

Bob, annoyed, looked at Robert Schurer and said, "What's this all about, number 4 and 6?"

Schurer feeling victorious, "We won. They wanted you to undergo a psychological evaluation. I got them to agree to a family evaluation like we discussed. Your wife will be evaluated. You said that she had a mental breakdown."

"But I have to pay for everything?" asked Bob, irritated.

"You might not have to pay. We can reserve a decision for a court hearing."

Though Bob had pain in his heart and head, he still had a functional brain. "These conditions are all in her favor. What's to my advantage?"

"You wanted to see your children. I know Dr. Soble. I've worked with him before. He'll work with us." He noticed the disappointment on Bob's face. "Do you want to see your children? Do you want to wait two to three months for the social services report?" He paused. "Sometimes it could take up to six months. I thought that I had explained it to you. We made it an order, a 730, stipulating our professional in lieu of the social services."

Bob shook his head and said, "No."

"All the other conditions could be changed later. You want to see your children. We had to give a lot so that they would agree." Reluctantly and irritably, Bob agreed.

Mr. Walsh walked over. "Counselor, my client has reviewed the document. She accepts the terms."

"How about the sale of the restaurant?" asked Bob. "The buyer wants a reduction in the price."

The two attorneys glanced at each other. Walsh asked, "How much?"

"I think about 20 percent," replied Bob.

Walsh said, "I don't think that you have much of a choice."

Schurer added, "Mr. Walsh, I think that it'll be best if Mr. Dorsete contacted the buyer." Walsh stared in silence. Schurer smiled. "Bob, you finalize the sale."

It was late in the afternoon, and the courthouse was almost empty. The parties were in a courtroom. The judge was looking at the document, entitled "The Stipulation."

Schurer stood next to Bob and said in a low voice, "When the judge asks you questions, answer yes to the questions."

The judges addressed the two attorneys. "Are your clients here?"

Both attorneys responded, "Yes."

The petitioner and respondent were asked to step forward. They were asked to raise their hands and swear to "tell the truth, the whole truth, and nothing but the truth." They sat down, and the judge asked, "You two have read this document?"

Both Bob and Ann responded yes. "Do you agree with this document?" Ann and Bob responded with a yes. "Are these your signatures on this document?" Both responded with a yes. The judge banged his gavel and said, "It is now a court order," and he signed the documents.

Quietly, the parties left the courtroom; Bob glanced at Ann. She turned the other way. They all walked toward the elevator. Robert Schurer wore a complacent look that suggested that he had done a good job for his client. He suggested that they take the stairs. As they walked down, he said, "You did good. You behaved very civilly, and I'm proud of you."

"Thank you!" Bob said, not sure why he was thanking him. Bob was not sure if he was not better off this morning than this afternoon. This was his third time in this court building, and he still had not seen his children.

Schurer continued, "Now, you have to move out of the house. Just take your personal items. Don't take anything else."

"Nothing else?"

"That's correct. Just take your clothing and your personal items and leave the house by Friday. By the way, my retention was for five thousand dollars. You only gave me two thousand. When can I expect the balance?"

Bob, not quite sure where he was going to get the money, said, "I'll have it for you next week."

Robert Schurer had been practicing family law for a number of years, and most of his clients were fathers. He understood that there was little he could do for Bob Dorsete at this time because of the allegations of abuse. The system practiced in playing it safe than being sorry. He knew the scenario. Very seldom do the fathers win over the issue of custody. The mother bears the children and, at divorce, keeps them.

The hot July days did bring the warm and caring Cancer or Leo nights. It had been an empty void of an existence for Bob. Two days later, Bob was packing his clothing into two suitcases, preparing to leave on a reluctant journey to nowhere, thinking it had not been a happy summer. There were no summer barbecues or family outings. He made his way downstairs and placed a letter on the table next to the flowers he purchased. He grabbed the front doorknob and stopped. He dropped the suitcase on the floor. He decided to take one last look around the house. He walked into the kitchen and stared at the rings she used to wear. Throughout the hallway were the family photographs on the walls.

Bob made his way to a chair. Tears flowed from his eye as he thought of the rings, the photographs, souvenirs of days together, and trophies of games the children played. The memories of love not long ago, signs and symbols of long and deep love. He said a prayer that in her heart she would find a trace of love that was once there, and he prayed for a second chance that she would come back and drive the tears from his eyes. He cried in silence, hoping for a miracle.

Chapter 9

Ann and Bob Dorsete's first year of marriage had been fun and fulfilling. They were coming out of a theater into the October wind as it whipped through the mall parking lot. They had seen a sad movie about love and tragedy. He noticed that she was shivering. "Let's race to the car," Bob said and started to run. Ann chased after him. Laughing, he opened her door. As they waited for the car to warm up, he observed the sad look on her face. In a concerned tone, he said, "It got to you. The movie was sad."

"Yes," she said, hesitating.

He felt that something was not right. "What's the matter? Was it the movie, or is it something else?" She did not answer. "Is it me? Are you happy with me?" He looked at her, admiring her girlish features. Her pretty face was edged by her lush reddish-brown hair.

"No, Bob. I'm happy with you. I love you very much." She unbuttoned his coat, put her hand on his chest, and massaged the hard, well-defined mounts. She gently kissed his cheek and said, "It's just that I'm disappointed that I don't have a teaching job and you've working so hard for your degree. I can't get a decent job. We both worked so hard for our college degrees, and all we have to show for it are low-paying jobs. All those years we went to college."

"We have each other," he said cheerfully, placing his arms around her. "This is only temporary. Give it time. You'll see." Ann was working as a secretary/typist, and he was working part-time at a retail store as a clerk while attending school full-time. He was optimistic and had a positive outlook. She saw things for what they were. She was disappointed and worried about the future.

Ann said, "All those courses and time, and I still don't have my master's degree. I completed the courses requirements, passed the major comprehensive test with an A. I failed the minor comprehensive test twice, and I don't know what else to do."

Bob squeezed her tighter and rocked her gently back and forth and said optimistically, "Don't worry about it, you'll get it." She started to sob. Trying to cheer her up, he said, "That movie got to you. It was sad, but it's only a movie."

She moved away to dry her tearing eyes. Shaking her head sideways, she started to sob harder. "There's something else I think." She hesitated ominously. "I think that I'm pregnant. It's two weeks… I'm late."

"Pregnant!"

Jolting her head, she said, "I'm not sure. I might be."

Trying to ease her distress, he said, "Well then, don't worry about it until we know for sure." He wanted to cheer her up. "Why don't we go down to the shore tomorrow? You always enjoy the beach."

Ann, in a half smile, said, "What are you, crazy? This is October! It'll be cold."

"Think of it," he said, smiling, "no traffic. We don't have to fight for parking spaces. Do you know that we met seven years ago around this time? So let's celebrate."

Bob was always adventurous and romantic. She never had to ask him to take her places. Where ever they went, they always had a good time and happy memories. It was unusually warm for October. It was midafternoon, and the sun was shining brightly. Ann and Bob went to their favorite beach. There were some people lying on the sand, absorbing the year's last rays of sunshine, but no one was in the water. They walked on the boardwalk, stopping at their favorite stands for something to eat and to play the games of chance. The sun had moved further west, causing the temperature to drop rapidly. Ann said, "I feel cold. Let's leave."

"Okay." He grabbed her hand and started to run, pulling her along. Once inside the car, he said, "What would you like to do now?"

"Let's go home for some hot coffee and dessert."

He smiled and said, "Why! It's too early. And besides, this is your day out. I promised you a good time."

"I'm having a good time."

"The evening is too young. The moon isn't out yet."

They drove along the beach until they found an isolated area and parked the car. They embraced and kissed until it was dark. There were no sounds except for the serene ocean rowing on the beach. The ocean brightly reflected the moon like a mirror. "Isn't it peaceful and beautiful?" Bob said. "Let's drive on to the beach."

Ann cautioned, "Please don't go on the beach. Suppose the car gets stuck in the sand."

Bob, laughing, said, "Ah, this is a light car. We won't get stuck. This is a VW an unconverted dune buggy."

Ann, believing yet frighten, asked, "Are you sure? There's no one around if we get stuck." He drove on to the beach, heading straight for the ocean. He shut off the car lights. "Bob, please put the lights on. You might go right into the ocean."

"It's okay. See the reflection of the moon," he said, pointing. "See how bright it's reflecting on the ocean. I can see the entire beach."

Ann looked carefully. She was frightened. "Bob, please stop. Let's get off the beach."

Bob reassuringly said, "It's okay. I know what I'm doing." He stopped the car and shut off the engine. They sat quietly, enjoying the view. Bob broke the silence. "I've been thinking about what you said last night about possibly being pregnant. How do you feel about it?"

"I don't know. After last night, I just told myself that I wasn't going to worry about it until it's definite."

With a serious look, he said, "We've just been married a little over a year. We're not financially secured. I don't think I'm ready to be a father."

"What are you suggesting?" Ann asked with a dumbfounded expression on her face. "I don't understand what you mean."

Bob paused and stared away from her. He had difficulty in speaking. "An abortion."

Ann was surprised. The thought had never entered her mind. Abortions were legal but had been a controversial a few years earlier. She never had any reasons to think about it before. She said, "Isn't that killing the baby?"

He turned toward her and, in a serious tone, said, "If you're pregnant, what, three or four weeks. It takes nine months. It's just a fertile egg right now."

"I don't know. I never thought about this. I don't know if I want to do it. But last night, you said not to worry about it or to think about it until I am sure."

Bob felt melancholy, thinking that he had said something profaned. "Yes, you're right. Hey, let's go home for a nice warm cup of coffee."

"I would like that."

Bob started the car engine and shifted the stick into gear. The engine raced, but the car did not advance. He shifted to reverse and forward, causing the car to rock slightly until there was no movement. Ann asked, "What's the matter? I told you. But no! You had to prove something. Now, we're stuck. I warned you."

"Okay. So we're stuck. Now, let me think."

Ann was scared as she looked at the ocean only a few feet away. She yelled, "I told you! I told you not to drive on the beach! You had to be a daredevil. You said, 'The car's too light, it won't get stuck in the sand.'"

"Okay, stop yelling," Bob said, chuckling. "I'll get us out of here. You'll see." He stepped out of the car and saw that the rear bumper resting on the sand and the rear tires were buried. "Ann, you have to drive, and I'll push."

Ann, in astonishment, said, "This is a stick shift. You know that I can't drive a stick shift."

Laughing, he said, "No better time to learn than now. Get in the driver's seat."

"But, Bob!" she said as she walked around the car. "I don't think that I can do it."

"Look around," he said as he moved her shoulders. "Who am I going to ask?" She sat in the driver's seat. Pointing, he said, "There are three pedals down there. Right? You know how to use two—the gas and the brake. The third is the clutch. The gas pedal is the same, and so is the brake. Here are the gears."

Lacking confidence, Ann said, "I'm afraid. I've never driven a stick shift. What happens if I can't stop?"

"Then I'll meet you in New York," Bob said, laughing. "No, I'm only kidding you. You step on the brake."

"I don't think that I can do it. Let's get help."

"You can do it if you put your mind to it," Bob said slightly annoyed. "Please listen. You use your left foot for the clutch. You use the right just the same as in your car for the gas and the brake. You put it in gear by pushing down on the clutch. Try it." Ann pushed on the clutch and moved the gear shift. "See how easy it is. That's how you get the car to move."

Ann did not understand a single word. "Bob, I don't think I can do it."

In a stern voice, he said, "There's no one around. Do you want to do walk for miles to find a tow truck and pay seventy-five dollars? You can do it. Just give it a try. Listen to me and push down on the clutch. Put it in gear and give it gas. As you start moving, give it more gas, and keep moving until you're off the beach."

Ann was not as confident as Bob. He got directly behind the car. He planted his feet into the sand and shouted, "Okay, put it in gear!" He pushed hard in anticipation that the wheels would rotate. But they didn't turn. He shouted, "Ann, what's the matter? Put it in gear!"

Ann nervously shouted back, "I can't move the stupid stick!"

Bob walked toward Ann and bent over. "That's first!" He paused. "Are you ready now?" She motioned with her head. He went to the rear of the car and shouted, "Put it in gear!" Ann pushed down the clutch and forced the stick shift forward. She pressed hard on the gas and quickly let go of the clutch, causing the wheels to turn. Sand was flying in the directions of Bob, landing on his clothing and face. Bob shouted out for her to stop. The wheels continued to rotate until the car stalled.

Ann stepped out of the car, and in a proud girlish excitement, she hollered, "I did it." Bob, trying to answer, spat out sand. His entire body was covered with sand. Ann laughed at the sight of the sand figure. Chuckling, she said, "Oohh, my poor baby." She wiped the sand from his face and kissed him. "I love you." Bob opened his eyes and started to laugh. Ann said, "Do you have any other bright ideas?"

"You know me, I don't give up." He walked away.

Ann yelled, "Where are you going! Don't leave me here by myself."

Bob continued to walk and answered, "I'm going to look for things." He walked slowly and stopped to bend down.

"Please hurry back," she howled out.

She sat nervously in the car, fearing that they would not be able to get out. The cold breeze was causing her to shiver. She felt better once he returned with a bundle of driftwood. She watched in silence as he started to dig the sand away from the front of the tires and laid the wood in front and under the tires. She stared in admiration for his determination and resourcefulness. He cleared the sand from the rear body of the car. She loved his persistence and felt confident that in just a few minutes they would be out of the sand and out of danger.

Bob got into the driver's seat and said, "Get out and push."

Ann, with a shocked look on her face, said, "What?"

"I'll drive, you push."

"I'm not strong enough," she said in bewilderment. "I can't push the car out."

"Well, if you don't want to push, you have to get out. I don't want any extra weight in the car." So she stepped out. Bob slowly put the gear in first; the car moved slightly. He eased up on the gas, and the car rolled back. He got the car rocking in a back-and-forth motion. As soon as he felt the car moving slightly forward, he gave it more gas until he was out of the pit. He slowly drove off the beach.

Ann shouted, "Hey, stop! Wait for me!" Bob stopped and moved in reverse. "You had me worried. I thought that you were going to leave me here."

Bob stepped out of the car, smiling. He put his arm around her and said, "I love you too much."

Holding him tight, she said, "You're my hero. I never would have figured out how to get out of there. Let's go home. I want to show my hero a good time."

Ann and Bob were lying in bed side by side. Bob squeezed Ann's tight, firm round buttocks, burying his fingertips into the thick skin and maintaining the rhythm, waiting for signs and sounds. He slowed down only to delay his own rapturous delight and ecstasy. His head was resting on the bed next to hers, turning occasional to gently nibble on her ear. Perspiration was forming on his neck and head as exhaustion was taking over him. He continued the plunging, hoping for shrieks of pleasure. He felt her fingers pushing into his back, digging deeper, and he knew it was only a matter of seconds now. He slowed down his thrusts and pushed his penis deeper into her wet passage. Her vaginal wall encompassed his shaft, sucking like a vacuum cleaner. Her dry month open and screamed sounds of enchantment delight. He pulled out and dropped the hot seeds on her thick hairy tiny forest. He squeezed forward, releasing all the secretion from his body.

Ann Dorsete had looked beautiful in her French red lingerie. She wore a demi-cup bra, enriching the fullness of her breast, and bikini panties styled in chiffon with lace and sequin trim. They were both naked, exhausted, and in ecstasy. Ann asked intimately, "Bob, do I satisfy you? Do I make you happy? Do you love me?"

In a content tone, he said, "I'm very happy with you. I enjoy making love to you."

"Did you like the sheer teddy I had on? Was it sexy?"

"You looked very pretty. Just lavishing."

Ann, satisfied, said, "Nothing like that plain one on our wedding night."

Laughing, Bob said, "I didn't want to tell you then, but it didn't do you justice."

"You were reluctant to make love that night."

"I wasn't. I was just too tired."

Ann was laughing and leaning over his fatigued body. "Yeah, the Italian Stallion was just too tired." With a changed tone, she said, "Tomorrow, I'm going to make an appointment to see a doctor. I just can't think of having an abortion."

He raised his head closer to her face and placed his hands on her shoulders. She turned away. He placed his hand on her chin and gently turned her face to his. Looking into her eyes, he said, "I'm just going to tell how I feel. Financially, we're okay, but we can't afford a baby now. I'm not ready to be a father. We've just been married a year. We're having a good time. We can go anyplace we want, do what we want to do. I just don't want to give that up right now."

Ann was saddened. "I can't think of killing a baby."

"You're not killing a baby. It would be different if it were five or six months." They were both silent for a while, and then he said. "Ann, it's your body. I'm just telling you how I feel. The choice is yours. If you want to have the baby, it's okay by me. I'll quit school, and I'll get a full-time job. It'll work out. I'll get two jobs if I have to."

"I hate to see you quit school," Ann said sadly. "But I don't know if I want an abortion. I feel like it's wrong. I'll be so embarrassed." She did not want the abortion and was angry at herself for not being careful.

Bob did not respond. Then he said, "I also feel embarrassed. We don't have to tell anybody. It will be our secret. I promise in a year or two we can have a baby." They embraced each other.

"I love you very much. I'll love you forever," said Ann as she kissed him. "Let's not talk about that now." Smiling seductively, she asked, "Do I satisfy you?"

"Yes!" Bob said reassuringly. "You were very good tonight."

"Do you love me as much as you did when we first met?"

"Yes, I love you more today than yesterday." He put his arms around her. "Making love to you is so fulfilling. All of time stands still. What more can I ask for? There is nothing else I desire. I couldn't wish for anything more than your love. You're all I need."

Hearing these words made Ann totally content mentally and physically. She kissed him. "I will love you for ever and ever and ever." They peacefully rested in each other's arms.

Ann hated that day at the abortion clinic. She felt guilty and depressed for months. She never mentioned her true feelings to Bob. Never again, she thought. Bob, too, felt the guilt and embarrassment. Yet he believed what is done is done. He tried not to think of the past. Two years later, Ann thought that she was pregnant. This time, she did not tell Bob until she was certain. She worried that he would suggest that she have another abortion. She had a good job, and Bob needed twenty credits for his MBA degree. Financially, they were on a tight budget and saving money for a house. Perhaps, she thought, that he would now feel differently. She hoped he would. She was nervous and apprehensive to tell Bob. But she had to. After all, in a month or two, he would know.

That evening, Bob noticed that Ann was quiet and made little conversation. He asked, "What's troubling you?"

Ann said, "Nothing." She was frightened. "I just had a bad day at work."

"It's more than that. It's written all over your face. That is something." In a concerned tone, he asked, "Please tell me."

Ann started to weep. "I'm pregnant." There were tears running down her face. "I don't want an abortion. I want this baby."

Bob hesitated in answering. With a big smile on his face, he said, "That's great!" He hugged and kissed her.

Ann, in near shock, withdrew and said, "Are you sure? Do you really want to have the baby? We live in two rooms. With the baby, we'll be so crowded. You know that I will have to quit my job, and you're still in school."

He smiled and said, "I want the baby. How pregnant are you?"

"Two months—not exactly two."

"It'll work out. In a few months, I'll be finished with school. You have a good job with benefits."

"I'll have to a take a medical leave of absence." Sadly, she said, "We'll need all kinds of baby stuff, a crib, walker. We'll be too cramped here. I don't want to have the baby in this two-room apartment. I'm worried that you won't find a job."

Bob, smiling, said, "Come on, cheer up. Remember what the insurance guy said? That we had potential. We've kept our expenses low. I believe that we saved enough for a down payment to buy a house."

Ann was not sure. "How? How are we going to qualify for a mortgage?"

"Things have changed." Thinking positive, he said, "Banks now take into consideration a woman's income. You've been working for the same company for almost three years. We can qualify on your income."

In the following weeks, Ann gained weight and ate for two. Her petite body showed her swollen stomach, and it was obvious that she putting on weight. In the mornings during breakfast, she experienced nausea. She often ran to the bathroom, trying to vomit what little she had in her stomach. Seeing and hearing the sounds of pregnancy, Bob also felt some of the pain. She was feeling a little low because their lovemaking became less frequent and less intense. She started to think that perhaps Bob didn't think that she was attractive or desirable to make love to. Bob thought that she was beautiful and attractive in a different way. He was pleased and excited that she was having his baby.

They found a small house a few blocks from their apartment. Bob and Ann were anxiously awaiting approval for the mortgage. A month after filing for the mortgage, they were called to the bank to clarify a few questions on their application. Ann and Bob considered that they might be denied the mortgage if the bank knew that Ann was pregnant. She wore a big heavy winter coat.

It was a special pregnancy coat made by her mother, able to expand as she got larger. It was a warm November day. She felt ridiculous with the bulky coat inside the bank. She nervously sweated that the man would notice that she was pregnant. She was so uncomfortable breathing heavy and couldn't wait to leave. She thought that she was going to passing out. The more the man stared at her, the more nervous she felt. The man noticed the perspiration on her face and asked why she did not remove her coat. She told him that she had a cold and felt chilly.

Their mortgage application was approved, and Bob suggested that they celebrate. They were on a tight budget, so they settled for a moderate celebration at their favorite pizzeria. Ann was excited about having her own house. She felt contented and believed in her man and that everything would work out.

In was January of 1977, and the eastern part of the country was in severe winter freeze. The temperature had been near zero for the past month and the wind-chill factor dropped the temperature below zero. There was a great demand on energy, and costs were creeping upward and supplies were diminishing rapidly. Many states were placed in a state of emergency. All public places and businesses had to keep their thermostats at sixty-three degrees or lower. Residents were requested to maintain their thermostats at sixty-five or below.

Ann and Bob Dorsete had recently moved into their home. They had little furniture, just the bare essential, a bed, kitchen set, and one couch. It was early Sunday night. They had just returned from Ann's mother's house. Once inside, Ann complained of how cold it was as she exhausted warm air from her mouth. Bob agreed as he tried to find the cause. He checked the thermostat. It read thirty-five degrees. He went downstairs to the basement to check the furnace; it made no sounds. He was unfamiliar with it, and he did not know what to do. He returned upstairs.

"What's wrong?" asked Ann, still wearing her coat.

"I don't know." He was wearing a dumbfounded look on his face. "The furnace is not running. It could be out of oil." He paused to think, and then he said, "I'll call the service guy." He called and got an answering service, so he left his name and phone number, stating that it was an emergency.

They sat in the kitchen in silence with their coats and hats. The cold was affecting Ann more than Bob as she started to shiver. "We can't stay here," Ann said. "It's too cold."

"It's not as cold as outside," Bob said, trying to make her laugh. "We'll be okay. We'll sleep in our clothes and cover ourselves with all the blankets we have. We'll be okay." He widened his lips to give a smile. "And we can cuddle together."

Ann was cold and pregnant. She was concerned about the baby. She said, "Let's go to my mother's house."

Bob did not want to sleep at his mother in-law's house. "I don't want your mother to think that I can't take care of you. I don't want this incident as another one of her lectures." He stood up and paced the floor to relieve the tension. "We have been married for three years. I know that we've been struggling, but we're happy." Continuing in a bitter tone, he said, "I hate when she says things like that we were too young to get married, that we should have waited until we finished school and had jobs, that we should have moved in with her. She was disappointed that we lived in a two-room apartment. I don't like your mother telling me what to do. I'm not one of her children."

Ann proudly said, "I tell her how hard you work and that we're happy." She desperately wanted to be in a warm place. She was not being selfish. She was only thinking of her unborn child. Pleading, she said, "Please, Bob. Let's go to my mother's house."

"You want to go?" he said, mad. "Go ahead and go. I'm not coming. Believe me, we'll be okay."

"Please, Bob." She did not want to go without him. She was cold, and her nose had turned to a flush red.

Bob thought he was the man and it was his responsibility to take care of his wife and their baby. "It's still early. I'm going to call some oil companies. Don't stand around worrying. Make the coffee and get more blankets."

He called several oil companies with the same response. Due to the severely cold winter, they were busy servicing their regular customers. The best that they can do is tomorrow. Bob was disappointed and aggravated. He tried humor to vent his frustration. He promised to be a regular customer if they serviced him tonight. He thought that since there was a declared state of emergency, there might be some agency he could call. He found and dialed the number several times before he got through. He explained his predicament. He was told that they were assisting only low-income families with minor children. Disappointed and out of ideas, he thought that perhaps they should go to Rose Pellone's house.

Ann was on the couch canopied in blankets, watching television to calm her mind. He told her that perhaps they should spend the night at her mother's. She changed her mind about leaving. They snuggled together under the blankets and watching TV. Later in bed, they slept closely clinging to each other. The next morning, the house was colder as the thick gray clouds hid the sun's ray. They lay awake in their warm bed and embraced with no desire to get up. They were disturbed by the sound of the telephone. Bob quickly jumped out of bed, hoping that it was an oil company. Bob hung up the telephone and shouted, "Ann! It was the serviceman. He'll be here in an hour."

Gus had serviced the previous homeowners and was happy to service the new owners. Bob watched as he dismantled the furnace/burners, cleaned the components, and assembled it. He showed Bob the primer button. He put in ten gallons of oil and started the furnace. He had scheduled an oil delivery by early afternoon. He instructed Bob to make sure that the pipe to the tank was exposed so that the driver can get to the tank.

Later, Bob was outside. Everything was covered with snow except for the street and narrow paths on the sidewalks. He put on his boots, coat, scarf, and hat. The lawn was covered with over one foot of snow. With a shovel, he started in the center of the lawn, removing the snow. He shoveled a small area, hoping to get lucky. When he reached the ground, it was frozen hard. He cleared the snow with his fingers in search for a two-inch-diameter metal pipe that should be penetrating two or three inches. He was disappointed that he did not see anything. He shoveled a larger area, clearing the lawn of snow; and with his fingers, he searched. He stopped to rest, examined the lawn, and murmured in frustration. He noticed a young man on the porch of the house next door. The man strangely glanced at Bob as he walked by. Bob greeted him good morning. It was the first time that they saw each other.

Bob continued to shovel. The task was becoming more difficult because he had made larger piles of snow. He stopped to take a breather and to drink the coffee that Ann brought to him. Bob had no place to put the snow. The driveway was the only place. He had cleared most off the lawn. Some green was showing, but it was mostly white. He was in the middle of the lawn as he examined the area in search for the pipe. He cursed in defeat. He spotted the man that he saw earlier. The man stared at Bob as he entered the house. Bob waved, and the man waved back.

Bob raked the frozen white ground in frustration and anger. He raked vigorously, lifting the dormant grass. Standing on the porch, the stranger watched with interest. Bob murmured curses as he continued to rake the white lawn changing to brown/green. The man continued to stare at Bob, thinking how strange it was for someone to rake their lawn in January. More strangely, why would anybody be removing snow from the front lawn? Bob got on his knees, and with his fingers, he carefully felt and raked the grass, searching for the mysterious pipe. The stranger thought, *Now he's praying.* The man went inside, convinced that he had a strange neighbor.

The long-awaited spring had finally arrived, and Bob and Ann were anxiously looking forward to the birth of their first child, and Bob completing his MBA. Bob was delighted that Ann wanted to name the baby after Bob if it was a boy. He wanted to name it after her if it was a girl, but Ann did not want that because girls don't carry the family name while boys do.

Ann was in the kitchen, preparing dinner, and he walked in savoring the pot roast. "You're a great cook, babe."

She enjoyed to make him happy and was pleased to hear that he appreciated her cooking. Being pregnant, she felt inadequate that she had no sexual appetite. She feared that he would seek sex elsewhere. Her friends at work had told her numerous times that Bob was handsome and wished they had a husband like him. She was eager to give birth to regain her figure and to enjoy sex again. "Thank you," Ann said, thinking that now was the time to tell him. "Bob, I have something to tell you."

Bob, reserving himself, asked, "What's the matter?"

Ann disappointedly said, "I was informed by the personnel manager that the baby is not covered."

Bob asked bluntly, "What do you mean the baby's not covered?"

"My pregnancy is covered, but since we don't have a family plan, once the baby's born, it's like another person. The baby's stay in the hospital is not going to be covered by my insurance company."

Bob was baffled by the bad news. He stopped washing the dishes to be more attending. "I don't quite understand it. Are you sure?"

"Yes, it's been bothering me all day. We're on a tight budget, and this might cost us thousands. Where are we going to get the money from?"

Bob drew back his lips, holding back his displeasure. "Did you check your policy? Maybe he's mistaken."

Ann shook her head and said, "No, I did. The baby is not covered."

He walked toward her, and warmly, he grabbed her hands. "Ah, don't worry about it," he said, smiling. "It's just another bridge. We'll worry about it when we get there."

"But we don't have the money, I'm worried."

"Look, you're pregnant. Don't get upset. We'll get by. You'll see."

"That's more bad news. I got a call from a man, a bill collector. He said that I have an outstanding student loan from college."

Bob, with a puzzled look on his face, said, "I thought you paid that off. I haven't seen a bill in over a year."

"Yes, I thought we did. I…I am sure. I haven't seen a bill in a long time."

"How much was the balance on the loan?" Bob asked, irked.

"I don't remember. When the bill came, I paid the monthly payment," Ann said, defensive. "The guy said that they wanted immediate payment."

"How much?"

"I don't remember. I was so nervous. He insisted that I make payments, plus interest and handling costs."

"Well, the hell with him. Let them take us to court. We don't have the money." Bob expressed displeasure. "You're too quick to panic, reacting without thinking. Just like the time the furnace was out, you panicked and wanted to run to your mother. And the time with your degree. For a whole year, you were miserable and cried. I helped you with that. You always dump the problems on me."

Ann was hurt and upset by his comments. She said, "It's just that I was nervous for the baby. I am proud of you and the way you took care of things. I know that you are very smart and clever." She leaned forward to kiss him. "Wait until after the baby is born. I'll show you a good time."

In a calm tone, Bob said, "Next time he calls, tell him to contact me. Tell him that you husband handles the finances."

It was Bob who came up with the idea to assist Ann with her master's degree. Bob had instructed Ann to work closely with her advisors and to meet weekly. Pick their brains, show them your ability and sincerity, and demonstrate that you are working diligently. She got to know them, and they got to know her. Ann's confident and desire was heightening. She never had this type of help before. They were very helpful by giving their time, additional supplemental books, and personal notes. A week before the test, one of her advisors gave her a list of ten questions and told her that three would be on the test. The test was so easy that she was done in a half hour, where the previous times she struggled for hours.

Two days later, while Bob was home studying for his finals, Ann was escorted home by a male coworker. She was weak and had difficulty in walking. She could not stand on her feet. Bob helped her to bed and removed her coat and shoes. She had been badgered by the collector. He called her a liar and threatened to garnish her salary. She feared that they would lose their house. She became nervous with hot flashes, causing her head to spin, and she passed out on her desk.

Bob was upset and angry. He shouted words of revenge and swore to get him. Bob called the man. He told him to stop harassing his wife and they always paid their bills. He explained that perhaps there had to be some kind of error and that they haven't seen a bill for over a year. He tried to reason with the man to try to work something out. The man was cold and arrogant, stating that according to his records, no payments had been made for two years. Ann Pellone had moved several times in an effort to avoid payments. The conversation changed into personal insults. Two growth men acted like adolescents, ready to fight. Bob defending his credit called the man a jerk. He told the man that he was not going to take his crap. His blood pressure raised, and his adrenaline flowed with anger. Bob threatened to go to the man's office to kick his ass.

Ann was disturbed by the shouting and called out to Bob to stay calm and not to do anything foolish. She raised her head weakly, trying to get a peek at Bob. She saw him as he paced the kitchen floor, shouting threats and cursing. Bob was angry that the man hurt his wife. His mind was filled with rage that he could not study, and he contemplated of some way to resolve the problem.

The following week, Bob Dorsete had contacted Ann's college and made an appointment with the person in charge of student loans and collections. Bob honestly and openly explained the problem. He reassured the woman that they had no intention to default on the loan. Bob had made a very convincing point, explaining that Ann enjoyed her college days and wanted to be loyal to the school. This situation was a bad reflection on the college. He justified that they were currently struggling and were willing to resume payments at a later date. The woman was overwhelmed by Bob's reasoning that she researched the problem. She was convinced that it had been an oversight or an error due to the change of their computer systems. Without making any effort to contact Ann, the loan was turned over to a collection agency.

They had worked out an agreement that the Dorsetes would make monthly payments with no accumulating interest. Ann praised Bob for his cleverness and his ability to confront a problem and resolve it in a civil manner.

Bob had just completed his requirements for his MBA in finance. Ann and Bob's thoughts were on the birth of their first child. They had agreed on a boy's name but were uncertain on a girl's name. They had taken Lamaze classes, so they had a general idea of what to expect. They had trained together. Ann was the participant, and Bob was the coach. They both hoped for a boy.

They quietly watched television. Ann said, "I feel very tired. I'm going to sleep."

Bob looked at the clock and said, "It's only eight. It's early."

"I have to go lie down."

"Are you all right?" Bob asked, concerned. "Won't you stay and keep me company for a little while?"

Ann said, smiling, "I'm fine. I just need to lie down."

"Do you want company?"

"No." Ann smiled and kissed him good night. This was Ann's first experience in childbirth. However, she felt something. Call it instinct, passed from birth to birth and still unexplained by science. She had just visited the doctor early this week, and he told her that she won't be due for at least two weeks. She did not want to worry Bob, so she did not tell him of her intuition. She had packed her bag earlier.

Bob entered the bedroom quietly and observed that Ann was in a deep sleep.

How uncomfortable she had been for the past month, and he humorously thought that he was glad he was not a woman. He was amazed how a woman's body changed. Her breasts had swollen to almost twice her normal size. Her hips had become wider. Her stomach had fallen and expanded out; her legs were spread apart. She appeared to walk like a duck. It was humorous to Bob, but he did not laugh or insult her. He silently slipped into bed, moved closer to her, and placed his arm around her.

"Bob, Bob!" said Ann, nudging him. "Bob, please wake up." She shook him hard.

In a daze, he opened his eyes and said, "Yeah! What's the matter?"

Ann said excitedly, "I think I'm having labor pains."

"Oh, oooh." He rolled over to sleep.

"Bob, did you hear me!" She shook him vigorously. "I think I'm having labor pains."

"Oh, okay," he said as sat up slowly, still unconscious. "What's the matter? Why are you bothering me?"

"Didn't you hear me? I think I felt pain."

"Are you sure?"

"Yes! I think so."

He looked at the clock, and its red digit numbers were all that was illuminating the room, and it showed 4:12. "Gee, Ann, it's four in the morning. Are you sure? Can't you wait a couple of hours?"

Ann, thinking that Bob was only kidding, said, "C'mon, Bob, I think it's the real thing. Help me time them."

"All right, I'll watch the clock. What time was the last one?"

"I'm not sure." Getting a little bit nervous, she said, "I was busy trying to wake you up."

"Okay. I'll watch the clock." He rested his head on the pillow with eyes fixed on the clock and watched, 4:16, 4:17, 4:18 until his eyes closed.

"I felt the pain," Ann said excruciating. "Oooh, it hurts."

Bob opened his eyes and looked at the clock. "We have a long way. You're ten minutes apart." He had mistaken the last number.

"No! The pain is five minutes apart. You fell asleep again." Stepping out of the bed, she said, "Take me to the hospital."

"Ann, if the pains are five minutes apart, we have plenty of time. It could be twenty hours from now. Do you want to spend twenty hours in the delivery room? Do you remember all the stories we heard about false labor?" He clutched her hand. "C'mon, settle down." He rested his head against the pillow and closed his eyes. Ann cried out in agony. "Get up! Take me to the hospital! This one was two minutes apart."

"Okay, I'll get the car out." He quickly dressed. "You just sit down. I'll come back for you."

Bob drove the car by the side house door, and Ann walked out. Bob shouted, "Let me help you. Why didn't you wait for me?"

"I'm okay."

"Put the bag down," Bob said. He helped her to the car, opened the door, and gently helped her in.

Ann screamed out in pain, "Please, hurry!" Bob went to get the bag and returned. She looked at him. "You can't go that way. Look at you. You have slippers, no socks, ripped pants. Get changed."

"But you said you can't wait." Ann stared at him. "Okay, I'll be back in a moment." He ran inside and changed into the first decent pair of pants he found. He grabbed a pair of socks and placed them in his pocket. He put on his shoes without tying them, and he ran outside. "Ready to go." He backed the car out of the driveway and turned the wheel to drive forward.

Ann shouted out, "The bag is in the driveway!"

Bob placed the car in park and ran out to get the bag. He turned. "Okay. Here we go," Bob said enthusiastically.

It was Saturday morning, not quite six and still dark. There were no other cars on the road. They were on the highway driving over the speed limit with no fear of being stopped. Each time the car bounced, Ann screamed out in pain and annoyance. "Please watch those bumps. All this bouncing is putting pressure on my uterus." Then she shouted, "Hurry up, the pain hurts…Oooh! Take it easy! Don't make the car bounce!"

Excited and concerned, he said, "I can't do both. Hold on to the seat."

He drove to the hospital emergency entrance. There were two ambulances parked by the entrance. He paused, undecided to where to park. He parked along the side of the ambulances. Two paramedics wheeled a stretcher inside. "Wait here!" Bob said. "I'll be right back with a wheelchair." He ran through the door, chasing the paramedics looking for help. He ran into an orderly. "My wife is pregnant!" he said. "She's in labor! I need a wheelchair!"

"Calm down," said the orderly, realizing that this was a first-timer. "Can she walk?"

"No, she's in a lot of pain."

"Where is she?"

"Outside," Bob said, pointing.

"I'll get a chair."

Bob ran outside to the car. He opened the car door, and Ann was not there. He looked around dumbfounded.

The man approached with the wheelchair. "Where is she?" he asked.

Bob looked around. "I don't know! I left her here." He stared at the empty seat.

They entered the emergency room and spotted Ann sitting on a chair adjacent to a desk. An elderly woman was interviewing

Ann, giving all the particulars for admission. Bob walked to Ann and asked, "Why didn't you wait?"

"You went through the wrong door," Ann said. "You were in the supply section."

The woman smiled. "Okay, that completes everything. Please get in the wheelchair, and we'll take you up to the maternity ward."

Ann was in bed with a tube attached to her arm, a monitor to her stomach. Bob watched the digital movements of the monitor. "Oh, Bob, I'm so excited," Ann said. "It's going to be a boy, I know it, but I can't stand the pain."

Bob replied, "I just want a healthy baby."

Ann's doctor entered the room, observed the monitor, and examined her. "You're doing fine," he said, smiling. "We get you into the delivery room within a few minutes. Mr. Dorsete, do you still intend to be in the delivery room?"

"Yes!"

The doctor examined Ann's stomach. He pressed down gently. He moved back a couple of steps and turned to Bob. "Mr. Dorsete, follow me." They walked out of the pre-room. "Mr. Dorsete, your wife is having irregular labor pains. Her pelvis is expanding properly, but the baby, it's in a breech position. Please wait here. We are going to move her to the delivery room."

Bob nervously waited in the waiting room. Bob was devastated and frightened for Ann upon hearing that they would have to operate. They were going to perform a C-section. Bob was not prepared for this. The doctor informed him that this is quite normal. One in every four births is a C-section. It had been a long wait for Bob. It felt like an eternity. He felt depressed worrying about Ann being cut and thinking that they will never be able to have another child. The doctor entered the waiting area. He smiled and extended his hand to congratulate the proud father of a baby boy. Bob was exuberant that Ann and the baby were okay. Bob saw Ann in the recovery room. She was resting.

Bob watched as the nurse cleaned his son, took measurements, and recorded them. Bob thought that the baby was beautiful and felt proud. He left the hospital with a feeling of euphoria that he never experienced before. One that cannot be explained; it has to be experienced.

Ann spent seven days in the hospital after the birth of their first son. The operation had been painful and excruciating for her. She had difficulties walking, and it took her over a month before she could go up and down the stairs. It saddened Bob to see her in such pain. Ann was having a difficult time breastfeeding the baby. The baby had a tremendous appetite and would suck rapidly and hard. The baby changed the lives of Ann and Bob. Bobby Junior was six months old. Bob was in the kitchen, reading. Ann was in the bedroom, feeding the baby. She shouted out, "I can't take this anymore! He is driving me crazy!"

Bob entered the bedroom and asked, "What's the matter?" Without warning, she flung the baby at him. He reacted quickly to catch the baby. He cradled him close to his body, trying to quiet him down. She briskly left the room. Bob walked slowly, holding the baby close to his heart in an effort to stop the crying. Once the baby stopped crying, he went after Ann. She was sitting at the kitchen table with her face buried in her hands. Bob held the baby in one hand, and with the other, he grabbed her hair from the back. She gave out a scream. He tightly clenched her hair and, in an angry tone, said, "What the hell is the matter with you? You threw the baby at me. I could have dropped him."

Ann, frightened, started to sob. "I can't take it anymore. He's driving me crazy. I'll never have another baby."

Bob noticed that she was emotional and sad. "He's only a baby. He's our son. He's our responsibility."

"I haven't had a night's sleep for months," Ann said, weeping. "I'm up every three hours, feeding him."

"But I'm helping as much as I can. I need my sleep because I have to go to work in the morning."

"I know you're helping, and I appreciate it. But I'm doing it around the clock. He's always crying. He always wants to be held. My breast are so sore that I can't even wear a bra because it hurts my nipples."

"Okay, calm down. Why don't you supplement his feedings with the formula to alleviate the pain of your breast?"

"I love the baby. I know that he is ours. But I'm so tired. I don't have time for anything else. It's always the baby."

The baby started to cry. Bob raised him over his shoulder and gently patted his back. Bob felt sympathy for Ann. He didn't know what to say. It hurt him to hear her say that she will never have another child. He couldn't blame her after all she has been through. "Ann, I'll help you as much as possible. Rearing children is both our responsibility."

They made it through the first year, learning to be parents. Bob was earning a good paycheck, and Ann was working a couple of day per week as a teacher. They were happy and content. By the time their first child was two years old, they talked of having another child. A month after celebrating their first child's third birthday, Ann gave birth to their second boy. They named him Tony. Ann was disappointed that it was not a girl. She had another C-section, so they decided that this was their last child. Her recovery was slow but not as long as the first. The second child was not as demanding as the first. Maybe it was because they were more experienced as parents. Little Bobby accepted and loved his new baby brother. Ann and Bob were proud parents of two handsome boys.

They lived in a changing community, and the school system had diminished in quality. Bobby was a year away from starting school, and Ann was very adamant that she did not want her children to attend the city's schools. Their little house was now becoming crowded. Bobby slept in a tiny bedroom, and the baby's crib was in the master bedroom. Six months later, they purchased a house in the suburbs. It had three bedrooms, a full basement, and large grounds. It was an admirable community, suburbia America. Bob was doing well in his career, gaining a lot of experience and confidence. He was doing some traveling, and Ann was still working a couple of days a week. She enjoyed her job because it gave her the opportunity to socialize and make friends. She felt fulfilled both as a mother and having a career.

Tony was two years old. Ann consulted her doctor about having another baby. He assured her that it would be safe. Bob and Ann decided to have another child. Ann desperately hoped for a girl. A woman's fertile stage can vary from seven to ten days in between her menstrual cycles. Ann and Bob engaged in sex for the purpose of fertilizing an egg. After a month, Bob felt that it was more of a chore than pleasure. Ann was pregnant and happy that she was going to have a daughter.

It was cold and snowing outside but warm and cozy inside the Dorsetes' home. It was Sunday morning. Ann was in the kitchen, making breakfast, and Bob was in the next room, playing with the boys. Ann was interrupted by the sound of the telephone. "Bob!" called out Ann. "It's my brother, Frank. He wants to talk to you." Ann shakily handed him the phone.

"Please, come here, right away," said Frank Pellone. "They're at it again! They're fighting and chasing each other around the house with scissors. It's been going on all morning, I'm exhausted. I can't take this shit anymore."

"How about Uncle Lou?" Bob asked.

"He's not much help. He's yelling and chasing after them."

Bob, feeling helpless, could hear the shouting in the background. "There's a least six inches of snow on the ground and coming hard. It could take me over an hour to get there… Call the police?"

"I can't do that. It's my mother and aunt."

"Then I'll call the police."

"No! Don't!"

"But you're concerned that they might hurt each other. Can you stop them?"

"I don't know! I'll try," said Frank uncertain.

"Okay, I'll come over. It's going to take me some time. I have to get dress and clean the car. It is still snowing here, and I don't know about the conditions of the roads." Bob hung up the telephone.

Ann stood nervously, watching Bob. She asked, "How bad is it this time?"

"They're fighting. Frank can't stop them. I am going over."

"How about breakfast?"

"Just coffee. I'm going to start the car and clean off the snow." As Bob stepped outside, he noticed that the snow was coming down faster, and visibility was getting worse. He decided to call the police.

Rose Pellone was sixty-one, and her sister Mary was sixty-five. They had always been close. Rose did not drive and relied on Mary for transportation. They were both working part-time because of the lack of work. Most of seamstress worked had moved to the Carolinas. Rose appeared more like a hag with her unfixed hair and the ripped clothing she wore around the house. She was experiencing health problems—diabetes, cataracts of the eyes, and at times, some loss of memory. She was annoyed that she could not function the way she was accustom.

She kept it to herself, and it was difficult for her to cope that her last child was leaving her nest. His wedding was planned for this summer. She felt a void that she would not have any of her children living with her. She had been a committed and dedicated mother rearing three children alone. All her life, she was needed. Rose was only thirteen when her mother died, and she took care of her young brothers and sister.

Mary was overweight and bigger than Rose. Her husband died many years ago. Rose's children were like her own. She had helped rear them and had been a second mother to them. Rose felt in competition with Mary for the children's affection. Rose was constantly having verbal and physical fights with Mary. She accused Mary of taking her undergarments and other ridiculous items, moving things around to make everybody think that she was crazy and trying to take her children away from her. The arguments had escalated to fights. As the wedding was nearing, Rose had more setbacks and more fights with her sister. Frank Pellone had installed a bolt lock on Rose's bedroom door to safeguard her belongings.

Bob noticed the police car in the driveway as he neared the house. He ran to the door and rang the doorbell. Uncle Lou opened the door and said cheerful, "Well, hello! Come in quick before you catch a cold."

As he stepped inside, Mary shouted, "Why did you call the police? You had no right." She appeared exhausted with cuts on her face and arms.

"Calm down," said the large intimidating policeman with an oversized waistline. "I think you're nice people. There's no need for fighting."

"Thank you, Officer, for coming. I'm Bob Dorsete. I called."

"Well, I think they're all right now. Are you gonna be here for a while?"

"Yes, Officer."

"I'm not making a report. However, if I come again, I will." The policeman left.

"I told you not to call the police," said Frank harshly.

"I was concerned that someone would get hurt." Bob was a little annoyed but decided not to aggravate the situation. He left after all appeared to be calm.

After this incident, Bob called for a family meeting with Ann's brother and sister to discuss their mother's behavior. Ann's sister suggested that they commit her to an institution for observations and evaluations. Bob and Ann were adamant against committing Rose. Bob cared for Rose as if she were his mother. Bob suggested that Rose and Mary needed to be separated. Ann and her sister had children. They should take turns in having Rose stay with them. Rose would be around her daughters and grandchildren. Nothing was decided.

Rose Pellone spent the majority of her time with the Dorsetes'. She helped Ann with the cooking and cleaning. She enjoyed taking care and playing with the children. As much as Bob cared and loved Ann's mother, he felt he had very little privacy with Ann. However, he felt it was more important to help Rose. Frank's wedding was splendid. Bob was the best man, Ann was in the bridal party, and Bobby was the ring bearer. It was a happy occasion for the entire family. Rose Pellone looked attractive, and her mind was on the happiness of her son.

The fall was approaching. Ann was in her final month of pregnancy and had taken a one-year leave of absences from her job.

Her job was guaranteed for September the following year. Bob was recently laid off. He was feeling the pressure and responsibility of providing for his family and thinking of another mouth to feed. He desperately did everything he could to find work. They were on a tight budget. The little unemployment he received barely paid for the weekly expenses.

Ann was disappointed that she had a boy and displayed the tears in the delivery room. They could not agree on a name. Bob wanted to name the child after his father. Ann again refused. Bob was vexed that she named the child without his consent. Though he was annoyed, he did not want to upset her. It was Ann who went through the pain of delivery, and it was Ann who was more disappointment. Bob did not press the issue and accepted the name, but inside he was hurt.

With each passing week, Bob became more melancholy. He missed getting dressed in a suit and tie and doing something productive. He was starting to dislike the fact that Ann's mother was with them. He tried looking at the positive side: Rose was helpful and company for Ann, they had a healthy newborn, and Ann had recovered more quickly than the other two previous times. Ann was also depressed. She tried not to show her disappointment and gloominess. She kept her true feelings to herself. Ann tried to understand the pressure that Bob was under, and he tried the same for her. They both were entrenched with their own feelings of depression and despondency. They became less sensitive to each other's feeling, and they argued more frequently.

Bob was willing to take any kind of work. With each letter of rejection, he become more anxious. Ann was also looking for work. She had two job offers—a full-time position and a part-time tutoring position, starting in the new year. She did not want to work full-time. However, she did not want to put the total burden on Bob. She was troubled that Bob would insist that she take the full-time position. "I don't want to work full-time," Ann said.

"It's up to you," said Bob openly. "We sure can use the money, but I understand that you want to be with the baby. I'm also concerned about your mother. She could have a setback. I don't think that it's fair that we burden her as a full-time setter." Bob smiled. "Hey, something is better than nothing. It's your decision."

Ann was delighted. She was totally wrong to think that he would insist that she take the full-time position. She put her arms around him and said, "Thank you. I love you very much."

"What are you thanking me for?" said Bob, surprised.

"Ah, nothing."

Bob pressed, "I really want to know what you mean by that."

"Okay," said Ann reluctantly. "I thought you were going to force me to take the full-time position."

Bob was perplexed by her statement. "Why would I force you to do something you don't want to do? I listen to what you have to say."

Ann, smiling, feeling good, said, "And you thought I couldn't get a job. I had more calls for interviews than you did."

Bob was again surprised by her comments. "I have all the confidence in the world in you. I know you're smart. You're capable of doing anything you want to do." He showed a big grin on his face. "Except for beating me up." He grabbed her hands and held them tight.

Ann gave out a howl, "Hey, you're hurting me." She made a fist and gently struck his shoulder.

"You might be prettier and smarter than me, but I'm stronger than you are." He seized her to place his arms around her. Kissing her neck, he asked, "Now what did you mean about the comment that I didn't think that you were capable of getting a job?"

"Well, you know."

Bob questioned, "What do you mean I know?"

"Well, it's just…" Ann hesitated. "It's just the way you are so assertive and I'm just a teacher. Look how well you have done in your career, how you have advanced in responsibility. I can't make the kind of money you're capable of making."

Bob proudly said, "That's because I'm the breadwinner. I'm the man of the house. It's my responsibility."

"Well, it's other things too."

"Like what?" asked Bob.

"Well, every time we have problems, you have always resolved them. You're so smart the way you get things done. You do an outstanding job for your company."

Bob smiled. "But that's my job. What does it have to do with us?" He moved his arms to her waist. "Three children and you are still beautiful, and I still love you very much. I'm confused about what you are saying. I don't understand why you feel this way. I just want you to know I love you."

Ann embraced him, kissed his lips, and said, "I guess I was just being silly. I'll take the part-time job."

She held back from telling him that she felt subservient to him. It wasn't that Bob was bad or mistreated her. She felt that she was not as capable as him. She sometimes felt worthless. She was not trying to compete against him. She tried to submerge these feelings, but she could not help it. She was a woman with emotions. She also felt jealous that he had three sons and sometimes she felt out of place. Her involvement in their lives would be reduced as they would become older, she thought. She would have a secondary role to Bob. She noticed the bond that Bob had with them as he toilet-trained them and played with them. When Bob worked around the house, Bobby would try to imitate his father. As they would get older, they would spend more time with their father playing sports and doing other boy things. In time, he would have a closer bond with them than her. She felt cheated and wished for a daughter.

Ann and Bob had a simple Christmas with little to cheer for. They were still on a tight budget. They purchased small gifts for the boys and nothing for themselves. They looked forward to Marion Philip's visit tonight. He was coming to see their new baby. Marion was Bob's friends, but Ann had known him since she was seventeen years old. Bob looked up to Marion in some way as his mentor, his big brother. Bob had always kept a close contact with Marion. When Bob struggled in college, it was Marion who kept giving him the confidence that he could do it. Weekly, Bob would stop by Marion's store, and they would talk about everything. Bob was not embarrassed that he had a gay friend. He never saw Marion as gay but as a good friend who had been like a brother. Ann and Bob always enjoyed Marion's company and looked forward to having their cards read. From an educational and logical perspective, they thought it was nothing but a bunch of hocus-pocus. But some of his predictions had come true.

Marion complimented Bob and Ann on their new beautiful baby and how attractive and handsome the boys were. Marion read tarot cards for them. He told them that it would be several more months before Bob would find a job. Ann would have several job offers, and financially, they would be fine. Their love for each other was strong, and within the next eight months, their financial pressures would be a little easier for them to deal with. "I'm starting to feel confident about palm reading," said Marion.

"I didn't know that you were into that," Ann said.

"I been studying for some time. Let me see your palm." Marion delicately held Ann's hand and, with his fingers, followed the lines and studied their meaning. "Well, I see everything in your palm that I read in your cards, but I'm very puzzled about this line, the family line," said Marion in astonishment. "I'm looking at the line for children." He paused to look at Ann's face and said, "You had a baby girl some time ago."

Ann, shocked and horrified, looked at Bob. Then a moment later, in a choked voice, she said, "No."

"I feel confident in what I saw," said Marion in a puzzled tone asked. "Did you have a miscarriage?"

Ann stared at Bob and replied, "No."

Marion was perplexed. "I don't understand it. It shows here that you were pregnant four times, but you have three children. Maybe I'm wrong."

That evening, Bob and Ann were in their room, getting ready for bed. Ann was placing extra blankets on the bed. "Bob, I was shocked. I didn't know what to say."

"I was also embarrassed," said Bob. "I didn't know what to say. I hated to lie to Marion. What could I say?"

"God's punishing me," Ann said, dejected. "That's why I have three boys...because of the abortion."

Bob walked to her, put his arms around her, and said, "Don't think that way. That was a decision we made some time back. It was the right decision at the time."

"Perhaps it was," Ann said, shaking her head. "But it was wrong. I'm being punished for it. That's why I had to deliver by C-sections. That's why I have three boys… I killed my daughter." She started to weep.

Bob held her firmly. "Please don't cry. Don't make me feel bad. We have to accept what we did. Just be thankful for the three health boys we have."

She could not accept his reasoning; it was wrong. She did not respond. They got into bed without further discussion.

In January, Ann started her new job working four and a half hours per day, four days a week, as a special instructor. Rose watched the children. On the weekends, she returned to her house. Bob was still searching for full-time work. He worked the midnight shift as a forklift operator at a trucking company. He was on standby. He would call an hour before if there was work. He did not like the work nor the hours. It paid more than unemployed compensation, and he had the day for job interviews. They earned sufficient income to pay the monthly bills, yet they were both were feeling stressful and argued over little things.

Ann became more melancholic. There were days when she was in a deep depression, thinking and convinced that the baby she had aborted was a girl and she would never have a daughter. She didn't tell Bob her thoughts because she thought that he did not want to hear it and would say that she was being silly. He had other things on his mind. Bob was annoyed that he had no job offers. Ann complained that she missed her regular job and wished that she was home instead of working. Bob, weary of hearing her tribulations, in a loud voice, said, "You're a nag sometimes. Sometimes you piss me off. You complain about the winters being too cold, the summers being too hot, and the kids being too much for you to handle. You're an adult. I come home from work. I'm happy to be home. I'm happy to see you and the children, and the first thing out of your mouth is what a tough day you had. How you don't like your job."

Ann was intimidated by the tone of Bob's voice and his yelling. She became frightened. She wanted to quiet him down. "Bob, I love you very much… Please calm down. I know that you're under a lot of pressure."

"You're right." He noticed the frightened look of her face. He lowered the tone of his voice. "We both have been under a lot of pressure. I think we need to get away."

She was more at ease now. "Sometimes you frighten me. Your words sometimes cut worse than a knife."

He walked toward her and gently put his arms around her. He put his hands on both sides of her cheeks and looked into her eyes as he kissed her. "I love you very much. But you know this is the way I am…the way I vent. I say exactly how I feel. Please judge me by my actions, not my words. Perhaps you're right. Sometimes I do say horrible things."

Ann was overtaken by his words. "I have something for you. I was going to give it to you next week for Valentine's Day. Wait here." She went into their bedroom and returned with a card. It had a heart on the cover and written below.

Bob and Ann forever and ever. She opened it and read:

> Dear Bob,
>
> Happy Valentine's Day! Today is the day that lovers are supposed to express their love. Well, I just wanted you to know I love you just as much now, maybe even more than I did when we met. We have been through some very rough times and through some very happy times. We stayed together all the way through. We are now in a slump. I just wanted you to know that I love you very much, and I always will. I know that right now you are feeling very worthless. In my eyes, you are still very much a man. I have a lot of

respect for you. You are very responsible, loving, and ambitious. You are an excellent father. No matter what happens, I love you and will stick with you and try to support you. I am very lucky to be loved by such a wonderful person. Someday we will look back on this and remember what we went through and wonder how we did it. The most important thing is that we have each other and we have three beautiful, healthy boys. As long as we have that, we will be able to make it through anything. Remember, I love you, no matter rich or poor.

All my love,
Ann

Bob took the card from Ann's hand and looked at it. He was taken by her words. He put his arms around her and said, "I'm sorry. I love you very, very much." They kissed and hugged.

Rose noticed the stress and strain that Bob and Ann were experiencing. She suggested that they needed a break. Perhaps a weekend at the Poconos. Ann told her that was impossible since they were still on a tight budget. Rose suggested that go out some Saturday and that she would watch the children. They accepted her offer.

It was a warm April night. Ann wore a dress and underneath a garter belt and stockings. She was sure that Bob would be pleased. She enjoyed arousing him. They went to a nearby restaurant. In the beginning, neither one struck up any real conversation. They both acknowledged that it had been a while since they had been out alone. "I'm glad we have this night out," Bob said. "It's been a long time."

Ann smiled and said, "You're right. It has been a while since we had a date. Just the two of us. Last time it was just the two of us was our vacation to Hawaii."

"That was three years ago. Just the two of us. I loved Hawaii. I was so overwhelmed by it. It was beautiful."

"Yes, it was so beautiful and warm," acknowledged Ann. "The weather is the same all year long. No snow, sleet, or freezing weather. Oh, I would love to live in a place like Hawaii."

"It was beautiful, and so were you." He held her hand in his. "You looked attractive in your bathing suit. I got so turned on I could hardly wait to get you to bed."

Ann smiled, feeling content, and said, "Pretty soon it's going to be ten years that we've been married. I'm very happy that you still can't keep your hands off me."

"That's because you're so beautiful," Bob said, smiling. "Hey, how about taking a ride to our old necking grounds."

"Sure!" Ann said with a gleam. "Why not?"

They drove to the place where they had spent many nights before they had a place of their own. As he parked the car, Ann said, "This brings back a lot of memories."

"It sure does." Bob said as he laughed. "Boy, we were crazy kids. How many times did we try doing it in the car? I was so turned on, and you were so nervous. I had to keep peeking to make sure that no one approached the car. Every time you heard a sound, I stopped to look around and reassure you that it was okay."

"You're right. I was very nervous. Now that I think about it, it was kind of exciting."

They stepped out and walked around holding hands. They walked toward the terrace wall. It was near dusk, and they could see the lights below and across the way, the lights of lower Manhattan. They decided to walk. They entered the woods walking on the small dirt path. They stopped and looked around. No one was around. They were surrounded by trees. It was almost dark. Bob put his arms around her and gently kissed her lips. Their lips pressed hard as his hands moved all over her breast, crotch, and buttocks. She unbuttoned his shirt and touched his well-defined chest. She stared at his hard-upper abdomen and explored the hair running from his chest to his belly. She stroked and intertwined the hair with her fingers and kissed his chest. They embraced tightly and kissed hard. Ann, breathing heavy, whispered, "You excite me. It's been a long time. Make love to me."

Bob looked into her eyes. "We can go home to our nice comfortable bed."

She closed her eyes, kissed his lips, and gently bit his ear. She whispered, "This brings back a lot of memories. It excites me. Let's do it here."

Ann backed up against a tree. Their bodies pressed hard as they moved in rhythm. He squeezed her tightly, his chest against her breast. He slowly lifted her dress, moved his hand between her thighs, and rubbed her crotch, gently at first, then pressed hard and tender. He placed his hand between her red bikini panties and gently poked his finger inside her. He dug deeply into the flesh. She moaned in delight. He stopped to squeeze and rhythmically stroke her crotch. Her breathing became deeper and more rapid as she muttered, "Make love to me!" In a weak, excitable whisper, she said, "Fuck me, baby." She undid his zipper, grabbed his hard erect penis, and with her entire hand, squeezed it firmly. "I love you, I love you. Give it to me. I want it."

Bob seized her panties, pulled vigorously to tear them off. He made a passage. He placed his penis between her thighs. With his hands, he held her head, pressed his lips against hers, and placed his tongue into her mouth. His penis was between the lips of her lira. She placed the hard hot human rod by her moist passage. Gently, he thrust forward as he entered her wet vagina. He pushed her hard against the tree, penetrating deep inside. Ann's breathing become heavier with each pounce as she moaned and grunted. She lifted her legs and wrapped them around him for more of him. Her mouth was opened wide, and her nostrils expanded as she struggled for more air. Her moaning changed to loud screaming. Bob quickly put his hand over her mouth and whispered, "Not so loud. There might be someone around."

Satisfied and exhausted, Ann said, "I couldn't help it… It felt so good… It's been a long time since I have felt this excited."

Bob, smiling, said, "You're crazy."

Smiling, she said, "I'm your sex nymph. I'm for you anytime."

A year later, Bob, was hired by Bennix, and Ann was teaching three days a week. The days she worked, she had to drop off the two older boys at a friend's house, and from there, they would go to school. Chuck was two years. Ann would drop off Chuck at a babysitter near her workplace. Bob watched as Ann walked in her bra and bikini underwear. He thought, *How sexy she looks.* At thirty-five, she was just as beautiful as she had been at twenty-three when they were married.

If I didn't have to go to work, I would grab her, throw her on the bed, and make love to her.

"Oh, shoot," Ann said in an annoyed tone.

"What's the matter?" Bob asked.

"I don't have a blouse to go with these slacks."

"Are you okay? You seem uptight this morning."

Ann did not answer. Bob slowly walked toward her, gently took her hands, and kissed them. "Are you okay, beautiful lady? You look really sexy in your undies."

Ann smiled and said, "Not now, I have to go to work."

"You're right." He kissed her and walked out to warm up the cars. The days she worked were hectic for her, and Bob tried helping her as much as possible.

Bob was back inside and noticed that the boys were not fully clothed. He shouted upstairs, "Ann, what's the matter? It's getting late. Do you need some help?"

Ann yelled back, "I can't find a blouse to match my slacks."

Bob yelled back, "You're still looking for a blouse! What's the matter?"

"Nothing. I'm okay. I'm just running a little late. I'll be okay. Go ahead, you go to work."

Bob was happy with his new job. He enjoyed the work and the people. But today he could not concentrate on his job. All day long, his thoughts were of Ann. It wasn't like her. She usually has everything in order, her clothes for the next day, the clothing for the boys. However, this morning she was running late and appeared nervous. Bob and Ann parenting three young boys was a full-time job—bathing at nighttime, bedtime stories, all day Saturday laundry, watching children's moves, half-a-day grocery shopping. Socializing was with family on birthdays and holidays and less with friends. Bob was involved in coaching Bobby in soccer.

Bob felt that he and Ann had little time for each other for dialogue that did not involve the house or the children. With each additional child, it required more time for nourishing and caring. Their private time had become less spontaneous and required advance appointments. And when they didn't have sex, they cherished the little time alone before sleeping. Ann enjoyed when he removed her underclothing and massaged her back and buttocks. She, in turn, would rub and scratch his back. They would hug and kiss and told each other how much they loved each other. He never doubted her love. Yet he wondered if all was right. He knew that when a woman says that nothing is wrong, there is something wrong. It wasn't like her. He truly loved her, and he was concerned.

Ann enjoyed her teaching job. She was home a couple of hours before Bob. That gave her time to pick up the boys and prepare dinner. It was a warm April evening; they took the boys to the park to enjoy the fresh sweet air of the blooming trees. They took the boys to the Jungle Jim section. The boys were having a good time running through the tubes and playing on the log-bridge steps. Ann and Bob took turns holding their little son. Bob turned to Ann and asked, "Are you okay?"

"Yes."

"You weren't yourself this morning. You were like a chicken without a head. I can tell. This morning and other times, your head is shaking back and forth. What's the matter?"

"You don't want to hear it. We've talked about it before."

Bob was astonished. "What do you mean 'I don't want to hear about it'? I love you. I'm your husband. Tell me what's bothering you."

"It's Delaney," Ann said in a very subdued voice.

"Now what?"

"He wants to make my position a full-time position. I love my job, but I also want to be a mother. I like working part-time. It breaks up the week. I don't want to work full-time."

Bob raised his voice a little and said, "Look, babe, I'm getting worn out of this. We've been through this many time. I've been telling you for months. I earn enough money. You don't have to work. You're letting this thing get to you. You're letting it eat you up inside that you can't think clearly. You're all tense. I hate to see you like this."

"That's why I didn't want to mention it to you," she said, saddened. "I know that you're tired of hearing of it, but I can't help it. It bothers me. I don't want to lose my job. I like my job. I have friends that I enjoy socializing with. But I love my children. I don't want to raise them like my mother did. My mother raised us working full-time. I hated coming home to an empty house."

"I know that," Bob said softly. "I hate repeating myself, but it's making you a nervous wreck. Your head is always shaking. I'm getting more concerned about it. I want you to find out why. See a neurologist or a psychologist to find out why."

"It's just a nervous twitch. That's all it is."

Bob gently kissed her cheeks and lips. "I love you too much. I don't want to see anything happen to you. You're getting nervous for nothing. Wait for the year to end. If it happens, then worry about it. But please stop worrying about it now."

"I know you're right," Ann said, trying to be honest. "But I can't help it."

"You get nervous too easily. We don't need the money. Stop worrying about it."

"I'll try."

"Here I thought you were upset because I didn't want another child."

Ann was saddened. "That too."

It was a month before the end of the school year. Ann was happy and relieved that the status of her teaching position did not change. Her principal, Mr. Delaney, told her that he was very satisfied with her work and that he wanted and hoped that she would return in September. Ann saw a neurologist. He told her that it was just a minor nervous twitch. He recommended mild tranquilizers. Ann refused to take them, concerned that she had three children to care for. She did not want to be impaired by any kind of medication. Her body had other manifestations. After three births, she knew. She decided not to mention it to Bob until she was certain.

Ann and Bob had just left the office of Ann's obstetrician. They were both in deep thought and silent as Bob drove. Ann was the first to speak. "I want to have this baby."

"I don't know," Bob said sadly. "I'm concerned for you having a fourth C-section. I want you healthy. I need you. I don't want to see you in any kind of risk."

"What risk?" she asked. "I'm healthy. It's been over two years since the last birth."

"Four C-sections! I don't know. It's the way your doctor said that this is the last. He suggested that you have your tubes tied."

Ann, smiling, said, "He said that four C-sections is not uncommon, and he doesn't anticipate any complications."

"I never heard of anyone having four cesareans. I'm very satisfied to have three healthy, handsome boys. I want our children to have a quality life. I want to be able to spend time with them. I also want time for us. I don't know if I want to go through another pregnancy, being up late at night and changing diapers. Another child means less time for you and me. I was hoping, now that the boys are getting older, that you and I could start going out alone. However, with another infant, it means another three years of being tied inside. You know how hard it is to get a babysitter for three young children. It will be worse for four."

Ann, reaching for his hand, said, "I understand all that. I desperately want a daughter. You have your sons, but I don't have a daughter."

"Ann, there's no guarantee that it's going to be a girl. I hate to see you go through another disappointment. Are you up for it? Can you face it? How are you going to feel afterward? Look how disappointed you were when Chuck was born. For months, you feeling highs and lows, mostly lows."

"I know, but I feel strongly that this is a girl. I don't want another abortion," Ann said sternly.

Bob slowed down, pulled to the side and stopped the car. "I understand you feeling strongly against abortion." He looked at her and softly said, "But seriously, think about it. What if it's another boy?"

Ann smiled. "I'm confident it's going to be a girl."

"But if it's a boy?"

Ann replied, "I will love the baby and accept it if it's a boy."

"If that's the way you feel, we'll have the baby."

Ann put her arms around him, gave him a kiss, and said, "Bob, I love you very much. I'm so happy to have you for a husband."

Bob continued to drive, and all he could think about was how much he hoped that Ann was being honest and, for her sake, that it would be a girl.

The Dorsete family were outside the airport terminal. They removed their coats as they marveled over the sight of palm trees and the bright, warm afternoon sun of late February. They were excited at their first sight of California. They were enthusiastic and happy to leave behind the cold winter of the east, the snow, the frigid winds, and freezing wind chill. Ann believed it was the closest she would ever get to paradise or Hawaii. Ever since her vacation to Hawaii, she often thought of the bright flowers, comfortable weather, and blue ocean. When Bob mentioned a possible promotion to California, she immediately responded with a yes. He told her that the happiness of his family was more important; the choice was hers. Bob cautioned her to think carefully about moving away from their friends and family. He told her, "Once we move, I don't want you to have any second thoughts or regrets." Ann, with no hesitation, said, "California is the closest I will ever get to Hawaii. Let's go."

It had been a hectic and exhilarating three months. Ann had little time to reflect on her fourth son. She was too preoccupied with the move to California. They would have to wait ten days for the arrival of their furniture. Bob took the first three days off from work to spend time with the family at Disneyland. After the third day, Bob showed Ann their new house. It was a big two-story building with five bedrooms. Bob hoped that the house would be to Ann's liking. As they entered the house, Ann was taken by the cathedral ceiling and the open staircase to the second floor. Bob gave them a tour of the house, inside and outside. Ann was reserved and did not make any comments.

"So what do you think?" Bob asked. Ann did not answer as she searched around. Bob was bothered by her silence. "What do you think of the giant kitchen? Let me show you all the counter space." Ann followed Bob into the kitchen. He noticed the blank expression of her face. Trying to cheer her up, he said, "The boys seem to like the house." They were outside running around the pool. Ann did not reply. "What's the matter? Don't you like the house? I know that it needs some work to personalize it."

Ann looked around and sighed, "You took me three thousand miles for this? In New Jersey, I had a brand-new kitchen, including the dishwasher and stove."

Bob replied, "They are not that old. They just need a good cleaning."

"So I have to spend the first week on my knees cleaning the appliances?"

Bob displeased in hearing that. "But look at the potential. With four children, we would need a bigger house."

Ann turned her head to look around. "I liked my house back East."

"Goddammit!" Bob said, annoyed. "What did you expect from me? I worked my balls off for the past months, finding this house, renting the property in New Jersey, getting things situated here. This is the thanks I get. I spent weeks cleaning and painting this place." He raised his voice in disgust. "Who the hell needs this bullshit?" He turned and walked away. He went into one of the bedrooms and lay down on the floor. He was weary and hurt.

Ann did not chase after him. She stayed in the kitchen, glancing outside, reflecting on the past six days and living in motels. She became melancholy as she thought of her former house, friends, and family. She felt homesick but could not tell Bob. She had to get out.

"Bob, let's go!" Ann shouted out. "The children are hungry. Let's get something to eat."

Bob was reluctant and slow in moving. He felt hurt and did not want to talk to her. They quietly left the house, and Bob avoided making eye contact with her. They stopped at the first fast-food restaurant. The boys eat happily except for Bob and Ann.

Once they arrived at their motel, Bob said, "You and the boys get out."

"Where are you going?" Ann asked, surprised.

"None of your business. Just leave me the hell alone."

Ann made no comment, realizing that he was annoyed. She took the children and made her way to the rooms. Bob stopped at a bar. He drank briskly to wash the hurt and pain of feeling unappreciated.

The twelve days in transit were becoming more difficult for Ann. Bob was at work, and she was alone with the boys. With each day, the boys became bored because there was little to do in the motel. Ann became tensed. She called Bob daily to express how difficult it was for her, and she couldn't wait for the furniture to arrive. Bob kept reassuring her that the furniture would be arriving shortly, telling her to be patient. (Bob had been informed that the driver took a three-day layover at his home in Missouri). They had stopped going to quality restaurants for dinner because the boys did not like the wait and become jittery. The boys gawked at the fancy garnishing and vegetables, so they slowly would pick their plates. They hated the smell of fish. The baby would cry out. Once back at the motel, the boys complained of feeling hungry. Bob had to go out in search of a fast-food restaurants. They had to settle for family restaurants and fast-food types. The boys were happy with simple hamburgers and French fries.

In the months to follow, Ann was making the adjustment of her new home and neighborhood. She appreciated her large, spacious house. As the fall passed, she felt comfortable, and as the winter approached, she was happy to be in California. Bob and Ann were at the park. Ann was in shorts and a skimpy top. The children were running and playing. Ann said, "I'm happy to be here. It's so pretty with the flowers all over the place, and there's no sign of winter. If we were back east, we would be wearing coats and preparing for the snow, sleet or freezing weather. Here it is January. We're in shorts." She tightly put her arms around Bob and said, "I love you very much. I'm happy, and so are the boys."

By the second year, Bob and Ann made the adjustment to California lifestyle. They were happy and comfortable in their home. He was happy with his job and the challenges. The boys were actively involved in sports—soccer in the fall, basketball in the winter, and baseball in the spring. Ann and Bob were popular in the community because of Bob's involvement as a coach. He was well-liked for his exceptional coaching ability and in dealing with the kids.

Bob had a close bonding with his older boys. They played together, talked sports, and watched games together. Ann was bored by sports. She sometimes felt that she was not important in their lives. She felt a little jealousy that Bob had the four boys and she didn't have a daughter. She told Bob on many occasions. He encouraged her to get more involved and to participate in sports with them. She wanted a daughter so badly and remembered his words of caution. She tried to put these feelings aside and accept the fact that she would never have a daughter.

She made efforts to get more involved in the boys' sports activities. She joined housewife's sports activities. At first, she was very apprehensive. But with time, she enjoyed the running and competitiveness. It was the first time in her life that she had ever enjoyed sports. The women played soccer, basketball, and volleyball. She expressed to Bob her desire to possibly coach their youngest boy when he starts to participate in sports. Bob encouraged her, saying that he would assist her.

Chapter 10

It was a warm, clear night. Tom Connelly was outside his house, drinking beer and listening to music. He was feeling uneasy, awaiting the arrival of Bob Dorsete. Wearing only cutoff shorts. He paced in and out of the darkness of his garage. He had mixed feelings about Bob moving in. His wife, Liz, did not like the idea. Tom had insisted that Bob come stay with them; he had no other place. Tom looked up to Bob because he was educated, a family man, and a good father. Tom envied Bob and wished he had those things, but he was not jealous of him. He knew that Bob had worked hard and earned those things. Bob had been kind to him, always advising him and criticized him with cause. He had to help his friend, the older brother that he never had.

Tom was reared in Chicago (Irish father, Italian mother) in a predominately Irish/Italian neighborhood. At a young age, he was forced to work in his father's liquor store. His father had a habit of drinking and getting intoxicated and abusive. Tom despised and feared his father. At nineteen, he enlisted in the army. He had the opportunity to travel all over the world. After three years, he returned home and worked for his father. His father was still abusive. Tom feared confrontation with him since so he reenlisted in the army and served mostly in California. Tom had highs and lows in the army. He did get some technical training.

After a four-year enlistment with the army, he resigned and stayed in California. He attended a technical school learning to repair and built electrical components. He was hired by Bennix as a test equipment technician. He was married to an illegal alien, Liz.

Their marriage was based on a mutual agreement for her to obtain a green card, and he would have a steady bed partner. They gradually learned to respect and care for each other to some degree. Liz was more mature and less reckless with the spending of money.

At Bennix, Bob had helped Tom prepare financial statements for the purchase and justification of test equipment. From small conversations, their relationship slowly grew into a friendship. Tom liked doing physical work and had helped Bob in the maintenance of his house. He enjoyed going over to the Dorsetes' house to eat good Italian food and to play with the Dorsete boys.

A year ago, Tom was daily engaging in verbal arguments with his co-workers. One late afternoon, Bob called Tom into his office. Bob, in a calm voice, said, "Please sit down." Tom quietly sat down and watched Bob as he closed the door. Bob slowly made his way to his high-back chair. He sat back, placed his feet on the top of the desk, and said, "I am not your boss. I am your friend. What is going on? You're getting a bad rap. Your mouth is getting you in trouble. This 'F you' and 'F everybody' stuff is not appropriate in this environment. It's not the army.'"

"It's not me," Tom said defensive.

"Your boss mentioned that he is ready to write you up."

"Well, fuck him!"

Bob sat forward and looked directly into Tom's eyes. "What's going on? I know that sometimes we bring our personal problems to the job, and sometimes we take our work problems home. What's going on?"

Tom was trying to find the words. "My father passed away a couple of weeks ago. My mother and sister are pissed that I did attend the funeral."

Bob looked at his watch and said, "You know it's quitting time. Do you want to leave or continue our conversation?" Tom shrugged his shoulders. "Better yet, let's go for a drink. I'm buying."

They went to a nearby bar. It was a blue-collar's bar with two small pool tables and a strong fragrance of stale beer. The decor was old, dilapidate, and in need of repairs. They found two seats at bar and ordered a couple of beers. They were served by a female bartender. She was dressed in snug shorts and a tight-fitting low-cut top. Every time she bent over, she exposed a large portion of her enormous breasts. Tom's eyes and attention was fixed on the bartender's healthy chest. With a gleam in his eyes, he smiled with content. He wiggled his eyebrows up and down and said, "Do you like that? She's got some chest."

Bob did notice but did not stare. He wanted to focus on their conversation. "Come on!" Bob grabbed Tom's elbow. "Let's move to a table."

They picked up their drinks and went to a table. They sat on wobbly chairs. Bob, probing, asked, "How is your mother taking your father's death?"

Reluctantly, Tom said, "She's okay."

"Why didn't you go to his funeral?"

Tom shrugged his shoulders and said, "I don't know." He paused to drink. "I couldn't stand the asshole. I hated him. He did mean things to me and mistreated my mother. Sometimes, he got so drunk that he would throw things around the house. He would call my mother "a whore and a lazy Italian guinea." He would yell and scream at me, call me lazy. He used to say that I didn't know shit and how could he have such a dumb son. One time…" He paused to lay his hand on the table. "See this scar?" he said pointing to the back of his hand. "He told me to stick out my hand. He grabbed it and took his cigarette and pressed it hard against my hand. I have this scar to remind me of him. As soon as I was old enough, I left home. After my first hitch, I returned home. I tried to get along with him." Bob thought of his father. "The bastard didn't change…always drunk."

"Do you have any good memories of your father? Did you ever have a good time with him? Was he ever nice to you?"

Tom said in a hostile tone, "Sometimes! He tried to make up for all the bad shit he did to me."

"How!"

"Well, he took me fishing to Florida. We saw a couple of Notre Dame games." A slight smile creaked in. "Once, at the Florida Keys, I caught this big fish. He was so proud of me. He said that the fish was the biggest he ever saw."

Bob felt a little jealous. "You're lucky. My father was poor and truly an old man when I was growing up. We never did things together until I was an adult."

Tom continued, "When I graduated from high school, he bought me a brand-new car."

"You lucky son of a gun! What kind?"

"T-bird. Well, I worked for him all those years, and he never paid me."

"He gave you a place to live. He prepared a home."

"Yeah, but he was a mean bastard."

Bob, with a serious face, looked at Tom. "I'm not a psychologist, but I think you're feeling guilty because you never made peace with your father. You didn't go to his funeral." Eyes were getting watery. "My father passed away a year ago, so I understand. When my father passed away, I was at peace with myself. As a teenager, I disliked my father because he was different from other fathers. He didn't speak English, and he was old-fashioned. He never came to any of my games. But when I became a father, I started to understand what it is to be a parent. The responsibility of bringing a newborn in the world." Bob paused. "They are beautiful but very demanding. The night feedings, the crying, and diapers." He placed his hand on Tom's shoulder. "Then I started to appreciate my parents. Six months after my first child, I thanked my parents for putting up with me, for raising me, and for their love. When my father passed away, I was saddened but at peace with myself because, as an adult, I was there for my father and mother. Despite our philosophical differences, we began to understand and respect each other as best as a father and son could ever do. I believe that you have to make peace with your father."

Tom, with a bewildered look on his face, asked, "How do I do that? He's dead!"

Bob paused. He took a drink and said, "It's a tough one." He took another drink. "You're right. Your father is dead. You can't make peace with him; however, you can make peace within yourself." He paused to read Tom's face. "Get all this anger that you have for him out. Try understanding his actions, and perhaps you'll come to love him. You don't know what it's like to be a father. You don't have any children. It's difficult. No one goes to school to be a parent. It's on-the-job training. Parents make mistakes. My boys are young now. Once they become teenagers, we are going to have disagreements and arguments. But my intent is to do the very best I can."

"Well, I've seen what kind of father you are. You're the kind of father I wish I had. You don't get drunk. You're always playing with them."

Bob interrupted, "I'm not apologizing for your father. I'm not making excuses for him. All I'm saying is, try to understand the responsibilities that he had. I don't care how mean he was. He never abandoned his family. He was a good provider. He tried to spend time with you. Every father at one time or another is disappointed in his children. Maybe your father was unhappy. Maybe he was unhappy with your mother. But the fact is, he never left her. Did he run around with other women?"

Tom was feeling a little confused. "Not to my knowledge."

"You see? There are positive things about your father. Don't just look at the negative."

Tom never forgot that conversation. From that day on, he viewed Bob as a big brother. Shortly thereafter, he understood what Bob was trying to say. He found some kind of peace with himself and his father. He no longer blamed his father for his problems. He called his mother and apologized for not being at the funeral. He told her that he loved her and invited her to California.

Tom saw headlights of a car pulling into the driveway. The driver got out. Tom slowly walked to the car. He embraced Bob and said, "Hey, man, I want you to know that I feel bad. We got the room all set up."

"Thanks, Tom," Bob said in a hollow voice. "I appreciate you and Liz allowing me to stay here."

"You want something to eat?"

Shaking his head, Bob said, "No thanks. Help me bring in my things." Bob had taken with him two suitcases, a radio, tapes, books, and a box with documents. In addition, a gallon of wine, a liter of Scotch, and a carton of cigarettes.

"I hope the room is okay," said Tom. "We had a border once." He placed the suitcases on the floor and reached into his pocket. "Here's the house key. Liz goes in and out of the house. I would appreciate it if you would park your car in the street." Bob surveyed the large room. It had two small beds, two large windows over the beds, and a small window on the opposite side. Tom noticed the disappointed look on Bob's face. He knew that Bob was under a lot of stress.

"I have a house. Now I have a room. Why?" said Bob, distressed.

"I don't know." Tom was thinking of how Bob had changed this past year, short-tempered with the children. "I didn't tell you before. But the week before we went to New Jersey, Ann made a comment that if it wasn't for the children, she would leave you."

"Believe me, I didn't hit her or the boys." Bob was annoyed at himself. "I stopped loving her. I was just so angry. She's scared and confused. She doesn't know what she's doing. I know that she snapped."

"Hang in there, buddy. I want you to know, I'll help you any way I can." He moved closer to Bob and placed his hand on Bob's shoulder. "Hang in there. Maybe she'll change her mind."

Bob unpacked his suitcases. He started to feel sorry for himself and thinking that he had reached a crossroad of his life that led nowhere.

Two days after Bob left the residence, Ann Dorsete and the boys returned to their house. They had been away for more than forty-five days. Ann was delighted to be back in her big spacious house. The shelter had been cramped and crowded for her and the boys. She was happy to be back in her own kitchen. The boys hated the shelter and missed their home, friends, and swimming pool. The boys immediately ran to their rooms and started playing with their toys and games. Mark walked throughout the house in search for his daddy. Ann was a bit apprehensive and concerned that Bob would violate the restraining orders. Worse yet, he might physically hurt her. Ray Ditler had assured her that he would be on the lookout for Bob. He had changed all the locks on the doors. She walked throughout the

"Well now, he could. I'm telling you this for your own safety. Your father will get better, but now we have to stay away from him. We have rules to follow." Bobby and Tony motioned their heads in acknowledgement.

As Ann was preparing for bed, she thought of Bob. He might break in the middle of the night. She examined every window to make sure that the locks were in place. She placed chairs in front of the doors. The only place that she was concerned about was the side garage door. It only had one lock. When they went on long trips, Bob had barricaded the door. She did the same. She lay in bed, trying to sleep, but her mind was on Bob and her fear of him. Although she didn't like the shelter, at least there she felt safe. She tried to assure herself that she was safe for the night. *But what happens tomorrow or the next day? If I go out shopping or simply outside the house. The children alone in the park. Supposing he comes by and abducts them? What would I do then?* These thoughts tremendously frightened her. She was interrupted by the sound of tiny footsteps. It was Mark. He quietly entered the room and climbed onto the bed. Without saying a word, she kissed and hugged him. For the past weeks, he had slept with her. Ann turned to kiss him again, feeling love and compassion for him and the other children, feeling strong with her children around her. She finally fell asleep.

It was a splendid late July morning caused by the strong bright sun. Bob Dorsete was outside the post office, awaiting the arrival of Ann. He was dressed in casual shorts, a tank top, and sunglasses. He was looking forward to finally seeing her alone. He hoped that perhaps she would have the boys with her. He nervously surveyed the parking lot. His hands were trembling, and the perspiration was forming on his shoulders. It had been almost a week since he left his home.

Ann and Bob had agreed to meet to sign the termination lease for the restaurant. Bob had wanted to meet at the house, but Ann refused and demanded to meet at the local post office. He had no choice. He spotted her, and his eyes followed the car as she parked. Ann walked toward Bob, holding Mark's hand. She wore tight-fitted shorts, skin-firm blouse detailing her bra and large sunglasses. They were within twenty feet of each other when Mark recognized Bob, and he shouted out, "Daddy! Daddy!" and he went running to his father.

Bob picked him up, hugged him, and smothered him with kisses. "I love you. I missed you so much." Bob couldn't hold back his tears. He turned toward Ann and noticed a glimpse of a smile on her face. He thought that she was pleased to see Mark happy. Bob asked, "How are you doing?"

She replied, "Fine," and quickly said, "I don't have much time. I brought an envelope. Let's sign the papers." They went inside the post office, signed the papers, and mailed them.

"Ann, please," Bob said, hesitating. "Let's talk. Let's talk about this whole thing."

"It's too late." She took a breath and held back her tears, forgetting Mark for an instant. She snapped back, "Do you know what a mess you left the house? All the bills. None of the bills have been paid for months. The gas, the electric, the mortgages, and we still have bills coming in from the restaurant."

"How much money are you talking about?"

"Over seven thousand."

"Can we get together to review them?"

"No!" In a controlled tone, she said, "I'll send you a list."

Bob ruefully said, "You have all the money. You cleaned out the savings and checking accounts."

Aggravated, she said, "It cost me money to live at the shelter. Whatever cash I had, I gave to my attorney." She showed a little sadness. "We got a letter from the mortgage company that we have to pay the mortgage in a week or face foreclosure."

"I can borrow against my credit cards."

Ann was delighted to hear this and asked, "When can you get the money?"

Bob was happy that she was receptive to him. "Follow me to the bank to make the withdrawal and deposit."

Ann in reserve paused then said, "No. You go to the bank by yourself and give me a call when the money is in the checking account."

"Ann, please…let's talk."

"I'm sorry, I don't have time. I have things to do." She picked up Mark, turned, and walked out.

Bob stood, uncertain of what to say or do. He chased after her, shouting, "Ann, let me carry Mark." He caught up to her and picked up Mark. "Ann, please give me a chance," said Bob, pleading. "I'm not the same without you. No one can make me feel like you do. I love you. I realize that I made mistakes… Please give me a chance."

Ann stopped. Feeling strong and confident, she turned to face him and said, "I've changed. I'm not the same person. I don't think you'll like me the way I am." She felt her newfound strength. "I'm not the same little puppet you thought I used to be for you to control and to dominate."

Bob, for fear of saying the wrong thing, was lost for words. "Please, think about it. Why can't we talk? Please give me a second chance." She grabbed Mark and turned to walk. Bob followed, pleading. She continued walking. She opened the door and entered the car. Bob again asked, "Ann, please think about it!"

"You get help. I'll think about it." Ann turned the key, shifted into drive, and drove off. It gave her immense satisfaction to see and hear him beg.

That night, Bob could not get Ann out of his mind. He thought how sexy she looked in the tight shorts and blouse. She appeared pleased when he embraced Mark. He debated with the thought of calling her. He had reservations about it. After all, there was a restraining order against him not to disturb her peace. He logically thought that she broke the restraining orders by calling him and meeting him at the post office. So he felt confident there would be no danger in making a phone call. He called the house, and to his surprise, she had installed an answering machine. He left a message expressing his love, how sorry he was. He understood the pain that she went through, and he did not want a divorce. She never picked up the telephone. He called every night and left a message stating how much he missed her and the boys and how badly he wanted to see them. And for her to call him back.

A week later, Bob received the list from Ann. He was amazed at how quickly the restaurant bills had accumulated. The rent alone was over three thousand dollars. Using the bills as an excuse, he decided to call her. He nervously dialed the number and wondered if Ann would talk to him. He got the recorder, and he proceeded to say, "Ann, please pick up the phone. I am only calling to discuss the bills."

Ann picked up the phone and calmly said, "It's me."

"Have you gotten my previous messages?"

"Yes," she said coldly.

Bob hesitated, then said, "I was hoping you would call me."

"I don't want to talk to you."

"Please, hear me out." He tried holding back the emotions. "I'm hurting. You're hurting me. This whole thing is very painful. I love you and the children so much."

"You hurt me really bad," replied Ann. "If you love us, you wouldn't have done what you did."

"I didn't mean it. Whatever I did, it was the pressure and thoughts in my head. I was all stressed out."

Ann interrupted, "You called regarding the bills. Let's talk business."

"I can't believe all these bills. Did you get the check from the restaurant?"

"I gave it to my lawyer." She paused, waiting for a sarcastic remark. "If you agree, we use the funds to pay the bills."

"Yes, I agree. Let's pay all bills." Bob paused. He sensed that Ann was feeling a little bit more comfortable now that the bills were going to be paid. He nervously asked, "Can we see a marriage counselor?"

"No. I want a divorce. For over fifteen years, you treated me like shit."

Bob remorsefully said, "Maybe, I have in the past year. You have always been my catalyst. You were the one that gave me the motivation for working hard, going to school. You were my reason for—"

Ann interrupted, "I don't want to hear that. If you want to talk about business, I'll talk to you."

"You want to talk business," Bob said, annoyed. "Ray was hired by Bennix. He is making money from us." She did not reply. Bob continued, "How's Ray doing? How often do you see him?"

"I'm very busy. I don't have time to socialize," said Ann, offended. "I am going to hang up."

"Don't. Please listen," Bob said, trying not to upset her. "What have you done regarding the sale of the house?"

"I'd like to sell the house on our own without getting a real estate person involved to save money." Ann, feeling strong and poised, said, "I want to make you an offer so that we could resolve things and save money regarding the properties. You take the house in New Jersey and give me this house."

In a half-chuckle, he said, "That's not fair. There's more equity in the house in California."

"I have the children to raise."

"Why can't we raise them together? After all, I am their father."

Ann, in a cross tone, responded, "Yes, you're the father, but you're a sick person. You were teaching the boys to be violent. I don't want you raising them. They never listen to me because you always belittle me in front of them."

Bob was not sure what to say. The echoes of her voice were wistful and pugnacious at times. Bob implored, "I'm hurting all over. I miss you and the boys very much."

She snapped back, "Well, you hurt me for a long time. For many years, you made me feel so small about myself. I want my independence. I want to feel good about myself."

Bob sensed the impasse and held back the tears. "I did everything for you. I love you."

Ann sobbed. "I wanted to be treated like a princess."

"You were my queen. I always cared for you."

"No, you were selfish. You did everything for yourself!" Ann yelled. "You controlled me like a little girl. You wanted me to be your puppet. I don't need you! I don't want you! I don't love you!"

In a low voice, Bob said, "Please, can we get together? I don't want a divorce. A divorce will make us enemies. By the time it's over, we're going to hate each other."

She was not touched by his words. "You need help. Go to that place for violent behavior. Get yourself cured, and maybe after the divorce, maybe, I'll remarry you." She hung up the telephone.

Bob called Ann often, leaving messages for her to talk to him. He searched for answers to Ann's changed behavior. He spent the days at the library searching through articles, journals, and books on battered and abuse women. He found a guide for the abused woman. It provided him insights of dos and don'ts. He thought that Ann was following the manual to the letter. All the material implied that the women have no faults; it was all the crudity and violent behavior of men.

Bob researched books and material on divorced children and suicide. Bob contemplated; it was just last year that he talked with acquaintances about a popular baseball player Donnie Moore, who had played for the California Angels. He was earning a million dollars a year. He had just retired. It was reported that after shooting his wife, he turned the gun on himself. He was thirty-five, only three years younger than Bob. Bob could not understand why someone would commit suicide.

At night-time, Bob watched television and read books. His drinking increased to improve the taste of cigarette smoking. He perpetually thought of Ann and her soft lustful body. He had the continuous pain in his head and neck. He felt distressed about the unpleasant but inevitable consequences of his predicament. He felt like he was in an endless pit, feeling a sense of doom, and contemplated of death. To deal with the pain, he started taking the pills that were prescribed, Prozac for depresion and Xanax for anxiety. Bob now understood why someone would take his life.

Tom and Liz were concerned about Bob's behavior. Liz was more disturbed because she was in and out of the house. Liz pleaded with Tom that she did not feel comfortable with Bob in their house. Tom did not know what to do. He could not tell Bob to leave. Tom knocked on Bob's door and walked in and was immediately hit with a heavy cloud of smoke. Bob was resting on the bed, watching TV and smoking. Tom was uncertain of what to say. "How are you doing?"

"Hey, Tom, I want to thank you and Liz for putting up with me. It's really nice of you."

Tom was disoriented for words. "I'm concerned about you. This is not the buddy I knew. You're turning into nothing. You drink and smoke too much."

"Yeah, I know. But you don't know how much it hurts—the pain…no torture or pain that hell contains can compare. What the hell would you do if you were me?" Bob said in a raised voice. "What the hell do I have to live for?" He raised his cigarette and said, "This is my friend. All twenty." He picked up the bottle of rye and toasted, "This is how I get by, with my friends."

Tom, concerned that Bob was drunk or near drunk, tried to be careful with his choice of words. "Bob, there is still hope. You and Ann could get back. Don't let this destroy you. Be the guy I used to know. Be tough, hang in there."

"That's easy for you to say!" Bob shouted. "You didn't lose your children, kicked out of your house." He paused to drink. "You don't have fucking children. Do you know what's it like? Bring them into the world… They're my children, and I can't see them. Why? I don't understand why Ann is doing this."

Tom had no reply. He stared in silence. Bob was hurting. In a lot of pain. "Bob, I don't know what to say."

"Do you know why I stay up late at night? For fear of facing the next day."

Tom could not deal with Bob. He felt uncomfortable. "You got fucked! I have to go to work tomorrow."

Liz and Tom were in bed, disturbed by the noise of the slamming door. Tom, in briefs only, left the room. He opened the front door and saw Bob by his car. He quietly walked toward Bob and called out his name. Bob did not respond. He was trying to put the key into the lock. He was having a difficult time putting the key in the lock. Tom grabbed Bob's hand. "Where are you going?"

house and was pleased that everything was in order. She noticed the flowers on the table, opened the envelope, and read the note.

> Marriage can at times cause intense emotional relationships of bitter differences. A life cycle that brings out the interplay of love and hate to a crisis. Arguments and divorce create tension between man and woman, with neither's attitude understood as wrong but as different.
>
> Comparison, fairness, understanding, and willingness to view the other's point can bridge the difference. Resulting into resolutions of problems peace and friendship. Without the love, there can be no understanding between the heart and the mind. Divorce is a permanent solution to a temporary problem. You can choose the dagger or the olive wreath.

Ann thought it was another attempt of Bob to control her. She took the flowers and threw them in the large garbage outside. She spent most of the day putting the house in order and cleaning. She cooked a special dinner for the boys. After dinner, she had a meeting with the boys to explain the rules. "Your father is not supposed to come around the house, nor at school or the playgrounds. If you see him, report it to your teacher. Don't go near him, and tell me right away."

Chuck, not understanding what Ann was saying, asked, "Why, Mommy? I want to see Daddy."

"You will," said Ann in a controlling tone. "Your father is not the same person." She paused as she examined the blank looks of their faces. "You have to listen to me."

As Tony had asked many times, "Why? I don't think Dad wants to hurt us. Daddy loves us."

"You don't know your father. He has changed. Remember the times that he hit you?" She gazed at Bobby.

Bobby replied, "He didn't hurt me."

Bob slowly turned and pushed Tom back. "Leave me the hell alone. It's none of your business." Bob again tried to put the key in the lock.

Tom quickly snatched the keys from his hand and said, "You're not going anyplace." They struggled for the keys. Tom clenched the keys tightly in his hand. Bob tried to grab the keys from Tom.

"Give me my fucking keys," Bob said, antagonistic. "If you don't give me those fucking keys, I'll kick your ass."

"I don't want to fight you, but you're in no condition to drive." Bob threw a punch. It caught Tom's shoulder. Bob lifted his fist to throw another punch. Tom quickly moved out of the way. Bob stumbled, fell toward the ground, hitting his shoulder on the hard concrete. Tom quickly bent over Bob. "Hey! Are you all right?"

Bob was crying. "I was thinking of killing myself… I was going to drive off a cliff. I don't want to live anymore. You don't know how painful it is to be without Ann and the children."

Tom slowly helped Bob up, putting his arms around him, said, "You're like a brother to me. Don't do this to yourself." He helped Bob back into the house. "Think about your mother. Do you want to break her heart? They all think—Ray, Ann, and her lawyer—that you are in the brink of a nervous breakdown. Don't give them the satisfaction. Think of your children. Don't give Ann justification for all her actions."

Bob slowly said, "Thanks, Tom, thanks." Bob found new strength to continue to live.

August 5, 1990

Bob Dorsete was currently in the entrapment of the legal system, separated from his wife, children, and possessions. He was now entering the psychological world again, more intrusion into his life. He sat peacefully in the reception area of Dr. Soble's office, reflecting on the past two months. Bob was thinking of all the people that were involved their lives and profiting. He was trying to make sense of the situation and understand Ann's actions. He hoped that Ann would stop the divorce proceedings and talk to him so they could resolve their difference. He tried to read a magazine, but his eyes and mind were searching throughout the office. He avoided staring at the mothers with their young children. He gawked momentarily at the young pretty receptionist dressed in the off-blue uniform. She was fair-skinned with straight blond hair, light makeup around her eyes, and a pretty friendly smile. Bob probed the degrees and the certificates of achievement on the wall and noticed the children's toys in the corner. He felt optimistic that Dr. Soble could help. He closed his eyes to rest.

Jule Soble grew up in Flatbush, New York. His father owned a dry-cleaning business and their apartment was upstairs. His father and mother wanted Jule to be a doctor. At a young age, his parents emphasized the importance of school and money. His early involvement in the family business made Jule a business psychologist. He had three offices and worked with several associates. His practices were prosperous. With the years of experience, he was at a level in his career in which he made decisions without extensive or intensive research into his clients' background. Jule Soble was in the office bathroom, washing. He stared into the mirror. It reflected a solitary suntanned man with neat curly black-gray hair, long thin face, and brown eyes with a piercing gaze.

Dr. Soble was dressed in casual pants, button shirt, and tie. It had been the usual day listening to the problems and emotional of clients. He was reading Bob's questionnaire as he pushed back the glasses hanging over his thin nose. He paused as he repeated the name Dorsete. He searched through his notebook pages, "Dorsete, Potential New Patient," and found a scribbled note. Last week, he had a conversation with Mr. Schurer that his client will be visiting. Mr. Schurer had told him that his client was taking the divorce pretty hard. The wife and children had been in a shelter. He focused on the information sheets. He thought this could be a complicated case, a long marriage, and fight for custody of the children.

Dr. Soble walked into the reception area and called out Bob's name. Bob stood up; Dr. Soble politely extended his hand and said, "Good afternoon. I'm Dr. Soble. Please follow me." They entered his office, and he closed the door. "Please sit down anyplace." Bob sat on the small couch. Dr. Soble sat on the chair next to his desk and, in a soft tone, said, "I spoke to your attorney. I have some understanding of your case." Staring at his notes, he said, "However, I need more information." He raised his head, and with his eyes concentrating on Bob, he asked, "How are you going to pay for my services? Do you have medical insurance?"

"No," replied Bob disappointedly. "I will pay you cash a little at a time. I am currently unemployed."

"The charge for my services is four thousand dollars. This includes the entire evaluation of the children, the parents, and the written evaluation. If I am asked to appear in court, that will be an additional cost."

Bob acknowledged, "I understand."

"I am going to need a retainer of some kind."

"I can pay you five hundred today."

"Good," Dr. Soble said. "I want you to complete these forms. It's a profile for each one of your children and your relationship with them. In addition, I would like a list of names, telephone numbers, and addresses of five individuals that know you and your family. I would also like for you to take some psychological tests." He paused to stare at Bob with his piercing eyes. He showed no expression as he waited for a reply. "Make an appointment with my secretary for the psychological test. Be prepared to stay for a few hours." Dr. Soble turned downward to the questionnaire. "Can I reach you at this number?"

Bob replied, "Yes."

"Good," Dr. Soble said with a slight smile. "Then I'll see you in two weeks."

Bob did not move as he stared in confusion. Bob handed him a copy of the letter from Dr. Bergren and said, "I was in a hospital. I was evaluated for five days. I'm okay, just stressed."

Dr. Sobel read the letter. "I have the responsibility of young children. I want to conduct my own evaluation."

Bob asked, "Dr. Soble, we haven't talked about seeing my children." He cleared the lump in his throat. "When do I get to see my boys?"

Dr. Soble eyed Bob critically. "I haven't seen your wife and children yet. I have to interview your children."

Bob interrupted, "Mr. Schurer assured me that I would be seeing my boys." Bob said in a firm tone and with a tough facial expression.

"Are you taking medication?"

"No," Bob passionately said, "I was in a lockup unit for twenty-four hours. I was evaluated for five addition days. I did not take medication."

Dr. Soble analytically said, "It's going to take a little time. Mr. Dorsete. You have to understand, I am responsible for the well-being of the children. I have to make a written report to child social services." Bob, disappointed, stared in silence. "You will see your children soon. You have to be patient, and I will do everything possible to make it happen."

"This fuckin' system sucks," Bob said aggravated. "They're my children. It's been over two months. How about my rights!"

Dr. Soble waited a moment, then said, "I cannot do anything until I see your children and their mother. I will try my best to expedite matters." He stood up and extended his hand out. The two politely shook hands, and Bob left.

A week later, Bob completed the questionnaires. One regarding his background and relationship with parents and one each for each for his children. He was given a test entitled Minnesota Multiphasic Personality Inventory (MMPI). The test was developed in the late thirties and early forties by a team of psychologists and psychiatrists working at the University of Minnesota hospitals. The team had hoped that they had devised an efficient and reliable way of determining and diagnosing a person's mental state. Today it is the most widely used and heavily researched personality inventory. The test consists of over five hundred questions about one's feelings that can be answered either by true or false. The answers to the questions determine to what extent each of the ten selected qualities or emotional problems called scales is present. These include depression, hypochondriac, male and female attributes, and seven other categories contributing to personality. Participants that dabble in the human mind believe that this test has significant value in identifying emotional trouble areas and suggest the direction of psychological treatment, if necessary.

Ten days later, Bob was back in Dr. Soble's office. Today was a special day, Bob told himself. It had been a long and painful period not seeing the boys. Mark was growing fast. He had all kinds of mixed emotions, how to react. He was trying to read a magazine, but time was just going to slow, and he was too anxious. He stepped outside into the hallway to smoke. He paced back and forth like an expecting father. He reflected to the time when his children were born. But that was another time and place. Then he hoped for healthy children and now he hoped to embrace them.

Dr. Soble's secretary opened the door. "Dr. Soble will see you." Bob walked through the reception area toward Soble's office. The door was open. He heard voices of children. He recognized the voices. Mark ran to Bob, shouting, "Dad! Dad!" Bob picked him up, tightly held him, and kissed him. In an emotional tone, he said, "I love you. I missed you so much." Bob had tears as he saw the most important people in his life.

Ann watched as Bob held Mark. Her lips widened, showing a slight smile. "Hi, Ann… You look nice," Bob said as he examined her clothing. She had a cream cardigan jacket with cranberry-colored piping with gold-tone buttons, and a slim bright cranberry skirt. Bob's heartbeat increased, causing an elevation of his blood pressure and respiration. The palms of his hands were starting to sweat. The boys approached Bob. Bob placed Mark down and put his arms around the other three boys. Bob hugged Chuck, Tony, and Bobby tightly. The boys were cautious. Their embracement was lukewarm and not in the same enthusiastic manner as Bob's.

The two youngest boys made their way to the corner for the toys and began to play with them.

"Bobby, how are you doing?"

"Fine," responded Bobby in a flat voice.

Bob asked Tony, "How are you doing?"

"Oookay," Tony said.

Dr. Soble extended his hand to Bob and said, "Mr. Dorsete, I would like to see." Bob nervously followed Dr. Soble into the office. Once inside, Dr. Soble said, "The boys are going through a very difficult time, and I know that it's also hard on you." He paused waiting for a reaction. He continued, "Please, don't ask the children any questions and don't talk about the situation. Are you ready to see them?"

"Yes," Bob said anxiously, not knowing what to expect.

Dr. Soble left the office, and within a few minutes, he returned with Bobby and Mark. The boys walked in, and Bob placed his arms around them. Dr. Soble sat behind his desk and grabbed a pen and pad. Bob and the boys were sitting on the couch opposite of Dr. Soble. The silence was broken by Dr. Soble. "You can talk to them."

Bob was in a loss for words but not for affection. He could not hold back the tears as he hugged and kissed them. "I missed you guys so much him. Oooh, I love you so much. Bobby, why don't you hug me?"

"Mr. Dorsete!" intruded Dr. Soble as he stared with a no.

"Hey, Dad," said Bobby. "I got some neat baseball cards." He opened the notebook to show his father the cards. Bob examined the cards.

"I got cards," Mark said with a big smile as he pulled them out from his tight little pocket. He handed the mingled cards to Bob. Bobby and Bob talked about baseball teams and players. Bob had his arm around Mark as he sat quietly holding his toys.

After five minutes, Dr. Soble stood up and said, "Okay, boys, I would like you to leave and join your mother." Mark seized the toys, and Bobby gathered his baseball cards. Dr. Soble turned to Bob and said, "I'll be right back."

Within a few minutes, he returned with Tony and Chuck. Dr. Soble sat on his chair and picked up the pad and pen.

Bob embraced Tony and held him tight. He kissed him on the cheeks and asked, "I don't get a kiss?" Tony replied with a tiny kiss to Bob's cheek. Bob turned to Chuck, embraced, and kissed him. Chuck stood motionless without saying a word. Bob rotated to Tony and asked, "How are you doing?"

"Fine," replied Tony.

"Are you playing any sports?"

"Yes, I just started soccer practice."

"Who's your coach?"

"Mr. Waters."

"I don't think I know him."

"This is his first time he's coaching."

"Oh, I see," Bob said. They talked about sports as Chuck occupied himself on the floor, rolling the cars. Then all was silent. Bob, trying to keep his composure, broke the silence. "Whatever is going on is not your fault. It has nothing to do with you. It's between your mother and me. We both love you ver—"

"Mr. Dorsete," interrupted Dr. Soble, "remember our conversation," Bob stopped talking and placed his arm around Tony as they looked through his baseball book.

"This concludes our session for the day," Dr. Soble said as he stood up. "Mr. Dorsete, please wait here." He escorted the boys out.

Bob sat quietly, but inside, his thoughts and emotions were racing and steaming, burning of anger and still trying to understand why. The session with his children had been disappointing. He had no real time with them. They appeared okay, but he wondered about their emotional state, specifically what they were thinking of him and why they were so cold to him. He tried to understand their feelings. At the same time, he was having a difficult time coping with his own.

Dr. Soble returned and, in his usual soft voice, asked, "How do you feel?"

"A little hurt," Bob said, grasping for words. "They were a little cold. It wasn't like this before. They were always affection to me. I'm worried about them."

"They're doing fine. They miss you and want to see you. I think that we can schedule visitations with your children." Bob's heart started to beat with excitement as he wanted to jump up and down. Dr. Soble continued with pierced eyes fixed on Bob. "You have been under a lot of stress, and you should be in counseling. In addition, I recommend that you take a course in parenting. It will help you to be a better parent, to understand your children, and to learn what you did wrong."

"What did I do wrong?" From happy, Bob's feelings changed to resentment and frustration, and it showed on his face. "Yes, I have been under a great deal of stress. You know that. I just don't understand her actions. She always said that she loved me," Bob said as his eyes become watery. "There has to be something wrong with her. What's wrong with her?"

"There is nothing wrong with her. She doesn't want to be married to you. She's a little distressed, but other than that, she's doing fine."

"Sure, she's doing fine," Bob said, testy. "She has the boys, the house, and basically everything. How would you feel about that?"

"Are you angry?" Dr. Soble asked.

"No, I'm not angry, just frustrated and pissed off."

"It's okay to feel anger. It's an emotion. It's okay to show your feelings."

"I'm not angry!" Bob said with a raised voice. "I'm just frustrated about everything. I can't believe what's happening. Can't see my children."

"It's okay to be angry," Dr. Soble said, hoping to calm him. "It's okay to admit that you are angry."

"Yeah, I'm angry," Bob said in a raised voice.

"I'm here to help you. I know that this is very hard for you. It's important that you be in contact with your children. You can start talking to them. You can call on Monday, Wednesday, and Friday for ten minutes. In two weeks, you can start visitations with a monitor."

"A monitor? Bob asked dumbfounded. "What for!" What do you think I'm going to do to then?"

"It isn't that I think you're going to hurt them. Your wife wants precautions. I agree with her. The children are a little afraid of you."

"Sure, they are! She tells them that I want to hurt them. She runs to a shelter. They haven't had any contact with me in over two months. They're children, confused, and they don't know what is going on. After all they have gone through, how do you expect them to react?" Bob, feeling in the right, stared into Dr. Soble's eyes. "It doesn't take much intelligence to figure it out. At the shelter, they have been counseled as abused children." Bob paused, pledging. "Dr. Soble, I don't think you fully understand what our life was like. Did she tell you that I was the disciplinarian? There were times that she would yell and scream at the boys, and they totally ignored her. She couldn't handle the two older boys. They are very competitive. Sometimes they would bicker and argue over the silliest things. She would often call me at work to complain about the boy's behavior, mostly when they fought. She had difficulty in dealing with it. There were times that I left work to rush home to reprimand or disciple them. Regularly, she would nag and complain of the boys' behavior the moment I entered the house. I had no problem in controlling them. They are typical boys, getting bigger. Hence, she become less involved in the disciplining of the children. I was the enforcer."

Bob paused, hoping for support. Dr. Soble stared in silence. Bob continued.

"They thought that I was powerful. Now, Mom gets rid of Daddy. I haven't had the chance to explain anything to them. So they believe everything she tells them." Bob raised his eyebrows, and with a tensed voice, said, "In plain English, she has scared the shit out of them, and they blame me."

Dr. Soble said, "The children have got through a great ordeal. You have to accept the situation. You need to be in counseling to learn to accept it and to deal with your emotions. You need to talk about your animosity of blaming others for your problems."

Bob did not respond because both his thoughts and emotions were sprinting in confusion. He felt perplexed. He wondered about Dr. Soble and the contradictions he stated that his children miss him and they want to see him, yet why a monitor?

August 22, 1990

The weather was changing. The days were getting shorter, and the temperature was dropping. As Bob approached the courthouse, the same feelings appeared—the numbness of the body, nausea in the stomach, and the limbs becoming weak and helpless. His brain functioned at a slow incoherent tempo. Oh, how Bob hated seeing *Dorsete vs. Dorsete* posted on the courtroom door of cases to be heard. The purpose of this hearing was to solve the issues of child support and to pay outstanding bills. For Bob, the chance to see Ann. Bob had a lot of confidence and trust in his new attorney. Bob hoped that perhaps he could talk to Ann to reach her. In their last conversations, she made it indisputably clear that she didn't want anything to do with him. He hoped that today he could demonstrate his love, adoration, and appreciation to her.

Bob noticed the usual swarm of people, mothers with young children, the phone booths all in use, and the noise of human chattering all around, a human zoo.

Ann and Bob and their respective attorneys were in the courtroom, waiting their turn. After an hour, the judge called out *Dorsete vs. Dorsete*. The attorneys approached the bench. The whispered conversation lasted for five minutes. The attorneys were instructed to work out settlements.

Just as the previous times, the majority of time spent was in the cafeteria. The tables were occupied by respondents, petitioners, and counselors. Ann and Bob had agreed to pay all their outstanding bills from the process from the sale of the restaurant. This was done in a cooperative manner. When all the accounting was done, there was over twelve thousand dollars remaining. The respective attorneys agreed to pay themselves three thousand dollars each from the community funds.

Mr. Walsh was persistent over the issue of child support. Walsh insisted that Bob resigned from Bennix without cause to avoid paying child support. He argued that Ann didn't have a job and she had four minor children to take care of. Schurer rebutted that Bob had been offered a job by Ann's cousin and he was planning to go to

New Jersey. Walsh complained that $500 was half of Bob's previous earnings.

The two counselors engaged in private conversations. Ann and Bob were civil toward each other and tried to be friendly. It was as two strangers meeting for the first time. She told him that at the shelter there was a girl that liked Bobby, but Bobby didn't make a fuss over her. The ladies complimented her on how handsome the boys are and how good they behaved. Ann expressed her concern regarding the finances and asked why Pete was only paying Bob $500 a week. Bob explained that he would have to take time off to make monthly returns to California to see the boys. Bob reassured her that he would send her as much as possible. Ann told him that she would be busy in trying to sell the house. Bob asked about seeing the children before he left. She responded that she would think about it. Early afternoon, an agreement was reached that once Bob starts working, he would pay $500 per month for child support. The attorneys found a judge to sign off, making it a court order. Ann was disappointed because she needed more.

By the time they left the courthouse, it was late afternoon, and the place was nearly empty. Mr. Schurer told Bob that the decision to go to New Jersey was a good one. He told Bob that he did good. He was proud of the way he conducted himself. He also advised Bob that they would be in court sometime in November, then he would be divorced. Schurer suggested that he go on with his life.

Ann was frightened about the future, a single mother with four children. She wished that there could have been another way. She believed that Bob was too stubborn and he would never change. If she went back to him, he would seek revenge on her someday to make life miserable for her or bodily harm her. She feared Bob because he was bigger and stronger than her and she did not want to be hurt like the women from the shelter.

California had been too superficial for Bob. He never had a chance to enjoy the sun and activities. Life for him had been the same as back east, working and caring for his children. He had little time with Ann and for himself. At least in New Jersey, he had happy memories of familiar places and faces. He was a little apprehensive of leaving California, but what choice did he have. He had been so uncomfortable living with Tom and Liz. Bob's life was in limbo, waiting for each calendar day to go by. The days went by so slow, and the nights were so long. At least in New Jersey, he would have a job to keep busy and to occupy his mind as a means to subside the pain and sorrow. There were other reasons for returning to New Jersey. The distance apart would give Ann space. He knew that she was still frightened of him. He hoped to demonstrate that she had no real reasons to fear him except for her own fears and perception. However, he still felt remorseful about leaving the children and Ann behind.

Ann and Bob had agreed that Bob would leave his car at the house. He would take a shuttle to the airport.

Bob arrived at the house a little earlier. He rang the bell, and Tony opened the door. He turned his head to yell, "Mom, Dad's here!" and he quickly ran off. Bob waited for instructions.

Ann appeared dressed in a long plain nightgown. "Come in, I'm cooking breakfast for the boys," Ann said benignly. "Would you like some?"

"Sure," Bob said, pleased at the invitation. He walked to the table, reflecting on the many weekends they had breakfast together. It seemed like a long time since he had sat down with his children. The boys were seated waiting for more pancakes. "Hi, guys."

"Hi, Dad," replied Bobby.

Mark hollered out, "Daddy! Daddy! Sit here." Bob was happy to sit next to him. He cut the pancakes into small pieces for Mark. Ann was by the stove, making more. Pancakes were the boys' favorite breakfast. Bobby and Tony were busy eating; hence, they ignored Bob's presence. Once they ate to their heart's content, Bobby, Tony, and Chuck quietly disappeared from the kitchen. Bob was disappointed by their behavior. Mark enjoyed his dad's attention and smiled as he ate.

"Aren't you going to eat?" Bob asked Ann.

"No, I'm not hungry." Her head was low, and her voice was saddened as she cleared the table.

Bob stood up, walked toward her, and gently embraced her from the back. "What's the matter?" Mark followed and grabbed Bob's hand.

Sobbing, she said, "We have no money. The mortgage is due for the house."

"We took care of that in court. Al the bills are paid up."

"No, it's for the next month."

"I'll send you money, whatever I can… I can borrow if necessary." He gently tightened his hands around her waist.

"Stop! Don't do that."

He let go and asked, "Can we talk?"

"Let's go upstairs," Ann said. Bob followed her up the stairs, holding Mark's hand. Once upstairs, Mark left to play with his brothers.

They entered the bedroom, and Bob closed the door. "Ann, what do you want me to do?" Bob said, caught between pleading and weeping. "I want you, I need you, I love you so much. I love the children. We were such a happy family."

Ann paused to think. "I did everything for you. You didn't appreciate me, you only took advantage of me. You hurt me. You hurt me very much." She turned to sit at the edge of the bed.

"I'm sorry," Bob said. "I didn't know."

She asked, "Why did you hurt me? You made me feel so small, so worthless."

Bob sighed. "It was not intentional. I never meant to hurt you. I was just so frustrated about the whole situation. I was just annoyed by everything. Sorry for taking it on you. I let my anger get out of control. But I always loved you." He got on his knees. "Three months ago, you got on your knees and begged me to forgive you. Now, I'm on my knees, begging you to forgive me. To give me another chance. While in New Jersey, I'll always be true to you. I love you. I want to be with you forever."

She tried to fight off his words to gain control of her composure. She thought about the pain and said, "I don't mean to disappoint you, but half the times we had sex, I faked it. And another thing, I first contacted an attorney a year ago, twice."

Her words hurt him. He did not want to aggravate her. Again, he pleaded, "Give me a chance." He placed her hand over his chest and said, "This heart needs a second chance. Can't you see I love you? Remember all the good times we had."

"There were a lot of bad times too," Ann curtly broke in.

Bob made no defense. He did not want to give her any cause to get upset. He placed her hands between his and held them firmly. She sat quietly as her eyes started to fill with water. He wanted so much to put his arms around her, to kiss her, and to get on top of her like he'd done so many times in this room. However, this was not the time. Ann moved her hands away to wipe the water from her eyes.

Bob stood up, pulled Ann up, put his arms around her, said, "Please, don't cry. We can work it out. Just give me a chance." He gently kissed her on the lips. He kissed her again longer without opening his mouth. He pushed her gently on the bed and got on top of her. He stroked her hair, moved his hand over her breasts, and kissed her cheeks. He closed his eyes and placed his lips on hers and opened his mouth.

She firmly pushed him away and said, "I don't want to be married to you anymore! I don't want you! I don't love you!"

Bob felt hurt. She hollered, "Get off the bed!"

He stood up and said, "Baby, I love you." She turned her eyes away. He walked to the dresser, searching through the clothing and withdrew a stack of letters. "How about all these? Letters we wrote to each other. How we talked about being together forever and ever. How strong and special our love was." They were letters that he had read many times over these past months.

"That was years ago!" Ann said bluntly. "They don't mean a thing now. Things have changed."

"So that's it. Love is like a box of candy. It has an expiration date."

"That's another thing I don't like, your wisecracks."

Bob was at lost for words; hence, he did not reply. He stared at her as he placed the letters on the dresser. He noticed the time on the clock. "I don't have much time. I have to get a few things. I'll stay if you want me to."

"No, I want you to go," Ann said coldly.

As Bob was gathering some ties and dress shirts, his thoughts were of her. How he wished he had some magic word like *abracadabra* or something to change her mind. There was no magic for his burning desire. He finished packing and walked out. As he walked down the stairs, he heard someone call, "Dad." He turned to see.

"Dad, come here," called Tony as he motioned with his hand. They entered Tony's room. He took Bob's arm and led him to the edge of the bed. In a low voice, he said, "I have a plan for Mommy to take you back. Wait here, I'll get Bobby." Bob sat motionless as he waited. The two boys returned. "Go ahead, Bobby. Tell Dad our plan!" said Tony in an excitable whipper.

"No, you tell him," Bobby said.

Tony said, "Bobby and I have a plan." He paused to sigh. "You leave Mommy alone and don't bother her, then she'll stop being so mad. Then Bobby and me will ask her to take you back."

Bob did not answer immediately. He thought how much he loved them. They were his boys, and they still loved him. He embraced them. "Give it a try."

They were interrupted by Ann's voice shouting, "The shuttle is here!"

"Hey, guys. I have to go." They made their way downstairs. They hugged and reluctantly said goodbye. Bob was holding Mark. Mark had his arms tightly around Bob and did not want to let go. Deep inside, Bob's heart was breaking, but what else could he do? He had to respect her wishes and accept that she was in control. Bob handed Ann an envelope, and kissed her cheek and said goodbye. He wrote a letter to express his feelings in hope of softening her heart:

> Dear Ann,
>
> I want to tell you just how I feel. I just want to tell you how much I love you, miss you, and want to be with you and the boys. I want to be with you at your side. My feelings are real. Nothing can please me, and my thoughts are few.

However, words cannot express how much I love you. So here it goes:

I love you. You are the one that made my dreams come true. You made me happy when I was feeling low and alone. You gave me the confidence and the strength to withstand life's challenges, and the love you have given me, I can never repay. I'm saying these words that come from my heart. I have always loved you, and I will never love another.

I know that these words push and shove in endless winds. These words are to the one that I love, always did, and always will.

Love,
Bob

Bob was in the airplane on his way back to New Jersey, back home to his friends and family. The past three months have been one hell of an ordeal for him, but now, for the first time, he was a little more relaxed and optimistic. Ann appeared a little more receptive, and perhaps she would come around. Yesterday's conversation with Dr. Soble was hopeful. He told Dr. Soble about the evening at the amusement park with Ann and the children. It was like a family outing. He and Ann talked, and the boys had a good time. After the park, they went for coffee, and the children had doughnuts. He told Dr. Soble that Ann planned to return to New Jersey. Dr. Soble expressed pleasure to hear that Bob had spent time with the children. Bob informed Dr. Soble that he would make arrangements to return to California, at least once a month to see his children. Dr. Soble made the comment that this marriage could be saved; there was a chance for reconciliation. Bob hoped that Ann would keep her promise to talk to him. Bob was optimistic and hoped that the separation would save their marriage. The pain in his head subsided as he reflected on happier days together. They had been together too long, been through so much, and loved too much to end.

Chapter 11

It was early September in New Jersey. The hot summer days were gone. The low-hanging clouds made it a cool windy day. *It's too cold for this time of the year*, Bob told himself. Bob was living with his mother, who was in her late seventies and independent. She was old-country thinking and had a difficult time understanding Ann's action. Ann was her favorite daughter-in-law, and she loved her as her own.

It was Pete's plan to put the divorce on hold by having Bob in New Jersey. Pete had assigned Bob the responsibility of production and material control. The situation at Micro Research was not improving. Sales were low, and the company was hurting financially. Pete Devigne had employed friends and relatives in responsible positions. He gave them big titles, but some of these individuals were not competent in performing their responsibilities. Production had ceased due to lack of sales and insufficient parts in the house. The retail stores were losing money because of mismanagement, no advertising, and out of stock merchandise. The investors sought interest payments. Pete, as president, had to address all the problems. Despite all these probems, Pete was always optimistic and talked of new business ventures and potential investors. Vinnie Radice showed no optimism for Pete's plans, always pointing to the financial limitations.

Bob tried to keep his personal problems to himself and concentrate on his work. He was saddened and dishearten that Ann would not talk to him. Pete called Ann many times, but she never answered the telephone. Pete left messages. He was bewildered by Ann's action and felt a little annoyed that she did not return his calls. He thought that she was acting immature and wondered what was going on in her mind. Bob and Pete had known each other since Bob started dating Ann. They had always been friendly but never close friends. Pete complemented Bob for behaving civil and being patient. "You know, Bob," said Pete. "I'm disappointed that Ann won't take my calls. I had hoped that the separation would calm Ann's fears of you. I had hoped that Ann would reconsider, think things out, and consider returning to New Jersey. When she was in the shelter, she said some weird things, like 'You don't understand, there are rules… I should not be talking to you.' The few conversations I had with some of females, they sounded like neo-Nazis. I have nothing against feminism, you understand."

Bob said, "I have done a lot of reading on abuse women and shelters. I found a guide for the abused woman. It cites dos and don'ts. They encourage them not to have any contact with the husbands and his friends and family. There are dealing with weak females that depended on men. Their aim is to get them to break away from men."

"The little conversations I had with Ann after she left the shelter, she said nonsense things: 'My mother was controlling, you were controlling, I couldn't do anything without his permission.'" Pete laughed. "That's a joke, because our wives control us. It's these neo-Nazi feminists. I think that they hate men. They blame men for everything. Look at the new domestic violence laws. The man is removed and jailed for three days. I mean this is bullshit. How many times did they make false allegations? That's why I cautioned you when you went back."

"That's because of all the propaganda. They quote stats of millions of women beaten by men, thousands of women killed each year, all for public sentiment. They blame men for the violence. All the material I read, the women have no faults in bad relationships. It was all the violent behavior of men. Like females don't kill their husbands or their children."

"Yeah!" Pete said. "That's rubbish. I thought that Ann was following rules like a puppet. Yeah, she is the poster child for the shelter—a white college-educated woman claiming that she was abused.

You have done nothing violent, yet the law forbids you to see your children. The pendulum has gone the other way, no equal rights for men."

Ann Dorsete was relieved that Bob was in New Jersey. She was busy taking care of the boys, running them to soccer practices and cleaning and maintaining the house. She was worried about money and confused about returning to New Jersey. She sought employment. She was angry and blamed Bob for forcing these responsibilities on her. Bob called his children every Monday, Wednesday, and Friday night. Bob felt that the boys acted estranged to him. Their conversations were superficial and lasted for only a few minutes, talking about school and sports. Bob realized that it was a difficult time for the boys, and he did not want to add any more pain to their lives. He tried not to think badly of his children, wondering what they thought of him. During one conversations, he asked his oldest son, "Bobby, let me talk to your mother."

He called out to his mother. "She doesn't want to talk to you."

"Please, tell her it's very important," Bob said, pleading. "I need to talk to her."

Ann got on the phone and, in an aggravated tone, asked, "What do you want?"

"I thought that once I was in New Jersey that you and I could talk."

"I have nothing to talk to you about."

"What did I do now? I'm three thousand miles away. I thought you were going to talk to me. You promised."

"Don't tell me what to do." She was talking in a loud voice. "You manipulative son of a bitch! I want nothing to do with you."

Bob asked, "What did I do?"

"You are a schemer! You were at the house early. You forced yourself on me."

He hesitated, not knowing how to respond and not to upset her. "Was it so wrong that I wanted to see you and the boys? I just wanted to talk to you, to spend a little time with the boys."

"You're manipulative and controlling!" Ann shouted.

"What did I do that was so terrible? What do you mean by calling me manipulative?"

"Look it up in the dictionary."

"Ann, please list—"

Ann interrupted, "I don't have to listen to you! I want my divorce! Get a life."

"That's easy for you to say," Bob said, inflamed. "You're living in my house. You have the boys. Look at all the money we are wasting."

"My attorney told me that you'll be responsible for my legal costs."

"The attorneys," yelled Bob, "are the only ones who are making money!"

"I don't have time to talk to you." She hung up the telephone.

Bob couldn't understand her behavior. It was just a couple of weeks ago that he was at the house. She was calm and receptive to him. Now she is worse than ever. There was no way he could talk to her in her current state of mind.

It had been over thirty days since leaving California; Bob Dorsete had returned to California to see his children. Ann and Bob were in conference with Dr. Soble. Bob was apprehensive about this meeting because Ann had not softened toward him. Ann was sitting a few feet to his right. He wanted to put his arms around her and tell her how much he loved her. He tried to make eye contact with her. Her eyes refused to meet his. Ann was like a statue of Venus—beautiful, restrained, and lifeless. His letter had fallen on deaf ears. He glanced at her ivory ruffled collar blouse. The blouse lined the top of her breast. Bob thought, *Just months ago we made love. How beautiful she looks. How slim she is for her age. How much I love her.*

"Bob would like to see the children this Sunday," Dr. Soble said as he stared at Ann. "Is that okay with you?"

"Yes."

"What is a good time for a two- or three-hour visit?"

"From ten to one," replied Ann.

Dr. Soble asked, "Bob, do you have a planned activity where you and the children could do something constructive and have fun?"

"The boys always enjoyed going to the swap meet. Afterward, I can take them for lunch."

"Good," said Dr. Soble. "Do you two have a mutual friend that could act as a monitor?"

Bob's heart sank low. He thought, *Why a monitor? What the heck is going on?* Trying to stay calm, he asked, "Why do we need a monitor? What's the reason?"

"The children haven't seen you for a while. It's best for them. They're a little frightened."

Bob was infuriated, but he wanted to see the children under any conditions. He suggested Tom Connelly.

Ann stated, "I have no objections with Tom."

"Good," said Dr. Soble.

Bob moved closer to Ann, clutched her hand, and said, "I love you very much. Please don't do this. Give me a chance. We have been together for too long. You just can't go through this without giving me a chance." Ann was cool, calm, and in control. She did not respond nor move. Bob got on his knees. "Ann, I'm begging you, please give me a second chance." Ann sat quietly and satisfied, feeling like David in the slaying of the giant.

Dr. Soble interrupted, "Stop it! She is not interested in reconciliation."

Bob stood up and shouted, "Who the hell do you think you are? We've been together for over twenty years! We've been through so much. We had four children." He lowered his voice. "She doesn't know what she's doing. She doesn't know the consequences, the long-term effects on the boys. They need a father and a mother. Not one parent. Not a divided family. The family is the most important thing in our lives, and she's destroying it without giving it another chance."

"Bob, get ahold of yourself," Dr. Soble said, concerned about his outrage. "She doesn't want you! You have to accept it." Bob did not reply as he quietly sat down. Dr. Soble continued, "Divorce is a stressful thing. It also could be very costly. There are a lot of issues—community assets, family support, and custody of the children. You can save money if you work out some agreements." Satisfied to have their attention, he resumed, "The children are going through a major drama. I'm concerned about their well-being. Let's try to think about the children and what is in their best interest. I recommend that Ann and the children stay at the residence and you take the New Jersey house."

"I'm not going to give her the house," Bob said, bothered by his comment. "It's worth more than the New Jersey house." Ann said nothing, feeling comfortable in letting Dr. Soble speak in her behalf.

"I think it's a fair property settlement and beneficial for the children," Jule Soble said.

"And for her," Bob shouted sarcastically, "what do you know about real estate? You're not my attorney." He paused, feeling tense. Dr. Soble backed off, thinking of other things to discuss. Bob asked, "Ann, I need some additional clothing and things." Ann did not answer.

Dr. Soble suggested. "After you see the children, you can go to the house with your friend. Is that okay with you, Ann?" She acknowledged with her eyes. "Bob, give her a list of the things you need. You two should think about saving money. Your attorneys are very expensive." Ann and Bob did not reply. "That's it. Have fun with the boys."

Ann and Bob stood up to leave. Dr. Soble called out, "Bob, please wait."

Bob stopped by the door. "Yes!"

"I don't want you to leave with her. Please wait five minutes in the lobby."

Bob left Dr. Soble's office, feeling dejected, angry, and betrayed. He trusted and believed Dr. Soble. He reflected of the things that Dr. Soble had stated—that the children miss him and wanted to see him. Yet why was he recommending a monitor? The session had nothing to do with reconciliation.

Bob had a restless night in anticipation of seeing his children. He talked himself into making sure that he would do the right thing and not say anything against Ann. Knowing that he was underneath the microscope and anything negative could be blown out of proportion into some gigantic misbehavior or misconduct. He knew that the children were going through a difficult time. He had to do what was best for them.

As planned, Ann dropped the boys off at the local park. Tom and Bob were there, waiting. Bob approached the boys, hugged, and kissed them. They responded lukewarmly and with little affection. They spent the first hour at the swap meet and everything the boys saw they asked for. After the swap meet, they went to a diner and had breakfast. Tom Connelly was given instructions by Dr. Soble to make sure that Bob was following the agenda of the visit to stop him from saying anything negative against Ann and not to discuss any issues regarding the divorce with the children. Tom felt out of place. He had been around Bob, Ann, and the children and knew them well. He could not comprehend why a monitor was needed. He knew that Bob would not hurt the children, and the visit should have been with Bob and his children alone.

It was early Monday at the law office of Schurer and Saylor. Some of the staff were just arriving while others were drinking coffee and having light conversations in the hallways. Robert Schurer called out to his secretary and asked, "What time is my first appointment?"

She closed the magazine and cleared her throat. "Ten, Mr. Krupnick."

"Please, get his file."

She walked in, thrusting her young girlish body contours before him. "Here is the file. Oh, by the way, Mr. Dorsete called several times last week."

"What did he want?"

"I have several messages. He said that he was in California. He wanted to see his children. He was unhappy about monitored visitation."

Robert Schurer took the messages from his secretary. He examined the dates and time, lit a cigarette, and reflected on the relaxing weekend he had with his family. He finished the cigarette. He grabbed his telephone directory and dialed the number. "Dr. Soble, please…Robert Schurer."

"Hello, Mr. Schurer," Dr. Soble said. "How are you doing?"

"Fine, Doctor, fine. I need an update regarding the Dorsetes. The father is in California and wants to see his children. Can he start seeing them?"

Dr. Soble paused and then said, "I had arranged for visitations this past weekend?"

Schurer said, surprised, "That's good. So he is seeing his children."

"Somewhat…Mr. Schurer. You're not going to like what I have to say. Mr. Dorsete can see his children, but it will have to be with a monitor."

"Why?" Schurer asked in astonishment. "The guy is not dangerous. He hasn't been charged with anything. I have no information of any prior incidents of family violence. No medical records of children hurt by father, no incidence reported by the schools."

"I cannot jeopardize the safety of the boys," Dr. Soble said in a calm business manner. "Mr. Dorsete is having difficulty accepting that she wants a divorce. His psychological reports and tests show that he is overtly angry and paranoia. He also has a dysfunctional personality. He has been under a tremendous amount of pressure and demonstrated the potential of slipping at any time. He needs professional help. Justifiable, Mrs. Dorsete is fearful of him. I can't allow unmonitored visitations."

"Okay, you're the doctor. He's not going to like this."

"I don't care. I'm in charge of this case, and I'm not going to take a chance."

"All right, I understand. You're in charge." Schurer hesitated, then asked, "Is the guy that bad?"

"If you want to help your client, strongly advise him to get himself in therapy."

"Thank you, Doctor. Oh, by the way, are you going to give me a formal report?"

"Yes, it will probably be after the father has had a couple of visits with the children, and then I need to interview the children. I have to know how they interacted with him."

"Sounds good. Thank you. Goodbye." Robert Schurer was surprised and disappointed of Dr. Soble's conclusions.

Bob Dorsete returned from California from his second monitored visit with his children. The visit with the boys was just that, a visit. The time was limited to three hours. Dr. Soble had provided a young man in his early twenties as the monitor. Bob was restricted to the park. He and the boys played tag and football. The monitor participated in football. After an hour, the two oldest boys told Bob they were bored, and they wanted to go home. Mark was tired and fell asleep in Bob's arms. Bob was hurt that the older boys demonstrated little desire to be with him. He didn't feel like it was quality time with his children. He felt that a monitor was a negative reinforcement to the children, that there was something wrong with their father. He swore that he would never see the children with a monitor. He was disappointed with Dr. Soble. He was content that Ann was a good mother, and the boys were healthy physically. They were still actively involved with their sports, but Bob wanted to be part of their everyday life. He was angry and frustrated. He hated Ann for what she was doing. It was becoming obvious to him, that the divorce was inevitable and he had to accept it. All this caused him pain and stress. He prayed to God to give him the strength and help to make it through the day.

It was late, and everyone had left work. Vinnie Radice, Bob Dorsete, and Pete Devigne were in Pete's office. Pete said, "You know, I'm not taking sides, but Ann's family have accused me of siding with you. I don't get it, her own family, her mother, Aunt Mary and Frank and her sister. They don't want to get involved. They say it's between them. I told them there are psychologists, lawyers, neighbors involved. These are all strangers. Aunt Rose said, 'Poor Ann, she is all by herself, trying to raise her children, and he won't send her any money. Why doesn't he just leave her alone?'" Pete stood up, pointing a finger to his head. "They're small-minded people. Don't they realize that they are your children as well?" Pete shook his head.

Bob said, "I'm not surprised. I have always considered them as my family. They were not happy about us moving to California. In three years, not once did any of them visits us in California. I offered to pay for her mother's ticket. My mother contacted Ann's mother and begged her to get involved to mend the marriage."

Pete excitedly said, "Just last week, I saw Frank. The moment that I mentioned your name, he jumped all over me, saying that it was none of my business, and to stop defending you. He said you both got what you deserve. She's getting her divorce, and you ended up in the nuthouse." Pete raised both his hand as his eyes widened. "Her own fuckin' brother." Pete paused, lighting a cigarette. "I just don't like what Ann has done. Keeping the children away from you. Going to a shelter and saying all the BS. I just don't get it. I don't understand why you are to be subjected to the monitored visitations. You have not been charged with anything. I told you not to trust that Soble. He's on her side. Is he fucking her?"

"I don't know," said Bob, crushed. "I will never subject myself to monitored visitation. It makes me feel like I am guilty. I have to be careful of what I say. And the boys, they are confused as heck. No! Never again!"

Pete said, "She just won't talk to me. It is sad that she's listening to all those strangers. The feminists at the shelter have convinced her that she was an abused wife. That's California, too many wackies."

Bob interrupted, "She won't talk to any of our friend or my sisters or my mother."

"I have to agree with you about California," Bob said, feeling no love for it. "It isn't that California is not a beautiful place. It is a beautiful state. It has a lot to offer—comfortable weather, sunshine, and activities all year long. My lifestyle did not change—going to working, spending time with the boys, doing house chores, no time to vent and relax. I missed New Jersey."

"Why?" Vinnie asked puzzled.

"It's the winters," said Bob, thinking his thoughts out. "Here in the wintertime, we hibernate. We're forced to stay inside, and socializing is limited. We have to deal with the elements. Families are more important here. In California, people are active all year long, always on the move."

"Hey, Vinnie, get some cups," Pete said as he surfaced a bottle of whiskey from his desk drawer. Pete paused. "Let's go to the club!"

Bob replied, "I'm not in the mood to see girls dancing."

"Just trying to cheer you," said Pete as he grabbed the cups from Vinnie and laughed aloud. He had difficulty finding a clear area on his desk to lay the cups. His desk was crowded with letters, books, unopened mail, and two filled ashtrays. "Here, you have to hold your own cups," Pete said, laughing. "You know what they say about California?"

"No," replied Vinnie and Bob.

Pete filled the glasses. "The females have half the money and all the pussies." Pete rocked back on his chair as he laughed hard. "Females, they're hard to figure out. They fuck you in bed, and they fuck you when you get divorced. You know, Bob," Pete said in a serious tone. "Ann is my cousin, and I have known that family all my life. And I love her. But they have a weird way of looking at life." He paused to find a light for his cigarette. "You fucked up because you were always there to carry her."

"I loved and cared for her," said Bob, a little upset.

"I'm not saying that you did something wrong." Pete paused to think. "I've known Ann all my life. She was always the nervous type. See, Aunt Rose was protective of her children. She did everything for them. You did the same for her. You were always there to catch her." Pete stopped to clean the ashes from his shirt. "I can't believe that family of hers."

"I…I made mistakes. It's easy to see that now," said Bob, feeling hurt.

Pete looked at Vinnie. "Have you ever seen so much shit piled on Bob?"

Vinnie motioned with his head in agreement and said, "I still can't believe it. It was just last year that I visited you. Ann was excited about opening the restaurant. Now, she won't take my calls."

"Bob!" Pete paused to light his cigarette. "I'm going to tell you changes Vinnie and I discussed while you were in California. No one knows yet." He hesitated. "Things are not getting any better. The investors have cut off the funds. We decided to close all the stores and lay off half the staff. We will consolidate all the business activities to this location." Bob was not surprised. Vinnie had told him that the company would cease to be in business by the end of this year. Pete explained, "We're just barely making the payroll. Starting next week, everybody will have to take a 20 percent pay cut and 50 percent for the executives. We're planning a major layoff after Thankgiving. I know you have personal problems, but I have no choice. I can't pay you. You can file for unemployment." Bob was surprised to hear that he was laid off. Pete continued, "I'm thinking of starting a new company. I can't give you all the details now. We still have some marketable assets, such as the inventory. I have the okay from the board of directors to transfer the assets to a new corporation. If business picks up, then I could put you back on the payroll."

"Pete, I need to be busy to keep my mind from going insane."

"I know. I wish I could talk to Ann. She has a right to a divorce. I just don't like the way she is going about it. The way she is hiding behind her attorney. They're going to eat you and her up. Keeping you from the boys, that pisses me off."

"I was involved in two divorces," said Vinnie. "I was hire to do the accounting of assets. It was my observation that if you got money, the attorneys will spend it. The attorneys were requesting all kinds of documents related to income and assets. One attorney told me to get the divorce done as quickly as possible, or they will stretch it out for years." Vinnie was totally discouraged with the company and Pete. He worried about Bob. "Bob, if you need money?"

Bob felt that he had real friends. "Thanks, Vin. I settled with Bennix. I expect a check soon."

Pete asked, "How much?"

"Eight thousand. It's already gone…to my attorneys, Dr. Soble, and credit cards."

Pete tried to cheer Bob up. "You know that San Francisco got all the gays and LA got all the attorneys." They laughed lightly.

Pete noticed that it was dark outside. "Well, guys, I got go. You can have the bottle."

"I got to go," Vinnie said. "Bob, are you okay?"

"Yeah, I'll stay here for a while. You guys go, I'll lock up." He wanted to be alone. He poured the rest of the bottle and was disappointed that there was only a drop. He opened the desk drawer and grabbed another bottle. He turned on the radio and lay on the couch. His mind was running with the thoughts of what Pete said. He thought of Ann and the boys. He missed them and his former life. He wanted to be at her side, to touch her, to kiss her, and to feel her tenderness.

Bob thought it would be best to push forward for the divorce. He contacted his attorney. Robert Schurer assured Bob that he was in contact with Will Walsh and things were proceeding and that by the end of December, the divorce would be final. The reality was that Schurer was not being honest. Dr. Soble was not on his client's side. Why the monitored visitations. Walsh was stalling the process by sending a barrage of requests and the filing of "orders to show cause" pursuant to the provision of California Code 20121 and 2025, request for the accounting of trust funds, request for imbursement, request for transfer of title of station wagon. Schurer ignored Walsh's petty stipulations and subpoenas sent to Bob's former employer and renters. He had other cases that required immediate attention. He had higher aspirations to consider.

Psychologists have acknowledged that during the holiday period of Thanksgiving and Christmas, more people get depressed than any time of the year and Bob was one of the depressed. As the holidays were nearing, he felt more depressed. He was not looking forward to the holidays at all, especially Christmas. In the past, this had been one of the happiest times of the year. Bob was receiving unemployment payments of $180 per week and continued working at Micro Research. He was in need of money and peace. Dr. Soble was asking for payments. The trips to California had cost him thousands. He spent his evenings reading and writing, depicting his feelings of love for Ann.

From the onset, Joanne was more asserted and called Ann weekly. She had helped rear Bob as a child, and they had always been close. Ann gives very descriptive details of Bob mistreating of her and the boys. Joanne was half convinced. Ann told her that she did not know how bad Bob had treated her, and she desperately needed to be free. If Joanne really loved and cared about Bob, she should help him seek professional help because he seriously needed it. Bob's sisters were constantly nagging Bob to apologize to ask for forgiveness and promise to do whatever Ann wanted. Bob explained that he did everything possible and was tired of quarreling with them.

Bob contended what is a psychologist going to do for me? Fix the entire situation: pay my bills and to get Ann back for me? He debated with the thought of seeking counseling. He knew that he was in a very stressful situation and felt unhappy. To get his sister off his back, Bob decided to seek counseling at a county institution. After two visits, the counselor told him that it was obvious because of the circumstances that Bob was slightly depressed and under a tremendous amount of stress. However, Bob was coping with the situation as best as possible. His behavior was totally normal and acceptable. Since it was a county institution and he was not in serious need, he was advised that they could not see him. If he felt that he needed counseling, he would seek a private psychologist.

Christmas had always been a special time for Bob and the family—the decorating of the house and the smell of the tree. Also, Ann would cook a special dinner with all the trimmings. Christmas morning, the boys were excited as they opened their gifts and played for hours and hours with their new toys.

A few days after Christmas, Joanne related to Bob that Ann's actions were not right. She was disappointed that Ann stopped taking her calls. Joanne said that she was sorry for not believing Bob. Ann was wrong for not letting Bob see the boys. Joanne associated her children opening their gifts on Christmas: "It made me think of all the Christmases you had spent with your children and the pain you were feeling. That's when I felt your pain after seeing you here all these months by yourself. You have been under a lot of stress and pain for your family. I know that you were a good father and that you love your children. I'm sorry. I truly am. This whole thing is crazy." Bob was touched by her words. He now felt good that after all these months she finally believed him.

Ann was too busy to think of love and romance. She was too occupied in taking care of the children and trying to make the holidays special for the boys.

She was annoyed that Bob stopped sending money. She received gifts from Bob for the family. She saved the gifts for the boys for Christmas. She examined the blouses that Bob send. She was not going to keep them. She decided to wrap them for her new friends from the shelter. She did not want anything to do with him. She was disappointed that there was no check. She opened and read the enclosed letter:

It was the spring of our lives,
We met so innocently.
Was it the warmth of your smile?
We quickly fell in love.
We turned spring into summer.
As the summer's evenings grew, so did our love.
You became the sunshine of my life.
We sowed all our summer's dreams.
We enjoyed the music of the Byrds and the Beatles.
The magic of songs lifted our spirits and souls.
The flowers bloomed into the colors of the rainbow.
And together we lived the summer of our lives.
It is the fall of our lives.
Winced words cause all to fall.
The sun's light is blocked by clouds,
Causing all the colors to turn gray.
And the day's length dwindles down.
It is the winter of my life.
All my days have turned to nights.
The day's motions have frozen life's time.
The frost of dawn chills the winter's sun,
Causing all the flowers to perish.
Are seasons the reasons for our emotions.
Is this the wonder of the seasons' emotions?
Love, Bob, forever and ever…

Ann crunched it up and thought, *He just won't give up. I hate him, I don't love, I don't need him, and I'll never take him back.*

It was a cold cloudy January afternoon. Bob Dorsete felt warm around his friend Marion Philips. It comforted him to visit with someone who was so knowledgeable and sympathetic. Marion, who was now in his fifties, with more weight on the front of his medium body, thinning hair on top, sporting a ponytail, and a small diamond earring in his left ear. He was still handsome with the complexion of a young man and boyish smile. Bob was at Marion's office. It was a simple office with three chairs, a desk, and bookshelves. The walls were plastered with symbols of the zodiac. Marion was delighted to see Bob. "You know, I just don't understand Ann's drastic actions. I thought you were both very happy. You both went to college and had four children together. You worked hard and did very well, but when she told me all those things you supposedly did, I was horrified. She was so convincing—you yelling at her in front of the kids and calling her stupid, immature, and dumb. You threaten to hurt her and the children. It was hard not to believe her, but I had my doubts. Ann said you had a nervous breakdown and needed professional help. We all believed her and hoped that she would take you back. She made it sound that you were so terrible. Yet you have be civil about the whole thing. You've done nothing to hurt her or the children. I'm proud of you... There was no need for what she has done."

Marion paused as he looked downward. "Give me a few minutes to study these charts," Marion said, examining two papers with a large circle with various letters and signs. He looked up at Bob. "Let me explain. This is your natal chart. It's divided into twelve equal sections called houses, representing everyday activities. Each house is occupied by zodiac signs. The chart also shows the location of the planets at the moment of your birth. The major consideration in assessing a chart is the planetary location in the zodiac and to the houses." Marion continued to exam the charts. Bob smoked as he waited patiently.

"You see," Marion said with his finger on the chart, "the love partners were in jeopardy for about two years, but it didn't take effect until Saturn moved into your fourth house, the home and family. Saturn can build or destroy. The fourth house rules your family, and it was squaring your seventh house of partners. A square is a negative aspect, a conflict. Mercury was also squaring your Neptune. Mercury deals with communications, and Neptune deals with the self. Neptune is in your first house—again, the self, the individual. All the while, this squaring deluded you for the last two and two and a half years, thinking that you were strong in the marriage situation. This Neptune business deceived you and you were not aware of the problems."

Marion, feeling satisfied, lit a cigarette. "In August, Jupiter went into Leo," continued Marion, "causing opposition to your fifth house, loved ones. An opposition and a square are difficult aspects that cause tension. The fifth house also deals with children. This pressure took away your children. Jupiter deals with morality and ethics. It squared your eighth house, which deals with sexuality and money. Remember that things came out about your sexual activities, and you were restricted from using your money. That is what Jupiter is doing right now—not allowing you to make money. That is why you lost your job and can't find one. Jupiter in the mid-heaven deals with authority and career aspiration. This squaring is a deterrent to your reputation. That's why people believed things that Ann said about your reputation this past year. She said you were going to kill people, you abused the children, and you were sexually perverted. Ann said all that bullshit that hurt your reputation."

Marion stared at Bob and said, "The slow-moving planets moved into the sign of Capricorn in December. For about the last two years to two and half years, they were in Sagittarius, which they were before. In that sign, everything was smooth with your marriage situation. There was no major problems. Neptune moves fifteen years through each zodiac, Uranus seven years. They were in Sagittarius for seven 15 years. You been married for sixteen years, right? So they allowed you while in this sign, to be free, to rule in your marriage with whatever types of situations you wanted. You had control, right?" Bob nodded. "They allowed you that cause of where they were. You understand! Now, as they slowly moved into

Capricorn, they started to oppose your goals. They squared your home and your love situations and yourself. This is why you were nervous. This is why you were losing control over yourself."

Marion looked up at Bob. "Do you understand?" Bob sat in silence. Marion staring at the charts. "With these aspects," said Marion, shaking his head, "this is definitely not a good chart for you at this time of your life. So the divorce could take place. It is very evident."

Bob sadly said, "It's no surprise right now we are getting divorced."

"Yes, we know. This is telling us through your chart why it happened. I couldn't understand it at first. You and Ann indicate that all was well in California and you were happy. I never looked at your charts. The planets had control over your home. This is why you had all that erratic thinking and confusion around yourself. Neptune was eluding you, making you think that things were going to work out, that you thought that you were in control."

Marion rested. "I know that a lot of people don't believe in this stuff. It's not for fortune-telling. It cannot predict any definite event. However, it does exert a strong influence on every moment of your life, pleasant and unpleasant. But you ultimate have your own free will to decide. With astrology, you can gain an understanding of favorable and unfavorable aspects and deal with them better."

Marion, examining the chart using a ruler, drew a line. "Let's see what's going to happen. Now Saturn is going to leave your fourth house by February and go through the fifth house of your chart. It's going into Aquarius, which is still going to square here, keeping you away from the family. This Saturn transit could last two years. It will trine to Neptune in your first house. A trine is an easy aspect; it harmonizes. You're going to see things about yourself. This is what's going to straighten you out, with your mind and your thinking. Saturn is going to give you more control and direction where you are going with yourself. You're going to find everything out about yourself that you want to know and get it corrected. This is the time when you will correct things in your life." Bob stared in bewilderment. "You will! You'll have more time to yourself and to think things out."

Marion contemplated, "You got to wait until the summer, as Jupiter moves closer to Virgo. Then you won't have Jupiter in opposition to your fifth house, the children. This will help to give you back your children. You'll be able to see them and have more control with these kids than you had in the past year. You have to wait."

Bob, not sure if that was good or bad, said, "So I won't see my children for two years?"

Marion said, "Wait, there's more. Jupiter will move into your eleventh house, the house of hopes, dreams, and wishes. This will bring you other nice aspects. I will trine your moon, Mars, and the sun. These planets will stimulate positive feelings for you. They will also trine your fourth house, your home." Marion paused to stare at Bob. "I don't want to give false hope, but there could be a chance." Marion stopped to check. "You could go back! Saturn will trine Venus, your loved one, your wife. With Venus in the ninth house, it means a love in a faraway place. If your wife stays in California, there is a chance for you to have a reconciliation with this marriage. Now you can get it back, possibly with the Saturn where it's going. It might allow you to do that. Before you do that or go back to her, you're going to have to work at it, and you're going to have to get yourself straightened out, which you will. The Saturn trines your Neptune, which will allow you to see things as they really were. You will see yourself and what really happened. You'll be able to get everything back into focus again."

Marion stopped to think. "The fact that Ann is a Gemini will help you because you will be a favorable aspect to her sun. But she's a late Gemini, almost a Cancer. This means it will take more than a year or more. So if you get yourself back in order and you can get yourself together, you have a chance. There is a second chance!"

Marion rested to light a cigarette. He looked at Bob and, with a serious tone, said. "Listen to what I'm saying. You have to be very careful of your reputation. I want you to listen carefully. Mars on the twenty-third of next month will be in Gemini for a while. It's going to square your sixth house of work and your twelfth house of unconsciousness. That could make you get a lot of nervous energies and make you want to drink more. So be careful of that. You have Pisces in the sixth house. That's why you're drinking a lot. When things don't go your way, you drink. It's a delusion. It's a way of diverting your pain."

Marion noticed the disappointment on Bob's face. "Now, it's not so bad," Marion said. "Saturn is also going to be able to stimulate better-working activities for you. That won't take place till after March." Marion pointed to the chart. "You got this triangle in the mid-heaven that always brings you nice aspects. That's why you always worked, progressed, and succeeded." Bob smiled, liking what he heard. "After March, Mars will go into Cancer. It will be a little softer. In fact, after March, you'll be able to generate a new job. That's when something will come up and you will start to get involved with a career."

Marion paused as he sat back. "Remember that I have always said that you're stubborn sometimes. This is where your stubbornness comes in. The planet Mars, the sun, and the moon are in Taurus, your eighth house. This house is a very fixed house. When people make up their minds they don't change easily. They are determined, and they also assume responsibilities. They have broad shoulders and capable of carrying almost any load. You know that. That's also why you're very sexual, and sex is so important to you."

Marion paused to look at the chart. Marking with the ruler, he said, "Once we move into the sign of Aquarius, it's going to square all your Taurus planets again. What you're getting here is a double whammy with the Saturn business. You had it for two and a half years while it was in Capricorn, squaring your rising sign in your seventh house of partners. Now unfortunately, you're a Taurus, so now when it goes into Aquarius, it will square your sign for another two years. The transit here to your ascendant sign, the rising sign, which is you, personally. This why you feel so much pain." Marion saw that Bob was confused or in deep thought. "I'll try to explain in another way. While Saturn is in Capricorn, it always takes away. It teaches you a lesson. It's why we call it the taskmaster of the astrological chart. He is there to break you down and to rebuild you again. While he is breaking you down, he is teaching you a lesson of some sort that has to be taught in life. Wherever Saturn is in the chart, it teaches you a lesson at that time. This time, it happened to be through your fourth house, the home. He has taught you a lesson here, the importance of your family. That's what he has done. The fact that you personally felt all this pain is because it squared the rising sign of your chart. The first house on the rising sign of everybody's horoscope chart is that person, the self. So it will teach you things about yourself. You've learned some lessons already."

Bob asked, perplexed, "What have I learned about myself? Other than that, perhaps I took my marriage for granted. I worried more about money instead of my wife. I had all the responsibilities of providing for the family that I vented all my frustration to Ann. Perhaps I was loud. Perhaps this is my fault. I said some terrible things."

"You have changed. I can see that." Marion paused to think. "I know you since you were a boy. You'll become more mellow, less critical, and more understanding. You have learned something through this shit. So now it will give you a chance to rebuild. It will restrict you with money situations for the next two years. It will restrict you with some sexual activities in the next two years. After a square, it will trine. Do you know what I am saying?" Bob motioned in agreement. "A trine makes things easy. It will give you a chance to rebuild and make things easier for yourself, to make you understand where you came from and where you're going. It'll trine to your Venus in the ninth house, which is your wife and love. The ninth house deals with faraway places. So your wife is in a faraway place. She is not in your neighborhood. This transit will make you aware of what happened and give you the opportunity to make corrective changes. But it will take one to two years."

Bob was discouraged. "How am I going to survive? Every day I exist with pain. No job. No house. Every day it gets fucking tougher and tougher. I can't see myself living like this. We have wasted the money. Not seeing my children is driving me crazy." Bob was irritated and uncomfortable. "I'm fighting with myself to control my feelings. Sometimes, I get thoughts of revenge. I have to force them out if my mind. I just can't. I can't see myself living this way."

Marion felt sympathy for Bob. "I know that. Nothing is going to happen right away. You have—"

Bob interrupted, "I just can't sit. Let the attorneys eat us up."

Marion interjected, "You'll take care of it! You'll find things to do. You have your family here, friends that care. After March, not before then."

"My mother, God bless! She has been understanding. It hurts her that…that…I am the youngest of her six children and the only one facing a divorce. She still doesn't understand… She's no comfort to me."

Marion broke in. "No mother is. A mother is a mother… You love them, but they're not a companion."

Bob added, "And my sisters. They have been supportive, but they have doubts. They insisted that I call Ann to apologize. To tell her that I would do anything she wants. They just don't understand that I already have begged, apologized." Bob paused to light a cigarette. "At Christmas, my sister was disappointed that I would not participate and dress up as Santa Claus to give out the presents. After we finished eating, I had to get away. I went downstairs to be alone. She came after me and begged me to go upstairs with the family. I refused. She was annoyed, calling me stubborn and childish. She complained of my drinking and smoking."

Marion chuckled. "Oh, Bob, you and your women troubles. I'm sorry for laughing. Let me tell you about a woman. The three stages of a woman's life. First, a maiden, second, a mother, and thirdly, a hag." Bob gave out a light chuckle. Marion, trying to be positive, said, "You have another saving grace here. In the summer, Jupiter, moving out of Leo, will start to ascend to your seventh house of partners and your third house of neighborhood. This might generate a relationship. There's a good chance of you finding a relationship by then. You might even be able to go back to your neighborhood where you came from and start to rebuild."

"Do you know how painful Christmas was?" Bob said. "The first time without Ann and the boys. They didn't send me anything, not even a card."

"Don't blame the children. It's not their fault."

"I didn't call the boys for two weeks. Last week, I spoke to Bobby and asked if they received the presents that I sent. He was so cold. I felt rejected and annoyed that I told him that I wanted to be there for Christmas, but his mother won't let me." He shouted back, "Don't blame Mom. It's your fault." I got so pissed. I spoke to Ann. I asked her why she turned the boys against me. I told her that I was going to get her. She shouted back, "I hate your guts! If you were right here, I will stick a knife in you." Then I asked her why she was so angry and keeping me away from the boys. I get the same reply, that I am manipulative, a controlling son of a bitch. She said, "I'm glad that you're hurting. Stay with your mother and leave me alone. I hate your guts. I wish you were dead. Better yet, I would like to stick a knife in your fuckin' balls!" And she hung up.

Marion noticed the despair on Bob's face. "She, too, is having a hard time because of Jupiter. Nothing is working out. It's also affecting her personally, her inner feelings. Jupiter is squaring her house of partnerships and also her first house. Jupiter is causing her a lot of stress. She'll be under a lot of pressure for the next two years. Her worst is yet to come. She'll have problems in relationships and in rebuilding her life. She has a lot of conflicts… Don't believe all this stuff she's saying, that she's happy and everything is wonderful. Personally, she's having conflict within herself. She is a Gemini with two hearts—one in her chest, the other in her womb." He rested to think.

Marion continued, "Things will get better for you. Give it time, and all your court matters will clear up. Once everything is done with the lawyers and the courts you'll feel better. Give it a chance. Believe me, I know what I'm talking about. You'll have good transits happening. You have two working planets. Jupiter in the seventh house with Mercury ruling there can help you do that. And with Saturn moving into the Capricorn sign, it will lose its power. The destruction of Saturn is over. You will start to feel more at ease with your mind, thinking more constructive than destructive. You will start to feel better by the end of March. You'll have less pressure with the opportunity to rebuilt what was taken away from you. Remember, with thorns there are roses. It's up to you."

The following days, Bob continued to think of Marion's reading. Bob had hoped for an easy fix. There wasn't any, only an uphill battle. The reading had helped Bob with a better understanding of himself and the situation. Bob had little contact with his boys. The conversations were short because the boys were not engaging. Bob pleaded with Ann to see the boys. She told him to contact Dr. Soble to make the arrangements. They argued, and as usual, she hung up on him. Bob did want visitation with a monitor. He was in deep thought that required some decisions.

The thought of dying would drift through Bob's mind. He pondered about the different ways he could do himself in—overdose, cutting his wrists, or simply putting a gun to his head. The thought of a gun made him think how horrible it was. If he could find a painless way to kill himself, he would have done so. The more he thought of suicide, the more self-pity he felt until he become angry and frustrated. He decided to express his feelings in a letter to Ann. He wrote:

> You let me to believe that our love and marriage was tight and you were my friend and my greatest supporter. It was never my desire or intention to ever hurt you. I was only doing the best I could with one objective, to take care of my family. That is my one and only crime. Mistakes and demands I made. Can you remember my last words: Your health and safety come first and take care of the boys? If you can't handle the business, close it and place a sign "Closed for Vacation." Set the alarm every night.
>
> I never had any desire to control or restrict you. I have always been proud of you, bragged of your outstanding qualities, and supported you. You don't have to prove anything because you are capable of everything. I became less tolerant not because I loved you less. It was because of the busy schedule and concern for our finances, which you placed totally on my shoulders.

Life is not always smooth, and every marriage at one time or another has problems, especially the way I complicated ours.

The obstacles of life are intended to make us better, not bitter. It takes mature tough individuals to work through the obstacles.

Do you remember the times I said, "Judge me by my actions, not my words?" Did I ever do anything to hurt you?

It's obvious that you are running on fear, anger, and revenge. Anger improves nothing and is an uncontrolled feeling that betrays what you are. Fear is the opposite of courage and will always find a philosophy to justify it. Revenge does more for the legal profession than any other human emotion. Time spent in getting even is better used getting ahead. Revenge is sweet to the sour.

You have no cause to fear me. Have I ever hurt anyone physically or sought revenge against anyone? I understand and accept your actions.

You have no reason to seek further revenge against me. The loss of your love is the greatest pain that I can ever experience.

With time, I have accepted the initial shock, the perplexity, and all the confusion of what has happened. I have nothing but deep concern for you. Throughout this ordeal, I have done nothing that would indicate that I am dangerous or seek revenge. I have difficulty understanding the loss of your love and friendship. How you can love me in May and hate me in June. There is only one thing stranger than love at first sight; that is divorce at first fight. Nothing is more true than the fine line of love and hate.

You are quitting on your marriage. You don't have the maturity to face me. How long are you going to run on the fuels of anger, fear, and revenge? People can change if they want to. You did!

You can never change the fact that I am the father of our children. Can you remember when I stated that you shouldn't hold things in and you have to feel good about yourself to feel good about life?

We shared the same bed for twenty years. If only you shared your thoughts! From the beginning, I only wanted the chance to talk to you honestly, civil and openly.

Sincerely,
Bob

Chapter 12

February 1991

Pete Devigne had successfully dissolved Micro Research and started a new company with the remaining assets. The new company was struggling and barely making payroll for its six employees. Pete spent the majority of his time contesting lawsuits and the creditors of the former company. He had little time to think of the Dorsetes, and he made no further efforts to contact Ann.

Bob Dorsete was outside the airport terminal, feeling the warm heat of the February California sun as he waited for the shuttle. Just six hours ago he left the bitter February winter of New Jersey. He saw the palm trees and thought that it was just four years ago that he moved his family to California. The paradise that had turned to his hell. California was just another place on earth, no better and no worse than any other place in the world. For Bob, he viewed California as the place that he lost his marriage, children, career, and possessions. His mother pleaded with him to stay with her. She gave Bob a thousand dollars. She feared that in California Bob had no place to live and he would be alone, too much anxiety. He came back to California with just two suitcases. He returned to fight for his rights, his children, and his property. He had no dreams for the future. How could he without Ann, he thought. He was on his own, facing the greatest challenge of his life, his love and friend turned adversary. Where he would go and do, he didn't know. He was trying to be strong and take one day at a time. His first objectives were to find a place to live and a job.

Ann did not want him at the house, so she parked his car two blocks away. Bob spent two weeks in a cheap motel before he found a place at a boarding house in Anaheim, ten minutes from his house. The house was located in a blue-collar residential area. He had his own room and shared the rest of the house, which included a living area, kitchen, and bathroom. Bob was feeling melancholy as he unpacked his suitcases. There was nothing in the room except for a dresser, a bed, and a small lamp.

Bob walked in the office of Robert Schurer. He extended his hand out and, with a mechanical smile, said, "Mr. Schurer, hello."

"Bob, nice to see you. Welcome back. How are you doing?"

"All right," said Bob, lying with a slight smile.

They walked into a large office, and Robert Schurer said, "I'm glad to see you. We have a lot of things to discuss. First of all, do you have a job?"

"No, I just got back a couple of weeks ago. I am looking for work."

"Good, good," said Schurer satisfied and smiling. "They're really making a big issue about that. Mr. Walsh continues to make an issue that you quit your job on purpose."

Bob interrupted, "When is this divorce going to be finalized? When am I going to see my children?"

"Your case is complicated," said Robert Schurer, no longer smiling. "I have Dr. Soble's report, and it's very damaging. Did you force you wife to make porno films?"

"What the hell are you talking about?" Bob asked, annoyed.

"Take a moment to ready this." He handed Bob the document. "Perhaps you'll understand better." Robert Schurer lit a cigarette.

Bob started to read:

> Ann and Bob Dorsete were married for approximately sixteen years. The marriage appeared to be one of an overly controlling and subservient style. Bob would be overly controlling and demanding. Ann would be very subservient and dependent and would not, to any great extent

> early in their marriage, protest or assert herself, as she indicated. She would avoid conflict at all costs. Even if she did not assert herself, Bob's personality dysfunction would not allow him to perceive that he may have any problems but would project those onto others and would continue to badger, manipulate, control and abuse to get what he needed.

Bob quickly skimmed through the rest of the pages and stopped at the final page, entitled "Recommendations."

Keep in mind that with all the aforementioned, as well as other information reviewed, the following recommendation is in the best interest of the boys:

1. They remain in their residence in the area which they feel accustomed to.
2. Sole custody is given to Ann Dorsete.
3. That the boys have an opportunity to participate in counseling if it appears they need to participate; however, at this time, it appears that the boys are doing quite well. As they become a little older, they need to understand better why their father was not able to be in their lives in a positive way. This can only be obtained through counseling. That is, because the boys may often be blaming themselves for the father's abandonment.
4. Bob is not to have any visitations until he has completed a course in parenting and has begun a course of psychological treatment. Once completed, he can then begin moderate visitation. That visitation schedule is to be for four hours every second Sunday per month. The monitor is to be selected and approved by Ann Dorsete.
5. It is recommended that Bob Dorsete be immersed in an intense psychotherapy program to help him understand his own behavior in hopes that he can be more involved with

other people and his own children on an intimate level. There is no doubt that Bob is going through a lot of pain and hurt, but he has to begin somewhere and the safest place for him would be in an inpatient program.

6. One year after Bob has completed the above recommendations, he may request a reevaluation.

Bob was inflamed. He was not surprised that Dr. Soble had sided with Ann. Yet he was shocked by the severe recommendations. He slowly looked up at Robert Schurer. Trying to stay cool, he said, "This is absolute bullshit. I don't understand why… What are you going to do?"

"I don't agree with this entirely," said Schurer sincerely. "I have worked with Dr. Soble in the past, and I was surprised to get this kind of report for my client."

"I thought that he was in our corner," Bob's voice raised. He stood up and turned toward the window. His body had become numb. His mind was on overload. "This is absolute nonsense…inpatient program, in a hospital, for how long? Who's going to pay for it? I don't have health insurance. I don't have this kind of money. I don't have a job." Bursting out in a loud voice, "Who the hell does the son-of-a-bitch think he is. Why is he doing this to me?"

Schurer paused, fearing the Bob might snap. "Bob, do you think that perhaps you need help?"

Bob quickly responded. "Yes, I need help. I need money. I need for all of you parasites to get out my life… I need to get this shit over with… Let's talk about that."

"All right then," said Schurer, feeling a little a more at ease. "Mr. Walsh has really been nagging me. They're looking for some kind of family support. He wants close to about fifteen hundred a month. However, I think I can successfully get him down to about twelve."

Bob was uncertain if he should cry or laugh. "Family support?" he said, chuckling. "I don't even have a job… The number is zero. In fact, I would like to go to court and request spousal support. I understand that she is working."

"Forget it. Don't even waste my time with that. We got more important things to do."

"Okay," said Bob. "Let's get to the issues."

Robert Schurer lit a cigarette. He searched through the files and handed Bob some papers. "This document is entitled 'Petition of Request for Admission of Facts Propounded to Respondent.' Take a moment to look at the questions. We have to respond in two weeks. I also received your wife's financial records, wages, and expenses. I got to admit"—pointing to a stack of documents—"it's a well-detailed package. Normally, I don't get this type of complete information. We have to do the same."

Bob looked at the documents. The telephone rang, and Schurer picked it up. "Yes, I'll take the call." Bob started to read the document:

You are requested to admit within thirty days after service of this request for admission that each of the following facts is true:

1. Admit that during the period you were married and living together with petitioner. You earned the following additional educational degrees—an MBA and engineering degree.
2. Admit that your gross monthly income was about five thousand dollars for a period of four years prior to the date of separation.
3. Admit that you do not currently suffer from any psychological stress that has caused or caused you to become disabled from work.
4. Admit that prior to the date of separation, you threatened the petitioner that should she ever leave you or file for dissolution of marriage, you would do all within your power to make sure that she and the children would be poverty stricken.
5. Admit that you are intentionally not working in order to fulfill your threats of poverty to petitioner.
6. Admit that, since the date of separation, you have applied for loans with financial institutions, gave false information to obtain a loan, including falsifying your gross monthly

income, a felony punishable by fine or imprisonment or both.

7. Admit that you do not tell the truth when the truth of the matter asserts, does not benefit your interests.
8. Admit that you have a reputation for dishonesty in making false statements.
9. Admit that you have willfully violated orders of this court by mailing nonlyrical and sometimes bad poetry to petitioner at her residence.
10. Admit that to the parties four minor children's interest will best be served if the petitioner has sole physical and legal custody.

Bob stopped reading after the tenth item, looked up, and stared at Schurer. He was still talking on the telephone. Bob waited for Schurer to finish. "This is nonsense," Bob said, tossing the document on the desk. "It's absolute bull."

Schurer, pointing at Bob, said, "Like it or not, they can request that we answer these questions."

Bob was infuriated. "Give me a copy. I'll give you my answers." Bob frowned. "When do you think this divorce will be over?"

Schurer benignly said, "By the end of April."

"How about the children?"

Schurer, with a blank look on his face, said, "That's going to be a problem. Perhaps Dr. Soble will allow monitored visitations."

"No way," Bob quickly responded.

"We can send you to another doctor to get a reevaluation."

With a half-smile, Bob sarcastically replied, "I don't have the money to gamble with another psychologist."

"Then you better get yourself into therapy and take a course in parenting. Like or not, that's his recommendation. The choice is yours if you want to see your children."

Bob was defeated. "I'll complete the questionnaire and return it to your office in about a week." He laughed ruefully. "Soble is full of shit."

Bob left his attorney's office, feeling low and aggravated. He thought that if he didn't have bad luck, he wouldn't have any luck at all. He felt more alone than ever before. He was discouraged by the way his case was progressing. He started to lose confidence in his attorney, believing that Ann's attorney was very pushy and was doing everything to make Bob appear as the bad guy. His anger focused on Dr. Soble, thinking that one day_I'll get him.

Bob was adjusting to his new place. His new extended family was made up of a middle-aged man and a young man. For dinner, Bob did take-ins because the kitchen had a foul odor. The garbage was piled high and uncovered. The stove was blanketed with greasy spots. The sink was loaded with dirty dishes and pans, and the refrigerator was dirty and smelly.

Bob Dorsete's second thing to do was to find work. Every week, he searched through the classified ads and responded to any potential job that he was qualified for. No matter how hard he tried, he could not get Ann and the children out of his mind. In an effort from not going crazy, he forced himself to find ways to keep active. He found a local bar, the Fox Hunt. It was a dingy place. The majority of patronizes were men, blue-collar workers. The parking lot was usually cruised by hookers. Bob would routinely have a beer or two and shoot pool by himself. He was not interested in socializing. He kept to himself.

It was near dusk as Bob Dorsete stared at the large blue building. After walking up and down the block several times, he was sure that this was it. He looked for a sign or address number. It was not at all what he had expected. It was an old residential house, two-and-a-half stories. It was recessed over two hundred feet from the curb. The front lawn, close to the porch, was crowded with children's bicycles and other riding scooters. Bob opened the screen door and slowly entered. A woman walked past him. "Excuse me," Bob said. "Is this the place for parenting classes?"

"Yes," said the woman as she pointed to the stairs.

Bob slowly and nervously walked up the stairs. With each step, he heard the sound of the creaking of the floor. Downstairs, he got a glimpse of some young children eating in the kitchen. He felt jittery as he entered a large room filled with people sitting on single school chairs. They all stared at him as he stood quietly. An elderly woman asked, "Can I help you?"

"Is this parenting class?" Bob asked tensed.

"Yes, is this your first time here?"

With a lump in his throat, Bob replied, "Yes."

"Have you completed a form?"

"No. I called yesterday. I spoke to a woman, Milly."

"Am Milly. We just started class. Take a seat and see me after class to complete the necessary information." Bob felt uncomfortable and didn't want to be here. He wanted to leave but kept saying to himself, "It's for my children." He barely paid attention to the lecture as he looked at the strange blank faces of men and women. Bob thought that they were less fortunate, people who lacked discipline or had difficult times with the law, drugs, or alcohol. Bob was not accustomed to being around these types of people, not since his days in Newark.

Tonight's class was on anger. Bob was slightly incoherent. She lectured on the different types of anger and how people show their anger. The nagger that goes on and on and simply complains about all his or her frustrations. The slammer—when things get too hot to handle, he simply storms out. The crybaby—instead of letting the anger show, she simply dissolves into tears. They read articles about child abusers. The thrust of the lesson was the out-of-control anger that can lead to abusing helpless children. It was a long three hours for Bob and for the rest of the class.

"This concludes tonight's session," said Milly. "Next week's lesson, number 7, we'll talk about children's self-esteem."

Bob was led to a tiny room with one desk, one chair, and bookshelves. Milly asked, "What is your name?"

"Bob Dorsete. Sorry that I was late. I had a difficult time finding the place." Bob was trying to be friendly. "I didn't expect to be in a house." Uncertain of what else to say, he smiled.

"Yes, I know," the woman replied. "The name of this organization is COPES. It's a nonprofit organization that offers family services."

"Oooh, that explains the children downstairs."

"Yes, we have about six children now. Cared by adult staff members twenty-four hours, seven days a week. We provide parenting classes in English, Spanish, and Vietnamese. The course covers ten topics. Each is a three-hour session. There is a five-dollar fee per session. It's mandatory that you attend all ten sessions to get a certificate. If you miss any of the sessions, you have to wait until it comes around again. Classes are held every Tuesday, seven to ten." She paused to look at Bob, then asked, "Are you here on court orders?"

Bob very proudly said, "No."

Milly was uncertain and asked, "Then why are you here?"

"My wife and I are involved in a divorce. She made allegations of child abuse. But I have not been charged with anything." Bob paused. Milly turned her head to the side. "There was a family evaluator. A psychologist recommended that I attend a course in effective parenting."

Milly stared at Bob, thinking that it was usual. Again, she asked, "Were you court-ordered?"

Bob, thinking that either she was hard of hearing or just surprised that he was here, said, "No! I was not ordered by the courts." Feeling a dislike for Dr. Soble, he continued, "A shrink recommended that I take a course in parenting so that I can see my children."

"Is social services involved?"

"Yes, but I have not heard a thing from them."

"Do you have an attorney?"

"Yes."

"What does he recommend?"

"That I take a course in parenting."

She paused to examine Bob. He did not appear nor speak like the typical student she has experienced. She widens her lips to smile. "Are you from New York?"

"No, New Jersey."

"I'm from New York. It's obvious that you're for back east."

"Small world," Bob said, feeling a little at ease. He liked the woman. He found her to be sincere. It was obvious that she was a retired person volunteering her time.

Milly handed Bob several pieces of papers. "Here is some information about the purpose of COPES and the other fact sheets. Will you attend class next week?"

"Yes," Bob said as he stood up walking toward the door, and he turned to ask, "Milly, is this course recognized by the Orange County Courts?"

"What!" Milly asked. "You have to speak louder. I'm deaf in one ear."

Bob was in his room, looking over the documents that he had received from Milly. The basic purpose of COPES is the prevention of child abuse and/or neglect. It shelters and cares for abused and neglected children of ten years of age and below. COPES provides a safe home environment for children while working with their families to resolve immediate crises, as well as chronicle problems and economic difficulties. It also involved in assessing the appropriate type of long-term placement necessary if returning home is not appropriate. Children at risk may be placed in COPES voluntarily by the parents. The average stay for this type of placement is one to three weeks. The social service department placement at COPES averages three to five months. During the stay, the child's assessment is completed, and the child is stabilized to return home or to enter long-term placement. COPES provides counseling with professional social workers, monitor visits, and appropriate interaction with children.

Bob drank as he reflected on the sad state of child abuse. He thought of incidents that make the five-o'clock news—a husband shoots ex-wife, a man kidnaps his kids, a mother drowns kids. He never experienced or witnessed child abuse or neglect.

He lay in bed, trying to sleep. He wanted to think pleasant thoughts. He thought that it was just a year ago that they had their last date. Bob had told Ann that it was more difficult to have a date with his own wife than with a stranger. Ann wanted to please him. Ann had arranged to leave the boys with a young neighborhood girl that had spent a great deal of time at the Dorsetes' house.

It was four thirty; Bob was outside his workplace, anxiously waiting for Ann. He finally spotted the car. Ann stopped the car and slid over to the passenger side. As he entered the car, he froze with eyes fixed on her and said, "You look beautiful." Ann gave a big smile and kissed him. "Happy hour time. Let's get happy."

After a couple of drinks and some appetizers, they drove to San Pedro. They parked in an isolated area facing the ocean. Ann said, "This is beautiful. I'm glad we have this chance to be together."

Bob stroked her legs and stared in fascination. "You got pretty legs… You look appetizing in stockings and garter belt." He moved his hand to the end of her stocking and felt the skin of her upper thigh. He lifted his face to kiss her and whispered in her ear, "I love you." Ann didn't say anything, She closed her eyes to enjoy the kissing, caressing, and touching. With one hand, he held her head as he pressed hard against her lips. The other hand was between her legs and between her panties. "You're wet," said Bob softly.

"I have been wet all afternoon just thinking about being with you and getting dressed… Do you like what I have on?"

Bob teasingly said, "Let me see what you have on." Ann turned her legs toward him, lifted her dress above her stomach, and opened her legs. She stroked her hands over her light red stockings that ran up three-quarters of her thighs. They were attached to strips leading to a dark-red garter belt beautifully styled in chiffon and satin. She had on sheer bikini panties. She rubbed her crotch with one hand, and with the other, she cupped her breast. She bent her head toward her breast and opened her mouth to withdraw her tongue, extending it as far as it could go to reach her bosom. She raised her eyes to stare at his to see his burning desire.

Bob watched with approval and satisfaction as he glanced at her legs and face. He was immobile as he smiled and licked his lips. He appeared like a little boy eyeing the different flavors of ice cream at an ice-cream parlor. Ann placed her hands behind her back to lower the zipper of her dress. She placed her hands to the inside of her shoulders and lowered her dress to the top half of her breast. "Do you like what you see?" asked Ann, knowing that she was in full control. "Do you want more, little boy?" Bob did not move except for the widening of his lips. She moved the front of the dress below her bright red bra with demi-cups, giving fullness to her breast. Bob was captivated as he continued to stare. "You want to see more?" She moved her hands to her crotch. She lifted and held her panties with one hand and inserted her finger between her pubic hair. "Oh, it feels so good," she said as she closed her eyes. After a moment, she raised her finger close to his face. The fragrance of her womanhood made his head spin, stimulating and arousing his manhood to its fullest. Ann was excited with energy. Her mind and body were one, a woman in her fullest with desire and power. She was master and in control.

Ann slowly and, in charge, placed her hands to the front of her bra and released her swollen breast and erected nipples. She cupped them and pressed inward and up, presenting maximum completeness to the eclipse of her nipples, near-perfect hemisphere. Without uttering a sound, her eyes and smile commended. Bob lowered his mouth to her breast and swallowed her nipple into his mouth. Her head spun with desire and delight as her thighs ran with moist electricity. She felt helpless and captured wanting the highest thrill of human emotion and feeling. She wanted him inside. She unzipped his pants, found his manhood, and positioned herself to receive its delight. Immediately, she was thrilled by its heat and hardness. She melted into enslavement as his body covered hers. She muttered out, "Aha! More! More!" Bob moved with the power of a locomotive and the strength of a bulldozer until she shouted out with excitement. He placed his hand over her mouth. The master turned to slave to the desires of needs and prerogative.

Tom Connelly had referred Carmen Conte to Bob. Tom had met him at a Zen Center, a Buddhist retreat. Tom had told Bob that Carmen was a cool guy from New York, not your typical psychologist. He served in Vietnam, smokes grass, and loves females. Bob was in the reception area of Dr. Conte. There was no secretary, no receptionist. By the inner door, a sign read: "RING BELL." Bob sat on one of the three chairs. There was a small table with magazines.

After ten minutes, the door open. A clean-cut young man walked out, followed by a tall, bulky man. He said, "See you next week." The man was nearly six feet tall with a good head of long graying hair. His face was oval and smooth, with heavy forehead and eyebrows, high cheekbones, unshaved. He had a thick neck and an earring in his left ear. He turned to Bob with a slight smile. "Bob?"

"Yes!"

"Come in." The man was dressed in a flowery shirt and baggy shorts. He wore sandals with no socks. They entered the simple office decorated like a normal household living room with couches, coffee table, and end tables with lamps. "What's happening with you?"

"Well," said Bob, chuckling, "I don't have a job. My wife is divorcing me, and I have been separated from my children."

Dr. Conte interrupted, "Okay, okay. I started with that to be funny. Relax. So you are a friend of Tom? Still living with that crazy Phillippe woman?"

"His wife, Liz."

"Tom told me that you are going through rough times."

Bob relaxed. "Yeah. A real hell."

"Who is the psychologist?"

"Dr. Jule Soble."

"Never heard of him."

"His office is in Mission Viejo."

"Who is your attorney?"

"Robert Schurer."

Dr. Conte, looking deep into Bob's eyes, said, "How can I help you?"

"Dr. Soble recommended that I not have any visitations with my children until I have completed a course in parenting and begun a psychotherapy program."

"That's harsh. Who did you kill? I am kidding. Tom said he knows your family. You guys were involved in some kind of business."

"A computer company in New Jersey, out of business now." Bob opened his briefcase and presented Dr. Soble's recommendations.

Carmen looked over the document, shaking his head. "Heavy. Have you started parenting classes?"

"Yes."

"Give me your attorney's number. I want to talk to your attorney." He paused. "Tom told me something about you acting crazy. Any thoughts of suicide?"

"No! I'm just having a hard time not living in my house, with my wife, with my children. I am still having a hard time understanding my wife's action. This divorce is bullshit."

"That is why I am not married or have children. *Love* is a cheap four-letter word that rhymes with *fuck*! Marriage does not hold the same values as it did in the past. The children suffer the most for their parents' egotistic behavior."

With a slight smile, he said, "Don't let it destroy you. Tom said you have a family back east that care and support you. Think about them." He paused. "You recently came back. Why?"

"I want to see my children. I need to get the divorced finalized." For the next twenty minutes, Bob summarized the past eight months of his life: Ann filling for a divorce, his stay at the hospital, going back to New Jersey, Ann's zealous lawyer, Dr. Sobel and the monitored visitations, etc. Dr. Conte felt the compassion and deep sympathy for Bob. He scheduled the next session in two weeks.

The nights were difficult for Bob Dorsete. He would usually drink himself to sleep while watching TV or listening to music. He spoke to his children once a week. The conversations were brief and superficial. He tried to adjust and accept his new way of life, although he hated the situation. Bob cleaned the kitchen, washed the pans and dishes, and cleaned the refrigerator. He purchased food and cooked. Ann is an excellent cook, and Bob is no stranger in the kitchen. He had done the cooking the first year of his marriage. Bob made attempts to be friendly with his roommates. Bob invited them to eat dinner with him. Chet, a young man, was friendly and accepted Bob's invites. Chet was a tall thin man with thinning hair and big sunken eyes. Tim, a middle-aged man, wore a large cowboy mustache and wore thick glasses. He was medium height and walked with a limp. Tim was timid; he continued to eat in his room.

After a couple of weeks, Tim joined Bob and Chet for dinner. The men shared in the purchase of food and all kitchen items. Bob did most of the cooking, and the other men shared the cleaning of the kitchen. Chet ate very quickly and ran outside for a smoke. Bob tried striking up conversations with Tim to no avail. Tim ate slowly and methodically. He was a nonsmoker and complained about the cigarette smoke. He was single and never married. He claimed he was an engineer. Bob had his doubts.

Chet worked for the Salvation Army as a clerk at a warehouse. Sometimes he would come home excited, showing Bob the great deals he got. His room was filled with stereos, cameras, all kinds of knickknacks, figurines, old coins, sports cards, music albums, small pieces of furniture, wallets, and clothing. Bimonthly, he would go to the swap meet to sell his collection. On a good day, he made up to four hundred dollars. Chet sold Bob a stereo, TV, bookshelf, and albums.

Every Wednesday night, Chet attended AA meetings also attended by those with drug problems. Bob started to have some concern of his excessive drinking, so he accompanied Chet to several meetings. He was overwhelmed by the sad stories of people hitting rock bottom, homeless and penniless. Some individuals told their stories of unsuccessful suicide attempts. Bob was touched by one individual's story: "You know when you've reached the bottom. When you dig in your pocket and you come up with nothing but a few coins. You count every one of the silver and copper coins. You're in your glory when you can reach in your pocket and find a green bill." Another individual told his story. He put a gun to his mouth. With finger shaking, he slowed pulled the trigger. The gun jammed. He was glad he was still alive.

After one AA meeting, Chet and Bob were drinking beer in the living room. Chet very proudly said, "I don't have a problem with alcohol, I can drink beer. My problem was drugs. I have been clean for two years now." He paused to take a drink.

Bob was interested in hearing more. He asked, "Why did you do drugs?"

"I lived in Florida. My parents got divorced when I was about thirteen years old. Within two years, my mother remarried. I didn't like the guy. He was a jerk. When I was seventeen years old, I ran away from home. I've been on my own since then." He stopped to drink. "When I was a kid, I just did grass, casually. I lived in Dallas for a while."

Bob interrupted, "How did you live?"

"I did some panhandling, crush in drug houses. There I met some guys that were dealing. I started with the heavy stuff, coke, heroin, crack. You name it, I did it. Then things got too hot in Dallas. I got tired with the scene, so I came to California. I was up in San Jose. I got in with some bad mothers. That's when I got into some massive shit dealing. I was buying and selling. I had all kinds of money… It was great! I was dealing with this guy, Lou. He was bad, doing real heavy buying and selling. I was dealing for him." Bob listened with interest. "Hey, man, I need another beer. Want one?"

"Sure," said Bob.

"Boy, you should have seen the cash I had," said Chet as he returned with three beers. "A thousand a day was easy." He handed Bob one. "Man, I had some fucking money…and cunt. Just give the babes some dope, and they'll fuck like rabbits. I use to get all the stuff I wanted."

"Like what?" Bob asked.

"My favorite was baked coke."

Bob had never done drugs and never associated with users. Very inquisitive, he asked, "What's baked coke?"

Chet very proudly said, "Well, you take a soda can, rip out the middle, put some water and coke on top, and heat it up. The coke starts to form into balls. You take the little balls and put them in a glass pipe and smoke it. You inhale it like grass while you heat up the pipe. Boy, that stuff was good."

Bob asked curiously, "What does it do to you?"

Chet paced up and down the room. "I don't like to do needles, they leave marks. If you snort coke, it's not a good high as when you smoke it. It gets you high quick. It goes right to your head." Chet paused. "Did you ever do grass?"

Bob admitted reluctantly, "Yeah, when I was a kid but not regular."

"Well, man," said Chet, "coke is stronger. It gives you a real crazy high. It's a short high, about twenty minutes. It really makes you feel good. You have to be careful. Sometimes, depending on your mood, you can have a bad trip. I've seen people go wild, especially babes. Man, I had a bad trip once. It scared the hell out of me."

"Why did you leave San Jose?"

"I had to."

"Why?" Bob asked again.

"Lou was getting crazy. He had a fallen-out with one of the guys we were dealing. Well, not really a falling-out. The guy got caught with some stuff. He had a record, so he made a deal. He ratted on Lou. I had just finished my deliveries and went back to the apartment. The police were all around the place. I wanted to warn Lou. I thought about making a phone call. But I thought the telephone would be tapped. The police stormed the apartment, and within minutes, they had Lou and two babes in handcuffs. They found quite a bit of stuff, grass, pills, coke. You name it, they had it. They were smoking and tripping all day. That day, I had two thousand in cash and about five thousand in stuff. The van didn't belong to me. It was in the name of one of Lou's friends. It really belonged to Lou. He had no job. He didn't want anything in his name. I was lucky that day. I stayed away from the area. I moved in with some friends across town."

Bob asked, "What did you do with the money and all that dope?"

Chet lit a cigarette. "I sold some of the stuff, and some of it I used. Finally, the money and the dope ran out. Things were hot. The police were busting everyone I knew. I couldn't get any stuff. I stayed away from Lou's friends because the police were busting them. So I decided to come down here. I lived in a homeless shelter for a couple of months. Man, I was low, rock bottom. I use to stand in the street with a sign "Will work for food," panhandling. I was looking to get high, but I didn't have the money or the connection. Man, I was going crazy. So finally, I decided to get help. Got into a place for six weeks, got cleaned up. That was my third time. They found me a job with the Salvation Army."

Chet held up the can of beer. "You see, alcohol is not my problem. Drugs! This I can handle."

Bob confused asked, "What's the different?"

"Hey, I don't do drugs anymore. I'm clean. I stay away from that stuff. It's poison, and I'm not an alcoholic." He raised the beer can. "I can put this shit down anytime."

Bob, in support, said, "I give you a lot of credit. You really got to be proud of yourself for admitting you had a problem, finding help and keeping yourself clean."

Chet grinned. "Yeah, yeah, I'm glad I don't do that shit anymore. I want to show you something." He headed for his room and returned with some papers. "Drugs fucked me up!" He handed the papers to Bob. "Read it. It's in there." Bob looked at the papers. He started to read but was interrupted by Chet. "Dope is bad shit. It's all around. Once you get hooked on it, it's a hard habit to break. Lots of people try, but it's real hard. Yeah, you got to be careful of that shit. Chet pointed with his finger over his back. Man, you go out there on Lincoln Avenue, you can get anything you want, all kinds of drugs. All the girls there are whores and druggies. They will do anything for drugs and money. You can pick up a whore for twenty dollars when they're desperate. Some of them have a man. They refer to him as "their man." He protects, gets drugs, and pimps them. As quickly as they make the money, they're high."

Bob was surprised. He had gone past that section many times and never thought anything unusual about it. That street was lined with stores, apartments, and motels. Chet continued, "Yeah, they're always looking to get high. They move from motel to motel. You got to be careful of those people; they're just slime. The only time they're friendly is when you got dope." Chet stopped to look at the clock, "Oh shit, it's late. I got to get to bed." Chet swayed as he made his way to his room.

Bob was in his room, drinking and looking at the papers that Chet gave him. The report was two years old. "Chet Miller a thirty-three-year-old white male with light-brown hair, tall and thin with a skinny face, bony nose." Bob thought that Chet was older. He continued to read.

"He dropped out of school in the tenth grade because he was a rebellious kid. As a child, he was seeing both psychologists and psychiatrists. He was in special education in the seventh and eighth grade. He also had tutoring for reading and speech. He started using drugs when he was twelve years old. He began using cocaine approximately twelve years ago, and for the last five years, he was constantly using drugs daily. He had lived in an adult rehabilitation center of the Salvation Army, and he was placed on employment status with them. He was having a difficult time. He felt embarrassed and concerned over what he calls his lack of comprehension of the use of textbooks. It frustrated him that he was not able to understand the material. He was suffering from some type of memory problems, which is related to drugs."

Bob stopped reading to turn the page, feeling sympathy, thinking what a sad life for such a young bright guy. He continues to read: "The subject had gone through some psychological testing. The results placed him toward the top of an average intellectual classification. Although his performance on the verbal comprehensive test was inferior, he did very well on the verbal reasoning and some of the other tests utilized. He did, however, express himself very well. On an Altus intelligence scale, he rated an IQ of 105. On a Wechsler Memory Scale Form, in mental quotation, he rated a 135. This placed him in high superior classification, and it did not demonstrate difficulty with either long- or short-term memory. He was able to repeat eight digits forward and six backward, which is almost a perfect score. When shown a design for ten seconds, then removed, he had to reproduce it from memory. He did very well except for some of the items. He might have problems with memory, but it was not supported by the tests. According to patient, he was using cocaine for several years, and he may have developed a habit of laziness and not trying his very best. Because of all the years of drug abuse, he apparently suffers from some type of a memory problem."

Bob reflected and felt sorry for Chet, thinking about what Chet had stated about his parents getting divorced. He thought about his children, and he hoped that this would not happen to any of his boys.

Bob was attending his third night of parenting class. Milly was lecturing lesson 1, the introduction to the course. It dealt with the purposes of the program and the need for effective parenting, for the protection of children and preparing children to survive in today's complicated society. She talked about punishment as being negative and the positive ways of dealing with children and structuring the child's time. Milly encouraged and tried to get comments and participation from the students. Bob Dorsete and another student, Shelby, were the only ones to participate. Shelby and Bob did not always agree with Milly's viewpoints. The discussions sometimes turned into debates and even light disputes. At times, Milly displayed her dissatisfaction. Shelby enjoyed challenging Milly.

After class, Bob went over to Shelby to engage in a conversation. They walked out together. Shelby suggested that they go for a few brewskies to a local bar. Shelby was a couple of inches taller than Bob. He was average looking, but not very distinctive, with lively almond-shaped eyes, strong nose. He had a fleshy jawbone, wide mouth always smiling, and a strong sense of humor.

"Two more sessions and I'll be done," said Shelby, smiling. "It's taken me eight months. Milly means well. I had private conversations with her."

"Congratulations," said Bob, "I have five more sessions."

"So you volunteered because of a shrink."

"Yeah."

"Well, that's very unusual," said Shelby. "The majority of us are here because court-ordered."

"Why are you here?" asked Bob.

Shelby, still grinning, said, "My old lady is screwed up. She and I were into drugs. One night we got so high, I don't know how it happened, my little infant daughter, she was six months old at the time. She got burned by the portable heater. The left side of her face."

Bob, very curious, asked, "How did it happen?"

Shelby, no longer grinning but had a serious look on his face, said, "I am not sure. Me and my old lady were asleep. What I think happened... We had the baby in bed with us. My three-year-old daughter probably thought the baby was cold and put the baby next to the heater. Poor kid's face was burned. She's doing better now. She's three years old. She's had plastic surgery, but you can still see some of the scars." Bob thought, *Poor kid.* Shelby continued, "We were at the hospital. The social services were called. They took the kids away from us for three months. We had to get into a rehab program to get the kids back. We stopped doing drugs. We were both clean for two years. My old lady was having a hard time doing a lot of drinking. Her mother dies, and she started doing drugs again. I told her to cut that shit out… I told her I would leave her if she didn't. One day, I caught her and her friends doing drugs. So I left her. She was doing drugs with friends and fucking other guys." He paused to drink. "The social workers found out about it and took the kids away. The social worker told me about my older daughter being sexually molested by one of the guys. I didn't know until later." Shelby stopped to drink.

"How old was you daughter at the time?"

"Almost six. I was pissed," said Shelby sadly. "I went back to the trailer. I kicked the shit out of the guy. I told her that she better get her act together. She was high. She was out of it. I couldn't talk to her. I tried to get my kids. The social services had placed the kids in a foster home. They charged me for neglect. I told them I had split with my old lady because she was doing drugs. They didn't care. My kids are under the protective custody of the court. I'm trying to get my kids back." Shelby stopped to stare at Bob.

"How about your wife?" asked Bob.

Shelby, in a low voice, said, "I don't give a shit about her. She didn't give a shit about the kids or me. After I finish this course, I'm going to try to get custody of my children."

Bob patted Shelby on the back. "I hope you get your kids back. Good luck to you. Do you have a lawyer?"

"The best," said Shelby with a big smile.

"I don't think my attorney is doing much for me," said Bob meekly.

Shelby was beaming. "I got a great attorney. The children's attorney wanted to charge Patty and me for child abuse. My attorney got the charges dropped. To look at him, he doesn't look like an attorney. He dresses very simply. But he's a genius."

"How did you find him?"

"He's a friend of the old man." His mouth widens. "My old man has money. But he's a cheap son of a bitch. I had a problem with my license. I got caught driving with a suspended license. My lawyer kept me out of jail, and within two weeks, I got my license."

"Is he really that good?"

"He got all the charged dropped against Patty for selling drugs and child molestation. That was my father's idea. I was pissed that she didn't go to jail."

Bob, thinking that they were both guilty, asked, "Do you care about her?"

Shelby frowned. "I did until I found out she was pregnant with another guy's kid."

"I think this parenting class is good for you," said Dr. Conte. "Are you learning anything?"

"Yeah," said Bob in a half laugh. "A lot of bad parents. I think that I was a good father." Bob had made his second appointment through an answering service. It had been three weeks since he first met Dr. Conte.

"What are you doing for relaxation, recreation?"

"I work out. I joined a gym. I go to the library frequently. I do a lot of research on divorces on children, battered women, and I listen to music."

"How about friends?"

Bob said in a gloomy tone, "Well, I am friendly with my roommates. Met a wild and a kinda crazy guy in class."

"How about Tom?"

"I have not seen Tom in weeks. Too busy looking for work. I'm responding to menial jobs, such as warehouse work." Bob stopped to light a cigarette. Showing some disappointment. "I prepared a different résumé depicting different type of work experience. I watered down my educational background, stating I have an associate degree in business. I am walking the pavement, filling applications at retail stores." Bob smiled. "I did have two interviews."

Dr. Conte motioned his head. "Well, that's good. I'm happy to hear that at least you're making friends. Sounds like you are doing okay." Dr. Conte did not take notes. "Dating?"

"I have no interest."

"Any contact with your wife?"

Bob's mind lapsed. The pain and hurt surfaced. His face became flush, and his shoulders perspired. "I still have a hard time understanding her action." Tears started to form. "I don't understand why I can't see my children. I don't understand why Dr. Soble wrote such a report."

"You have to accept what is going on. You have to let go of her. And with time you will. You'll see, it takes time. You had a long relationship. Keep busy, continue doing what you're doing." Dr. Conte, believing that Bob was making every effort, could not make any suggestions. He asked, "What's the status of your divorce?"

"I've been trying to get in touch with my attorney. The last conversation I had with him, he said that by June the divorced would be finalized. As much as I want to believe that, I doubted it very much. I see no progress, no negotiations, no settlement of property." Bob shook his head. "Fucking attorneys! They have a license to steal."

"You got to push him. You need to get this thing over. Once it's over, you'll have less pressure, and you'll feel better."

"Don't you think I'm trying?" said Bob annoyed. "He tells me that everything is progressing. I keep telling him that I want to see my children. I told him that I was attending parenting classes and I was in counseling. What the fuck am I paying this guy over two hundred dollars an hour for? I don't think he's done shit." Bob paused, sadly. "I want to see my children. I feel that my attorney has abandoned me. Perhaps if you can contact him."

Conte frowned. "I did talk to your attorney regarding visitation. He said that Dr. Soble was in charge. You're the professionals. You guys work it out. I contacted Dr. Soble." Carmen shook his head. "I can't figure him out."

"He's an asshole," interrupted Bob.

"I told him that you have accepted the situation. You should be seeing your children without a monitor. This separation is not good for the children. He wouldn't agree to visitations. However, I did get an agreement that he would consider the possibility after you complete the parenting course. Once completed, he wants to see you to reevaluate you."

"I don't like the asshole," said Bob, grinning his teeth. "I don't want to see him."

"You have to." Looking deep into Bob's eyes, he said, "Hey, you want to see your kids?"

"I hate that shit head. I just might lose my cool and tell him how I feel."

"Just play the game. You're smart enough to know what he wants to hear. Don't argue with him."

Bob felt relaxed that he had a friend. "I'll do whatever is possible."

Dr. Conte said reassuringly, "I'll push him. This shit pisses my off. Give me a cigarette." Carmen lit the cigarette and puffed a sigh of relief. "Under the circumstance that you are going through, you're doing great. Visit me on a needed basis and pay whatever you can afford. I'll tell Soble that I'm seeing you regularly."

Bob completed the parenting program. Bob had a job in his field with BP Carbons (earning less) located in Lakewood. Bob was stunned that his attorney, Mr. Schurer, notified him that he had been appointed a judge. Schurer informed Bob that he had to resign his practice. His partner, Mr. Saylor, was currently handling his case. Schurer had suggested that Bob had three options—let Mr. Schurer's partner handle the case, though he was currently busy. He could recommend another attorney without requiring a retainer or get his own attorney.

The telephone conversations that Bob had with his children were frustrating and unfulfilling. He was in his room drinking heavily. He picked up the telephone and dialed. He listened carefully to each ring. After the fourth ring, the recorder answered, "Ann, it's me, Bob. Please, I need to talk to you. I just want—"

"What do you want?" broke in Ann.

"Thank you for picking up the phone," said Bob nervously. "This Sunday is Easter, and I would like to see the boys. Please, let me see them."

"Talk to Dr. Soble," said Ann sharply.

"I hoped that we can work something out. Just for a couple of hours."

"I'm sorry, but I have plans."

"Can I just come by for an hour?"

Ann, in control, said, "Don't come by the house. You have a restraining order to stay away."

"A restraining order is only as good as I want to respect it. I just want to see the boys for a little while."

Ann was jittery. She responded, "I'll talk to Dr. Soble."

"Ann, why are you doing this? It's important that I have a relationship with my children."

"Yes, I agree," said Ann calmly.

"Then why are you preventing me from seeing the children?"

"It's you, Bob. Not me."

Bob, in a stern voice, said, "You had no choice. You didn't have a father. Your father died when you were young." Bob pleaded, "Please, our boys have a father. They're going to need me… I want to be in their lives. They need to be around me. Don't you realize the psychological damage you're causing?"

Ann shouted back, "Oh, you're going to blame me for everything. You're going to tell them it's my fault."

"When they're old enough, they will ask questions."

Ann hung up. Bob called back and listened carefully to each ring. The recorder answered. Bob shouted, "You've really turned into a bitch. A real bitch." And he hung up.

Bob was so overwhelmed by frustration, and he needed to vent. He called Marion, no answer. He called Vinnie and Pete, no answer. Bob was stewing. He was disturbed by the sound of a loud bang coming from Chet's room. Bob quickly opened the door. He caught a glimpse of a woman and Chet following. He heard voices coming from the living room. Bob was curious to get a better look at the woman. He went into the kitchen to get some ice cubes. Chet and the woman were in the living room with beer cans in hand. The woman called out to Bob, "I hear you're from New York."

"No, New Jersey," replied Bob.

"Well, it's close enough," she said, smiling. "I'm from New York. My name is Kim."

The room was dark except for the light coming from the kitchen. Bob thought, *How could Chet get a woman like that; a pretty face and attractive body*? "My name is Bob Dorsete. Nice to meet you." Bob noticed that Chet was annoyed by his presence. "Well, I guess I'll leave you two alone."

"No, don't leave," Kim said with a smile. "I enjoy talking to people from back East."

Chet, fidgeting, said, "Bob is separated from his wife. He has five—or is it six?—children."

"It's four boys. I'm waiting for my divorce to be finalized." It was obvious to Bob that Chet wanted to be alone with Kim. "I have to prepare for work tomorrow. Nice meeting you. Good night."

"What are you drinking?" asked Kim.

"Scotch...Would you like some?"

Kim stared at Bob with sensuous eyes. "Sure."

"How about you, Chet?" Bob asked.

"I'm good," he said, holding up the can.

Bob went to his room with Kim following. He felt a bit nervous as he poured her glass. Kim smiled. "I would like to give you my number."

Bob grinned. "I would like that very much."

"Hey, I'll have some Scotch," said Chet as he entered the room. Bob handed him the bottle. "Let's go to my room," Chet said, grabbing Kim's hand.

"No, it's getting late. I have to go." She turned to Bob. "Good night." She turned and left. Chet followed her out.

Bob was driving slowly, researching for house numbers. He stared to make sure that it was the right number. It was an old wood frame building in need of repairs. He carefully walked up the steps and knocked on the door. A man opened the door. He had a beer in one hand and stroked his long hair back with the other. Bob examined the unfriendly blank face. "What do you want?" asked the man.

Bob regained his speech to ask, "Is Kim home?"

The man turned around and shouted, "Kim, your date's here!"

"Let him in!" Kim shouted back. "I'll be down in five minutes."

Bob was uneasy as he waited impatiently, thinking about what to say and do. Kim entered the room. Bob stood up and stared in silence. She smiled and moved in rhythm, giving him a good look at what she wore. She had black high heels, a black leather miniskirt and halter, and a black hat with a bright red band. She was in all black except for bright red lipstick outlined with a dark line and the red band around the hat. Her clothing matched her short dark curly hair, enhancing her round smooth face of olive-brown tan skin.

As they got into the car, Bob said, "You look great! Where would you like to go?" All that he could think about was how gorgeous she looked.

"Not to your place. I don't want to run into Chet. The guy that answered the door rents the place with his girlfriend."

"Would you like to go to a bar?"

"Where?"

"There's a bar close to my place. I hang out there to shoot pool."

"Sure! I shoot pool."

"Great. They serve some food." Bob felt awkward and strange, unsure of what to say. It had been a long time since he had been with another woman. He did not want to say the wrong thing nor make a bad impression. They were silent as he drove.

It was a weekday, and the place was nearly empty except for a few customers. Bob led Kim to the far end of the L-shaped bar. The times that Bob had been here, he never made friends or acquaintances. He made small talk with the bartenders. Kim was drinking double martinis, and Bob was drinking Scotch. Bob tried making conversation by asking questions. Kim, in a firm annoyed voice, said, "What's with the sixty-nine thousand questions?"

"I'm only trying to get to know you," said Bob, feeling uncomfortable.

"All right. But no questions."

Bob moved closer to her and put his arm around her waist. "Hey, what's with the arm?" said Kim. "Do you mind keeping your hands to yourself?"

Bob felt strange with her. He thought, *This is it. I'm ready to take her home. I'll give it five minutes. I'll make one last effort.* He asked, "So you shoot pool?"

"Yeah, I want you to know. I'm pretty good for a girl."

Bob, in a half chuckle, said, "Good, I don't mind competition." There were two pool tables. One was occupied by two man. Bob placed two quarters in the coin slot. Bob racked the balls, and Kim broke first. Every time Kim bent forward, the two men stared. They were doing more watching than playing. They gawked like hungry wolves smelling the scent. The bigger man with long hair and an unshaven face walked over. Looking at Kim, he turned to Bob and asked, "Play partners. Me and my friend against you and your lady friend."

"Sorry," said Bob, "we'd like to be by ourselves."

The man stood still for a moment. Then he turned to Kim and asked, "Hey, sexy lady, what's your name?"

Holding the pool stick with arms crossed, she said, "Marilyn Monroe. What's it to you?"

The guy smiled and said, "Just wanted to know." He turned and walked away.

Bob stood in silence and thought, *Boy, this lady is hard.* After a couple of games, Bob and Kim returned to the bar. Bob ordered nachos and more drinks. They ate in silence. Bob broke the silence by asking, "How do you know Chet?" In a hesitant tone, he asked, "Are you two…uh…dating?"

"We're friends," Kim said firmly. "No, just business."

"What kind of business?"

In an angry tone, Kim said, "Business! That's all, just business. Stop with the questions."

"Well, I'm sorry." Bob was not concerned about making a bad impression and ready to take her home. "I'm not trying to be a busy-body. I was only trying to make conversation."

"Look! All night long, all you've been doing is asking questions. Maybe I want to keep my personal life private. I don't know you."

"I'm sorry. I didn't mean to pry into your personal life. I honestly just want to get to know you." Bob paused. "I'll be honest. It has been a long time since I have been with a different woman." Bob ordered another drink. "Chet and I talk a lot. He never mentioned any business. I know that he's hurting for money since he got laid off. He sold just about everything he had. I share my cigarettes with him, paid for food. I want to help the guy."

"He's a loser," said Kim without emotion.

Bob was surprised by her comment. "I thought he was your friend."

"I told you, it's just business with us." She grinned. "The night that I met you, I was in his room. We were smoking grass. He says that he enjoys smoking in the nude. He starts to undress. He took off his shirt and started to undo his pants. I told him to keep his clothes on or I would leave. He told me to relax, to take off my clothes. I refused. Then he tried to kiss me so I walked out of the room."

Bob said, "Yeah, I was distributed by the sound of the door and how quickly you were walking. Why didn't you leave the house if you were upset?"

Kim moved closer to him, stared into his eyes, and said, "I saw you, and I wanted to meet you. I was glad that you came over and started talking to me. I saw you once before. Chet told me you were a decent guy with education and a good job. I think you're that—you're a handsome Italian."

Bob smiled. It pleased him to hear such words. "Well, thank you." He placed his hand under her chin and moved closer to meet her lips. He gave her a gentle kiss.

Kim said, "I'm half Italian from my mother's side. I'm originally from New York… I'll tell you, the men in California think they're hot stuff. They're not like the guys back East. The guys from the East are more down-to-earth. They don't have to prove anything."

Bob kissed her gently on her lips. Kim put her arms around him as they kissed hard. Bob noticed that everyone in the bar was watching. He stopped and said, "Kim, everybody is watching."

"So what? Let them eat their hearts out... Tell me about the work you do."

Bob, talking very discreetly, put his hand on her knee and gently rubbed it. He slowly moved his hand inside her inner thighs. She did not object. He tried to move higher, but her skirt was too tightly wrapped around her body. A further movement was impossible. Kim said, "Order me another drink. I'll be right back."

Bob glanced at the patrons. One of the men lifted up his beer bottle. Bob lifted his glasses in acknowledgment. The man asked, "Is she your lady?"

Bob replied, "Just a date."

"Man, she's some hot chick. And that leather. Wow!"

Kim returned, sat on the bar chair stool, and whispered into Bob's ear, "I took my panties off for you."

Bob felt the movement in his pants. He wanted to be in a private place with her. "Why don't we leave and go to my place?"

"I'm not ready yet," said Kim, smiling and displaying her freshly painted lips. Her eyes fixed on Bob as she raised the glass to her lips.

The same guy from before approached them. He looked at Kim and said, "Lady, you look hot. If you and your friend have time, I'd like to get to know you."

With confidence and a smile, Kim said, "Hey, big guy. I got a lover." Looking at Bob, she continued, "He's the best and all I need."

In disappointment, the guy turned and walked away. Kim put her arms around Bob. Kissing his neck, she said, "Let's go to your place." Bob smiled favorably at her and took her hand in his. Amused by her astonishment, they walked out.

Bob nervously unlocked the door to his room. He was apprehensive if he could perform. As soon as they entered the room, Kim put her arms around him and started kissing him. She opened her mouth, searching for his tongue. Bob responded. Her hands were all over as she started to undress him. They kissed while they undressed each other. Kim had her back against the wall as he bounced on her. She wrapped her arms and legs around him. He placed his hands on her buttocks. He turned and carefully walked to the bed and fell forward with Kim underneath. He gently cupped her tiny breasts and gave specific attention to her large erected nipples. He had her entire breast in his mouth, biting gently at first. The harder he bit, the more she moaned with excitement. "The door's open," said Kim, giggling. Bob got up to close the door.

His fears were suppressed by desire. They eagerly engaged in a long hot session of love. He felt like a whole man, believing that he had satisfied her. "Would you like a drink?"

"What do you have?" Kim asked.

"Scotch and bourbon."

"I'll take the bourbon."

Bob draped a towel around his waist and left the room. He returned with two glasses filled with ice. Kim was in bed with the sheets up to her chest covering her breast and tucked beneath her arms. As he poured, her eyes were fixed on his naked body. She watched his every move. "Please hand me my cigarettes," asked Kim. Bob lit a cigarette. She stared into his eyes as he placed it between her lips. "You have a nice ass," said Kim, beaming, "and a sexy chest."

Bob, smiling, handed her the glass and moved between the sheets against her naked body. He gently nuzzled and bit her nipples as he stroked her naked body. Feeling very satisfied, she said, "You're v-very good."

"You're not just saying that to make me feel good."

"I mean it. I knew you were good."

"It's been a long time for me. Almost a year since I…" said Bob as he kissed her. "I made love to a woman."

Kim was surprised. "A guy with your looks. You're telling me it's been over a year. You don't have a girlfriend, at least two?"

"I'm in the middle of a divorce. I still have feelings for my wife." He stopped touching her. "I have four children that I haven't seen in over a year."

"Don't stop." She placed his hand on her body. "Yeah, I divorced my old man two years ago. He's still chasing me. He still wants to get me in bed." She rolled over Bob and started to kiss and bite his lip. They embraced and made love again.

Exhausted and satisfied, they lay in bed, talking. Bob told Kim about his entire situation. She was very sympathetic. She also expressed the same dislike for attorneys and divorce. Bob glanced at the clock. "Oh, shit! It's one in the morning. I have to be up at six for work."

Kim said, "Call in sick. Let's spend the whole day in bed."

It was noon when they got out of bed. They got dressed to get something to eat. As they walked out of the room, Chet opened his door. He gawked at Kim and said, "What are you doing here? I've been calling you for days. You haven't returned my phone calls."

Ignoring Chet, Kim said, "Bob, let's go."

Chet looked at Bob and said, "Oooh, I see. I understand." He returned to his room and slammed the door.

Daniel McGrath did not want this case, especial a friend of Shelby with possible drug problems. He didn't think that it was just love gone bad. He did not like this case because of the allegations of abuse and monitored visitation. There were so many documents filed with the court. He passed over the documents of the court orders of June, July, and August. He found documents that had been filed and signed by the commissioner of the court for September, October, and November.

There was a continuation of restraining orders. Many subpoenas issued for information of Bob's payroll history and complete benefits, statements regarding his savings plan, retirement benefits, and pension. A stipulation to void the orders. *The case is a mess*, he thought, *but no drugs mentioned.*

Daniel McGrath was a big man in his fifties. His face was round and babyish-looking. His skin was white, reflected by his curly white-blond hair. His speech was soft and low. His voice sounded abnormal, too gentle for such a large man. "Mr. Dorsete, as I told you two weeks ago, I am currently busy. I don't have time to get involved in your case. I did have a chance to review your files. Do you want this divorce or not?"

"Yes," said Bob with a surprised look on his face.

"There hasn't been a date filed for the divorce. The petition was filed over a year ago, and no one has filed for "At Issue for Memorandum" to get a court date for the final divorce. Your entire case…it's like a plate of spaghetti. It has loose ends all over the place. Every time I pick up one string of spaghetti, it just doesn't go anyplace. Your case is a mess."

Bob sat in silence, staring at McGrath, and thinking about Schurer. What an asshole. Bob was astonished. "Have you been in contact with my former attorney, Mr. Schurer? I thought everything was in order. He told me the case was progressing nicely."

Mr. McGrath replied, "No, I made several calls, and he has not returned my calls. I have had several conversations with Mr. Walsh. He wants accountability of the community funds that were entrusted to your attorney. Do you know how much there was?"

"To my knowledge, I've never received any accountability. I think there is about twelve thousand dollars."

"Mr. Walsh stated that you have not made your family support payments and he plans to take you to court for contempt. Also, neither you nor your attorney have submitted the "Questions for Admission." He also said you constantly bother her by calling and upsetting her."

Bob interrupted, "That is bullshit! I call to talk to my children."

"Do you realize that you have restraining orders not to disturb her? I am confused. Do you have visitation or monitored visitation with your children?"

"Yes. Supervised by a Dr. Soble. I want to see my children."

"I'm sorry, I cannot address that issue until later. Perhaps in two or three months. There is so much I have to clean up before we can move forward. My first priority is to reply to Mr. Walsh's questions and allegations. Then I need to know their position. That is if we can negotiation various property settlements outside of court. This will determine as to the amount of court time we need so that I can file for 'At Issue for Memorandum' to get you divorce."

Bob was inflamed. "What about my children? That's my priority."

In a stern, robust voice, Mr. McGrath said, "I wasn't your attorney at the start of the case. Don't raise you voice at me for what others have done." McGrath thought, *I don't want another unhinged client.* "I'm telling you what I have to do. You have to be patient and trust me."

"Trust!" Bob stood up and paced the floor, repeating the word *trust* several times. "That's all I've been hearing. I trusted her. I trusted my attorneys. I trusted Dr. Soble. I'm not in a very trusting mood."

"I'm in sympathy with you, I understand. But before I can proceed forward, I need to resolve all these loose ends. You have to be patient. And most importantly, don't do anything stupid."

Bob was slowly learning the hard way, understanding the legal system. A system that is burden with too many cases and human emotions. A society with too many attorneys and not enough court time. Judges that don't have time to hear all the facts while the attorney meters continue to run, run, run. The mother is the direct beneficiary of society's overzealously desire to protect the children. Bob always believed in America and in equality. He believed women should be paid the same wages as men for the same type of work. He also believed in justice for all. His love and respect for America had diminished.

Bob and Kim spent a lot of time together. He had opened up to her and told her everything about himself, yet he knew very little about her. They were in his room, in bed, listening to music. "Chet's pissed off at me," said Bob. "Just the other day, he accused me of stealing you away from him. Calling you his girl."

"I was never his girl." She moved her fingers around his well-defined chest. "He's a goddamn fuckin' liar. He's a user. Let me tell you… His brain is so screwed up. The guy's been doing drugs for too long. He can't even think straight."

"I kind of like the guy. I feel sorry for him. Since he lost his job, I have been giving him money. He approaches me like a little boy asking for cigarettes, money to buy beer and food, money for transportation. He owes me about five hundred dollars."

In an annoyed tone, Kim said, "I wouldn't do shit for him. You know how many times he asked me to suck his dick. He's a perverted son of a bitch."

Bob asked, "Then why did you come over to see him?"

"Business. I told you it was business."

"Look, Kim, I'm not stupid. What are you involved in?" He felt concerned for her.

Kim held back the tears. "Okay, you want to know. I'm his dealer. I don't want to get you involved. I know you're straight. I sell drugs to him and other people he knows."

"That son of a bitch!" said Bob in an angry tone. "He told me that he wasn't doing drugs. Here I am, lending him money, trying to keep him away from that crap."

"You're a fool. With the money you gave him, he bought drugs. He's trying to do a little dealing just to support his habit. Chet is a customer and a rat. He ratted on some guys in San Jose to stay out of jail. I like to smoke grass, but I don't do that heavy shit anymore. My daughters were taken away from me. I had a difficult time keeping a job. With drugs, it's easy to make money. So why should I give it up? My ex-old man is a big dealer in the area. Chet might tell him."

"Are married you?"

"Yes! But we are not together. Never hired a lawyer to get divorced. He still wants me. I'm afraid if he finds out about you, he might hurt you."

"I'm not afraid! What the hell should I be frightened of? I'm not afraid of dying."

"Bob, you don't know these people. They'll do anything for drugs," she said with tears in her eyes. "I like you very much. You're very sexy and so sensitive to a woman's body. You're the best lover I've ever had."

Bob's ego was inflated. "Are you just saying that?"

"No, I mean it. You're very good. I have a good time with you. I didn't want you to know about my business." Sobbing, she said, "I didn't want you to get involved. You're a nice guy." She turned away from him. "I'm not good enough for you. You deserve a decent woman, not like me."

His hands encircled her face. "Let's put that all aside." He gently kissed her and held her tightly, trying to remove her fears and worries. They engaged in the simplicity of pleasure only experienced by *Homo sapiens*. They went beyond hedonistic pleasure only experienced by lonely people in need of love.

In the following weeks, Kim broke a lot of dates. Bob could not get in touch with her, and she did not return his phone calls. Late one evening, Bob was in his room, drinking and watching TV. The phone rang. He picked up the phone and said, "Hello." There was no reply, and then he heard the dial tone. Ten minutes later, it rang. Bob picked it up, and there was no reply. Five minutes later, it rang again. Bob picked it up and said, "Who is it? Who is this? What do you want?"

A low, distant voice said, "Bob, it's me…Kim."

"Kim, where have you been? I've been trying to get in touch with you. Are you okay?"

"I want to k-k-ill myself," said Kim, sobbing. "I want to die."

"Kim, I know life is tough. But we can all make it with help. What's the matter?"

"I've been doing some heavy drugs," she said in a fragile voice. "I'm sorry if I disappointed you. I didn't want you to see me this way."

"Where are you? I'll pick you up. We can talk about it. I'll try to get help for you."

"No! You don't understand. You don't understand. I've been to those places. They can't help me."

"Kim, please! Let me try to help you." Bob helplessly tried to find the words.

There was a long pause. "I want to die. I miss my daughters. I miss everything I used to have." Her sobbing was becoming heavy. "I'm not a decent person…I just want to die."

"No! You're a good person. Don't talk like that. You're just going through a rough time."

"Yeah, ten fuckin' years of it." In a stronger voice, she said, "Ten fuckin' years of running from the law."

"What do you mean?"

"They have warrants for my arrest." She stopped to collect her thoughts. "I was busted with my old man. They wanted me to testify against him. I didn't. I was found guilty of possession. After a month, I was paroled. He knows that the police want me to talk. Now he's concerned that I might testify against him. He's got powerful friends. He wouldn't have any hesitation about having me killed." She paused. "I'm tired… I've been smoking some coke just to feel better. To get the nerve to say…to say goodbye."

Bob understood. Many times he thought of dying. He drank to ease his pain. How could he judge her? "I'm your friend. I care about you. Let me help you."

"Thank you for being good to me."

"You got to listen to—" She hung up the phone. Bob was having difficulty sleeping that evening, thinking of Kim. Bob never saw or heard from Kim. He often thought about her. How exciting it was to make love to her. But she was not Ann. No one could ever replace Ann. He felt sorry for Kim. Life was taking him through a journey of new experiences of strange ordeals. He came to the realization that he could never judge anyone ever again unless he had been there. He was learning one of the lessons that Marion had predicted. It was not new; it's in the gospel.

Chet had received eviction papers to move out. While Bob was at work, Chet broke into Bob's room and stole the TV, portable radio, and Bob's suits.

Chapter 13

The days were getting warmer and longer. It was early May, the sign of Taurus, Bob Dorsete's sun sign. Good things happened around his birthday. Bob Dorsete was at the office of Dr. Soble. The two men quietly examined each other. One beaten and struggling for his rights and survive. The other was a twentieth-century Freudian Crusader.

"Have you seen my report?" said Dr. Soble.

"Yes," replied Bob.

"I know that perhaps you don't agree with its contents. I am in charge of this case, and those are my judgments."

"That's your opinion."

"I see that you are making progress." He was surprised that Bob Dorsete showed little resentment. He felt more at ease. So he continued, "You are attending parenting classes, and you are in counseling."

"I have completed the course," interrupted Bob.

"Oh, that's right. Dr. Conte told me. He recommends that you have normal visitation with your children." He paused to observe Bob's face. "I'm still concerned about you and your efforts to reconcile with Ann. Do you have that interest?"

"No," said Bob cold as stone as he lied. "I'm not interested in reconciliation. I want to get divorced. I want to see my children, and I want to go on with my life."

"Good," said Dr. Soble. "I'm very happy to hear that. I think you have come a long way. How do you feel if some of your children don't want to see you?"

"I'm not going to force them. I would like to see all of them. If any of them don't want to see me, I understand and accept it."

"Good," said Dr. Soble with some excitement in his voice. "Have you, in your sessions with Dr. Conte, discussed codependencies and barriers?"

Bob was uncertain as to what to say. "We talked about a lot of things, but we did not get into a course in psychology. I'm not sure if we did or did not talk about boundaries and codependencies."

"Well, Bob, I want you to continue your sessions with Dr. Conte and get into discussions regarding codependencies and boundaries. It will help you understand better."

Bob, in agreement, nodded, but inside he was a bit irritated. "Dr. Soble, what do I have to do to prove to you and the world how I feel about my children? You wrote a very damaging and negative report, but I'm here. I accept your authority, and I am willing to cooperate with you."

Dr. Soble was taken by his words. But the change was too quick, he thought. "I can see that you are making the efforts. I'm glad that you are complying with my recommendations. I believe that you are ready to see your children without a monitor. Let me get Ann in here so that we can discuss visitation." He stood up and left the office.

Ann Dorsete nervously entered the office. She made efforts not to look at Bob. She sat on a hard chair next to the couch that Bob was sitting. She kept her eyes and face fixed forward looking at Dr. Soble, and she vigorously chewed gum. Dr. Soble said, "I believe that Bob is ready to see the children without a monitor. Ann, do you have any concerns?" Ann jolted her head in silence. Inside, she was dismayed that he won ground. "Now I caution you," continued Dr. Soble, looking at Bob. "Don't put pressure on them and don't talk about the situation. Don't mention anything or ask questions about Ann."

Bob stared without showing emotions, nodding. "Yes."

Dr. Soble resumed, "Just have fun with them. I wanted to get a written agreement. For the first month, we'll start slowly. I feel that pairing off the children, the two oldest and the two youngest, will make the visits a lot more fun for the boys. Do you have any problems with that, Ann?"

Ann, in a soft voice, replied, "No."

"Ann, when and what time would it be convenient for you?"

"Sunday, from twelve to four."

Dr. Soble looked at Bob. "Is that okay with you?"

Bob nodded. "Yes."

Ann interrupted, "I don't want him at the house."

"What do you suggest?"

"We could meet at a local restaurant," said Ann with a little hostility.

"That's kind of childish," said Bob as he stared at Dr. Soble.

Dr. Soble said, "Bob, if that's the way she wants it."

"I'm renting a two-room townhouse. I'd like to spend more time with the boys in the summer when they finish school, perhaps one-on-one during the week."

"I think that's an excellent idea," said Dr. Soble. "Let's see how things go first. Another important issue." He paused and studied their faces. "I want you both to agree that you will not talk through the children. Don't relay messages or conversations with each other through them. Learn to talk to each other." Bob drafted, thinking of Ann. How badly he missed her. Her love, her tenderness, and her soft, sweet body. "Even though you are not married, you're going to have to deal with each other for a long time." Dr. Soble stopped to examine their faces. "If there are no questions, I'll make a copy of this agreement, and visitations can start immediately this weekend." He stood up and left the room.

Bob turned to Ann and asked, "Can I ask you something?"

"What?"

"I have not filed my tax returns. I need documents and information from you."

Ann, in an angry tone, said, "My attorney said I don't have to give you anything."

Bob replied in a strong tone, "That's where you're wrong. The rental property, the house you're living in. We still have joint ownership. I need to know the expenses and income to complete my taxes."

Ann said in a harsh tone, "There you are, always trying to control me. You haven't changed!"

Bob, in an effort not to get into a confrontation with her, stood up and walked toward the door. Dr. Soble reentered the room. He was puzzled and asked, "What's going on?"

Bob replied first, "I just asked for documents so that I can file my income taxes. She starts getting argumentative."

Ann's face flushed. "He's a liar!"

"Okay, calm down you two?"

Bob explained, "We have two properties. She has all the paperwork."

Dr. Soble said, "Ann, just make copies. He has a right to those documents."

Ann said, "My attorney told me not to give him anything."

Dr. Soble was a little annoyed. "You have to get along. You two should be in counseling."

Bob interrupted, "Dr. Soble, I accepted what's going on, but she hasn't, that's the problem. I can't talk to her. She has a difficult time dealing with me."

Ann was annoyed. "He is always telling me to stop the divorce."

Dr. Soble interrupted, "You have to learn to deal with each other. I'd like to recommend someone." He opened his desk drawer. He handed them a business card. "I recommend that you both seek counseling." Both Ann and Bob nodded. "In addition, as part of the visitation program"—he turned to Bob—"I want to see you every other week. Ann, I want to see the children every other week to monitor the progress. Bob, I have not received any payments in months. Can you make a payment before the next session?"

"Yes, I'll sent you a money order."

They all stood up. "Bob, wait here a few minutes while Ann leaves."

Bob had done this before, then distinctly replied, "No! I'll go first. Let her wait." Dr. Soble and Ann froze in astonishment.

It had been eight months since Bob had seen his children. He felt very awkward with them, and they felt strange with their father. Bobby, now fourteen, and Tony, eleven years old, demonstrated hostilities, addressing Bob as dude. Bob hoped that in time they would have a friendlier relationship. He accepted and understood that it was not their fault and that it would take time. Chuck was not hostile but not warm. They were like strangers. Mark was four years old and enjoyed embracing his father. Bob had to hold back his tears. After two months, the visitations had included midweek visits for two hours. The days were getting longer. Bob's heart was alleviated with warmth and hope that the one-on-one visits would enhance his relationship. Bobby on Tuesday, Tony on Wednesday, Chuck on Thursday, and Mark on Friday. Bob would pick up one of his sons at six. For a couple of hours, he would go to a local park and play soccer, basketball, or baseball. He also toss a Frisbee around. Other times, he would go to a restaurant and just talk.

On Sunday, Bob informed Bobby that they would be seeing each other on Tuesday and asked Bobby what he wanted to do. Bobby was less than enthusiastic about seeing his father alone. Tony heard the conversation and expressed his desire to see his father. I'll see you on Wednesday. Bob did not want to force Bobby to see him. He thought of discussing the switch with Ann. Bob changed his mind and decided to adhere to the agreement. Monday night, before the scheduled visit, Bob called Ann to confirm the time and place. Ann said, "You're taking both Bobby and Tony."

"That is not according to the agreement," said Bob.

"Well, you're the one who told the boys that you would see the two of them."

"No, that was not what I said. It's just that Bobby was a little more reserved while Tony was more anxious. But as Dr. Soble said, we're not to talk through the children. You're altering the agreement."

"Well, that's the arrangements," said Ann without fear of retaliation. "Like it or not, that's the way it's going to be."

Bob was in fury. "You can't do that. It's not right. You're acting like a bitch! I'm going to call Dr. Soble." And he hung up the telephone.

Throughout the night, Bob could not sleep. He was angry and annoyed that they were fighting over such a little thing. He feared Ann. He thought that she might complain to Dr. Soble. He was in a catch-22. If he did not follow the agreed schedule, Dr. Soble might withdraw Bob's visitation.

The next morning, Bob thought that they were acting childish. He was annoyed that Ann was acting so spiteful and that she wanted to be in control. The more he thought about it, the more he realized how immature it would be to go running to Dr. Soble. It would only demonstrate their inability to cooperate with each other. Bob decided to give in. He called Ann. No one picked up the phone, so he left a message that he was sorry for the argument and he would accept whatever plans or arrangements she wanted.

It was midmorning. Ann called Bob at his office. In a victorious and satisfied tone, she said, "I spoke to Dr. Soble. He said you can't see the children. And if you come around here, I'll have you arrested."

"What are you talking about?" asked Bob in a surprised tone. "What kind of pressure?" Bob quickly reacted to the slamming sound of the telephone by moving the receiver away from his ear. Bob was uncertain if Ann was telling the truth. He did not trust her. He did not want to see his children with a monitor.

"Dr. Soble called me to see you immediately because you were antagonistic with your wife, and she fears that you might act," Dr. Conte explained. "Dr. Soble said that you violated your visitation agreement."

"That's not true," said Bob, annoyed and irritated. "It was just a little thing."

"Your wife complained that you threaten her and using your children to get to her."

Bob yelled, "That's a lie!"

In a firm voice, Dr. Conte said, "I questioned Dr. Soble in that there are two sides to a story and that he should hear your side. He got exasperated, stating that he was in charge."

Bob was bothered. "I did talk to him. I told him that it was a trivial, silly disagreement. He stated that he would talk to Ann to smooth things over. That afternoon, I called her, and she refused to pick up the phone. How can I pick up the boys if she won't talk to me?"

Carmen was confused. "You had a conversation with Dr. Soble?"

"Yes!"

"When?"

"The same day. After she called."

Carmen was baffled. "He called me to see you immediately as if you might be going looney. This shit pisses me off. Give me a cigarette." Carmen lit the cigarette. "I quit smoking. It is times like this I get truly pissed that I need a cigarette. You have to get rid of this guy. He is not on your side."

"I told you that he's an asshole."

"You understand. If you want to see your boys now, it will have to be with a monitor. I'll contact your attorney, Mr. Schur—"

Bob interrupted. "I have a new attorney."

"Why?"

Bob laughed. "He quit on me. He's a judge now."

Carmen grabbed a pen. "What's his name?"

Bob said, "Here's his card."

"Daniel McGrath. Don't know this one."

Carmen chuckled. "Kid, you got no luck."

Bob smiled. "Better! Scherer hasn't done a thing in months. My new lawyer told me that my case is a mess. He doesn't want to get involved with visitation for at least two or three months."

Dr. Conte said in a serene tone, "If you want to see your children, it will be supervised."

Bob shook his head. "No!"

Carmen said sincerely, "I'll wait a week and call Soble to see if he'll cut you a little slack."

A week passed, and Dr. Conte had informed Bob that he was unsuccessful in restoring unmonitored visitation for Bob. That night, Bob was thinking, *That's not fair. It has been over a year since the separation. My oldest boy is angry and bitter toward me. Sure, they're going to side with their mother and see me as the bad guy.* Bob felt bitter at Ann for lying. He was pissed at himself for allowing a tiny thing to end his visitation. After drinking heavily, his rationality was overtaken by anger. He called Ann. He left a message. "Ann, why are you doing this?" said Bob in an angry and loud voice. "Why are you acting like a bitch?"

Bob continued to drink to numb his rage. He was too tense and uncomfortable, so he went outside for some fresh air. He looked across the street at the silhouette of houses and trees. He looked up at the sky, examining God's creation. He noticed the bright crescent moon and three bright stars. They were not stars but the planets Jupiter, Mars, and Venus. He uttered out loud, "I'm the master of what I hold—my glass of wine, the blood of your son. My cigarette, the body of your son." Slowly, he dropped to his knees, released the glass and the cigarette, placed his hands together, and said, "God, give me the strength to carry on…to forgive her. Please, God, give me the strength. I come to you in your temple, the open skies. Are you punishing me for twenty years of rejection, of denouncing the church? Please forgive me. All I ask for is the strength." Tears were forming as he continued, "Please give me strength. Give me a sign." Tears of sadness blurred his vision. He saw glimpses of vague, ephemeral images moving toward him. He closed and opened his eyes. He saw silhouette of children waving to him. He stayed motionless and watched as the images disappeared into the distance. His mind was in a trance as he envisioned. Why couldn't she forgive me? Why can't she give me another chance? His heart needed a second chance.

In an excitable tone, Bob told Marion that he was back to monitored visitation. "I'm going to kill that bitch. I'm going to be patient. Wait for the right time. I'll pay her back for what she's doing to me."

Marion was aware that Bob was drinking, and perhaps he had too much. "Don't drink so much," said Marion. "We care about you and don't want to see you destroy yourself."

Bob said, "It's just so difficult. I was a total waste last night. It's just this fucking life that I'm living."

"It will work out for you. Just be patient. I have your handkerchief with the Tarot cards. You do want me to read?"

"I'm anxious to hear what the cards hold for me."

"Okay, I'm going to press the on the speaker button. Can you hear me?"

"Yes," replied Bob.

"Now, you understand that a Tarot reading is a means to find answers to questions, to examine life, and to understand the inner and outer dimensions. This type of reading might not be as accurate as if you were here to pick the cards." Marion paused. "Okay, I laid a pattern of ten cards. They show that you will do well with money and with the courts. You'll get your possessions. But anyway, the Chariot card shows that things will work out well with the courts. Now I do see a new lawyer situation with you that is going to work out favorably. That is, you two will work well together. There are strong indications that you will soon have your troubles behind you in the winter, late winter. There seems to be conquests for you after the winter. Most of your struggles will be behind you."

Bob interrupted, "Another year of this bullshit."

Marion continued. "There are new beginnings or opportunities for you depicted by the Sun. The Rainbow card shows that you are going to go through a tranquil state before the year is up. You will have tranquility, getting most of what you are looking for, shown by the King of Pentacles. This card is a person that gets what he wants. I see the reentry of the children back into your life, and I see you dealing and working with them very nicely. You will have the opportunity to do what you want to do with them. Looks like things will turn around for you and that there will be healing with the children and yourself indicated by the Fool."

Bob calmly said, "Sounds nice, but I am so frustrated with the visits."

"I understand. It's been hard. I'm doing another spread, a thirteen-card spread. Okay, this shows a definite new beginning for you on the horizon. Again, after the winter. You're going to make changes. The Sun card came up again. I think toward the end of spring of next year. I see you setting in at your new apartment. There is an opportunity for you to find good things, indicated by the Page of Pentacles. It brings good news. I do see happiness for you with the children indicated by the Ten of Pentacles. There seems a better relationship, with at least two of the boys. They are coming around to your thinking level and being happy with you. You are happy with them. You'll have good health. Your health seems to be very strong. Again, you are going toward a period of tranquility. You will find tranquility within this year of this reading. There seems to be a lot of opportunities out there that are going to come to you in work situations and friends. It will be a year for growth. Growth with yourself mentally and physically."

Bob calmly said, "Sounds good."

"I'm doing a twenty-one-card spread now, a long reading. Okay, it does indicate that you are going to find a period of luck. You are going to have luck through the whole year. Now, there is a warning here about drinking. You can get involved in some sort of drinking or maybe sort of drug aspects. So be very careful. I don't want you to even think about that because the Tower sits over you. It could be very destructive. The Devil card keeps showing up. It does show a tendency for you to get involved with some heavy drinking to ease your burden. I don't want you to do that. I don't want you to do anything underhanded either, because the Devil card is not a good card. It signifies sneakiness. It shows something that is underneath, underhanded being done, or you are thinking about it. So be very careful. I don't want you to get too involved in any crazy shit."

Displeased, Bob said, "Are you making that up because I drink?"

"You know that I would not lie. Let me finish. There will be new beginnings for you to have an opportunity for love and romance, indicated by the Ace of Cups. There is a possibility." Marion paused. "It sounds far-fetched, but there might be some sort of reconciliation. But not right away. I'm talking maybe in the summertime of next year, signified by the Fool facing the Empress. The Moon is over them, which means that dreams and wishes come true. The Hanged Man shows that you will not lose what you thought you lost."

Marion went into a long pause. "I'm curious. The Queen of Cups keeps coming up. I'm going to do a reading of Ann. She is the Queen of Cups, which is the Gemini Queen. It shows that she is into a lot of problems. Like I've been saying, she is definitely not going to have a good year. I see a lot of struggle in front of her. I see a lot of sorrow around her. I do see maybe an illness that could come to her." Marion was true to his readings and would only tell Bob what he saw. "I wouldn't be too surprised," he said, hesitating. "The cards seem to show very favorably that there might be an opportunity for you to make some sort of peace with her. I'm not quite sure that you might get back with her. The Nine of Wands shows that you might be communicating, or she might want to communicate with you in a different level as the year progresses. I don't think it's going to be right away, looks more toward late in the year. Then she'll have a better attitude with you or toward you. I don't know if she is involved with another person, 'cause it does show another person sitting here. I'm not sure if that person represents you. It's the same card I used for you, but there is a dual aspect here—meaning, you or somebody else."

Marion paused. "I'm not sure if toward the end of the year or after the fall. There is some sort of way for her to be a little bit happier in the relationship but not now. It seems like she has a lot of difficulty around her. She is definitely worried about money and the courts. I don't think her career is going that well. She is finding difficulty in handling both career and house. It does show a lot of struggle around her, and she is going to have a difficult year."

Marion stopped to rest. Bob had mixed feelings hearing about Ann's struggles. "Well, that's it," said Marion. "You have to be patient. You are going to experience a good year of luck. Things are going to turn around for you. You will be contented and find yourself very strong by the end of this year of this reading."

Bob was disappointed. "Shit, I have to wait until next year. Nothing happening sooner?"

"Well, I've done several readings of the cards. They do show that you are going to have a promising year coming up. Just hold. Let things take their course. You'll get your children. The worse will soon be over, and you'll have control of your assets. Be patient. Give yourself time. I'm getting off the speaker. Now, as regards to the conversation we had the other night, I don't want to hear any of that stuff or talk from you. I don't want to have to worry about you all the time and what is going on in your head. Just take it slow. Take it easy. You can call me any time. We all love you."

On June 3, 1991, McGrath filed "Substitution of Attorney" from Schurer and Saylor. McGrath discovered that no one had filed an "At Issue for Memorandum" for the dissolution of the marriage. Walsh continued to send requests to McGrath while he was bogged with past-due requests for discoveries. There were past due family support, request for accounting of trust funds, community obligations now due, request for reimbursement, etc. McGrath spent the following months talking to Walsh, writing and filing counter-orders to show. McGrath had discussions with the court to address Walsh's ex parte (improper contact with a party or a judge) and request to deposit community property checks into his trust account. McGrath was meeting almost weekly with Bob to address all the open requests and issues. Bob wanted the removal of the restraining orders. McGrath advised that the removal of the restraining orders would be a waste of time.

Most of what Marion had predicted had come true, except for the relations with the boys and Ann. Bob's job, with BP Carbons, made life bearable. He had a steady weekly paycheck. He traveled biweekly to Northern California to visit his customers. He rented a two-bedroom townhouse. He was making the adjustment of living alone and making new friends. His job kept him busy, and he had found some kind of peace. He joined a bowling league and other clubs. He occasionally dated but no romance. He started gambling at the nearby casinos, playing Hold 'Em.

After three months, McGrath felt that he was sufficiently familiar with Bob's case and he had addressed the main issues. It was time to work on visitation for Bob. McGrath met with Walsh and Dr. Soble to discuss visitation. McGrath endeavored to turn the visitation matter to another professional for the purpose of reunifying Bob with his children. Walsh insisted that Dr. Soble remain since he had been involved since the beginning. Dr. Soble would consider visitation for Bob only after he evaluated Bob's current mental state. McGrath decide it was time to go on the offense. It was time to go to court. McGrath filed orders to show cause and "need for a present visitation" order.

In the behalf of his client, Walsh filed declarations, which delayed the scheduling of a court hearing. Walsh filed Demand for Production of Documents. The request was for income and employment information. The specific requests were for tax returns, copies of W-2, payroll stubs, all documents reflecting any/all efforts made to obtain employment, receipts for living expenses, all copies of profit and loss for investments, and all finances to real estate properties. In the weeks to follow, Walsh continued to file more motions. There was a Stipulation for Judgment, which the parties have stipulated to resolve all issue in the case, including the division of their community assets and obligations and visitation. McGrath argued with Walsh that the majority of these requests had been submitted. Walsh insisted that the previous submittals were a year ago and demanded up-to-date disclosures.

By November, McGrath thought if this was a deliberate tactic by Walsh to stall and frustrate his client. McGrath filed motions for a trial. In addition, McGrath made requests that Ann provide documents of income, accounting of funds held and monies from the rental property. On January 8, 1992, the court had scheduled a date for the trial, including McGrath's orders to show cause, "need for a present visitation" order. Ann had disagreed with the OSC; hence, the parties were required to participate in the mediation scheduled for February 13, 1992. A court hearing was scheduled for April 6, 1992.

In response, Walsh filed "Petitioner's Mandatory Settlement Conference Brief and Proposed Judgment" to a Mandatory Settlement Conference scheduled for March 31, 1992. Ann to have exclusive legal and physical custody of the children pursuant to stipulation of July 18, 1990. She requested that Bob paid for her legal fees, Dr. Sobel remain on the case, the residence be awarded to her, as well as all cash and property in her possession.

April 6, 1992

It had been over a year since Ann and Bob Dorsete had been in court. They had not seen each other for over ten months. Bob had infrequent conversations with his children. But today he had come to court on the issue of visitation with his children. Tom Connelly had agreed to testify for Bob. Bob had mixed feelings about seeing Ann, a love that turned to hate.

It was never made totally clear to Bob that a week before any hearings of visitation, the parties were mandated to a mediation conference for the purpose of discussing visitation with the court's mediators. Ann and Bob had attended one last week and another back in August 1990. Ann and Bob had the same two mediators. A man and a woman dressed in dark clothing like members of *The Addams Family* TV sitcom. Because they were so plain-looking, Bob viewed them as two lonely physiatrists who did even have children. Bob and Ann were interviewed separately and together. At the end of the session, Bob was asked to stay as Ann left. Bob never heard of any outcome or recommendations from the two mediation conferences.

It was past nine in the morning. Ann and Bob Dorsete and their respectful attorneys were in the courtroom, waiting their turn. *Dorsete vs. Dorsete* was called. McGrath and Walsh approached the bench. The whispered conversation lasted for several minutes. Mr. McGrath instructed Bob to go to the courthouse cafeteria.

Bob and Tom Connelly entered the cafeteria. The same place that Bob spent the majority of time. As usual, the tables were covered with papers, briefcases and pencils, pens and pads. The difference is that this is a new courthouse in Orange, whereas the other courthouse was in Santa Ana. Upon entering the cafeteria, Bob's eyes searched for a glimpse of Ann.

He spotted Ann. Bob and Tom sat at a table that was within eye contact of Ann. Bob stared at Ann. She noticed Bob the moment he walked. However, she avoided making eye contact. Bob thought, *Why all this anger? Why all this bitterness when there was so much love, so much caring, so much cherishing?* He placed his hands over his face to cover his eyes. He pressed his hands firmly against his cheeks, uncertain if to cry or pray. He spoke in silence. *Ann, can you hear my heart? Can you hear it calling to you? Trust your feelings. Feel the voice within. How many times do I have to say I'm sorry? Why all this destruction? Why all this confrontation? I want so desperately to…*

He was interrupted by a voice. "Bob! Are you okay?" asked Tom.

"I can't help it when I see her. Thanks for coming."

Tom very uneasily said, "I hate being in a courthouse. I hope Ann doesn't get mad at me."

"Don't worry about that. I only want you to tell the truth about my relationship with my children and how I treated them."

"Did you see Ann?"

"Yes, she's sitting over there," Bob said, turning slightly in the direction of Ann. She was sitting alone. "Would you like to say hello?"

Tom was reserved. He hasn't seen Ann since Memorial Day two years ago. He felt no animosity toward her. He disagreed with her course of action. "Sure!"

They approached Ann. Bob was the first to speak. "Good morning. Do you have any objections if I talk to you?"

Ann coldly replied, "No."

"How are you?"

"Fine," said Ann.

"How are the boys?"

In a stern voice, she said, "None of your business." With fire in her eyes, she turned to Tom and angrily said, "He twisted your arm, didn't he? He forced you to be here, didn't he?"

Tom was taken by surprised. He shrugged his shoulders. In a soft voice, Bob said, "Leave him alone."

"How did he force you?" Ann asked. "What did he tell you to say?"

"He's here of his own free will," Bob answered. "Stop harassing him." Resentfully, she looked at Bob and said, "Get out of here, or I'll make a scene!"

Making no reply, Bob and Tom walked away. "Boy, she is nasty," said Tom.

Bob replied, "What a bitch! She really has changed. It's sad to think that this is the same person that I once loved and cared for me.

This is the situation that I have had to deal with. I can't talk to her. She has become a bitter person and hates me."

Tom put his arm around Bob and, with a half-smile, said, "Well, today's your day. Fight for your kids. No matter what your relationship is with her, they're still your boys. I want to see you and the boys together."

Thirty minutes had passed before McGrath was in the cafeteria, informing Bob, "We're not going to have a hearing today. That Walsh is impossible."

Bob was disappointed. "No visitation? Why?"

"He's complicating things. Walsh insisted that Dr. Soble is in charge pursuant to California Code 730. Being in charge, Dr. Soble should appoint a reunification evaluator and direct and implement a reunification plan. Also, he appoints a visitation monitor to supervise visitations because you continue to disobey Dr. Soble's visitation recommendations."

"That is so bullshit!"

"I know. I told the judge that was nonsense. Walsh argued that the existing order provides a convenient vehicle for the court to establish, implement, and monitor visitation with Dr. Soble in charge. The judge was displeased that we had not settled the community assets. He stated that he would not have time to hear the case today. The judge instructed us to resolve the issues of community assets. He acknowledged that a trial was scheduled in thirty days."

"That is so fucking bullshit!" said Bob, enraged.

"I know. I have been auguring with that jerk for the past half hour. They want Soble to remain in charge. Walsh argued that you were arrears with child support and you intentional quit your job."

"That was in June 1990! I don't believe this shit," said Bob in an angry voice. He turned to Tom and continued, "You see the bullshit. This is the seventh, eighth time that I've been here. Nothing has ever been resolved in my favor. What rights do I have? Two years of this shit, and still, I have not had my day in court."

Tom, not knowing what to say, gently placed his hand on Bob's shoulder. "Hang in there. Don't let them break you."

"Ooooh, it's breaking me. Ooooh, I have thoughts of killing someone." Bob faced McGrath and asked, "What the hell are you doing for me?"

"I understand your frustrations," interrupted McGrath, upset. "I told you that your case was a mess. I have been in court many times, resolving old, outdated open orders to show cause regarding payment of legal fees, payment for Dr. Soble's fees, and a request for financial documents. Be patient." McGrath waited for Bob to calm down. He continued, "Your wife wants the house. She wants child support, retention of all the community cash, and sole legal custody of the children."

Bob hollered out, "She wants everything. I only want 50 percent of all assets and normal relationship with my children. What kind of bullshit is this! Yeah, I know what she wants. She wants to trade. I give her everything, then I get to see my children."

"Calm down," said McGrath. "I'm disappointed too. But I understand the judge's reasoning. Visitations is a complex matter, and Walsh did a good job insisting that Soble remain in charge. The judge strongly recommended that since we are here, we should make attempts to resolve the finances and reserve visitation for the trial."

Bob calmly said, "We had two mediation conferences with Mom and Pop Addams, the two so-called court psychologists. What were their recommendations?"

"As long as it was not negative on you, I never inquired."

"What guarantee can you give me that we'll be in trial in four weeks?" asked Bob.

"None!" replied McGrath, shrugging his shoulders. "You know that there are no guarantees."

"That's what I was afraid of," said Bob as he stood up and didn't care of the strangers' blank faces staring at him. "Did you explain to the judge that I haven't had normal visitations in almost two years."

"I presented the reunification plan with Dr. Reed."

Bob said, "Reunification! How many more psychologists do I have to see? How much more money do I have to piss away?"

McGrath interrupted, "As I explained before, your wife and her attorney want Soble in charge, and for reasons I don't understand, he's making it very difficult for you."

Bob replied, "Yeah, it's money. That's what he wants. He wants to keep his damn paws on the money coming in. I have paid his exorbitant bills."

McGrath said, "We have to face the fact that he is involved. If we can turn this over to Dr. Reed, we can get Soble off the case. Dr. Reed has worked with reunification programs, and he is an expert in the field. I have already been in contact with him regarding your case. He can't understand why you have been denied normal visitation. He'll work with us. He is a stronger believer that parents should have frequent and constant contact with their children."

Bob listened and tried to understand the new word that he heard and would have to deal with. He was confused and filled with frustration. He pounded his fist on the table. "Why should I even bother seeing my children? Look at all that I've had to endure." Bob stood up and paced back and forth. "How much more of this crap do I have to take? For almost two years, two years that I had little contact with my children, I don't even know who they are. I don't even know who they belong to. Am I their father? What is a father?"

Tom got up and held Bob in place. "They're your children. They love you, and I know that you love them."

Bob replied, "Do they really love me? Do you know how many birthdays, Father's Days, and Christmases have gone by?" Bob held up one finger up continued, "For the past year, not one phone, card, or any kind of a letter from my boys."

"Reunification is a start. A step forward," said McGrath. "We need to remove Soble. Trust me."

"Don't give up!" Tom added. "You're their father."

"Yeah," said Bob, venting. "More money to burn." He put his hands in his pockets and turned them inside out. "See my pockets are full of money. I'm loaded with money," said Bob sarcastically as he displayed his empty pockets. Bob looked at their faces. With all his emotions fired up and burning inside, he said, "Okay!"

The remainder of the morning was spent in the courthouse cafeteria discussing and disputing the division and amounts of community assets and expenses and child support and back payments. They exchanged documents and insults. Reunification was discussed. They broke for lunch. Bob wasn't really hungry, but he knew he should eat something. He ate a muffin. This was Tom's first experience in divorces. He felt so gloomy. He also ate lightly. Bob was pleased that this time he was not alone. Tom left the courthouse after lunch.

Mr. McGrath was on the fourth floor of the courthouse with Walsh following, scarching for a judge to sign off on a settlement agreement. They found a judge who had agreed to a short hearing scheduled for four o'clock.

The attorneys returned to the cafeteria. They agreed that Walsh could deposit the checks he had from Schurer & Saylor and other checks into his trust account. Walsh insisted that Bob pay Dr. Soble's outstanding balance and asked who would pay for Dr. Reed. Bob agreed to pay for Dr. Reed. Walsh then worried that if Bob was paying, Reed may be in his favor.

McGrath replied, "Your client does not want to pay. My client has agreed to pay, and you are not satisfied. Only in your mind, you would conjure any imaging of prejudice against your client? Walsh argued that Bob's finances were not totally complete, thus extorting favorable agreements by withholding information." McGrath rebutted that Walsh was using that as an excused to alter previous agreements. Walsh demanded that Bob pay for the appraisal of the New Jersey property. Walsh requested someone to make an appraisal of the furniture and furnishings and other personal property. McGrath stated, "I don't believe it is in our client's interest to pay to have someone appraise their personal property for which they agreed to divide in kind." Walsh and McGrath were disputing the wording of the agreement. Ann and Bob divided the household furnishings and had agreed to a primary plan for reunification and replacing Dr. Soble with a different professional.

A little past four in the afternoon, they were in a courtroom. Walsh and McGrath were at the bench quietly talking to the judge. Bob and Ann and sat silently. Bob genuinely believed in Daniel

McGrath and felt that McGrath was trying his best and cared about his rights. More importantly, Bob saw him as a good ethic man and a fair person. He had to trust McGrath.

Bob looked toward Ann's direction. Her head and eyes were looking straight ahead, totally avoiding any kind of eye contact with him. Bob thought that once he was in love with her, devoted to her and happy to be with her. How many times he thought to himself that he would give his right arm for her love. That made no difference now. It was in the past. One thing was certain—she had become his greatest adversity that he had ever faced. She has changed into a selfish and greedy woman. Why! He thought of the song "Stairway to Heaven."

> There's a lady who's sure all that glitters is gold
> And she's buying a stairway to heaven.
> And when she gets there, she knows
> If the stores are all closed.
> With a word she can get what she came here for.
> Yes, there are two paths you can go by.
> But in the long run.
> There is still time to change the road you're on.
> Dear lady can you hear the wind blow.
> And did you know
> Your stairway lies on the whispering wind?

After ten minutes, the attorneys talked with their respective clients.

McGrath had Bob sign some papers, such as title to Ann of the station wagon. Ann took the witness stand and swore in and answered some questions. Bob and Ann were officially divorced. Ann Dorsete had become Ann Pellone once again. Bob was saddening, and his mind froze into a trance.

A week later, Will Walsh had balked on the settlement of the household furnishings and on the discussions of reunification. Daniel McGrath was baffled and disappointed of the time he wasted in verbal agreements that were altered in written form by Walsh. He thought that Walsh was slightly deranged.

Dr. Soble had agreed to the reunification program with the supervision of Dr. Reed. He insisted that the first visits be with a monitor. He also wanted a written plan from Dr. Reed regarding the reunification program. McGrath had discovered that Walsh and Dr. Soble have been talking. McGrath contacted both Walsh and Soble to advise them that Dr. Soble should be impartial. Any conversation he has with one attorney, he should communicate to the other. He cautioned Soble that he might be liable for a lawsuit.

McGrath, at first, saw Bob as a just a client. Bob had been successful, owned property, and coached in his community. He liked Bob. An injustice had been done. In frustration, McGrath sent a letter to Walsh.

> When you withdraw the agreement or modify it, besides the chaos and conflict it creates to me, it also does not cause my client to believe that we are acting in a professional good faith manner. This harms our professional and increases the level of conflict in litigation, which is already fraught with emotion and conflict. We have negotiated in good faith despite your derogatory statements to the contrary.
>
> Short note about your name-calling. You have called my client a crook or thief and a liar. You said he is a coward. Now because we have a disagreement, you are calling me an asshole. I have cautioned you in the past of your ethical responsibility not to demean or antagonize my client. I state unequivocally that whatever your personal views of my client, I will tolerate no further name calling or other antagonizing. Further, any names you wish to call me, you may do so privately, but any further public derogatory

name-calling will evoke a response that will not make you too happy.

Apparently, the way your mind works, it doesn't serve to resolve the issues between this family.

There you have my lecture. I'm preparing for trial.

Chapter 14

May 4, 1992

California is a liberal state regarding divorces. It is a "no fault" state, and community property shared equally 50 percent. It is only one of thirteen states in which fathers have joint legal and custody rights of the children. After nearly two years, Bob Dorsete would get his day in court. Few men have every loved and labored so hard for their family as Bob. He was a man that had reached a status in career, property, and in the community. There was little that he had failed, yet he failed in the most important thing in his life, his marriage. He was now without family and possessions. Bob was in the hallway of Judge Ward's courtroom. He was uneasy but eager to get it over. His brain cells were in overload, thinking of the past two years. He wanted it to end today, but he did not want to lose. He never thought that he would have survived this long without Ann and the boys. He was nervous over the outcome.

There was a gathering of people. He saw Dr. Conte walking toward his direction. Bob was disappointed to see Dr. Conte dressed in an off-white loose shirt over the light tan casual pants, roman saddles without socks and earrings. They exchanged greetings. Bob was silent as he stared at Dr. Conte. "What's the matter," asked Dr. Conte.

Bob was reluctant at first, then said. "Looked at the way you're dressed. Couldn't you at least wear a suit jacket?"

Dr. Conte smiled. "Don't worry, I'm just as qualified as Dr. Soble."

Mr. McGrath interrupted, "Dr. Conte, good to finally meet you."

"It's my pleasure to meet you."

"Can you refute Dr. Soble's position?"

Dr. Conte replied, "Mr. McGrath, I'm sympathetic to Bob in that the unfair treatment of visitation. As we discussed, I'm dumbfounded that Dr. Soble has denied Bob normal visitations with his children. I don't understand Dr. Soble's motive and why he insists that Bob see the children with a monitor. The longer he's separated from his children, the worse the strain on their relationship."

Mr. McGrath said, "How about the fact that you have not seen or spoken to the Dorsete children, whereas Dr. Soble has?"

Dr. Conte placed his hand on Mr. McGrath's shoulder. "There's nothing wrong with Bob, just a lot of stress. No evidence of violence or abuse. He's not a danger to the children. And that's what I'm prepared to say today."

With a smile, McGrath said, "That's what I wanted to hear. Doctor, I was impressed by your outstanding qualifications."

Bob noticed a familiar face. "What is she doing here?"

McGrath turned. "Who?"

"Ms. Franken, the director of HR for my company. What is she doing here?"

"I don't know why Walsh subpoenaed her."

Bob commented, "The asshole."

Mr. McGrath addressed Dr. Conte. "Sometimes it gets tough representing men.

Most of my clients are men, and they do get the short end when it comes to visitation. It's mostly an uphill battle for custody. I had a client that almost lost it. He pointed a gun to his wife; it was not loaded. He gets slapped with restraining orders, monitored visitation, and ordered inpatient therapy."

Dr. Conte replied, "That is why I am not married or have children. I think of the quote, 'Heaven has no rage like love to hatred turned. Nor hell a fury like a woman scorned.'"

McGrath smiled. "I say it differently. I tell my male clients that it would be better to be in hell than to face the wrath of a woman who has been disparaged rejected." Both men laughed.

The small crowd entered the courtroom of Judge Ward. The judge called the two attorneys to the bench. The discussion was over in two minutes. Mr. McGrath made his way toward Bob. With a smile, he whispered, "Walsh was trying to delay. He wanted two days. I stated that one day would be sufficient. The judge said we'll be done today. He dismissed Ms. Franken from testifying."

Ann testified that Bob was physically abusive. He made threats of violence toward her. He would kick and batter her when he lost his temper. He would throw objects around the house. He threatened to kill her if she left him or dissolved their marriage. He demanded that she engage in sexual intercourse with him every other day. If she rejected his sexual demands, he would become hostile and belligerent toward her. Ann stated events that were partially true and partially false. She mixed descriptions of events that actually happened with other events that did not occur. Ann alleged that daily and weekly, without provocation, Bob would say, "You dummy, you idiot. I do everything for this family. If I left you, this family would be a bunch of nobodies." She attested to Bob, hitting Bobby on the face and buttocks. She stated that she feared for her life and had to seek safety at a shelter.

Dr. Soble testified that Bob had been too dominating and harsh with the boys. Soble said that he had had concerns that Bob wants to externalize and blame most of it on his wife and still is having difficulty with his own problems that he created with the family. In my opinion, "Bob has gained some insight into his own issues but still has no real understanding of the concepts of codependency and boundaries."

Dr. Conte testified that Bob was angry of not seeing his children. He was stressed due to the situation of dealing with the divorce, forced to leave his home. Bob had not harmed anyone and had no impulse to harm anyone.

"Dr. Conte, do you have other evidence or just your assessment?" asked McGrath.

"Yes, I have conversed with Dr. Bergren. He was the psychiatrist in charge of Mr. Dorsete's evaluation during his seven-day stay in Long Beach Hospital. He strongly stated that he had no reason to expect violent, impulsive behavior from Mr. Dorsete."

"Doctor, any other evidence?"

"Yes, I had several conversations with Dr. Soble. I have reviewed his written assessments. In all, I found no evidence that Mr. Dorsete poses harm to himself or others."

"Does that include Dr. Soble's written recommendations of January 8, 1991, Exhibit 12."

"Yes! Mr. Dorsete has complied with Dr. Soble's recommendations that he complete a course in parenting and seek psychological treatment. Dr. Soble had Mr. Dorsete complete questionnaires in determining and diagnosing Mr. Dorsete's mental state. There were no indications that Mr. Dorsete was a danger to himself or others. Dr. Soble makes no mentioning that Mr. Dorsete is a threat to his wife or children."

"Doctor, what is your overall opinion of Dr. Soble's testimony?"

"It's bullshit. Sorry! Excuse me. It is rubbish. His recommendation that Mr. Dorsete be immersed in an intense psychotherapy program to help him understand his own behavior is nonsense, especial his insistence of monitored visitations."

Mr. Walsh interrupted, "I object!"

Judge Ward asked, "On what grounds?"

"I object."

"Mr. Walsh, I can't rule. Give me grounds for objecting."

"I disagree!" said Walsh.

"Dr. Conte's opinion is his professional assessment of his patient. Do you have evidence contrary to his opinion?"

"Yes! You heard Dr. Soble's testimony."

"Overruled! Doctor, please continue."

"Mr. Dorsete's stress was due to over-involvement of activities of working full days, including weekends for the purpose of providing for his family."

Walsh cross-examined Bob. Walsh made statements and arguments that Bob Dorsete was a crook, embezzling money from his company. He accused Bob of verbal and physical abuse toward Ann and the children. Walsh stated that Bob was in contempt of court for nonpayment of child support, and Bob was a pathological liar in need of psychological counseling and anger management classes. Walsh made the argument that the mother should keep the resident to lessen the mental anguish of the children who have suffered because of their father.

Walsh asked Bob to admit that he willfully violated orders of the court by appearing at the petitioner's home with the city police department and intimidated her into letting you go into the house and take community documents during the month of November 1990. McGrath objected on the grounds of unimportant questioning. The judge sustained.

Walsh asked Bob to admit that he willfully violated orders of this court by approaching his children on the playground, near the residence during the month of February 1991. Admit that during the loan application process you gave false information, including the fact that your gross income was six thousand dollars per month. McGrath objected to all this line of questioning being immaterial. The judge sustained all.

"Mr. Dorsete, is it true that your father was from the old country?" asked Walsh.

"Yes."

"Is it true that your father was strict disciplinary?"

"It all depended."

"Please, a yes or no."

"He was fair."

"Yes or no."

McGrath shouted, "I object! He has answered the question."

Judge Ward asked, "Mr. Walsh, where is this going?"

"Well, Your Honor, it's just that Mr. Dorsete abused and hit his children because he was abused by his father."

"You asshole!" shouted out Bob. "My father passed away four years ago! You did not know my father!"

Judge Ward turned to Bob and said, "Mr. Dorsete, restrain yourself."

Bob, in a loud voice and excitable tone, yelled, "My father was a good person. He had a hard life. He raised six children and made a good life for us. He never learned to speak English. Some people tried to take advantage of him."

"Mr. Dorsete, that is enough."

"Your Honor," interrupted Walsh, "it goes to case that he admits that he was abused as a child. You heard from Dr. Soble that Mr. Dorsete was extreme jealousy. He was abusive. He blamed Ms. Dorsete for his stress."

Judge Ward said, "Do you have further evidence or corroborating witnesses?"

"Yes, Ms. Dorsete had to run to a shelter, she was in a shelter for forty-five days." Walsh moving closer to Bob.

"Mr. Dorsete's sisters have told my client that Mr. Dorsete was abused as a child. The cycle of abuse is repeated." Walsh placed his hand on Bob's knee. "Admit that you were…"

Bob stood up and yelling, "My father had to be tough. It was a tough neighborhood. He taught me to be respectful. That's the crap I have had to take from that asshole, calling me a crook, accusing of abusing my children, my wife, telling me I need to get help. I am tired and had enough of him pushing my buttons. He has been harassing me for two years with the same crap." The judge banged the gavel. Bob continued without stopping.

The judge banged his gavel, commanding silence, and said, "Mr. Dorsete! Mr. Dorsete seat down. Mr. McGrath, refrain your client or be held in contempt!"

McGrath forced Bob to sit down and be silent. All was quiet. The judge with a very firm look at Bob said, "I will not allow any outburst from you." He called out, "Counselors, please approach. Mr. Dorsete, you can take your seat."

The three were engaged in a heated exchange. Walsh, with a flush face, was rebutted by the firm face of the judge. After a few minutes, the judge standing up, composing himself, said, "Mr. Dorsete, you are excused. I have heard enough. I will be back with my decisions in thirty minutes. You all can take a break." He banged the gavel and walked out.

It was past five o'clock. Ann Pellone, Bob Dorsete, and their attorneys sat quietly, waiting for the judge to return with his verdict. All the witnesses had left. It had been a long day. The attorneys had presented and submitted various documents as exhibits. They engaged in discussions of the difference of opinions, at times erupted into arguments. It was ugly for Bob to hear Ann's testament of the alleged abuse and crudity. "Please, Bob, whatever the verdict," said McGrath, "don't go emotional."

Judge Ward entered the courtroom; all stood up. He fixed his glasses over the saddle of his nose and prepared to read his notes. Ann was confident that she would win. Bob was in a slight trance and worrying scared of the judge's decision.

Raising the papers, clearing his throat, the judge read, "Back on the record in the Dorsete matter. The parties' counselors are present. The court has some observations to make. I don't think that this court has ever had the misfortune to sit through a trial before involving the issue of custody and monitored visitation and have absolutely zero evidence presented as to the reason for monitoring and as to the reason why psychiatrists were appointed. The court doesn't have any idea as to why there has been a monitored visit. There's been no visitation and that request for monitored visitation, the lawyers have seen fit not to present any evidence to the court that's credible.

"Regarding visitation, the only thing that was presented was an exhibit of the respondent's entitled reunification for the Dorsete children. It is not specific. Based upon the evidence that this court has heard, the court orders that joint legal. Strike that! Sole physical, sole legal custody vested with petitioner, mother. Respondent is to receive reasonable visitation. That visitation shall be monitored. The parties through their attorneys are ordered to meet and confer and select an appropriate monitor. Visitation is to be consistent with the recommendation made by Dr. Reed as to time and place and length of visitation.

"Both parties are ordered to cooperate with Dr. Reed as it relates to the respondent's visitation. And this court has insufficient evidence whatsoever to order whether or not the respondent is to continue his therapy with Dr. Conte. The court declines to make the order."

He raised his head to look at the attorneys. "Is there any reason why Dr. Soble has to remain on call at this point in time?"

Walsh replied, "Well, because, see, I think he stated in his testimony that if he wasn't on it then somebody else would have to be there. And everybody stipulated to him being there because he had the breakdown."

The judge asked, "Is there a stipulation that Dr. Soble remain?"

McGrath replied, "No."

Walsh said, "Well, I thought there was, Your Honor."

The judge said, "Just a minute. The court's not making any order with respect to anybody staying on the case. If somebody wants to pay for it, they can pay for it. All right, so there's no continuing 730 with respect to Dr. Soble. With respect to any outstanding balances as it relates to Dr. Soble, Dr. Reed, each party is to pay one-half. Who's going to pay for Dr. Reed in the future?"

Walsh said, "I think we agreed that respondent agreed to pay it during the trial."

"All right, that's the order. On the issues of credits and charges, with respect to the request by the petitioner for Watt charges and Epstein credits, I'm going by the total lack of evidence. The petitioner is incompetent to present documents regarding credits and charges, so the court cannot make some findings regarding this matter. As to how much money she had at time of separation, the petitioner owes to the community sixty-two thousand dollars. This pertains to the petitioner and petitioner only. Since the petitioner has had the ability to earn income, I assess that she pays her own legal cost."

Judge Ward stopped to look at his notes. "With respect to the issue of support, there are four children. The guideline on the amount of child support is $1,230 per month. That's the order of the court, payable one-half on the first and one-half on the fifteenth of each month. The court finds, at this time, that the respondent has zero visitation, and the DissoMaster recommendation is based on that. With respect to the petitioner's request for Duke Order, 4700.10 as it relates to the California residence granted to the custodial parent, that's denied."

Ann made a ghostly sound. The judge looked up. "The court finds insufficient evidence to defer the sale of the family home to minimize the adverse impact on the children. The resident house is ordered to be listed for sale at the fair market price. Both parties are required to cooperate with the listing in the sale of the family home. With respect to the New Jersey property, the court also orders that it be listed at fair market value.

With respect to arrears of family support, the court obviously has continuing jurisdiction as it relates to any prior light orders that might exist. The furnishings are to be divided in kind by alternate selection. The petitioner to choose first, followed by the respondent. Alternate selections afterward. Jewelry: the court finds that there was a presumption of gifts made by others as well as the respondent to the petitioner. There's absolute zero evidence from a specific standpoint as to what items we're talking about except in general. Therefore, the jewelry is awarded to the petitioner. The matter regarding the life insurance: since no evidence was presented as to the value, the court reserves jurisdiction over this matter. The matter regarding cash of community assets held by Mr. Walsh, that is to be divided equally at the time of the sale of the properties.

So basically, no one gets any money until they resolve the credits and charges issues unless the parties stipulate otherwise. They've got the key. If they want to unlock it, they can. That's the order. Thank you, Counselors, and good luck, folks."

Ann showed no emotion, but inside, she was enraged at the outcome. The small crowd exited the courtroom. Once outside, Ann yelled at Walsh, "You told me that I wouldn't have to pay for my legal fees. I would get the house."

Walsh held her arm and whispered into her ear. He walked toward McGrath and politely asked, "Counselor, can I have a moment with you?" The two attorneys walked down the hall.

Ann and Bob remained stationary. Bob had mixed emotions. He was delighted of the judge's ruling, thus vindicating Bob of all the allegations of abuse. He was ecstatic that it was finally over. But he was saddened. There are no winners, only voluntaries that became victims. Ann stood like a statue. He turned to her. She avoided making eye contact with him. He finally got the nerve to talk. "Can we start talking now?"

Ann snapped back, "What for?"

"There are four children involved, and we are still their parents."

"If you really cared about the children, you wouldn't be throwing them out on the street." She walked away from Bob.

Bob did not respond. He thought for two years she has become a very bitter and angry woman. He thought that were no words to say. If only he could find a way to break that wall that she has created around her heart.

The two attorneys made their way to a small conference room. Will Walsh pleaded, "Mr. McGrath, there are four young boys. She's all by herself. She's working and taking care of the children. It will be a hardship for her to have to move out… Can we work out some kind of deal that we can buy your client out?"

McGrath, in a low, calm voice, said, "You can make an offer, and I'll take it back to my client, but it's his prerogative if he will accept it."

Walsh, grabbing a piece of paper with his glasses hanging over his nose, did some calculations. "Based on my numbers, we think twenty thousand in cash and your client keeps the property in New Jersey."

"Mr. Walsh," said McGrath, chuckling, "we've been trying to negotiate with you for the past five months. You always come up with some creative accounting that is unfair to my client. You only have viewed it from your viewpoint. Your arithmetic has been outrageous, and your offers have been totally one-sided."

"That's not true. I think that we have been more than fair. After all, she does have the children to raise."

McGrath calmly and forcefully said, "Listen for a moment. You're not going to like what I'm going to say, but you need a lecture." Walsh was taken by surprise. McGrath continued, "You've been practicing family law for a long time, and you know it's difficult and stressful on everybody involved, and mostly the children. Financially, it's been a drain on our clients. You have done everything to prolong and delay this matter and run up exorbitant legal fees. We had concessions and verbal agreements that you altered in written form. You forced us to bring every issue to court. All this time, your client has had control of the children and the parties' community assets. My client has had nothing. You called me an asshole. You called my client a liar, a thief, and a crook. That's unbecoming of an attorney and totally unethical… You heard the verdict today. Let's let them go on with their lives. I would not entertain any offer you have to make unless it's fair and equitable. None of these ridiculous proposals that you have made in past. Counselor, that's all I have to say to you. Goodbye!"

The courthouse was emptying. Ann, Bob, and their counselors made their way to the elevators. There were no smiles or sounds uttered. There were no words or glances exchanged as they waited for the elevator in solitude.

Dr. Reed was looking and sorting through papers. Bob Dorsete had met with Dr. Reed a week before the trial. Bob felt that he had his share of psychologists and psychiatrists to last a lifetime. He had to give it a chance for the boys. He just couldn't throw in the towel and give up on the boys. Dr. Reed said, "Sorry that I took so long in calling you in. I finally saw the boys and your ex-wife last week. She has been delaying for weeks. You've really got a bunch of handsome boys. They're good kids. I really enjoyed talking to them." Dr. Reed was an attractive man in his late forties. He had a well-trimmed short beard and medium-length hair. He spoke with a slight southwest accent. "It's been six weeks since I saw you."

"Yes, a week before the trial."

"I had conversations with Dr. Conte. He was direct that you were being fucked!"

"He's a New Yorker, very direct," said Bob.

"How are you doing? Any changes since our last conversation?"

"The best I have felt in two years. Just got laid off two weeks ago. I filed for unemployment compensation. The last time I got laid off, I had a wife and two children. I felt like shit. I was so nervous to tell me wife. This time, I felt no pressure or stress. I am looking for an apartment since I won't be able to afford the townhouse. Money stress."

"Feeling a lot of stress? Are you're not taking any medication?"

"No meds. Stressed, yes."

"I understand… I can't fathom why you have not had normal visitation with your children for two years. Are you some kind of serial killer?" he said with a mocking smile.

"No!"

"Of course. I'm only kidding. I don't understand why Dr. Soble would only allow monitor visitation for so long. The only time I would ever recommend visitation with a monitor would be if the father had been charged with abuse or if he was a murderer. The trial decision vindicated you of all her allegations of abuse. On Dr. Conte's suggestion, I have no reason to contact Dr. Soble. But I am perplexed as to why he insisted on the monitor visitations."

"He sided with her, and I refused to pay him. I don't know if, if I should tell you." Bob paused. "Last year, I was so frustrated with Soble. He was pushing my buttons. My lawyer was worthless. I hired an investigation firm. They reported that he did some free work at women's shelters. He has a realtor company. He has a brokerage license. He is a greedy man. It's all about money with him. I challenged his ethics as a psychologist. I think that he wanted to show that he was in charge."

"Dr. Conte is irritated and can't comprehend why Soble was so unreasonable. A lot of damage has been done to you and your relationship with your boys… I'm pleased that the trial went your way."

"The judge saw through her lawyer's BS."

Dr. Reed said, "The older boys are anxious to see you." Bob was happy to hear this and holding back the tears. "I spoke to her regarding visitation, and she agreed that a monitor is not necessary. Well, Bob, let me ask you a question. How do you feel about her?"

Bob asked, "What do you mean by that?"

"She said that you wanted to get back. Do you want her back?"

Bob smiled and chuckled. "I gotta be crazy to take her back." He shrugged and, with a frown, said, "No! She broke the most important thing in a relationship, trust. She's been trying to hurt me for the past two years. There's no way I ever want to get back with her." He paused to puff on the cigarette. "In order to deal with the situation, I have become hard inside. The boys have not been part of my daily life. I had to stop thinking about them, not to care about their daily activities. It's not that I don't love them. To not see them has been very painful. I had to get them out of my head and heart." Bob's eyes become watery. "Is that wrong?" He nervously smoked.

"No, it's nature. You have been through a lot. You were an involved father. You have been in a long relationship. Over twenty years. That's a long time by today's standards." He paused and looked into Bob's eyes.

"Twenty-two years."

"It takes a year for every ten years to forget. We got some problems to deal with. Mainly, their mother. In talking to her, she hasn't let go. It's not going to be easy. She is upset that the house has to be listed for sale. But that's okay. Your sons will understand as they get older. When you see them and if they ask why you're throwing them out of the house, just tell them that they don't have to worry about it. They'll always have a place to live. Just keep your answers simple. Okay, let's get started so you can start seeing your children as soon as possible. She has agreed for this weekend's visitation. Saturday, the older boys. Sunday, the younger boys. I suggested a minimum of four hours for this weekend. I told her that a break would be healthy for her."

Bob, delighted, interrupted, "After what I have experienced, four hours is good."

"I suggest that you plan a set activity. That way, there will be no controversy, no need for argument, and no debate. Do you object or have any problems with that?"

"No," said Bob, holding back his excitement.

"Good. She doesn't want you to pick up the children at the house. She wants a mutual place, a local restaurant."

Bob quickly responded, "Isn't that bullshit? We did that in the past."

Dr. Reed nodded. "She hasn't let go. She is an angry woman. She is upset over the court rulings. I don't want to force her. I want to gain her cooperation."

"She's still trying to hurt me by controlling visitations."

"Yes, I see that."

"It's an immature way to behave," said Bob. "It's more of an inconvenience for her." Bob was bewildered. "She has been in control for two years, but why is she still so angry? She got her divorce, custody of the boys, and me out of her life."

Dr. Reed said, "There are psychobiological differences between men and women. Research indicates that women stay angry longer than men and are much more inclined to harbor grudges and resentments. She thinks that she has justifiable hurt feelings from the past. If this is the case, she will always blame you."

"I just don't understand." Bob was feeling remorse. "Why can't we raise our children as divorced parents?"

"Until she gets the proper treatment, she will continue to be angry. I am not treating her. My task is to help your reunion with your children, have a good time with your children. I'll see you in two weeks."

Saturday, Bob picked up Bobby and Tony at a nearby McDonald's at twelve noon. He took them to a large pool hall. The place was filled with smoke and strong foul smell of beer. It was mostly filled with adults and some teenagers. The place smelled heavy of French fries and hamburgers. After an hour, the boys were hunger. They had hamburgers and fries. Bob had a beer, and as usual, Tony wanted a taste. After two hours, he called Ann that he was returning the boys.

Sunday, Bob picked up Chuck and Mark at a nearby McDonald's at twelve noon. Chuck was now eight years old, and Mark was five years old. He took them to a public pool. Bob spent the majority of time holding on to Mark and keeping an eye on Chuck. After an hour, he went to his townhouse, feeding the boys hot dogs and chips. They spent the rest of the afternoon playing with toy soldiers.

With each visit, the time was expanded to a full day. Bob entertained his boys by taking them to baseball games, movies, Knott's Berry Farm, and Disneyland. Occasionally, he was permitted to pick up the boys at home.

Chapter 15

It has been over two months since the trial. Bob Dorsete and Mr. McGrath were sitting in the courthouse cafeteria. As usual, the tables were covered with briefcases and papers. McGrath said, "As I have been telling you, Walsh has been delaying any settlement or meetings with me or us. Perhaps after the last lecture I give him. He suggested that your wife get a new attorney. I hope that he is more reasonable than Walsh."

"Good. I'm glad that she got rid of that asshole. Do you know him?"

"No. He's a young attorney, ten or twelve years of experience."

Bob spotted Ann walking with a tall big man dressed in an expensive business attire with short brown hair, combed neatly in place. Bob pointed with his head. "There they are!"

Ann and the stranger approached. The man extended his hand. "Mr. McGrath, I am Brett Johnson, nice to finally meet you."

McGrath stood up. "Yes, good morning."

The younger man said, "I have Mr. Walsh's files, a lot of stuff!" Brett smiled. "I think that we could resolve everything today. Can I have a word with you?"

The lawyers walked away. Ann stood by the chair. Bob stared at Ann and thought, *Why all this anger? Why all this bitterness when there was so much love, so much caring, so much cherishing?* He placed his hands over his face to cover his eyes.

After five minutes, the lawyers returned. McGrath said, "Before we start, we need set some rules? No arguing or shouting at each other. Let's all be civil. Perhaps we can get this done today. Do you agree?"

Ann nodded. Bob motioned his head.

Mr. Johnson said, "You are going to have to deal with each other for a long time, perhaps the rest of your lives, because of your children."

McGrath looked through his notes. "In accordance with court orders, we are here to resolve back child support, cash assets, and the furnishings to be divided."

Mr. Johnson said, "My client has determined that your client owes her $120,000. Here is a list. It includes back child support, expenses for the houses, and expenses for the four children."

Bob and Mr. McGrath looked at the documents. After a few minutes, McGrath handed them papers. "We disagree. Here are our figures. We have calculated that your client had over $150,000 of community funds."

Bob said, "You are very clever. You omitted the restaurant check, my retirement funds, and the $20,000 cash." Sarcastically, he said, "You poor thing with four children. You cleaned out the checking and saving accounts."

Ann was steaming. "For two years, I have been paying for all the expenses, the mortgages, the house expense, the children's expense, doctor's bills, school activities." She opened her purse. "Here are all the receipts of school activities and doctors."

McGrath said in a soft voice, "The house expenses are your responsibilities. The New Jersey property is community assets. You have received rents for two years. The children's expenses are part of the child support. You cannot submit a separate expense for those costs." He turned toward Mr. Johnson. "If you look at the documents, you will see that your client made the withdrawals while my client was in New Jersey. Also, Mr. Walsh had community funds in his trust account."

Ann shouted, "I had to pay my lawyer and Dr. Soble!"

Mr. Johnson said, "I am not aware of other assets. Give us a moment." The two were whispering. "Ms. Dorsete insists that we discuss the children's expenses."

"Ms. Pellone!" interrupted Bob.

They spent the remainder of the morning arguing over school trips expenses, clothing bills, doctor bills, and recreation expenses. The parties agreed that Bob would reimburse Ann $500. It was lunchtime. The lawyers left to make telephone calls. Ann and Bob were in the cafeteria. With a tray in hands, Bob walked over to Ann's table "Can I sit here?"

Ann nodded.

Bob was nervous. "My mother, my sisters, nieces and nephews, they all love you. For them, this is very difficult to comprehend. They want to talk to the boys. I just want to tell you that they all love you and care for you." Ann showed no expression. She stared in silence. Bob continued, "How is teaching full-time?"

She unemotional said, "That's none of your business."

Bob sighed. "I was only trying to be friendly. I'm not trying to probe into your personal life."

"Yes, I enjoy teaching, but it's hard raising four boys."

Bob interjected, "There's been a lot of hurt. Can we rebuild our separate lives and raise our children as divorced parents?"

"I never should have married you," said Ann, feeling annoyed.

Bob stared at her and said, "You know, that's a stupid comment. You can tell all your new friends all the bad things I did, but that comment doesn't fly with me or with people that have known us. Do you know how stupid you sound when you say that? We dated for almost six years before we got married. We were married for sixteen years, and we have four boys, one every three years. The choice was always yours. You could have walked out anytime."

Ann said, "I didn't know any better. I was raised that, once in a marriage, it's forever. But I'm different now, I've changed."

Bob shook his head. "Have you really changed? You haven't changed at all. The only thing that's changed is that you have a new religion. You have a new perception of life. You changed your name. You just substituted other people to carry you. Ray to protect you. Walsh, your mouthpiece. The shelter, your support group. And Dr. Soble to justify your actions. So how the heck have you changed?"

"See, you haven't changed," said Ann loudly. "You haven't changed. You're still trying to put me down. You're still trying to be that same old wise guy. I didn't come here to talk about the past."

They stood up to separate as Mr. Johnson approached. "Good to see that you are talking. Mr. Dorsete can we talk without your attorney?"

"Sure!"

"Your children need a place to live. Let Ann have the house."

Bob, in a firm voice, replied, "Let me quote, 'The court finds insufficient evidence to defer the sale, because of adverse impact to the children.'"

Ann was irritated. "The boys are going to hate you."

McGrath approached. "You started without me. I reserved a room on the second floor."

The parties were in the small conference room. The attorneys agreed to resolve the smaller issues first, such as the household furnishings. The parties had a list to divide the furnishings, with Ann choosing. At Bob's turn, he chose the dining-room set. Ann was annoyed. "Why the dining-room set? You don't have room for it."

"Because I want it."

At Bob's turn, he choice the VHS recorder and player (a purchase price of $1,500). Ann replied, "It does not exist."

"Where is it?" asked Bob.

"It didn't work. I got rid of it."

"Which part did not work? The camera, the recorder or the player?"

"All!"

"You liar."

Mr. Johnson jumped in. "Mr. Dorsete, no name-calling."

"She is a liar." Bob shook his head. "The grille."

"It's gone."

"What do you mean?"

"It rusted, I trashed it."

"You are such a bullshitter!"

McGrath interjected, "You both are paying us over $400 an hour. Stop arguing, let's continue."

The parties finished with the division of the furnishings.

Mr. Johnson. "I will need to check with Mr. Walsh regarding cash in his trust account. Here are our detailed numbers for back children support. In addition, her payments to Dr. Soble."

"That asshole. I agreed to pay for his initial involvement."

"But it was a 730, and Mr. Dorsete agreed to pay."

"Not after that lousy report. She insisted in seeing him."

Mr. McGrath interrupted, "If you look at the court order, Dr. Soble testified for your client at the trial."

The remainder of the afternoon was spent debating and arguing how much cash Ann had, reimbursement of back child support, and the house_expenses. The parties adjourned for the next day.

The next morning, Ann Pellone and her attorney were sitting in the courthouse cafeteria. McGrath and Bob approached. McGrath said, "I have reserved a small room. We can be in private."

The party made their way to a different floor and entered a small room with a table and four chairs. The lawyers emptied their briefcases with documents on the table.

Mr. Johnson said, "I spoke with Mr. Walsh last night. He does not recall how much Ms. Pellone had in cash. He mentioned that Ms. Pellone has been paying for Mr. Dorsete's health-care insurance for the past two years."

Bob was surprised. "I have been paying for Dr. Conte and Dr. Reed."

McGrath said, "I have presented a letter from his company that his retirement funds were sent to Mr. Walsh. Regarding child support, the parties had agreed to $500 per month in September of 1990. The recent stipulation of $1,229 was based on his recent job and no visitation. My client has no job and has visitation on weekends." McGrath was sorting papers. "As you can see, less payments made. He owes her $4,000 for child support."

Mr. Johnson reviewed the figures with his client. Ann, upset, said, "I had to pay for everything. I'm all by myself raising four children."

McGrath was silent as he glanced at Bob. He looked at his watch and said, "Let's break for lunch. You look at the figures." They all agreed to break for lunch.

The new courthouse was spacious. The cafeteria was on the first floor with an adjoining courtyard with tables and umbrellas. Bob and Daniel were outside, having lunch. Brett walked over with a tray. "Do you mind if I join you?"

McGrath said, "Not at all."

Brett said as he was sitting, "I know that she is my client. I need a break from her." Looking at Mr. McGrath, he said, "I was very impressed that you are in the law journal, your landmark case."

Bob stared in astonishment. Brett continued, "My associates thought that it was an unusual case."

McGrath grinned. "As usual as it gets."

Bob, in astonishment, said, "Dan, you never told me."

"It was kind of stupid," a very modest McGrath said. "I represented a client that had been divorced for two years. He decided to join the priesthood. He had about $300,000 in assets. He decided to donate the money to the church. His ex-wife was sued because he wouldn't have an income to pay for child support. They had two young children."

Brett interjected, "Things have become complicated."

Bob said, "Priests don't get salaries. They get allowances for living expenses."

"Her lawyer argued that he joined the priesthood to avoid paying for child support. Hence, the money should be awarded to her."

Brett laughed. "You lost the case. How were you able to win on the appeal?"

McGrath smiled. "My argument was that the man was a devoted Catholic. She had no calm to his assets since they had been divorced and settled on the community assets. In my briefs, I demonstrated the man was a devote Catholic. The assets were his alone, and he can do whatever he wanted."

Brett turned to Bob. "I read the trial transcript. You had no reasonable visitation with your children for over two years. Being denied visitation must have been a painful experience."

Bob nodded. "Thanks to her two friends, Walsh and Soble."

McGrath asked, "What happened to Walsh?"

"Walsh knows one of my associates. He referred me. He said that you two had some bad blood." Brett looked at Bob. "I have two young children. I don't know what I would have done if I were separated from them for two years." He paused to drink his soda. "For two days, she has been going on and on that she is all by herself raising four boys and working full-time. You want to kick her in the street. You quit your job to avoid paying child support, and you will not leave her alone. She won't give an inch. Was she always this imbalanced?"

It hurt Bob a little that Brett thought bad of Ann. "No! It was the California air and the people."

Reserved, Brett said, "Don't repeat what I said to her. She is my client."

The parties were back in the conference room. After over two hours, Mr. Johnson said, "My client gets the California property, your client gets the New Jersey property. They each have a house."

Bob interrupted, "But I plan to stay in California. What good would it do me? And I plan to buy a house here."

The parties paused. Brett and Ann were whispering. McGrath and Bob sat back in silence. Brett said, "Okay, you sell the New Jersey property. My client is willing to accept half of the expenses. You keep the money from the sale of the house, and we offer you twenty thousand dollars in the form of a note."

Bob replied, "That's not a fair offer. The resident is stipulated to be listed for $325,000 and the New Jersey at $180,000. That is a difference of $145,000."

"Bob, you have to consider." Brett had a pen in hand. "Ann is willing to share the cost—for the agent, legal, and closing cost."

Bob, in a raised voice, said, "She keeps the house. She saves on moving cost, cost for buying another house, and all the other inconveniences. Your offer is so unfair."

Ann said, "Well, think about the children."

Bob felt her angry eyes flush in his direction. He snapped back. "Have you thought about the children? Have you thought about my relationship with the children? With the help of Soble, you kept me away from my children."

McGrath interrupted, "Getting upset will not help resolve anything."

Irritated, Bob said, "Let me tell her. Lady, you got your butt beat. For two years, you had the house, the boys, and all the cash. Now, you know what a divorce is all about! There are no winners, only consequences and losses."

Mr. Johnson interjected, "We are on the meter!"

Bob yelled, "I don't give a shit. She didn't care about the attorney's fees when she thought I was going to get stuck with the bills. It didn't happen, did it? You didn't care about the cost then, all the money we pissed away."

McGrath grabbed Bob's arm. "Break time! Bob, come with me."

Bob snapped back, "Hey, baby, that's what divorce is all about. Everything chop-chop, half-half! The properties have to be listed and sold. I'm not throwing them out, I'm throwing you out. You can go back to the shelter." McGrath pulled Bob. The two left the room.

In the hallway, McGrath said, "I know an injustice happened to you, but we are here to resolve the financial matters. You stay here."

McGrath opened the door and stepped in.

Ann yelled, "You see, he wants to throw me out. He doesn't care about his children."

Mr. Johnson said, "Please calm down. Mr. McGrath, you have something to say?"

"Yes! Under the circumstance, I suggest that we adjourn. You have all our figures. You know our position. If you have no objections."

"Yes, I agree."

McGrath said, "We have directions from the court. List the properties as stipulated."

Ann shouted, "I will not list the house!"

McGrath said in a low voice, "Ms. Dorsete, the court has stipulated. You attorney is aware that I can file for an order to show cause, and you could be held in contempt. Mr. Johnson can explain it to you. Good day, Brett. I'll call you tomorrow."

Dr. Reed had increased Bob's visitation. Two boys at a time. Alternate visits with the oldest two and the youngest two. Ann was reluctant but agreed to overnight visitations. She complained that Bob had no beds for the boys. Bob had moved to a one-bedroom apartment. Dr. Reed felt confident that with the increase visitations, things would get better. Bob would pick up the boys Friday at six o'clock and return them before dark on Saturday.

It was Bob's second overnight visitation with his boys. He was caught up in heavy traffic and arrived thirty minutes past six o'clock. He knocked on the door. Tony opened the door, yelling, "He's here!" and closed the door. Ann opened the door, shouting, "You're late!" and closed the door. Bob knocked, pleading for her to open the door. After several minutes, Ann opened the door and allowed the boys to go with Bob. The following Friday, Bob was early. He parked the car a block away and waited until six o'clock. He thought, *Too early, she'll be pissed. How strange to be with my children, yet it doesn't feel the same.* The boys packed very little for the overnight visits with their father. When Bob asked Ann to assist the boys in packing a bag with clothing and toys, Ann shouted back that it was their responsibility.

After picking up the boys, Bob would take them for dinner at an Applebee's type of restaurant or fast-food place. At the last minute, there were changes to who would go with him. Bobby didn't show up once because he was going to a baseball game with his friends. Another time, Tony did not want to go. Bob purchased a VCR; he rented movies. He read bedtime stories to the younger boys. Bobby and Tony complained that they were too big. Chuck and Mark loved it. The boys slept in the bed; Bob slept on the couch. He would take them to the park to play basketball or soccer. He took them to amusement parks and swimming.

One Saturday as he dropped off the boys, Bob did not see Ann's car. He walked around the house staring at the work he had done. He thought that once it was his house. Bob drove off thinking, *one day to keep contact from becoming strangers. One day to play and have fun. Little time to let them know that I'm their father. Just as we start to know each other, it's over. They go back home and I am alone.*

"It's been weeks since we sat down to settle on the community assets. I have had many discussions with her attorney," said McGrath in disappointment. "She will not budge. She wants the house."

Bob replied, "I know. We still have not listed the residence. We fought over real estate agents. I finally agreed to her agent, but she still has not signed the contract."

"The New Jersey property?"

"Listed weeks ago."

"Good! Brett said that according to your wife, the retirement funds and the sale of the restaurant proceeds were split among the attorneys. Saylor final sent me an itemized memo of their fees and cost. The money was used to pay for your legal fees and cost. There is a zero balance."

Bob, annoyed, said, "Plus the $22,000 I paid…man, how convenient, zero balance."

"We have no way to dispute him unless you have bills."

"He only provided bills for the first two months."

"Then that money is gone. As a negotiator, you are aware that they are in a position of strength. She is in no rush. She has the cash and the house. Here is the reality if we go to court. It's going to cost you more money. I have to write an order to show cause. Her lawyer is going to delay. We might be in court in two or three months. Spend a day in court."

Bob shook his head. "You lawyers."

McGrath cut in, "I know that you don't like lawyers. There is the good, the bad, and the most in between. We deal with anger, bitter, and sometimes ugly clients, and sometimes things are not fair. I had a client that divorced his first wife twice."

Bob said, "He remarried his ex."

McGrath looked like the cat that ate the canary. He had Bob's attention. "No!" Bob stared. McGrath continued, "He divorced her twelve years earlier. There were little assets to divide at the time. She got custody of their two-year-old daughter. His ex-wife was going from one man to another. A year later, they made an arrangement that he had care of their daughter. He was working full-time and paid for day care. She visited her daughter twice or three times a month. During one of the visits, she begged him to let her stay with him because she had no job and no place to live. He felt pity for her. He offered her a room and board for three months in exchange that she would care for their daughter while he was at work. He thought that he was saving on day care. A month later, she told him that she was pregnant with someone else's baby. She was not sure who the father was and no place to go. He felt sorry for her. He allowed her to stay until she had the baby with the understanding that she not bring men to the house, not drink excessively, and they were not to engage in sex. She had a girl. She pleaded to let her stay, and she would care for both girls. In addition, for a small weekly allowance, she would clean the house and do the cooking. He agreed to let her stay for six months. He made it clear that he was not taking her back. Six months turned into another six months, into a year. Things were working pretty well. He was able to travel and earn more money. She talked him into adopting her second daughter. He had accepted the baby as his. They divorced two years ago. He had accumulated wealth; he had a house and a substantial retirement plan. The second time around, it was costlier for him. She was awarded half of the house, child and spousal support, and custody of the girls."

Bob shook his head. "No, the system can't be that bad."

"She won under common law. The court viewed their cohabitation as a common law marriage."

"What a disappointment," said Bob. "They had no sex, no sex. So the first time around, she gets nothing. The second time, she gets half plus. That sucks."

McGrath added, "He was so annoyed at the system that he became involved in a group called Fathers United for Equal Justice."

Bob sadly said, "The system is not fair."

McGrath said, "There are no easy solutions when children are involved. You have been in the system for over two year. You have experienced that it's not fair to the father. It's all about the children. The judges don't want to get involved in calculating finance. They are not accountants. That is why Judge Ward made no resolution to the finances. They leave that to the attorneys. The courts are sympathetic toward the mothers. Her attorney has argued that she needed the money to pay for the house expenses and children's expenses. It will be difficult to win."

Bob, displeased, said, "What happened to the fifty-fifty division?"

"You lost that money the day she took possession. I told you that I was an accountant before I became an attorney. I thought that my divorce was expensive and unfair to men." He paused. "Judges are reluctant to take money away from mothers because they are the beneficiary of the children." He paused. "How are the visitations going?"

"Difficult. Sometimes I had to take my five-year-old and my fifteen-year-old. It's difficult to do anything to interest both of them. After an hour or two, they get bored and want to go home. They bring no toys, no clothing."

McGrath, in sympathy, said, "The two years' separation was terrible. Let's talk about money. Their offer is you get the proceeds from the rental property. She keeps the house and a forty thousand cash settlement."

Bob shook his head. "It's not fair."

"Who said it's fair? You are not listening. I had a client that had weekend visitations with his six-year-old son. His stupid lawyer did make it a court order that his wife could not move out of state without his permission. After six months, she moved back home to Houston. She was not cooperative regarding visitations. We had to file visitation motions with the courts in Houston."

Bob was surprised. "Are you licensed in Texas?"

"Yes, that is why he retained my services. We obtained court orders for visitation in Texas. My client would fly to Texas on Friday and see his son for the weekend. After a few months, it became too costly for him to travel to Texas. He had to reduce his visits. She would not give the guy a break, so we filed to get visitations for his son to travel to California. She had to cooperate in that she had to deliver the boy to the airport. My client had to pay for all the expenses. After six months, he deleted his savings and his relationship with her girlfriend, and his job suffered. He now sees his son twice a year." McGrath saw that Bob was agonizing. "Bob, take the offer. This could go on for months and months. It could improve your relationship with her by easing the tension." Bob was uncertain with head down. McGrath said, "Let's wrap it up."

"Can I think about it?"

"What is there to think about?"

Bob became reluctant. "Okay."

"Good. Brett drafted this memo of agreement. Sign it." Bob signed. "Now you can focus on your relationship with your children."

Chapter 16

October 1992

Bob was sitting in the lobby of Dr. Reed. Ann appeared from Dr. Reed's office. She walked past Bob. She stopped and turned around. She walked toward Bob. Her eyes were furious, and her face was getting closer to Bob's face. In a raised voice, pointing her figure at his face, Ann said, "It's your fault. I should have never married you. It is your doing. Here I am working, raising four boys, and you want to take me to court? That's your plan? To take the boys away from me?" She stormed out.

Bob stood motionless and stunned. Dr. Reed stepped out. "What a tornado!"

Bob was amused. "What happen?"

"Come on in." The two walked toward his office. "I told her that she was not cooperating and making it difficult for the boys."

Bob was making his way to a chair. "To see her like that, the same person I loved and had children with, it's hard to believe that we were lovers."

"How are the visitations?"

"Odd."

"How."

Bob was uncertain. "They are my boys. I love them. I remember when they weighted eight pounds. But for the past two years, I have had more lows than highs. The visits with the boys didn't make me happy, especially after I have to leave them. Ann has not changed at all. She is still very bitter. She makes statements to provoke me or just to piss me off."

Dr. Reed said, "I had hoped that things would get better. It has been a shocking experience, the separation of your children because of false allegations. It has been difficult for you. Now you are a divorced dad and no longer living with your children. It has been truly devastating to your children to try to cope with their father not being home and having one parent. It is difficult. It is my task to help you unite with your children after a long absence."

Bob replied, "I know that. For the past two years, I have been doing a lot of reading and researching divorces and the effect on children, how the kids are caught in the middle. The importance of two parents. I have also researched abused woman and shelters, hoping to find insights into her behavior."

Dr. Reed said, "Absentee fathers have become an unfortunately common thing in our current society. Many young men lack not only a father in their lives but also a father-like figure. Thus, I encourage you to continue to see and spend time with your children."

"I read a book *Iron John*. There was a passage that made a persuasive impact." Bob paused to think. "Women can change the embryo to a boy, but only men can change the boy to a man. It makes me realize how important a father is to a boy. I need to be in their lives to help them grow into young men, but she makes it difficult."

Dr. Reed was impressed. "So you know that it is important that you be in their lives. Your involvement will shape their lives."

Bob lit a cigarette. "I can't believe it. For two years, I fought for my rights to see them. My oldest boy is almost as tall as me. My little one was just a baby. Now he's a little boy. I don't know their friends, their likes, and dislikes. I don't feel the same about them. I want to see them, but I don't want to see them. When I embrace and kiss them, there are times that they are not affectionate at all toward me. They sometimes cancel coming with me because they had other things they prefer to do. I have very little conversations with them. Strangers drop off my children and pick them up. How would you feel about that? My children spend more time with strangers than they do with me."

Dr. Reed said, "This is normal. The older boys are teenagers." Dr. Reed was in total sympathy with Bob. He too had been divorced. He had other male patients that were going through a difficult time and gave up. He did not want to see Bob quit. "An injustice was done. It has been a long separation. With time, you'll feel better."

Bob said in a sad tone. "I don't feel like I'm their father. I told her that I wanted to coach the boys. She won't let me. I have asked for the boys' activities."

Dr. Reed in sympathy said, "I know. I also have asked her for the boys' activities. She agreed, but I still have not received it. In some divorces, the man gets screwed, and some kids get messed up for life."

"Why does it have to be that way? From the time they were born, I have provided for them, and I provided a place to live. Going to the house is painful. That's the house that I purchased, worked on, and lived in. Do you know how much that hurts?"

Dr. Reed was encouraging. "It has been only a few months since you started seeing the children. It's going to take time. Just be patient."

Bob was agonizing. "All my dreams and desires were to be a good father and teach them things. I wished my father could have taught me. I wanted to be a great dad. I was in their lives every day. Now, I'm just a Sunday father. I don't like being a weekend father. I'm not a parent, but an Uncle Bob. Without the quality and quantity of time. I can't say to them, stop chewing your nails. Or say, eat the broccoli. I'm competing with her for their love."

Dr. Reed let Bob vent. "You know what I got for Father's Day?" Bob asked as the tears formed in his eyes. "I got a brush with no bristles and stating, 'For a bald man,' and a note saying, 'How do you keep a stupid Italian busy?' An arrow to turn, turning the other side, it read the same thing." Dr. Reed just listened with discontent. "When I picked up my furniture, it was outside in the driveway and a sign read, 'Do not touch. Merchandise belongs to a short, stupid, bald unemployed Italian that has no life nor hair.'" Dr. Reed did not respond. He was shocked. Bob resumed. "My children must believe that I was abusive."

Bob was becoming more emotional as he continued. "The boys have been_traumatized. The shelter, monitored visitation, her lies, and…and not seeing me. One weekend, I dropped off the boys at the house. Bobby and Tony were playing basketball in the driveway. Ann was not home. I joined in with Chuck and Mark. After five minutes, Tony told me to leave, saying that I did not belong there. I told him, "Let's just have fun." He left and went inside. Within a short period, a cop shows up. I explained that I was their father and I just dropped off two of my children. The officer was grinning as he asked if they were all mine. I proudly said yes. I guessed that my twelve-year-old son called the police, thinking that I had a restraining order."

Sympathetically, Dr. Reed said, "And you left."

"No. The officer said to have fun but to leave once their mother gets home."

With_compassion, Dr. Reed said, "Why didn't you call me about this before? I would have had the boys in. There's been a lot of damage done to your relationship with the boys. I don't expect any help from her. Be patient."

Bob's body temperature was rising, and he started to perspire. He stood up, raising his voice, "Patient, huh? Patient! For two years I hear from my lawyers, 'Be patient. Be patient.' I have been patient for two years! How much more of this crap do I have to take? Two years of psychologists, two years of people controlling my life…what to do, and it's still not over."

Dr. Reed acknowledged, "I know it's unfair and difficult for you, but you've got to be strong and hang in there. You'll have more time with the boys; they'll come around. I have given up on her. I suggest that you take legal action for permanent visitation. I will prepare my recommendations to Mr. McGrath."

Bob was bewildered. "Why is she still so angry? She got the house, the boys, and all the cash. I don't intrude in her life."

Dr. Reed said, "As I said before, eight out of ten women are angry longer than men. Your wife is one of those eight that harbors resentments. I believe that perhaps she is one of a thousand that never gets over it. She is doing all the heavy lifting when it comes to parenting. She is having a hard time dealing with the challenges of two teenagers and two young boys. She was a stay-at-home mother. You took care of all the finances, the house, and the cars. She gave up a lot for the sake of the principle that she was right."

Bob muttered, "She wants to be a martyr like her mother."

"She has manifested all that anger and bitterness toward you."

Bob, more in control, said, "It would be nice if we could just get along or at least be civil and do what is best for the boys, raise our child as divorced parents."

"But we know that isn't the situation." Dr. Reed was silent, not knowing what more he could say. He knew that Bob was hurting deeply inside. "That is why I suggest that you take her to court."

Bob walked out, murmuring, "I just want peace. I want to feel happy."

A week later, Bob received the following letter from Dr. Reed.

> Dear Bob,
>
> As I have stated to you previously, I feel that the separation you experienced from your children as a result of your marital dissolution was unfortunate. I am at a loss to understand why the mental health practitioners involved in your case saw fit to deny you reasonable visitation with your children over a two-year period. I believe this has been detrimental to the children and their relationships with you. I feel particularly adamant about this, given there have been no sustainable allegations of abuse.
>
> Despite these concerns, I think it is important to put the pain of the past behind you and concentrate on building your relationships with your sons.
>
> Sincerely,
> Patrick Reed
> Clinical Psychologists

A month later, Bob Dorsete was in the office of Daniel McGrath. "I have been in contact with Dr. Reed. I have his written certification for permanent visitation. I need your help to prepare an order to show cause for permanent visitation."

Bob said, "More cost!" Bob stood up and paced. "I don't have a job. The defense industry is so depressed that there are no ads to respond to." Then he laughed. "I sometimes think of standing on the corner with a sign 'Will work for food.'"

"Don't get melodramatic. I have your proceeds from the sale of the New Jersey property, $130,000."

Bob replied, "That's good news."

"Yeah, I'll finally get paid. Well, I can't release the funds until Mr. Johnson submits your wife's sign off. Your wife has not signed the release. I informed him that we were preparing papers for permanent visitation."

"How about the forty thousand?"

"He doesn't know."

Bob, in annoyance, said, "She knows the system 'Take me to court.'" Bob sat down and then, in a low voice, said, "I'm tired of the courts. The first six months, I was at the courthouse every other week, mostly spent in the cafeteria. I'm tired of all this shit."

"I promised you that you would win one step at a time. This order is for permanent visitation, and we'll include the release of funds."

Bob was still upset. "Attorneys! Psychologists are still involved in my life. I owe you over thirty thousand dollars. Oh! Add another $4,000. Coming from a poor family, I have always been prudent with my money. Never wasted money on extravagant vacations, expensive cars, or going out for dinners, yet that crazy woman and I have wasted over $150,000 on lawyers and psychologists."

Daniel was waiting patiently for Bob's emotional outburst. "You're wasting your money. Let's get to work."

Bob was shaking his head. "I want everybody out of my life."

McGrath said, "Come on, let's get this done so we can go to lunch." Bob and Daniel had become friends. During their meetings, they often had lunch. Daniel had invited Bob and his children to go sailing on his sixty-foot sailboat. Bob had been invited to spend Thanksgiving with the McGrath family.

Bob had overnight visitations with boys—sometimes one, two, three, or four of the boys. There were last-minute changes to who would go with Bob. Sometimes Ann was combatant and sometimes pleasant that she allowed two-night visits. Sometimes she made sure that they packed a bag. Ann invited Bob to one of the boys' soccer game.

On Friday nights, Bob would take the boys out for dinner, rent a movie, or play games. Bob purchased used mattresses at a swap meet. The boys did not mind. On Saturday, he would sometime take them to the park to play basketball, basketball, or soccer. He took them to the amusement parks. The boys enjoyed going to the large open swap meet, looking at baseball cards, coins, and toys.

Bob and the boys were becoming comfortable. Ann released the money from the sale of the house. McGrath got paid. Dr. Reed got paid. Bob spent Christmas in New Jersey with his eighty-year-old mother, sisters, brothers, nieces, and nephews. They all were very supportive. Bob visited friends. He felt relaxed. For ten days, he left all his troubles in California.

On February 2, 1993, Bob and Ann were in court once more. Ann sat next to her attorney, and Bob and his attorney were on the far side. They waited patiently, hearing other cases—a father not making his payments, grandparents attempting to establish visitations with their grandchildren. Bob thought all this could have been avoided. *What a waste of money. All I wanted was visitation with my children and to be involved in their lives, to help raise them.*

It was quarter to twelve. The judge had called the attorneys to his chamber. The only people in the room were Bob, Ann, the stenographer, and the court security officer. Bob moved toward Ann. Two seats away, he said, "Ann, this could have been avoided."

"Why don't you just leave me alone?"

Bob, with sincerity, said, "Because we have four boys. I am their father. Can we get along? Don't you think that we have spent enough money on attorneys?"

"You forced me to court?"

"No! You denied me visitation."

"No, no, no." Ann shook her head. "You did it to yourself."

Bob tried not to antagonize her. "Honey, we had something special. We had four boys."

Ann, in a temperance tone, said, "You never appreciated me. You controlled me. Men appreciate me."

Bob was disappointed. "That doesn't hurt anymore. For the past two years, friends have said to me, 'If you have a bird in hand and you let it go, if it's truly yours, it will return.' You have not returned. I have had to let go. I still have feelings for you… Please don't interpret that I love you or that I want you. You hurt me too much…and our children. I just want to raise our boys as divorced parents."

Ann's voice rose. "If you cared, why were you throwing the boys out on the street? Why are you taking me to court?"

"I'm wasn't throwing them out, I was throwing you out."

The guard walked over. "You two separate." He looked at Bob. "Move!" Bob moved.

Ann looked at the guard. "He forces me to court because he can't pay child support. I'm all by myself raising four boys." The guard was silent. Ann continued, "Do you have children?"

The guard turned around. "Yes, two girls."

"They must be beautiful."

"Yes. My oldest daughter is in college. She wants to be a lawyer. My daughter in high school wants to be a teacher."

"I am a teacher," she said proudly.

Bob was thinking she was trying to impress him that she has changed.

The attorneys returned to their respective clients. Bob asked McGrath, "That was a long time."

The judge entered. "I have reviewed the respondent's motion and the petitioner's countermotion. I have read Dr. Reed's recommendations. I have discussed the matter with your attorneys. I heard both arguments. I find your attorneys to be completive. For the purpose of not delaying Mr. Wilson's and Pan's lunch any further"—he looked at Bob and Ann—"I will not hear testament from the respondent or the petitioner."

He paused, staring at Ann. "Ms. Dorsete, I don't think that your ex-husband will deny feeding your children or deny them from participating in any extracurricular activities. I award Mr. Dorsete weekend visitation. Ms. Dorsete, since Mr. Dorsete is temporarily living in a single-bedroom apartment, I hope that you will be flexible in the number of children visiting."

The judge turned forward. "It is further stipulated that Ms. Dorsete will communicate with Mr. Dorsete to inform him of the children's school activities as well as any extracurricular activities. Inform him and provide children's school grades, any awards, and if they are ill. Mr. Dorsete, I encourage you to visit your children's weekend activities. I do not make that an order."

The judge paused to look at his notes. "Let the record show that Mr. Dorsete has received a check from Ms. Dorsete for $40,000. In an addition, he has received $130,000 in the settlement of the community property. Since it has been demonstrated that Mr. Dorsete has sufficient funds for child support, the court stipulates an amount of $530 per month."

The judge looked at Ann and Bob. "You have completive attorneys. Listen to them. Good luck to you both! Good day."

As usual, there were last-minute changes to who would go with Bob, the boys not packing a bag. Bob never knew which Ann he would encounter, the cooperative or combative Ann. It was midweek. Bob called Ann. "I had a discussion with Dr. Reed. I'm thinking that we need a break. There is nothing here for me. No job. I am living in a one-room apartment, and it is difficult having the boys."

Ann said, "That's your decision."

"I thought that we both need a break. I plan to go to New Jersey for a few months to sort things out."

"So you need a break!" Sarcastically, she said, "I am working full-time and taking care of four boys."

"I thought that a break would be good for us both. A chance for us to chill out."

Ann, in a loud voice, said, "So I'll be stuck with them on weekends."

"It's very difficult for me."

Ann was becoming belligerent. "I have been taking care of them for two years. After six months, you need a break!"

Bob was annoyed. "For two years, you would not let me see the boys. How many times have I offered to help you to give you a break?" Bob said calmly. "All the years I lived with you, you told me how much you loved me. What a good father I was, and how happy you were with me. Were they lies or the truth?"

"I said all those things because that's what you wanted to hear," said Ann in a loud voice.

Bob said, "No. That's what you thought I wanted to hear. All I ever wanted to hear was the truth. What happen to you?"

"That was before I realized that I was in an abusive relationship. You made me feel inferior. Your anger was getting worse. I was afraid that you might hurt the boys."

"You know that I was going through a lot of stress. We could have separated. I could have stayed in New Jersey, as Pete had suggested. No, you wanted a divorce."

Ann was very assured. "You blamed me for your stress. You said that we were the cause of your stress. Your treatment of me, by far, was the worst atrocity of a sick person."

It was times like this that Bob found the strength fueled by the fury of her hate.

"You take no responsibility for your actions. You take no blame. You have been crucifying me for two years. You wanted to crown my head with thorns for mental anguish. You want to see me on the cross with four spikes, one for each of the boys because they were not girls. You have punctured my heart, crushing my heart for the love I had for you. Drawing my blood was not enough until you tried pushing me into insanity."

Ann hung up the phone.

Bob Dorsete felt that he was a beaten man with nothing. The pain of being a weekend father dominated his thoughts Sunday through Tuesday. Thursday, the pain would start with the anticipation of the impending weekend to see Ann and the house in which he been a father to his boys. The past two years had changed everything. He had to adjust to not feeding, bathing, helping with their homework, reading bedtime stories, praying, coaching, and protecting his children. Everything had changed except for his feelings for someone he had loved, someone he cherished more than life itself. No matter how he tried, every time he saw her, his mind begged for a second chance. His heart cried out for another chance. He had to find a way to forget her.

Bob had discussions with Dr. Conte, Dr. Reed, and Daniel. Bob had opened all his inner feelings, thoughts, and the desire for peace and no more courts. Bob expressed how he and Ann had been together for over twenty years and had four children. How they had shared love, tenderness, and friendship. Now, she has transformed all her love to hate. Her hate was trying to destroy him and would affect the children's lives. His attraction, desire, and affection for his wife had turned to a sheer animosity. His dislike of the situation was so strong that he had thoughts that departed from the normal behavior. He had had it with the lawyers, the courts, and the psychologists. He needed to get away. He needed to find happiness, but he was not quitting. Dr. Conte, Dr. Reed, and McGrath were supportive of Bob's decision to take a break and that perhaps a break would be best for all.

The day before he departed for New Jersey, Bob took the boys to the amusement park. Bobby and Tony were off on their own, enjoying the rides. Bob supervised Chuck and Mark as they enjoyed the children's rides. He later took the boys for dinner. He explained his reason for leaving, to give their mother time, a separation that now all had been settled. He would call every night, and in three or six months, he would return.

Dr. Reed's last words to Bob were "Letting go of a relationship takes courage and strength. Heal your heart and move forward. Fathers don't abandon their children. They are driven away."

Postscript

Learning how to let go of a relationship is painful. It hurts, and there is no way around the pain. Bob Dorsete could not live in the past. He had to move forward. He found and attended single and parenting groups to socialize. He attended meetings with men and women who were going through similar life challenges. Bob attended weekend activities, such as dances and short trips. He quickly made new friends.

Bob, at forty-two, was living with his elderly mother, and it had its pluses and minuses. Bob threatened to divorce his mother unless she became less controlling and demanding. This was on the light side.

He called his children weekly. After only three months in New Jersey, Ann and the boys stopped answering the telephone. Bob left weekly messages.

Bob Dorsete met an intelligent, self-assured, and pretty woman with two young boys. She also was divorced. She also wanted to move forward, with new beginnings, with a new lover. They dated for a year and married. His new marriage also involved the rearing of her two young boys into manhood.

Bob never quit on his children. He left messages, wrote on their birthdays and holidays, and sent them gifts. Bob did not return to California and never saw his children again.

He found love again; his heart had a second chance.

About the Author

Tom Adornetto was raised in Newark, New Jersey. He is a graduate of Rutgers University (MBA) with residences in California, Pennsylvania, and Maryland.

Tom Adornetto has held various positions and responsibilities for many large companies in various industries. As a manager and company negotiator, he has had personal contact with people from all walks of life experiencing life's challenges.

For over twenty years, he wrote numerous periodic customer reports and internal business assessments, thus developing the unique talent to craft actual assessments to read with a positive overture.